Books by David Stout

Night of the Ice Storm
Hellgate (with Ruth Furie)
Carolina Skeletons

Published by
THE MYSTERIOUS PRESS

DAVID STOUT

NIGHT OF THE ICE STORM

THE MYSTERIOUS PRESS

New York • Tokyo • Sweden • Milan

Published by Warner Books

 A Time Warner Company

MYSTERIOUS PRESS EDITION

Copyright © 1991 by David Stout
All rights reserved.

Cover design by Jackie Merri Meyer
Cover illustration by Cathleen Toelke

The Mysterious Press name and logo are trademarks of
Warner Books, Inc.

Mysterious Press Books are published by
Warner Books, Inc.
666 Fifth Avenue
New York, New York, 10103

A Time Warner Company

Printed in the United States of America

Originally published in hardcover by The Mysterious Press.

First Mysterious Press Paperback Printing: March, 1992

10 9 8 7 6 5 4 3 2 1

For Ruth Furie, the tenth Muse

One

▲▲▲

January is a cruel month in Bessemer. The holiday decorations are gone, leaving the streets bleak, and winds off Lake Erie seem to cut right down to the cheekbone. Spring is an eternity away.

January is the month of snow. The snow is a blessing, at least in those brief hours when it lies fresh. It covers the gray ugliness of the factories and steel plants, covers the soot and the drabness of lives. But the blessing carries its own curse, because at some point each January, it seems, there is a brief stretch when the air hovers between freeze and thaw, and the snow that has lain pure and white begins to turn to slush.

At first the slush is a cold, gray pudding, but soon it takes on streaks of pink and orange from the mill and factory ash, so that when the ridges and valleys of slush freeze again, they lie like entrails in the streets.

Then the snow falls again, and the people of Bessemer, many of whom trace their seed back to the fields and

1

villages of Germany, Poland, Italy, and Ireland, shrug and long for the spring that lies over a far horizon.

This night, in January 1971, would be remembered as one of the cruelest of all. During the day, the temperature had shot into the midforties (it had been in the twenties less than twenty-four hours before), but after the early sunset it turned colder. The rain went on, and the drops clung longer to the trees. Anyone who knew winter at all figured that in a few hours the rain would turn to snow.

The temperature teetered between thawing and freezing, and the rain went on. Or was it rain? Those Bessemer people who ventured outside to throw out garbage or walk the dog felt the drops on their faces. Yes, it felt like rain, but when it touched the ground, it turned to a glistening crust. The drops clung longer and longer to the trees, and the limbs sagged as the drops turned to ice. The bent branches glistened and clacked against one another.

"Folks, the weather bureau says we're apt to get hit with a full-fledged ice storm. Now, what that means is that by late tonight, or maybe tomorrow morning, we're looking at downed power lines, loss of telephone service, problems with mass transit—"

"And lots of fender benders, Brad. The police have asked us to tell our listeners to use extreme caution if they have to go out tonight. The streets are getting very, very slippery, and they're going to get worse."

"Indeed they are, Phil."

"Now, the police are also advising our listeners to be sure they have flashlights and candles where they can find them if the lights go out."

"All in all, it's a good night to curl up in front of the fire with someone you like. You'll be a lot safer."

He turned off the radio. Curl up in front of the fire with someone you like. I would, he thought, except that I don't have a fireplace. Don't have anyone to curl up with either.

He did have a flashlight in a kitchen drawer, and he had made sure the batteries were good.

Some nights he did stay in his apartment, reading, watching television, reading the *Bessemer Gazette,* the newspaper he worked for. Many nights he cooked for himself. Other nights—and this was one of them—he had to get out.

He knew all the taverns in Bessemer. He chose taverns to match his mood: if he felt like shots and beers, and conversation to match, he would head over to the industrial section and the bars frequented by the plant workers. Other times he would feel like a thick cheeseburger or pasta or clams. Bars that served such food were one of the few charms of Bessemer. They dotted the streets of the ethnic neighborhoods, if one knew where to look. He did.

There were other places, in the university area. They offered beer, football songs, and a rich variety of food, for the university drew a lot of students from New York City, and the bars near the campus catered to them.

Sometimes he liked the university bars best. The carefree, iconoclastic attitude of the students was infectious, and some of the women so lovely that he ached just to talk to them. He seldom talked to the women, but fairly often he struck up a conversation with one or two of the young men. They talked about Nixon, Vietnam, football, golf, Kent State, the army.

He felt almost a generation gap with the students. It was not that he was so much older (there was only a few years difference) but that he had lived his own life differently, for reasons mostly beyond his control. Though he didn't like to dwell on it, going to the college bars gave him a chance to feed off the youth of others.

He put on his favorite pair of casual slacks and a comfortable pullover sweater and grabbed a windbreaker, pulling the hood over his head as soon as he stepped outside. The rain felt like cold spit on his face, and the footing was treacherous. A crust of ice glistened on everything he could see.

His car was at the curb, and he reached it without stumbling. He started the engine, turned on the defrost, and scraped the windshield while the car warmed up.

Just as he was getting into the car, he heard it: a piercing crash, followed by a series of smaller splintering sounds. Somewhere, probably within a couple of blocks, a big tree had just died, collapsing with the weight of the ice.

He drove cautiously, feathering his brakes and taking the turns slowly.

". . . so let us say it again, folks, if you don't have to go out . . ."

He snapped off the radio.

He parked on a dark street and locked his car. His windbreaker soon gleamed with congealing drops as he walked toward the Silver Swine tavern a block away.

He heard another piercing crash, like an ax handle being broken. The sound was to his rear, a few blocks away, and as he turned to look, he saw a blue-green flash of light, then nothing. Power line down, maybe a transformer, he thought.

The tavern's steamy window was decorated with a silver neon pig that winked and smiled. He pushed open the tavern door, instantly feeling the heat on his face. The place was full of the smells of onions, french fries, beef, chili, beer, peanut dust, bodies. The huge room throbbed with the babble of voices and background music and the clink of bottles and glasses from the long oak bar. Faded pennants from dozens of schools hung from the rafters. The wall behind the bar was plastered with political stickers from the previous presidential election: Nixon and Agnew, Humphrey and Muskie, "All the Way With LeMay." But a dart board with a smiling Richard Nixon for a target left no doubt about the politics of the tavern keeper and his clientele.

He took off his windbreaker, shook it so that the drops fell into the peanut shells on the floor, hung the jacket on a peg.

"What'll it be?"

"Bud draft."

Some of the people he worked with were regulars at the

Silver Swine, but he wasn't. It had been several weeks since his last visit and he had let his sideburns grow. He had also started a beard. He rubbed the stubble self-consciously, stopped when he saw himself in the mirror, took a swig of beer.

"What's it doing out?" the bartender said.

"Rain turning to ice. Slippery as hell."

"My girlfriend just called me," the bartender said. "She said trees are coming down right and left around North Park. Dragging electric and phone lines with 'em."

"I believe it."

North Park and the surrounding neighborhood had the oldest and biggest trees in the city. The park was near the lake, and bad weather often hit that area just before it swept the rest of the city.

He sat on a stool, finished his beer fast, ordered another. He felt warm, relaxed. Maybe he would order something to eat.

The television played soundlessly behind the bar. The weatherman stood smiling in front of a map of the city and touched one section after another with a pointer. Then the screen showed downed trees, sagging trees, power lines lying in congealing puddles.

He watched the weatherman, knew about what he was saying even with the sound down; he could tell from the silly smile that broadened now and then into a grin: ". . . so we are in for some really miserable weather. The kind even Bessemer doesn't get every winter, so unless you have to, please don't go out . . ."

Screw you, he thought. I had to go out.

To his left, two bearded university students wearing army fatigue jackets decorated with peace signs where there should have been chevrons were arguing about the Kent State shootings of the previous May:

". . . fascist, cold-blooded killers, no matter what . . ."

". . . only victims themselves, products of a sick system . . ."

". . . motto of the infantry. Follow me, I am the whore of battle . . ."

Suddenly, anger shot through him like an electric current; his temples throbbed with it. The students in the army jackets talked like spoiled fools. What had they ever had to do in their lives? He felt like shouting at them to stop their worthless little argument.

He drained his glass, motioned to the bartender to refill it. There, a long gulp to force back the bile. He felt better.

A man squeezed into the space between him and the students in army jackets. Good; the man blocked out the voices.

"Hey, all right!" the man clapped his hands softly.

He looked up at the television, saw Notre Dame's football coach, Ara Parseghian, smiling and shaking hands with several Bessemer Chamber of Commerce leaders.

He remembered: Parseghian had flown into Bessemer for a luncheon honoring his team's New Year's Day victory over Texas in the Cotton Bowl.

"I'm a fan of Notre Dame," the man said to him. "You?"

He was on guard. "Sort of."

"'Sort of,'" the stranger mimicked, though not obnoxiously. "Well, I gotta tell ya, I had a most happy New Year's Day. After the game, that is. During the game I was rattling the rosary beads right and left."

"It worked." He said that in a flat, almost offhand way without turning his head.

"This time it did," the stranger said. "But the Big Guy didn't come through when the Irish played Southern Cal."

"Maybe he had a bet on Southern Cal."

At that, the stranger chuckled. "My name's John Barrow."

"I'm Gary Price," he lied. He often used a false name in taverns, and he seldom mentioned his connection with the *Gazette*. It was too easy to get into a barroom argument over the war and politics.

"Glad to know you, Gary."

"Same here."

The stranger's handshake was strong. He was tall, broad shouldered, with swept-back, wavy, brown hair. He had straight teeth, a slightly crooked grin, blue eyes that had a touch of irreverence. He wore jeans and a plaid shirt over a white turtleneck.

"Buy you a beer?"

"Sure. Thanks."

"I forget sometimes that not everybody's a Notre Dame fan," John Barrow said.

"Well, a lot of people are in this town. Lots of Catholics."

"I know. Cheers."

"Cheers." He liked the stranger. "Actually, I wasn't surprised the Irish lost to Southern Cal."

"No?"

"No. Southern Cal gives the Irish trouble, especially in Los Angeles."

"So you believe in jinxes?"

"Sometimes. At least in football."

"Ah. I'm not supposed to believe in jinxes, but sometimes I think I do."

"Can't be too careful."

"What kind of work do you do, Gary?"

"I'm a newspaperman. With the *Gazette.*" He had surprised himself by letting his guard down; there was something about John Barrow he liked.

"Newspaperman! Do you cover sports?"

"I've done a little of everything. You?"

"I'm a social worker. It doesn't pay very well, but on a good day I get a lot of satisfaction."

"And a constant supply of problems."

"You got that right. Hey, check that out." John Barrow pointed to the TV set. The weatherman was pointing to the map of the city, and the words *Storm Update* flashed on the screen. Then came pictures of great, ancient trees lying ice-encrusted in the street, pictures of icy power lines hanging low, pictures of broken utility poles lying against cars.

"Jeez, look at that," the bartender said. The TV showed a transformer flashing blue-green, sending a cascade of sparks into a cold puddle below.

"A good night for the spiritual solace of a warm tavern, Gary. Good for the body and soul."

"You're right. Ready for another?"

"Does the Pope say grace?"

The beer felt good. He and John Barrow talked about college football, sharing remembrances of games played a decade or more ago.

"How come you know so much about football, Gary?"

"Frustrated jock." That was the truth.

"Me, too. You play golf?"

"I hack at it. I'm not very consistent, but I like it when I get a chance to play."

"I'm not bad. I can usually play at bogey level. When I practice a lot, that is. I live in an old house with part of the basement an old fruit cellar. Dirt floor, high ceiling. I can practice my golf swing all winter long."

"Damn. You mean you can actually hit a ball down there?"

"Sure. Tee it up and swing away. I got myself a few bales of hay and stacked them against a wall. Hung a thick tarp in front of the bales. Stops the balls nice and easy."

Two more beers had been set on the bar. He was caught up in the babble and music and personal contact. He felt warm and good.

"So," John Barrow said, "Bessemer's a terrific place to live in the winter, doncha think?"

"It sucks."

"Couldn't agree more. Which is why I'm flying out of here tomorrow. Couple weeks in Florida'll fix me up."

"Taking your golf clubs?"

"Silly question. I'm taking more golf clothes than street clothes. I really need this vacation, too. The holiday season's always so damn busy."

He was going to ask John Barrow why that was, but he let it go.

"You ever cover golf tournaments?"

"No. But I did meet Jack Nicklaus last summer. Some bullshit civic luncheon. A very nice guy. He even gave me a couple of tips."

By the time their glasses were empty again, he was hungry. He motioned to the bartender. "Can we get two more beers and a menu?"

"Guys, we're gonna close early," the bartender said. "Storm's getting worse. If you want another round . . ."

He was disappointed; he was hungry, and he was enjoying the company.

"You got any french fries and onion rings ready?" John Barrow asked the bartender.

"Yep."

"Good. How about putting a big serving of each in a bag. Throw in a six-pack." Then, turning to him, Barrow said, "We'll go to my place and shoot the shit for a while. Show you my new set of golf clubs."

"Why not?"

He carried the six-pack and John Barrow took the food. Then he followed Barrow into the icy night.

"You parked nearby, Gary?"

"Around the corner."

"I'm right here." John Barrow pointed to a white compact. "Blink your lights when you're behind me, and I'll lead the way."

The ice-rain stuck to his windbreaker. Once, his feet almost went out from under him. The world was wet, glistening. He had to step around several limbs and branches.

His car looked as if it had been sprayed with a fine mist, then plunged into a deep freeze. He had to bang the door with his fist for the lock to receive the key. He put the six-pack on the front seat, started the engine, took out the scraper. The ice clung to the windshield like skin and came off in strips only with repeated jabbings.

Suddenly, he felt panic: was he taking too long? Would John Barrow get tired of waiting for him?

In the distance, he saw a blue-green flash, like lightning, close to the ground.

Finally, with the defroster and the scraping, he had his windshield good enough to see through.

He turned the corner, feathered his brakes a couple of times, slowed to a stop, and blinked his lights when he spotted the white compact. John Barrow's car pulled out in front of him.

He stayed several car lengths behind the white compact, which made a right turn down Lethridge Avenue and a left onto the Ambrose Parkway. The pavement was slippery, but there were few cars. He decided he was in no danger of a DWI charge.

The white compact was leaving the university district. It stayed on the Ambrose as the parkway curved briefly along the edge of the industrial area, then exited into an old neighborhood whose mansions had gradually been converted to offices and boardinghouses as their grandeur faded.

He stayed close behind the compact. Some blocks were totally dark, and he passed one power-company crew where a huge old tree had fallen onto a utility pole. The repairmen's yellow raincoats glittered with ice in the glare of floodlights. Their chain saws growled as they ripped into tree flesh.

The white compact took one last right turn down a long street, slowed, and stopped at the curb. He pulled in behind it and shut off the engine. He had to urinate and wished he had before leaving the Silver Swine. The thought of asking John Barrow to show him to the bathroom made him feel foolish, childlike.

"Follow me, Gary. Watch your step."

He followed John Barrow up a dark, slippery walk toward an old three-story brick house. The ice-rain splattered on his face. A single lamp shone in a ground-floor window.

There was something familiar about the outline of the house.

"Just let me go in and get the hall lights, Gary."

He followed John Barrow into a long, narrow corridor with a tiled floor, high oak walls, and several huge doors.

"Those doors lead to parts of the house that I hardly ever go to," John Barrow said. "Down at the end there is a stairs. I never use the second floor at all."

Why would John Barrow live in such a huge house and only use a tiny part of it? How could he afford such a house as a social worker? And why had the house seemed familiar, even in the dark?

John Barrow slid open the oak door nearest the front entrance. "What do you think of my living room, Gary?"

"Big," he said, hoping his host didn't think him stupid.

"It's that, all right."

A huge marble fireplace topped by a mantel dominated one long oak wall. Next to a front window was an easy chair and a round table that held the lamp he had seen from outside. Between the table and the fireplace there was a large television set. Along the wall opposite the fireplace was a large sofa, and in front of that a long wooden coffee table.

At the end of the room farthest from the window was a round table on which rested a plant and a stack of mail. Over the far table hung a picture of Christ. John Barrow is a Catholic, he thought.

"Give me the beer, Gary. Why don't you spread your jacket on the floor next to the fireplace. Heat'll dry it off in no time."

He did as he had been told with the jacket.

"Make yourself at home, Gary. Sofa's comfortable. I'll get us some glasses and plates."

He was eager for some more beer because he felt the spell of camaraderie starting to crack under the strain of his own awkwardness. He saw John Barrow turn left at the far end of the room. Then he noticed suitcases and golf clubs lying on the floor underneath the table at the end of the room.

"I see you're all packed," he said, attempting levity as

John Barrow returned with a tray bearing steins, two cans of beer, plates, forks, paper napkins, and a bottle of ketchup.

"Yep. Now I just have to pray the airport stays open."

John Barrow nodded toward the front window. Ice crystals were forming on the glass, catching the lamplight and reflecting it in a hellish glow. "God's punishment," Barrow said.

"You must be Catholic."

"Indeed." John Barrow seemed eager to pour beer. "Cheers, Gary."

He took a big gulp, hoping it would restore some of the spell. But there was something he could not postpone. "Which way's your bathroom?"

"Back there. Light's on your left."

He passed a small, white kitchen and a dark bedroom. The bathroom was at the end of a short hallway. Its window, too, was ice covered. After relieving himself, he squinted through the icy window and saw a pale green flash of light, then nothing. More wires down. How far away? He couldn't tell.

Bottles of cologne and shaving lotion lined the back of the sink. For some reason, he had the urge to open the medicine chest, but after staring in the mirror for several seconds he forbade himself to do that.

His host was lighting a fire. "Dry your coat in no time," Barrow said.

"Good night for a fire." He sat down again on the sofa, took a gulp of beer. He piled french fries and onion rings on a plate. With the first nibble, he realized how hungry he'd been.

"You go to the Swine often, Gary?"

"Now and then."

"I don't think I've seen you there before." John Barrow sat down on the sofa and began eating and sipping beer meticulously.

"I envy you, escaping to play golf."

"Mmmm, I can't wait. Listen, let me get you a refill."

"I'm drinking faster than you."

"So what."

John Barrow brought him a beer, then took a large book off the top of the mantel. "Ever see this?" Barrow said. "A present to myself."

The cover showed a par-three hole protected by a pond on one side, a rock face on the other, and trees behind. He wiped his fingers thoroughly and leafed through the book: page after page of breathtakingly lovely fairways and brooks and pristine sand and velvet greens.

"Look on page twenty-six," Barrow said. "I've played that par five. It's a course in Florida."

"Do you travel a lot in your job?"

"Oh, sometimes." John Barrow smiled slyly. "To tell you the truth, Gary, I told a white lie. I'm not a social worker. I'm a priest."

"Oh. Well, almost the same thing." He had tried to sound blasé.

"You can understand," Father John Barrow said. "I get the same urges as anyone else—to go out and have a few beers, shoot the shit. But I have to be careful. You can understand, from the field you're in."

"Right."

"Tell me again what you do at the *Gazette*."

"Oh, I bounce around a lot. Cover this, cover that."

"Hmmm. Well, I cover a lot, too. A lot of sins and follies. Including some of my own."

"Everybody should have some."

"I'll drink to that. You ready again?"

"Not quite. . . . What the hell, I'm ready." He was drinking fast. He liked the priest.

Barrow laughed, went to the kitchen, and got two more beers.

"Who else lives here?"

"Just me. Your paper has run stories and pictures on this house. There's a debate within the diocese about what to do with it."

Of course. That was why the house had seemed familiar from the outside, even in the gloom and icy mist.

"The diocese is consolidating some parishes," Father Barrow went on. "They may close this building entirely, or do something else with it. Something. Until they decide, I'm sort of the caretaker."

"A big house to be alone in."

Barrow's face went stone serious. "You believe in ghosts, Gary?"

"I don't rule them out."

"Me either. You Catholic?"

"I was brought up that way."

"I figured, from the Notre Dame stuff. You believe in the hereafter?"

"Uh, I don't rule it out. That or ghosts."

"Ah, Gary, I'm with you. Priest or not, I'm with you."

From outside, against the house, came the sound of bumping and scratching. For a moment, he was afraid.

"It's a big old maple, Gary. Ice is getting heavier. Hope the storm doesn't kill her."

John Barrow put another log on the fire. The flames hissed and darted.

"Tell me, Gary. What do you do to unwind? Besides golf, I mean."

"Oh, read. Drink."

"No girl in your life at the moment?"

"Not at the moment."

"Plenty of time for that. You're young."

With John Barrow leading the way, they talked some more: about life and death and hope and what it all meant, about how springtime in Bessemer was so much sweeter than in other places, where winters were milder. They talked about love between parent and child, about how difficult that love could be, and how a person didn't understand some things until it was too late.

After a while, Barrow said, "Enough of this serious shit. You have to see my driving range. You have time, don't you?"

He looked at his watch. Almost midnight. "Sure, what the hell."

"Great. We can hit a few balls, then come up and kill off the beer."

John Barrow took three clubs out of the bag lying at the end of the room and led the way to a stairway off the kitchen.

"Watch your head, Gary." The priest turned on a light that revealed narrow stone steps.

He followed his host into a basement that smelled of mold hidden for decades in undiscoverable crannies.

"Check out that furnace, Gary. Big enough to heat a castle. Been here since the house was built. 'Course, we don't burn coal here anymore. This way."

He followed the priest through another door. His host flicked a switch, and a powerful light illuminated a room with a dirt floor and a high ceiling. The far wall was covered with a green tarp on which hung a white sheet with a saucer-sized red circle in the middle.

"Hay bales behind the tarp, Gary. Plenty of padding, so you can just swing away. Choose your weapon. Iron or wood?" The golfing priest offered the clubs; the head of the driver gleamed like dark cherry wood, the immaculate blades of the irons like silver.

"No, you go first."

John Barrow took off his turtleneck and shirt and tossed them carelessly onto that part of the tarp that lay on the floor beneath the target. His T-shirt covered a lean torso and a powerful chest. He had long, firm arms.

John Barrow picked up a handful of golf balls and tees from the floor under the target. Then he stepped to the center of the dirt floor and teed up a ball.

"Hand me the driver, Gary. I'm gonna need it on that par five in Florida."

The priest-golfer had a long, slow, clockwork backswing. He brought the club down in a smooth arc while shifting his weight perfectly. The ball rocketed off the club face and exploded into the target.

"Wish I could do that every time, Gary."

Barrow hit several more balls, sending each into the target center with thunderous force. Retrieving the balls from the floor, he did it all over again.

Barrow frowned with intense concentration, his face in a light sweat.

"Okay, Gary. Let's see what you can do."

He didn't really want to try. He had seen at once that John Barrow had a far better golf swing. "I'll try the five iron," he said. He was far less likely to screw up with that than with the driver.

He teed a ball and got a firm stance in the dirt. The club felt strange and heavy. He swung as slowly as he could and swept the ball cleanly off the tee into the target area.

"Nothing wrong with that, Gary."

"Respectable," he said, trying to sound casual. He teed up again and got off another satisfactory shot, then another.

"You're over that pond, Gary. . . . That won't hurt you."

John Barrow retrieved the balls and brought them back to him. "Gary, I might offer you one piece of advice. Get set up over the ball now. . . . Ah! May I?"

Without waiting for an answer, John Barrow put a hand on his forearm. "Gary, you've got real arm strength here, but you're not using all of it." Barrow paused, squeezed. "Strong. . . . Now try putting your arms a little closer together at address, so they make a tighter vee. Okay. Now swing."

He did, and noticed the difference.

"See? Try again, same way."

Again, he sent a good iron shot into the target.

"One more time, Gary."

This time he swung too fast and topped the ball. "I just went into the water."

"Your tempo was off. You're just rusty, that's all. Can I show you something else?"

He wasn't just rusty; he was tired of the basement. He wanted to go upstairs and have another beer.

"Gary, step back from the ball. Just an inch or two . . . there."

Barrow had gone around behind him. "Now, Gary, remember the arms. A good, tight vee does the trick."

Barrow reached from behind and put a hand gently on his right forearm. "You have good, strong arms, Gary."

He was getting annoyed at the hands-on teaching. Barrow was close behind him. He could smell the priest's sweat and shaving lotion.

"Okay, Gary. Standing a little away from the ball like that, still with that tight vee, you should get a lot more power. Try it."

He swung, but his annoyance had dashed his concentration. The ball flicked off the end of the club and bounced harmlessly off a far wall.

"My fault, Gary. I made you nervous." Barrow was still standing behind him. His voice was soft, apologetic.

He turned to look at his host and suggest that they go upstairs to have some more beer. What he saw in the priest's face startled him.

Father John Barrow's eyes were soft, watery, pleading. "Gary, I like you very much," the priest whispered.

The priest looked down—a signal. "Gary, do you think you could relax with me? Feel easy with me?"

He stepped back.

Barrow's erect, eager penis was jutting through the fly.

"Gary . . ."

"I'm leaving, okay?"

"Please, Gary. Didn't you feel some of the same—"

"No!" His shout echoed in the ancient basement. "No!"

"You must have. I felt that you did."

He backed away. John Barrow touched his own penis, then reached out to him. Watery, soft eyes. Pleading.

"No!" Almost by reflex, he swung the golf club. It was only a one-handed half swing, but the club struck the priest flush on the temple. Barrow put his hand to his head; blood seeped through the fingers.

"Gary . . ." Still pleading.

He could not bear the priest's voice.

"No!" This time he swung the club with both arms, full force, striking the side of the head. The priest dropped to his knees, a torrent of blood soaking through his hair and cascading into the dirt.

Barrow's eyes were changing, from watery soft to glazed. One eye looked away, but the other stared right at him.

"No!" He swung again, knocking Barrow off his knees. One eye had disappeared into a mash of tissue, bone, and blood. Lying on his side, curled in a fetal position, John Barrow twitched, then lay still, his penis in the dirt.

Don't you feel some of the same?

"No!" The club sounded like an ax hitting wood as it struck the corpse's head.

You must have.

"No!" With the next swing of the club, something splashed into his face.

"No . . ." His voice was a hoarse croak now, no longer echoing.

He had no idea how many times he swung. He stopped when the club became lodged in John Barrow's head. By that time, the grip of the five iron was slippery and his arms were exhausted.

"No . . ."

Blood on the walls, on the golf target, soaking his sleeves, drying on his face.

"No."

He turned the light out as he left the room with the corpse and went back through the furnace room. His legs felt weak; he was barely able to walk.

"No."

He stumbled up the steps, turned off the stair light, shut the basement door behind him. Past the kitchen again, back into the living room. He looked down and saw the golf bag.

He sat down on the sofa. On the table in front of him were spread the rest of the french fries and onion rings. He and the man he had just killed had shared a meal. He swallowed the urge to be sick.

Whom could he call for help? No one. The police would not believe it was self-defense. He had swung so many times; he had lost count.

The priest had lived alone. He was supposed to leave on vacation. It might be a long time before he was found.

He scooped up the remnants of the food and the dirty plates and napkins, tossed them into the fireplace, watched the flames hiss anew as they fed on the grease. Get out, he told himself.

He picked up his jacket, saw the gore on his hands, remembered the splatter on his face. He couldn't leave with blood on his hands and face. What if someone saw . . .

Get out, get out. No, wash your hands first, wash your hands.

He started toward the kitchen on wobbly legs, intending to give his hands and face a fast rinse, grab a paper towel, and run. He glanced at the empty beer cans. Fingerprints.

Get out, just get out.

He grabbed the tray with the cans and unused plates and napkins and rushed to the kitchen. He dropped the beer cans into the sink and threw everything else into the wastebasket in the cupboard beneath the sink. Then he ran warm water over his hands, shuddering as he watched the pink water run off his skin. He splashed water onto his face, reeled off several paper towels, dried his hands and face, wiped the beer cans with the wet paper towels, threw everything into the wastebasket.

Get out, get out.

Back to the living room. He was breathing hard, and his legs were still shaking. Get out.

His eyes fell on Barrow's luggage and golf bag. Can't leave them there; he's supposed to be going away.

A scratching, scraping against the side of the house, louder and louder, like claws trying to rip off the side of the house. The lights went out. Through the front window he saw a brief blue-green flash, then nothing.

The house was dark, except for the orange glow of the hissing fire. He was alone in the blackened house in which he had killed a priest.

He could make out the suitcases and golf bag in the firelight. He dragged them through the dark hallway at the rear of the house, shouldered open the bedroom door, slid the bags in with his foot.

He stood for a moment at the front of the little hallway, close to the living room, the kitchen, the door that led to the pitch-black basement where the priest lay curled on the dirt floor.

The flames flicked his shadow on this wall and that. He went through the living room, bumped the table in front of the sofa. He slid open the oak door.

And then he was outside, in the pure night. All around him was darkness; no streetlights, no house lights. The ice-rain pelted his face as he took slow, flat steps down the sidewalk. It was very slippery underfoot. All around him he heard the *click-click-click* of sagging tree branches. Then a cracking limb, somewhere.

With no warning, his feet slipped and he went facedown on the walk. The wind had been knocked out of him. His arm had come up by reflex and cushioned his fall. Had he hit his face? Yes, there was pain there, around his mouth. But no broken teeth, no broken nose. His contact lenses! Yes, they were still in place.

He lay on the ice for several seconds. From far away came the sound of a tree limb breaking. It was cold and wet on the ground.

Slowly, he stood up, got his feet under him. He made it to his car, chipped ice away from the lock, got in, and started the engine.

He had not dreamed it; there really was a dead priest in that house.

The defroster began to clear the windshield. He turned on the car radio.

". . . can hear me now, in fact, only if you happen to be listening on a portable radio or in your car. And if you are in your car, drive extra carefully. We're getting lots of disturbing reports here about accidents.

"Again, folks, much of Bessemer is without power at this time, and much of the community is without telephone service. Utility crews are out in force. Bessemer Electric is bringing in help from utilities in Pennsylvania and Ohio, but there's just no telling how long we'll be without power. We could be talking about days in some parts of the city.

"Now, police and fire stations are on emergency power. So are the hospitals. WSBC television and the radio stations are still in business, and the *Gazette* has told us they can publish tomorrow. I don't know how many people will be able to watch TV, because a lot of people won't have electricity. A lot of us may have to change our living habits, at least for a few days. We'll keep you as up-to-date as we can, not only on the storm's progress but on the progress of repairs.

"A lot of us here at the station may not be going home tonight, and maybe you're stranded where you're listening right now. You should think about staying there, folks. Better an inconvenience than a tragedy. One thing is certain. This is some weather, even by Bessemer standards. I think we're all going to remember where we were on the night of the ice storm."

He turned off the radio.

Two

▲ ▲ ▲

Sleep was a desolate kingdom. He had been afraid to close his eyes at first, afraid of what he would dream, but at long last, surrendering to exhaustion and beer dregs, his body yielded.

He had stripped off his spattered clothes in the dark of his apartment and tossed them into the bathtub to run water over them. As the cold water ran into the tub (there was no hot water), he squeezed the wet clothes and mashed them against the side of the tub. In the glow of the flashlight, he could see that the water running off the sleeves of his shirt was pink.

It was cold in his apartment. He stood for a few minutes in his flannel pajamas before the small gas stove as the orange-and-blue flame warmed a little cocoon of air around him. The flame reminded him of the priest's fireplace.

He turned off the stove and got into bed, curling himself in a fetal ball under the blankets. Once, twice, three times he awoke, and each time he thought he saw flames. He had to convince himself anew that he had not gone to sleep in the priest's house, that he was not staring into the dying embers in the priest's fireplace.

When he awoke, he shivered, yet his skin was wet. He felt his face with his fingertips, touching the little cuts from his fall in front of the priest's house. It had really happened; he had killed a priest.

On and on he roamed in the kingdom of sleep. Sometimes he groaned, tried to call for help, but he could not make word sounds.

Finally he opened his eyes not to darkness but to gray—the first pale hint of the January dawn.

His head ached from the beer, far more from the horror of what he had done. He did not want to get up yet, even though he knew he would not get back to sleep. He swung his legs onto the floor and stood up. The hangover was the worst he had ever had. He did not know if he would faint, did not know if he would be sick.

He was cold. He put on his robe and started into the tiny kitchen to make coffee. But first he turned toward the bathroom. If there was nothing in the bathtub, he had dreamed it all, and he could cry with joy.

Automatically, he flicked the light switch; nothing happened. But there was enough light for him to make out the sodden pile of clothes in the tub.

He went to the kitchen and put on a pot of water. He made instant coffee, as strong as he could stand it. From the small refrigerator (there was no light inside it) he plucked a piece of bread and nibbled at it as he sipped the coffee.

He had to go to the *Gazette*. The ice storm would be one of the biggest stories of the year, and he could not call in sick. It was out of the question. He was certain the *Gazette* would publish the next day: the newspaper had long ago bullied the power company into running underground lines into the *Gazette,* and in any power failure the *Gazette* got service as quickly as the hospitals.

He drank his coffee and thought, I have killed. I am forever different because I have killed. The thought alone was enough to make him shiver, even without the coldness of the room.

He had driven home safely, had negotiated the driveway with his car and then his feet, had made it into the darkened front entrance without meeting anyone.

He swallowed hard to keep the bread down and gulped some more coffee. He opened the curtains, gazed out at the gray streets and buildings.

Ice. Ice on the limbs and branches that hung low over the walks and street, ice on the cars that had been parked since before the storm, ice on the telephone and electric lines that lay like angel-cake frosting everywhere.

He was forever different now, different from the utility crewmen he saw across the street. How they slipped and slid, the utility workers, clumsy like children in snowsuits as they groped for footing and grips while stumbling about in their bulky yellow costumes.

He envied the utility workers: they would go home to wives and children who loved them.

He had killed; he was forever different.

Should he try to drive to work or walk? The *Gazette* was about two miles away. He didn't know what to do.

He fished a green plastic garbage bag out of the cupboard, went into the bathroom, and knelt next to the tub. There was enough light now for him to see the pink residue quite clearly. Trying not to look, he picked up the garments, one by one, wrung them out, stuffed them into the bag. When they were all in the bag, he turned on the water to rinse out the tub.

No hot water. Of course, no hot water. The furnace was out. How could he get himself clean? God, he wished he could stay home.

He would throw the bag full of clothes into a Salvation Army bin. But was that safe? What if they traced the clothing labels back to him somehow? What if—?

He had to wash them, with hot water and soap. And he had to get himself clean. He remembered how his hands had felt after they grew slippery from swinging the bloody golf club, how something had spattered into his face—

God, had he washed his hands last night? Yes, he had; he remembered. Before he left the priest's house he had washed his hands.

But this morning he felt dirty again, his body soiled from beery sleep and . . . from what he had done.

He heated another pot of water, a much larger one, and carried it into the bathroom. He put the plug in the sink, filled it with the hot water, and dropped the bar of soap in. Then he took a clean washcloth, soaked it in hot, soapy water, and ran it across his face. He closed his eyes; how good it felt, the cleansing.

He washed his hands, his arms, his armpits. Up and down his torso, across the shoulders, down his back as far as he could reach. He washed his entire body, trying to make himself clean. He had killed a priest.

As he washed and rinsed and toweled himself dry, he felt like a naked boy, ashamed.

He put on clean underwear, then socks, then a clean pair of corduroys and a heavy shirt. Warmer now. Better.

He made himself more coffee, gnawed at another piece of bread. He was stronger physically, though he could not stop the shiver deep in his soul, where he was afraid to look.

He went into the bathroom. After his stand-up bath, he had left most of the water in the sink. It was still warm. One by one, he took his wet garments out of the garbage bag and immersed them in the sink, wringing out the soapy water and putting each garment into the tub. He ran tub water over the clothes—the water was so cold it made his hands ache—then squeezed out as much rinse water as he could. It took him a half-hour to wash and rinse all his clothes, but when he was done, the clothes hung from the shower-curtain rod. He rinsed the sink and tub two, three, four times.

If the landlord should come in while he was away, and if he happened to look into the bathroom, he would see clothes drying over the tub. Was that so strange for a bachelor? No, at least not while the power was out, he told himself.

Besides, girls were always washing their panty hose and drying them in the tub.

He put on a sweater. It was almost eight-thirty. He had to go to the *Gazette*. He would call and say he was coming but that he might be late.

He picked up the phone. Nothing. Of course, no phone.

He put on a pair of thick, old work shoes and a heavy coat, grabbed his car keys, and opened his apartment door a crack.

Quiet, gloomy corridor. No one around.

He locked his door and started down the stairs.

"I think we're in luck."

The voice of the landlord, who was just coming out of a second-floor room, put him close to panic.

"Luck?"

"With the power. I hear from the electric company that we might be one of the first sections of town to go back on line. Old part of town, we got more than our share of police and fire stations. Could be tonight, tomorrow morning. Rest of town, who knows?"

"That's good."

"You don't sound too peppy."

"No." He turned to go down the stairs.

"Say, you work at the *Gazette*. You might be interested in this. Did you hear what happened?"

They found a dead priest in a house . . .

"No, what?"

"The oldest oak tree in the city fell over. The one up in the park. Saddest goddamn thing I ever heard. Be a great picture."

"Thanks. I'll tell the paper."

"Mister, I hope you're not planning to drive."

He had started to walk down the driveway when the booming friendly voice of the utility worker stopped him. He turned.

"There's hardly a block in the city that isn't clogged up with trees and wires and our trucks," the utility man said.

"Really?"

"Really. You're better off walking."

His shoes got decent traction, but his footing was still uncertain. He walked slowly, taking short steps.

The utility worker had been right. Telephone and electric wires, tree branches and limbs, lay everywhere. The wires and limbs were grotesquely thick with ice. Icicles hung from wires and limbs, from building gutters and signs, from the bumpers of encrusted cars.

He shuddered. What if he had waited even a little longer to leave the priest's house? Would he have found it impossible to get home? Suppose he had skidded and crashed only a few blocks from the priest's house. . . .

He had killed a man, a priest. With all his might, he tried not to think about how the body had looked, how the club had felt in his hands.

Had the body been found? If it had, that meant the police were looking for him. For him.

No. The body had not been found. How could it have been? No way. That meant it was still lying on the dirt floor of the basement, all curled up, with the golf club sticking—

Suddenly he knew he would be sick. He slipped and slid toward the curb, put a hand on the icy hood of a car, and threw up in the street. He stood, looked around. He was glad no one had seen him.

He wiped his face with his handkerchief, let the cold air dry the sweat from his forehead.

He started walking again. He felt a little better, braced by the cold air. He guessed the temperature was about thirty degrees.

A police car appeared from a side street, turned, and came toward him with its red light flashing. Right up on the sidewalk it came. His legs went weak, and the terror hit him square in the stomach.

The police car turned back into the street, then slowly up

on the sidewalk again to get around a downed pole, then back to the street. It passed him slowly, its light still flashing, the siren silent.

He had never seen the streets of Bessemer like this. The only sounds were the putter of chain saws, the drones of emergency generators and utility trucks, the occasional shout of one repairman to another. And now and then the soft tinkle of icicles being shaken loose.

Just ahead of him, an elderly woman, bird-thin and frail and bundled against the cold, emerged hesitantly from an apartment building. She had taken only a few steps when her feet went out from under her and she fell with a thud onto her back.

"Easy. Easy. I'm coming. Don't move. Don't move."

In his haste, he half-slid, half-skated toward the old woman, who sat up and turned her head toward him.

"Easy. Easy. Don't move yet. I'll help. Easy."

"Oh, I just . . . My legs just went right out . . ."

"I know, I know." He was kneeling next to her now. "Did you break anything? Can you tell?"

"I don't, I don't think so. My legs just went . . ."

"Okay. We'll get you up. Easy."

He planted his feet as firmly as he could, put his hands under her arms, slowly straightened his legs. She was so light, he was able to haul her up without straining.

"Easy now. Easy." He was afraid her trembling would send them both to the pavement. "All right now. You're okay."

"Oh, thank you. I, I need my prescription . . ."

A doorman came out of the apartment building, nodded his thanks, put his own strong arm around the old woman's shoulders, steered her back inside the building.

"Thank you, young man," the old woman said.

The *Gazette*'s parking lot had only a fraction of the cars it would have had for a normal weekday morning. Some of the cars were ice caked.

He gave a halfhearted smile to the security guard, who waved him through. He stopped at the men's room at the top of the stairs, hung his jacket on a hook, and turned on the hot water. Thank God the *Gazette* had hot water.

Even though he had washed earlier, he had to wash again. He washed his face, his hands, his arms all the way to his elbows. He started to dry his hands, then stopped, holding the palms in front of his face. These were the hands that had killed.

He dried himself, combed his hair, studied his face. He looked pale and tired.

The door burst open and in walked Ed Sperl, the police reporter.

"Lose your power?" Sperl asked.

"Yeah."

"Me, too. Son of a bitch, could be two or three days before we get it back. Goddamn big trees."

"Hmmm."

"Fall on the ice?"

"What?"

"Your face. It looks like you fell."

"I did."

Ed Sperl went into a stall and slammed the door.

He didn't like Ed Sperl. He hurriedly finished drying and left.

With a sense of dread, he walked down the corridor toward the newsroom. If they had found the body, he would hear about it right away. Everyone would be talking about it.

He couldn't think of it as a murder. A killing yes, but not a murder. It had been an accident, almost. Or self-defense.

"Hi!" Marlee West, a feature writer in her twenties, greeted him near the door.

"Morning."

"I was just on my way for coffee. Can I get you some?"

"No, no thanks." He dearly wanted more coffee, but

Marlee was by nature friendly and curious, and he didn't want to talk to her much just now.

"Lose your electricity?" Marlee asked.

"Yeah. You?"

"Sure did. I came to work dirty, like a lot of other folks. Oooh, what happened to your face?"

"Fell on the ice."

"Oooh. You okay?"

"Yeah. Well, I gotta see what I'm supposed to do today."

Marlee laughed. "That's easy. The only story in town is the ice storm. See you later."

The city editor, a potbellied, balding man a few years from retirement, looked up at him. "Check the hospitals," the editor said. "A lot of them are getting their phones back. Get a rough total of the injuries, serious and otherwise, and give your stuff to rewrite."

He nodded and went to his desk. He would stay on the phone, lose himself for hours.

Three

▲ ▲ ▲

CITY REMAINS PARALYZED
AFTER FREAK ICE STORM

By Gazette Staff Reporters

Much of Bessemer lies paralyzed under a glistening ice crust spawned by a storm that has made travel perilous or impossible and knocked out power and communications.

Travel is expected to remain hazardous for two to three days at least. Electric and telephone lines serving tens of thousand of homes and businesses lie in gleaming tangles throughout the metropolitan area . . .

Meteorologists blamed the ice storm on an occurrence one called "really quite unusual" for Bessemer. At ground level, temperatures were below freezing, and several thousand feet up they were colder still. But between the cold ground and the cold upper atmosphere lay a huge pocket of warm air.

Thus, snowflakes that formed in the upper air turned to raindrops as they fell through the warm pocket, jelled as they hit the low-level cold air, then turned to ice on the ground, pavement, wires and trees . . .

Travel in and out of Bessemer came to a virtual standstill.

Bessemer Airport was forced to close this morning, after airport crews ran out of the deicing compound that is sprayed onto the wings of jetliners.

One of the last planes to get out of the city was a charter "golfers' special" flight bound for Florida. "We had a lot of anxious-looking travelers standing around the terminal, wondering if they'd get out," said Airport Manager Ralph Goode. "They don't know how lucky they are."

Four

◢ ◢ ◢

Father Brendan Sullivan bumped the curb as he parked and was glad that no one saw. Son of a bitch, maybe he *did* need to get his glasses checked again. What had that smart-ass German optometrist said to him at the last exam two—no, three—years ago? "At your age, Padre, you may need to get your eyes checked more often."

Padre, indeed. At my age, indeed, Father Sullivan huffed as he climbed out of the car, slowly so as not to aggravate his back.

Lucky for him it was a clear, crisp morning. The wine from that morning's Mass was still hot in his blood, and the cold breeze that lifted his white hair and slapped his cheeks perked him up considerably.

He recognized Father Barrow's car, parked about fifty feet or so in front of his own. The younger priest's car was streaked with road salt and frozen slush. Goodness, lad, you're carrying this poverty stuff too far if you don't get your car washed at least once a winter. A fine messenger for the Lord you'd be, rolling up to a shut-in's house in a car like that.

All right, young Father Barrow. If you're here, you'll have some explaining to do. If you're here . . . Well, he must be, Father Sullivan thought.

Ah, me, he thought, heading up the walk. It's not my world anymore. Not my church maybe. . . . This Father John Barrow, he with the easy, breezy manner that appealed to the young Catholics, the young church . . . Father Sullivan couldn't help but like him sometimes, couldn't help being jealous, too.

Father Sullivan paused to glance at the strange new open space in the yard, at the sawed-off stump that had once been the foundation of a magnificent old tree. Until the night of the ice storm. Ah, me, he thought. Lots of trees died that night; no sense mourning them all.

Father Sullivan thought again of Father John Barrow and was annoyed. I never knew the church was supposed to be fun, Father Sullivan thought, pressing the buzzer and hearing it ring inside. The church sure wasn't "fun" for me, especially early on. That was the point, though. Whoever said being a Christian, being a Catholic, was supposed to be fun all the time? It wasn't for Jesus. . . .

He pressed the buzzer again, longer this time. Father Sullivan pressed his nose to the cold glass; he could see the vestibule inside clearly enough. Doors to the rooms closed. No sign of life.

He glanced back to the street, his eyes resting on the young priest's car. A disgrace, for a priest to be driving—

Father Sullivan saw the red slips of paper stuck under a windshield wiper. Parking tickets, for God's sake. He was puzzled: Father Barrow had lived in this house for some months, and he was certainly familiar with the parking regulations. It was foolish of him to have left his car on the street, rather than in the driveway, when he went away for his golfing vacation.

Father Sullivan studied the car. There were two long fingers of ice running from the roof down the side, then to the snow on the ground. For God's sake, that car's a disgrace. Young Barrow must have taken a cab to the airport, Father Sullivan thought.

Father Sullivan had come to investigate why the young priest hadn't returned from his vacation when he was supposed to. The sight of the car was just an extra annoyance. His excellency the bishop doesn't care much for his priests committing venial sins with the law. And God help you if you're thinking of trying to get these tickets fixed, lad. Purgatory'll seem like a picnic compared to what the bishop says to you.

All right then, young Father Barrow. I hope there's no monkeyshines going on in there. If you're here, I gave you time to answer the door, and I'm tired of standing in the cold, and furthermore, I don't like running errands for the monsignor. Not at my age, I don't.

Father Sullivan used the key from the diocese office to open the door. The vestibule was cold, and the air had a bad smell. Forget to empty the garbage before you left, did you?

His foot kicked a pile of envelopes and magazines, scattering them across the vestibule floor. Must be a week's worth, he thought.

Father Sullivan groaned as he stooped to pick up the mail. Then he slid open the big door that led to Father Barrow's apartment. On a chair just inside the door lay a couple of days of mail—right where Father Dino had put it when he came by to check after the ice storm.

Father Sullivan tossed the mail he had just collected onto the chair with the earlier mail. He felt sad and more than a little hurt. Young priests abandoning their calling (there had been more than he cared to remember) were apt to do things like this, not coming home from vacations.

John Barrow, don't you do this to me, lad. You're a good priest, all things considered.

"John? Father Barrow, are you here?"

Silence.

It was uncomfortably cool in the big room, and there was an unpleasant smell. Father Sullivan knelt before the fireplace and sniffed. Cold ashes, maybe that was it. Or maybe a squirrel had crawled into the chimney and died.

"Father John? Come on, lad."

He went to the kitchen; the smell was worse. The lad's got to learn some basic housekeeping, Father Sullivan thought. He's supposed to be helping to keep this place in shape.

"John? Father John?" But by this time he didn't expect an answer.

Father Sullivan knew where Barrow's bedroom was, and he knocked. After a few moments, he opened the door.

Wonder of wonders, Father Sullivan thought when he saw the luggage and golf clubs. You did come back. Bless you, lad!

He must have just walked a couple blocks to a deli or a newsstand, Father Sullivan thought. Relieved, resolving anew to scold the young priest for worrying him, Father Sullivan took off his topcoat and laid it on the sofa. Then he sat down in an easy chair to wait.

He was sure his young friend hadn't gone far; he hadn't even unpacked yet, hadn't picked up the mail. John Barrow, you're a good-looking lad and you've got the gift of gab, and I should know, being Irish. But you've got to straighten up, lad. I can't be covering for you every time you want to bend the rules a little to have some fun.

After sitting for ten minutes or so, Father Sullivan stood up. Too long in one place would aggravate his arthritis. Besides, he had waited long enough. Father Sullivan glanced at the golf book on the table. The golfing priest, he thought, not unkindly.

He went to the kitchen, picked up the phone, and dialed.

"Catholic Diocese of Bessemer. Father Morini speaking."

"Dino, lad, it's Father Sullivan. Has the boy priest checked in yet?"

"Not a word, Father."

"Ain't that strange. Well, his luggage and golf clubs are here, but no sign of him."

"Out for a walk perhaps."

"Perhaps. His car's been sitting out front, collecting parking tickets. Looks like it's been there all the while."

"You know—Father, perhaps I should have mentioned it—but when I stopped by days ago to check the place after the ice storm I was surprised to see his car."

"You were?"

"Yes, Father. I thought I recalled his saying he was driving to the airport and leaving his car in the garage there."

"Did he, now?"

"I'm sorry, Father. Perhaps I should have mentioned . . ."

"No, Dino. It's his car, his tickets. He can't just be going off any which way and keeping his own schedule, can he, now? Not if he wants to be a priest."

"No, Father."

"Tell you what, Dino. He's a lousy housekeeper, too. The place smells like a sty. Did you notice it when you were by here?"

"I thought, well, I thought it smelled unclean, yes. At first I thought there'd been a sewage backup, but I peeked into the basement and saw that the floor was dry. So I thought perhaps he'd forgotten to empty his garbage."

"Well, did you empty it?"

"Oh, yes. There was some garbage in the basket under the sink, although not all that much. I left it by the curb."

"Well, it still smells like the breath of hell. I'll just wait here a bit longer and hope to have a heart-to-heart with Father John. Good-bye, Dino."

The smell was stronger in the kitchen, no doubt about it. Father Sullivan bent over the sink and sniffed. Then he opened the cupboard beneath the sink, peering into the plastic refuse container. Empty, and with a fresh liner. Then what . . . ?

Father Sullivan moved closer to the closed basement door. Yes, the smell was worse still. Dino, I thought you said there was no sewage backup.

Father Sullivan opened the door to the basement and was overwhelmed by a stench.

"Dear God in holy heaven." He held a handkerchief to his nose, found the light switch, and slowly descended the stairs. He expected to see an ankle-deep pool of raw sewage, so overpowering was the smell, but the basement floor was dry.

He entered the furnace room, found the light switch. Nothing looked out of the ordinary, but the smell was almost unbearable.

Something familiar about it. What?

Another room. Father Sullivan found the light switch just inside the door. The first thing he saw was the golf target hanging on the wall. Dried streaks of brown hung on it everywhere.

Father Sullivan heard squeaks and the rustle of tiny feet as the rats fled the intruder. Then he saw the lump on the dirt floor and knew in an instant why the smell was familiar. He had been a battlefield chaplain in the Pacific in World War II.

"Dear God in holy heaven."

The swollen lump on the dirt was barely recognizable as human. Father Sullivan's eyes lighted only for a moment on what had been the head. Then they focused on the steel rod sticking out of the skull. Dear Jesus.

Dear God, I pray he has found the peace he's entitled to after dying like this.

Father Sullivan turned to go back upstairs and call the police. He had taken only a couple of steps when he fainted.

Patrolman Edward Delaney was chased back to his police cruiser by a biting-cold breeze. He put the giant cup of coffee and the hot Danish from Grossman's deli on the dashboard and watched as the windshield started to steam from the inside.

Coffee and Danish from Grossman's was one of the officially forbidden but much coveted freebies that went with patrolling in the university district.

The coffee cup was pleasantly warm in his left hand whenever he took a sip.

"All cars, prepare to copy," the radio said.

Delaney gripped the pencil in his right hand over the clipboard on the seat.

"Be on the lookout for a 1970 Mustang, color blue, license number . . ."

Good, he thought. I can finish my breakfast.

"Car sixteen, one-six, minor Code One on the Ambrose Parkway near University exit." Another patrol car had been summoned to an accident.

Edward Delaney was twenty-two and had come out of the police academy the previous autumn. He had grown up in Bessemer and his father, Brian Delaney, had been a cop. It had seemed only natural that the son would be a cop, too.

His father had saved a couple of lives and been written up in the *Gazette*. Now the father was a honcho on the State University security police.

Maybe he, Edward Delaney, would do something heroic, he thought as he finished the Danish.

"Car nineteen, one-nine."

Me, he thought.

"One-nine responding."

"Code Ten, repeat, Code Ten at forty-six Norwood Avenue. Please respond at once. Detectives on way."

Holy shit. A Code Ten was a homicide. Delaney's heart was racing. "Uh, roger. Will I, do I need backup?"

"Negative, one-nine. See a Father Sullivan at forty-six Norwood and secure scene, please."

There was no ice on the Ambrose Parkway or on the side streets, and with his red gumball and siren going he made it to Norwood Avenue in a few minutes.

He saw a man with a priest's collar standing on the walk in front of the house, waving to him. Jesus! The priest was holding a bloody handkerchief to his head. What the hell! They said I didn't need backup. My first homicide . . .

He braked so hard at the curb that the half-full coffee cup, which he had completely forgotten and which had survived the trip on the dashboard, tumbled back onto the seat. Son of a bitch, coffee all over the clipboard and upholstery and my pants.

Delaney got out, fumbling for his service revolver. The gun shook in his hand. I'm not ready for this. . . .

"It's all right, lad," Father Sullivan said. "I just knocked myself on the head, that's all. There's no one here. No one alive, anyhow."

"Show me," Delaney said, holstering his revolver with great relief.

The smell hit Delaney at once. It was so bad that he braced himself to see the body at any moment. Has to be an old corpse, Delaney thought. He wondered how he would react. All the bodies he had seen so far had been in coffins; he hadn't even investigated a fatal wreck yet.

The patrolman followed the priest into the kitchen. The smell was worse. The body must be very close.

"Down here, lad," the priest said at the basement door.

Delaney followed the priest down the stairs. What he had smelled upstairs was nothing compared with what dashed his senses in the basement.

"Through there, lad."

Delaney went through the furnace room, saw the target on the wall. Nothing he had imagined, nothing he had heard the veteran cops talk about, prepared him for the sight on the dirt floor. He swallowed as hard as he could, just in time to keep everything down. He felt dizzy as he turned and walked out.

I've got to act like a cop, he thought. So he said, "Did you touch anything, Father?"

"God no, lad. Except for the light switches. I'm afraid I fainted and banged my head."

"Yeah, well, you're entitled. Come on, let's get out of here." At least I didn't faint, Delaney thought.

"That's Father John Barrow," Father Sullivan said on his way up the stairs. "I recognized enough of him to be sure."

"*Father* John Barrow?"

"Yes. He was supposed to be on vacation. In Florida. When he didn't return on time, I came by to investigate."

"Yeah, well, it looks like he never left."

Back outside, Delaney breathed huge gulps of cold, cleansing air. Where the hell were the detectives?

Several people—men and women of retirement age—had gathered on the sidewalk in front of the house. Secure the area, Delaney thought. That's what I should do. Then he spotted four young boys crossing over the lawn, looking curious and smart-alecky.

"You guys should be in school," Delaney said.

"Going home for lunch," one boy said.

"Just keep walking, fellas. Okay?"

Delaney walked toward his patrol car, glad just to move away from the house. "Nothing to see here, folks," he said to the people on the walk.

Delaney opened the trunk, got out the coil of yellow cloth tape that bore the words POLICE LINE—DO NOT CROSS, and tied one end to a pole next to the driveway. He was unraveling the tape across the front of the yard when he saw the car full of plainclothes cops pull up.

Delaney stood on the sidewalk for a long time, shooing along the curious as gently as he could. It was cold enough to make his legs shiver and his toes tingle, but he was glad to be outdoors. His stomach was getting better by the minute. A little smugly, Delaney remembered that the old priest had passed out. Another patrol car had come by to take him to the hospital. He sure looked green around the gills, Delaney thought.

"Delaney," a detective hollered from the porch. "Captain McNulty wants you. In the basement."

Delaney's smugness vanished in an instant and was replaced by double-barreled nausea. Part of it was plain fear: Raymond McNulty was captain of detectives and known throughout the department as an iron-hard taskmaster who brooked no laziness or mistakes. Delaney figured he must have done something wrong. For a moment, he imagined that the old priest, Father Sullivan, had noticed his clumsiness and told someone.

The other part of Delaney's nausea was the thought of going into the basement again.

Delaney took some comfort from the expressions on the faces of the veteran detectives. Nobody was trying to hide how sick he felt.

"Come over here, Delaney," McNulty said. He was standing to the side of the golf target, about twelve feet from the corpse. McNulty was about six feet tall, gray haired, red-faced, and built like the linebacker he'd been in high school.

Delaney's knees were shaking, but he started to feel better when McNulty smiled slightly.

"That was okay, what you did here," McNulty said. "Good work."

"Thanks, Captain. I didn't do much."

"You kept people off the front yard. Now, that could be important, if we were dealing with a burglar, say. You think we are?" McNulty was speaking in a low, almost conspiratorial voice.

"I, I don't know, Captain."

"Now listen, Delaney. I know your dad, and I know how you did in the academy. You're not a career patrolman. Someday you might be a detective. That's why I called you down here."

McNulty took a couple of steps closer to the corpse, and Delaney followed, reluctantly. McNulty read his mind. "Where they do the autopsies, there's a stainless-steel room with a big air circulator," McNulty said. "Changes every last bit of air in the room in under two minutes. Did you know that? I've still been sick, and I'm not ashamed to say it."

"Right, Captain."

Near the entrance to the room, two men wearing rubber gloves held a large green bag.

"In a minute, guys," McNulty said to the men. More quietly, he spoke to Delaney. "We've been over this dirt floor with little rakes, like the kids use. No telling what we'll find. Understand?"

"Right, Captain."

"So what do you think. Burglar?"

"Could be." Delaney felt stupid.

"Delaney, anything could be. Why was he chopped up so bad?"

"I can't say."

"I can't either, for certain. But it looks like pure rage. Doesn't it?"

"Could be, sir."

"And why do you suppose his pecker was hanging out?"

"It could . . . oh, you mean . . ."

"Christ, you guys are naive nowadays. There's golf balls all over the floor, a couple of golf clubs lying over there, and he's got a golf club sticking out of his head. What's that tell you?"

Delaney felt increasingly stupid as well as sick. "I don't know, Captain. Some kind of ritual?"

The detective captain had to stifle a laugh. "Ritual, shit. Means he invited someone to the basement—a guy, most likely, though we won't take that for granted—to practice a little golf. Then . . ."

McNulty's expression invited Delaney to speculate.

"Right, Captain. Then maybe they, uh, got into some hanky-panky, and maybe . . . a lover's quarrel?"

"Could be. You're thinking along the right lines."

Delaney was feeling more confident. "Thing is, Captain, if they knew each other, wouldn't they most likely have been doing it upstairs instead of down here, dirt floor and all?"

McNulty nodded and smiled. "Good thinking. Which is why forensics is checking the sofa and bed sheets."

"So maybe they were strangers," Delaney said. "Maybe it was someone he picked up."

The detective captain nodded. "A stranger, or a fairly new acquaintance. Diocese says Father Barrow was supposed to go to Florida for a golfing vacation. So we'll check the passenger list on the plane he was supposed to take. Then check the motel in Florida—"

"To see if he was going to room with anybody who was on the plane," Delaney said.

"You got it. That's in addition to the standard routine: talk to neighbors, talk to fellow priests, retrace victim's last steps. All that. Understand?"

"Sure. Got it."

"And could be some beat patrolman will pick up something from a snitch, some talk about one faggot jilting another."

"Sure, Captain."

"Anything you hear, you report to detectives. Anything. At the same time, we don't let out everything we know. Any reporters try to talk to you about this, you tell 'em to call me. I'll decide what they get. Understand?"

"Right, Captain."

"Good. Now let's get out of here and let the rubber-glove guys do their thing."

Gratefully, Delaney followed Detective Captain McNulty up the basement stairs. McNulty stopped in the kitchen to confer with a couple of subordinates. Delaney stood to one side and saw two other detectives in the priest's bedroom.

"Look at these," one of the detectives said, pointing to the golf clubs. "Brand-new set of Hogans. Betcha they never been used. Damn, what a waste."

"You don't need good clubs, the way you play," the other detective said.

"Ain't that the truth."

McNulty finished giving instructions and led Delaney out of the house to the clean, cold air.

"How's your father, Delaney?" McNulty said just before getting into his car.

"Fine, Captain. Just fine."

"Good. Say hello for me." The captain opened his car door, then paused for a moment. "You're too young to remember Orville Smalley. He was coroner a long time. Well, he used to chew tobacco, see. And whenever he had a real stinker, like this one, he used to swallow his tobacco plug to keep from getting sick."

Delaney was tired when he changed into his civvies at the end of his shift. He was still wired up from the excitement of the corpse in the basement, and he had endured several jokes from older cops who knew that it had been his first body scene. Delaney had taken the jokes good-naturedly, buoyed by the memory of McNulty's friendly words.

Delaney did want to be a detective someday, and McNulty might be able to help. Have to talk to the old man about it, Delaney thought. Maybe stop in and see him tonight. Have a few beers.

The thought of a few beers was an inviting one, even though Delaney knew they might put him to sleep early: he hadn't had anything to eat after the Danish and coffee in the morning.

"Delaney," the desk sergeant said as Delaney came out of the patrolmen's locker room. "Stop at detectives' and see McNulty before you leave."

The detective captain was sitting at his desk, wearing half-rim glasses and thumbing through papers.

"Captain," Delaney said.

McNulty didn't smile, didn't look up right away, and Delaney smelled whiskey.

"You got any good snitches yet, Delaney?" the captain said at last.

"One or two, Captain. I've only been on the force—"

"I know, I know. Listen, we don't want to overlook any

possibilities in this priest thing, you know? So you got any snitches, you lean on 'em."

"Sure, Captain."

"You hear anything about burglaries in the university area, you pass 'em on pronto."

"Burglaries?" Delaney was puzzled. "Captain, in the basement, I thought you said—"

McNulty cut him off with a steel stare over the top of his half-rim glasses.

"We overlook no possibilities, Delaney. There's been break-ins before in the university area. You know that."

"I know that, Captain. But—" Just in time, Delaney was saved by a bit of advice he remembered from his father: know when to shut up.

"We overlook no possibilities," the captain repeated. "And we don't spread rumors. Rumors spread enough by themselves. You'll learn that, if you haven't already."

Delaney said nothing; he realized he was standing at attention.

"We don't spread rumors," McNulty said, looking down at his papers. "I don't want anyone spreading rumors about the condition of that priest's body. Understand?"

"Rumors, Captain?"

"Rumors," the captain said, again fixing Delaney with a stare. "We don't spread any rumors about the priest's private parts being exposed. We say nothing about that. Understand?"

Not for nothing was he a cop's son. Delaney knew the answer. "Understood, Captain."

"Good. That's all."

Delaney turned to go. He was hurt and bewildered and couldn't wait to get out of the stationhouse. He would talk to his father.

"This is a Catholic town, Delaney," the captain said in farewell.

Five

▲ ▲ ▲

PRIEST FOUND SLAIN
IN BASEMENT OF
DIOCESE-OWNED HOUSE

By Ed Sperl

A young priest was found battered to death with a golf club yesterday in the basement of a diocese-owned house near the Ambrose Parkway.

The victim, the Reverend John Barrow, was discovered slumped on the dirt floor of a basement room where the priest had erected a golf target, the police said.

Father Barrow, 26, had been dead about two weeks, according to the medical examiner's office.

Detectives said the walls of the basement room were spattered with blood. The victim's head had been battered severely with the club, which was found lodged in the corpse's skull.

Homicide detectives were tight-lipped about the case, though there were hushed whispers at police headquarters that even hardened investigators were shocked at the savagery of the crime.

Bishop Armand J. Ciccarelli said he was "shocked and deeply saddened" by the murder. The bishop described Father Barrow, a native of Sharon, Pa., who came to the diocese only last autumn, as a "vibrant and dedicated servant of the Lord who will be sorely missed."

Detective Chief Raymond McNulty said there were no suspects so far, but that "all available manpower" would be pressed into service . . .

A diocese spokesman said Father Barrow enjoyed the company of young people, and that his duties included teaching Confraternity of Christian Doctrine classes to diocese teenagers.

The spokesman said Father Barrow often stopped at taverns in the university district. "Father John liked nothing better than to talk to young people, for he understood and shared their vigor, idealism and desire for a world of peace," the spokesman said . . .

Six

▲ ▲ ▲

Early spring, 1971

Marlee West found a parking spot around the corner from the Silver Swine and got out of her rusting Volkswagen Beetle while balancing the gifts precariously in her arms. She almost dropped one, but she managed to hold on and kicked the door shut.

At least the sidewalks weren't slippery; Bessemer was enjoying a mild spell, and the steady drizzle that rinsed her cheeks was not too much of a price for the warmth.

She was the first to arrive. Only a couple of strangers—ham-faced afternoon drinkers—were at the bar.

A tall bartender came up to her, smiling. "You brought me some presents," he said. Coal-black hair, linebacker build—a hunk, Marlee conceded.

"No way," she said, setting a couple of them on the bar. She smiled and laughed, then was self-conscious because she felt her upper lip sticking to her teeth. When she smiled, the lip often stuck, right in the area of her childhood surgical scar.

"We set things up in the back room," the bartender said.

"Meatballs, rings, fries—we'll even throw in some cheese and crackers on the house."

"Well, that's very nice of you."

"Why not? Newspaper people drink a lot when they have a farewell party."

"That's true. And we've had a lot of farewells lately."

"Bigger and better things and all that. Here, let me give you a hand."

The bartender took the three heaviest packages from her arms, lightly brushing her right breast with the back of his hand as he did. No, he had not done it on purpose, Marlee decided. She didn't mind in any event.

She followed him past the end of the long bar, through a hallway into the back room. The room had booths on all sides and two tables—a large one for food, a smaller one where Marlee and the bartender set the gifts.

"So, you're a little early," the bartender said.

"I'm sort of the unofficial greeter."

"Well, you look well suited for it. C'mon, the first beer is on me."

"I'll make a stop first and then take you up on your offer."

In the women's room, Marlee stared deep into the mirror and tried to be happy with what she saw. She couldn't quite do it. Her light brown hair was too wavy and uncooperative in the damp weather, and her brown eyes, while huge and luminous, betrayed her shyness. Marlee took the jar of Vaseline from her purse and rubbed some on her teeth. Lipstick next.

There, the best she could do. The lipstick concealed most of the scar from the birth defect and the operation that had only partly succeeded, and the Vaseline kept her lip from sticking to her teeth. Chin up, Marlee. At least your nose isn't too bad.

The bartender smiled at her and nodded toward a stool in front of a foam-topped stein. Marlee smiled her thanks, felt a sting of disappointment that the bartender was engaged in shoulders-hunched man talk with a customer.

Marlee let her raincoat slide off her shoulders and took a sip of her beer. She studied the drizzle drops on the front window. Yes, she could understand why people didn't stay in Bessemer. If you weren't born and raised here, and you don't like winter . . .

Marlee was twenty-five and had been at the *Gazette* for three and a half years. It seemed to her that there were mostly two kinds of people at the *Gazette*: older people who were pleasant, ordinary, and would die there, and young people, some not very pleasant but some better than ordinary, who would not. Well, who was to say she had to belong to either group?

She had gone out with a few guys who had left the *Gazette*, promising to write her from Chicago or Pittsburgh or Atlanta or wherever their dreams had carried them. Some had even kept their promises and written to her, but not for long. Hey, their loss.

She had never gone out with Grant Siebert, who was the honoree of this farewell party. She would have, if he had asked her. Sometimes she suspected that Grant Siebert was more shy than he let on.

Grant Siebert probably did not think she was very smart or talented. He likely thought he was better than she was because he was a hard-news reporter with a real knack for finding the facts, or the jugular. And she was a feature writer, assigned to what the Gazette labeled "women's news." God, she hated that label; maybe she could get it changed someday.

Well, she might not be a terrific hard-news reporter, but she damn well was interested in writing about real people and real problems. And yes, that often meant women's issues. There was a lot of fertile ground there, especially in Bessemer.

She had to laugh at herself. Here she was, sitting on a barstool, feeling her feminist juices heating up her blood and making her angry—and all the while hoping the sexy bartender would give her the time of day. And feeling slightly sad that Grant Siebert had never asked her out.

Damn, it was tough sometimes trying to figure out what you wanted and how to get it.

"Care for another?" The bartending hunk had returned.

"Sure. Thanks." She slid a dollar bill across the bar.

"You write for the *Gazette*?"

"Sure do."

"What do you write?"

"I write for the women's section."

"Oh, you mean like recipes and stuff."

A moment of truth: should she indicate her irritation with his chauvinism or be tactful and pleasant? "Not just recipes. I try to get into other issues."

The bartender shrugged, rang up her drink charge, and walked away.

The door opened and in walked Will Shafer, shaking drizzle from a bright yellow windbreaker.

"Hi," Marlee said as their eyes met.

"Oh, hi. We're the first ones?"

"Yep."

Awkward silence. Up to me to fill it, she thought. "New jacket?" she said.

"Christmas present from my mom. I haven't worn it till today. She likes bright colors more than I do."

Will seemed stiff and ill at ease, as usual. "Well," she said, "you can always get a job as a crossing guard."

That made him laugh, a little.

God, Marlee thought, he's such a tight-ass Boy Scout. Oops, Marlee thought, do I detect the start of a beard? Can this be?

Will Shafer ordered a beer, took a big gulp, self-consciously wiped foam from his lips.

"So," Marlee said, "whiskers come to Bessemer. How does your mom like the beard idea?"

"She doesn't."

"Figures. Moms never do. All the more reason to grow it."

Marlee had to feel a little sorry for Will: facial hair had indeed come to Bessemer, to the extent that young men looked odd if they didn't have a beard or mustache or muttonchop sideburns or some combination of those. Will was damned if he did and damned if he didn't.

"I, um, just wanted to see how it would look, you know?" Will said.

"Looks fine. How is your mom?"

"Okay. She keeps busy." Will Shafer bit off a big gulp of beer.

No more talk about his mom, Marlee thought. "The guest of honor better not be late for his own party," she said.

"Mmmm."

She watched him drain his glass and nod to the bartender for another beer. After the bartender walked away, Will Shafer made a big project out of cleaning his glasses, frowning all the while.

Marlee gave herself credit for being able to put people at ease most of the time, but Will Shafer was a tough nut to crack. He was polite and he never seemed to lose control, no matter how much he might be keeping inside. But he seemed tight as a drum.

Will was different from the other young people on the *Gazette* staff. He was known as a clear, neat writer, though hardly a brilliant stylist, and a dependable, accurate reporter. But Marlee didn't think of him as having much of a cutting edge. Though he was about Marlee's age, he was older than his years.

Will Shafer filled in on the city desk once or twice a week and, Marlee had heard, was competent and conscientious. There was nothing of the iconoclast in him.

A perfect editor for the *Gazette*. And why not? He had been a paperboy, and the *Gazette* had awarded him a college scholarship.

Now that she thought of it, Grant Siebert was Will Shafer's polar opposite. He came across as pleasant, at least initially. But, Marlee thought, the more you got to know him (not that anyone did), the more you realized that the dancing light in his eyes wasn't just restlessness or humor or intelligence. Was it contempt?

Being in the women's section meant that Marlee had little direct contact with the city desk, the honchos who supervised the regular reporting staff. But she had friends throughout the paper, and she had heard how, time and again, Siebert's behavior had been one step away from insubordination. And he had become famous for his cruel imitations of the older editors, especially those who were myopic, raspy voiced, or lame.

He had come to the *Gazette* only two years before. He had majored in history at Notre Dame, which hadn't hurt when he applied at the *Gazette*. Catholic town, Catholic-slanted newspaper, she thought.

"Look who's here," Will said. Marlee could tell from Shafer's voice and the look in his eyes that he was not a fan of the man who had just entered.

No, Marlee thought, Grant was not half-bad looking, with the straight white teeth and the paradoxical crooked, wiseass smile, framed in recent weeks by a new mustache—and yes, the eyes with the dancing light in them.

Shoulders hunched in studied nonchalance under a fashionably shabby raincoat, Grant shuffled up to the bar and stuck out his hand. "Will," he said simply.

"Good luck in New York, Grant," Shafer said civilly.

"Thanks. Marlee, I appreciate your coming."

"Hey, everyone deserves a good send-off."

"I guess. Excuse me a minute."

The guest of honor headed toward the men's room.

"He seems a little down," Marlee said. "Must be a weird feeling, going to your own farewell party."

"Hmmm." Will studied the bottom of his beer glass.

"I admire him for what he's doing," Marlee said. "I mean, it takes guts, heading to New York with nothing solid lined up."

Will just nodded.

"You don't like him much, do you?" Marlee said.

"I like him just enough to come to his farewell party."

"That could mean you're celebrating."

Marlee saw Will's face change.

"No, I don't like him too much," Will said. "He's a real pain in the ass, from an editor's standpoint. I mean, I don't make the rules, you know? The *Gazette* runs some petty shit. Sure. Someone has to write it. I wrote it. Still do sometimes. And he's too good to? Bullshit."

"Ouch. I touched a nerve."

"Yeah, well, you asked me. Obits, golden wedding anniversaries, briefs—all staples. Okay, dogshit, some of it. But it's gotta be done. He drags his feet, and when he finally does do it, he's apt to screw it up. Like, like . . ."

"Like it's beneath him," she said.

"Right. And you know what? I don't need that shit, I really don't."

Mischievously, she pressed on. "You have to admit that story he had a year or so ago, about the police infiltrating the antiwar movement at the university—"

"Was a damn good story," Shafer said. "I admit it. He got his facts wrong in a couple of places but . . . yeah, it was. Of course, that's the kind of story he likes: thumbing his nose at authority."

"That's what some of the best reporting is, Will."

Shafer's face colored slightly. "Fair enough. Anyhow, I don't want to be a total hypocrite. I'm at his farewell party."

Time for me to be kind, Marlee thought. "I can see how he'd rankle you, Will. I know you're one of the more conscientious people around."

"And I get stuck doing over some of the work he refuses to do right."

"Well, if the other guys on the city desk worked as hard as you, we might have a more accurate paper." But still dull, she thought.

"Thanks." He paused for a gulp of beer. "Do you like him?"

"Oh, I think I'm the wrong person to ask," she said as

smoothly as she could. "I mean, I'm way back in women's."

"Well, I envy him in some ways. I envy his balls, excuse the expression. I envy his . . . selfishness. There!"

I already knew that, Marlee thought.

The guest of honor was returning. He was staring straight ahead, as if he was avoiding eye contact. I wonder, she thought. Damn. Wouldn't it be something if he was sorry he'd never asked me out? Of course, he never asked any other *Gazette* girls out either, at least that I know of. Could it be he's . . . No.

"Buy you a beer now," Will said manfully to Grant.

"Thanks. And thanks for . . . for . . ." Siebert paused, picking up the fresh stein the bartender slid at him. "Thanks for being such a careful editor."

"You're welcome," Shafer said.

"And good luck from me, too," Marlee said. "Are you all set to go?"

"No. God, no. My place is a shambles. Lots of packing to do."

Grant looked so troubled that Marlee had an impulse to kiss him, but she didn't. The moment passed.

The three glasses touched. Freeze this moment, Marlee thought. I see the envy in Will's face, I see the arrogance in Grant's face. And what shows in my face?

The tavern door swung open again. In walked a half dozen reporters in their twenties, smiling, sneering, eager to swallow beer and spew self-righteous wisdom. A lot of the people didn't like Grant that much, but any excuse for a party was a good one, especially after a tough winter.

The joy can begin now, Marlee thought, half sadly.

She lost count of how many beers she had had. I don't feel too drunk, Marlee thought. She threaded her way through the crowd and the noise to the food table. She filled a paper plate with meatballs, cold pasta, and coleslaw and sat down near the gifts. She nursed her beer, picked at her food, smiled when eyes met her eyes. She tried to imagine what it would be like if *she* ever had a farewell party. She would probably cry.

"How's it going, Marlee?"

"Hi, Arnie! Thanks for squeezing us in."

"Don't mention it. I gotta shoot some Chamber of Commerce bullshit later, so this is a nice break."

Arnie Schwartz was the *Gazette*'s chief photographer. A widower near sixty, he groused constantly about his workload, yet was never too busy to drop in on farewell parties to take souvenir pictures.

"Things gonna start pretty soon Marlee?" the photographer asked.

"It looks that way." Marlee took her tape recorder out of her purse and checked the batteries. In a little while, when it was time for the ceremony, she would tape the whole thing.

She had made it a practice to tape-record the ceremonies of the going-away parties, then mail the tape and the pictures to the person who was leaving. Sometimes she kept a copy of the tape. Occasionally, parts of them were funny enough to play again at Christmas parties or union picnics, or wherever people wanted to reminisce. Of course, a lot of things seemed funnier after a few beers.

She had heard that Grant reacted unenthusiastically to the idea of a farewell party, had hemmed and hawed about having it at the Silver Swine. So she had told him, as nicely as she could, that the Silver Swine was the best place because of the back room. Finally, she had had to tell him straight out that people would think it strange—would remember it a long time—if he refused to show up.

The music was turned up loud; someone had put a bunch of quarters in the machine out front so the music from *Hair* would play nonstop.

Cigarette smoke hung in the room now. Ah, not just cigarette smoke; there was a sweet smell. Someone had brought pot. Marlee had a good, warm, mellow feeling. Even Will Shafer looked as if he was having a good time. He was loosening up a little, talking to people, even though he was standing off in the shadows.

"Marlee." The voice was little more than a whisper. It came from the shadows a few feet behind her. There, Carol Berman, her friend from classified, smiling and beckoning. Marlee went over to her.

"Share, kiddo," Carol said, handing her the cigarette with the telltale wrinkle and small, bright ember.

I shouldn't, Marlee thought, not on top of beer. What the hell, one good drag . . .

Marlee tried not to sense the moisture from other lips, tried only to savor the light, out-of-herself feeling that marijuana gave her.

"Whee!" Marlee said. Impulsively, she kissed her friend on the cheek, then went back to her seat.

Oooooh. . . . She was feeling a little lighter than she had counted on. Better get the tape recorder ready to go while I still have my coordination, she thought.

The recorder felt thick, heavy like a brick. She put it on the table and concentrated as hard as she could. Yes, just hit "play" and "record" at the right time. That's all she had to do.

"All right, listen up, goddamn it!"

"Eat it!"

"Fuck off!"

Loud, derisive laughter from everywhere. The party organizers were signaling that it was time for the ceremony. There, Arnie Schwartz was in position to take pictures.

Marlee had a little trouble seeing straight, but she managed to turn on the recorder.

"All right, all right. Grant Siebert, front and center at this time." The emcee was a reporter whom Marlee knew slightly. "Listen, you people. We are here to say farewell—"

"Good riddance, you mean."

"Eat it!"

"Kiss my ass!"

"—farewell to—"

"Who gives a shit?"

Laughter, some of it drunken.

"—Grant Siebert!"

A chorus of catcalls, more derisive laughter.

Flashbulbs exploded, one, two, three, and it seemed to Marlee that the light almost had an echo. Marijuana dulled her sense of time.

Grant Siebert sat in a chair near the table of gifts, just a few feet away from Marlee. She thought he looked distant, insolent, and slightly sentimental all at once. Oops, yes, she could see better if she closed one eye.

"Anyone here from management?" the emcee asked.

"Sure as hell hope not."

"No one who counts."

In a corner, a beer glass crashed on the floor.

My god, Marlee thought, are these really the good old days?

He had worried about coming back to the tavern where he had met the priest. Finally, though, he had decided he had to come. Now, he felt more at ease than he thought he would. The bartender who had served him and the priest that night, the night of the ice storm, wasn't here. Besides, the bartender probably wouldn't recognize him anyhow.

He had not meant it to happen. He had even prayed for the priest the first few nights. The priest should not have unzipped himself like that, sticking out his . . .

No! He was losing himself in the beer and smoke and babble. He need not think anymore about the night of the ice storm.

But sometimes he did. For one thing, the inside of his mouth had been aching off and on since his fall on the ice that night. Besides, a bloody, terrible deed had a certain lure to it. He knew that. And carrying a great, dark secret filled him with an awe no one could imagine.

He was glad he had come. He knew he could keep his face

from showing too much. And a little levity might help his headaches.

"You, Grant Siebert, having elected to leave Bessemer for a larger city on the Hudson, are here in the bosom of your friends—"

"He hasn't any!"

"Shhh."

"—to drink, make merry, and get some cheap gifts . . ."

"Not cheap, I put in a quarter."

"Shut up, asshole!"

Marlee joined in the laughter. Her head was mellow, all right. It would be interesting to replay the tape and find out how it all *really* sounded. It was fun to be a fool once in a while.

". . . and so, Grant, to aid in your quest for glory in the Holy City of New York, we hereby present you with the following."

Light from flashbulbs burst in Marlee's eyes, filled her slow-crawling universe.

The emcee reached into one of the gift bags. "A map of the New York subway system."

Mild applause as the emcee waved the folded map.

"A copy of *Writer's Market* to help you in your free-lance endeavors."

Mild applause.

"Some food stamps, also to help you in your free-lance endeavors."

Laughter.

"A booklet listing the public golf courses in the New York metropolitan area."

A murmur of surprise. "I didn't know he was a golfer," someone whispered. Marlee had found out and suggested the gift.

"And finally . . . a copy of *The Kingdom and the Power* by Gay Talese, so you can daydream about the *New York Times* if you don't get a job there."

"You bastard," the guest of honor said.

"Hey, Grant. Let's see some imitations."

"Why not, Grant? There's nothing to lose now."

Marlee saw Grant smile sheepishly for a moment before catching himself. Of course, she thought, his imitations, his whole attitude are what he uses to keep people away.

"In closing, Grant, what else can we say, except break a leg and—"

"Eat shit!" Laughter, more of it drunken than before.

Marlee saw Arnie Schwartz poised to shoot again. This time she closed her eyes.

The ceremony was over, and some of the party quitters were drifting out. The more dedicated celebrants were sliding into booths or gathering around Grant Siebert. A case of cold beer had been brought into the room.

Marlee was able to focus pretty well, and by going slow on the beer she had regained some of her balance.

"You picked out the gifts?" Grant was standing next to her. God, Marlee thought, he looks as if he wants to smile.

"The Talese book," she said, feeling her heart leap. "Thought you might like it. I didn't tell him to make that snotty remark, though." Marlee hoped she sounded all right.

"Hey, it was on the money. I mean, the gift and the remark."

"Well, you're welcome." At least she *thought* he had said thanks. Say something else, she told herself. "I think what you're doing takes a lot of guts."

"I've been feeling it was time to leave." Something flashed on his face, then was gone.

Awkward pause; up to her to fill it, of course. "Do you golf much?"

"Oh, off and on."

He's embarrassed, Marlee thought. Must think golf doesn't go with his image. "I've always heard it's a game you can get hooked on."

"Yeah, it is. Takes your mind off things. I just haven't played much lately."

"Speaking of golf, wasn't that a gas about that priest getting whacked?" The braying voice belonged to Ed Sperl, a police reporter in his early thirties. He had a reputation for cozying up to the cops and taking their side in any controversy involving the police and students or the police and blacks. Marlee found him amusing in moderate doses. Right now, she had no desire to plumb the depths of his shallowness.

"A real gas, all right," Marlee said.

"I mean, Jesus, not just killed but . . . *splook!*" Sperl said.

"Ed, enough already," Marlee said. "It's bad enough you get off on that stuff. We don't need you to draw a picture."

"I hear the pictures are pretty good," Sperl said.

"That's disgusting, Ed," Marlee said.

"Hey," Sperl said, "everyone needs a hobby."

"Oh, yuk!" Marlee's friend Carol Berman said.

Marlee realized that a sizable knot of people had gathered near her.

"Maybe we should have followed up on it more," Ed Sperl said. "What's your opinion, Will? Should we have followed up on it more?"

"What's to follow?" Shafer said.

Marlee heard the defensiveness in Will's voice. She knew he disliked Sperl.

"You spend a lot of time on the city desk, you tell me. I heard a dark rumor at headquarters, on deep background, that the priest wasn't just golfing down there, if you get my drift."

"So?" Shafer said. "You're the one who's supposed to have the terrific police sources."

"Best in town," Sperl said. "But they quit talking on this thing, after the early rumor. Some of my sources pretend they don't know me."

"Maybe you should work on your personality, Ed."

Who said that? Oops, Marlee was really losing her sense of time and place.

"Could it have been a fag deal?"

That last was another voice; yes, Marlee was having trouble keeping the voices separate. They sounded far away.

"Oh, yuk!"

Marlee had no trouble telling Carol's voice.

"I heard his putter was out of his bag, if you know what I mean."

Sperl's voice? Yes, Marlee thought so. Or someone else . . . ?

"You bastard."

"The guy's dead, for God's sake."

"They held a mass of the resurrection, but it didn't work."

Cynical laughter from everyone. Or almost everyone. Even with her focus a little off, Marlee could see the discomfort in Will Shafer's face. She felt sorry for him; he was in a bad position, both right now and generally. He was too much of a straight arrow to fit in with the crowd of young, smart-ass reporters. Marlee also knew the *Gazette* was sending Will Shafer to some kind of management-training seminar the coming week-end over in Westchester County, just north of New York City.

Was she too sure of herself, too smug in her confidence about other people's desires and strengths and weaknesses? No, she didn't think so. It was a knack she had. Or did the pot make her feel smarter than she was?

Someone bumped the table. Back to earth, Marlee.

"Betcha whoever did it is long gone."

"Still hacking away."

"You sick bastard."

". . . yuk . . ."

Marlee's world was spinning, spinning, spinning.

". . . awful thing . . ."

Another bump on the table, and beer splashed onto Marlee's food. No matter; what she really needed was fresh air and coffee.

". . . a terrible thing . . ."

God, get me through this, Marlee prayed.

"You just committed a double mortal sin."

"Good. Two for the price of one."

Laughter, but far away. The voices around her were fuzzy. Was that all her fault? No, the voices belonged to people who were beered up. Stoned, some of them.

Marlee's table shook again. It was her friend Carol Berman who had bumped the table this time. "Marlee, honey, I'm sorry. For offering you that stuff, I mean. You look spaced-out, kiddo. Like me."

"Oooh . . . I think I need coffee," Marlee said.

"Me, too. C'mon, we'll go out front and grab a table and mellow out."

"Okay." Marlee was surprised to see that the crowd around her table had vanished. Not only that, but the crowd in the room had thinned out. She had lost track of time.

She stood up and steadied herself by putting her hands on the table. Her recorder was still there, still going. After a couple of attempts, she managed to shut it off. She got the machine into her purse without knocking over any glasses or bottles, though her sleeve got wet from beer on the table.

Out front, she thought. Carol is waiting for me there. Maybe that sexy bartender is still working. . . .

The air was better out front, and there was more light. Carol was waving to her from a table. At some other tables and sitting at the bar were some of the others from the party.

Marlee's head was clearing a little. She craved coffee.

The drizzle had stopped. Walking to his car, he savored the night breezes of spring. It was almost as if a rind of beer sweat and smoke were being washed gently from his face. Even his soul felt lighter. Listening to the jokes about the priest had been cathartic, in an odd way. He had even made some jokes himself; that made him feel lighter, too, though he had no idea why.

He had not had as many dreams lately about the priest.

Sometimes he could hardly believe it: the man had wanted him to, to . . .

"Goddamn dirty bastard!" he hissed. "Your own goddamn fault. Priest faggot."

Ouch. There was the ache again inside his mouth. He touched the spot with his tongue. Should he see a dentist?

Even if he had called the police that night, it would have done no good. The priest was dead.

"It wasn't my fault," he whispered into the night. "It wasn't."

He would try not to think about it anymore. It would just give him a headache.

He still had to pack.

Twenty Years
Later

▲▲▲

Seven

▲ ▲ ▲

As always, he felt awkward about using the side door so that he could bypass the receptionist and whoever might be in the psychiatrist's waiting room. Being executive editor of the *Bessemer Gazette* made him not only privy to other people's lives but vulnerable in his own.

"Come in, Will." Dr. Merle Hopkins was a short, rumpled man with thick glasses and curly brown hair that looked like wood shavings.

Shafer went into a small wood-paneled office that smelled of pipe tobacco and sat in a recliner facing the doctor, who took his place in a rocking chair.

"So," the doctor said.

"So. I was thinking on the way over that I had a hundred things to say. Now I don't. Why is that?"

The doctor shrugged. "Choose one thing."

"Oh, God . . ." Shafer let out a long breath.

The doctor waited, a hint of a cherubic smile on his face.

"I was thinking about what's become of me." Shafer laughed bitterly.

"And what has, Will?"

"I have become what I once despised."

"Which is?"

"A man on the wrong side of forty who . . . I don't know."
But he did, in a sudden, cruel insight. "I have become what
the undead me in his early twenties despises. Do you see?
The part of me that is young, or regrets not being, not
being . . ."

"Take your time, Will."

"No! That's the point. I spent my time already, my best
time, spent it badly."

The doctor lit his pipe and puffed.

"I feel like there's a rat inside my skull, trying to eat its
way out."

"A powerful image, Will. You have a gift with words—"

"A modest gift, which I squandered. Bless me, Father, for
I have sinned."

Will paused, the doctor waited.

"Do you know what that jerk told me to do today?" The
shorthand between doctor and patient was well enough
established so that Dr. Hopkins knew the jerk was Lyle
Glanford, publisher of the *Bessemer Gazette.*

"What, Will?"

"I'll tell you. But first let me tell a little more about my
sins." He paused, then felt the sins start to slither out of his
soul like maggots. "I'm a journalist—me—but I missed the
bus. When I was younger, starting out, when I should have
had a cutting edge—" Without warning, his voice began to
break, and he had to pause. "When I still had it, history was
being made. In the South, with the civil rights movement,
and in Vietnam. And . . . I . . ."

Through the blue smoke the doctor spoke softly. "You
missed out."

"Yes! The world offered adventure, a feast. I stood at the
table and . . . and . . ."

"You didn't take a bite. And now you hate yourself for it."

"Hate myself. If we were talking about videotape, I could

just rewind it, start over. But we're talking about life. My life. And my work."

"How is work, Will?"

The question, delivered in the doctor's studied, low-key manner, triggered instant laughter. Will laughed loudly, shook his head, giggled like a baby, and wiped the tears from his cheeks with a handkerchief.

"Laughter is good therapy, Will. Now, before I coax you to go on, I want to remind you of something. You're not alone in thinking you missed a bus."

"I know, I feel sorry for myself."

"I wasn't implying that at all. I'm only trying to remind you that just because you didn't do something in your twenties doesn't mean you are helpless in your forties. What we are talking about is control. Control, Will. Your ability to control your own life."

"Okay. So maybe I shouldn't be talking about petty shit. Especially at your prices. Maybe I should go right to the big stuff instead. Whatever that is."

"If it bothered you enough to make you this angry, it's not petty shit. So tell me, Will, how is work?"

Will told the psychiatrist about his meeting that morning with the publisher.

The summons had come just as Will Shafer was finishing reading that day's paper. Shafer had heard from a couple of subordinate editors about stories that had been messed up badly enough to require corrections. He wondered if someone with clout—a department store owner, a hospital trustee, a banker, an industrialist, the bishop—had complained to the publisher.

"Good morning, Will. Sit down and have coffee with me. I've thought of the name."

"Ah, the name." Will sat in the visitor's chair facing the huge desk. What name? he wondered. What the hell is he talking about?

"For the celebration, Will. What we talked about the other

day." The publisher leaned forward, winked conspiratorily, and whispered, "Breaking ninety."

"Breaking ninety . . ."

"You remember, Will." Glanford's blue eyes brightened slightly with impatience. "It'll be perfect. The *Gazette*'s ninetieth birthday celebration will be topped off by a golf tournament, the theme of which will be . . . breaking ninety."

A pun, Will Shafer realized.

"It'll be perfect, Will. Lucky for us the paper's anniversary falls in midsummer. I've already sounded out a few close friends at the club to work with you in setting things up. The *Gazette* is going to be the biggest story in town in midsummer, Will. My grandfather would be so . . . well, never mind. I just wanted to bounce the theme off you, knowing that you're a golfer."

"Not much of one, I'm afraid. But the name is clever."

"I want this to be a real triumph," the publisher said. "God knows, our community has had its share of troubles lately. But I really feel we're starting to turn things around."

Lyle Glanford's "sources," Will Shafer knew, were the merchants and industrialists who most wanted to see the city's economy get better and who were, to varying degrees, part of the problem.

"Anyhow," Glanford went on, "I know the remodeling of the clubhouse will be done on time. I mean"—the publisher leaned forward and winked again—"it is going to be done on time, if you get my drift."

"I do indeed."

"The movers and shakers of business and industry are human, even as you and I. When there's talk of locating a plant or a regional office in a city, a little thing like whether the country club is tip-top or tacky can make a difference."

The phone on the publisher's desk buzzed discreetly. He picked it up, smiled, and said, "How are you, Senator? . . . Good . . . good . . ."

As Lyle Glanford leaned back in his chair and turned

sideways toward him, Will Shafer studied the man. How very much like a publisher he looks, Shafer thought. How very much indeed, with his clear, shiny skin and ice-blue eyes and luxurious, gray-turning-white hair. The publisher always wore dark, classically tailored suits. He bought them out of town, and Will was sure there was not a clothier in Bessemer who made such fine suits.

Shafer hadn't seen the golf tournament coming, but he realized that the signs had been there. The publisher had mentioned wistfully from time to time that he wished the *Gazette* were approaching its one hundredth anniversary this year instead of just the ninetieth. What had the publisher said recently? "I'm sixty-six and I've already had one heart attack, so who knows if I'll be around ten years from now, Will."

Lyle Glanford hung up and swung his chair around again to face his executive editor. "So, Will, this could be fun, eh?"

"It certainly could be." Will tried as hard as he could to inject enthusiasm into his voice.

"You won't be too busy to put in an hour or two a week to make it all work, will you?"

"I'll find the time." More like several hours a week, Will thought.

The publisher's face turned solemn. "I know all the heavy hitters in Bessemer are looking forward to this, Will. But I want us to go a step further, to show . . . to, well, to blow our own horn a little to the whole world."

Will Shafer braced himself. There was no telling what that might mean.

"I'm talking about bringing back some of our famous alumni, Will. Bessemer alumni who have gone on to make good, people who have made it in bigger, though certainly not better, cities. That's where you come in. Look up some of the people who got their starts here at the *Gazette*, then went on to big things. Bring them back here for some golf and a good prime rib. A sentimental celebration, but one with a purpose. To show the world . . . well, you know . . ."

"You want me to see if, to see who might come back? To play golf?" Will Shafer was dumbfounded.

"Sure! Tap into your old-boy network."

I don't have an old-boy network, Will thought.

"It's a small world, the newspaper business," the publisher went on. "I don't have to tell you that. All it takes is a few people from the national press, put 'em in friendly surroundings, fill 'em with good food and good ideas . . . hell, we might even get a cover story out of it." The publisher beamed.

"A cover story?"

"Why not? On *Time, Newsweek* . . ."

Will Shafer was flabbergasted. What an unreal world the publisher dwelled in.

"I know I've seen stories like that, Will. On Houston, Miami, Los Angeles . . ."

"Those are major cities, sir."

"And we're not, you mean? Let's not lower our sights, Will."

"We'll do what we can, I promise you." Steady, Shafer told himself. Keep your voice steady.

"Great. I know your best will be tip-top, Will. Lyle can help you."

"Fine." Lyle Glanford, Jr., was the publisher's son. He was not an unlikable man, especially considering whose son he was.

"All right, then," the publisher said. "Full speed ahead and all that. We've got an opportunity here for horn-tooting and . . . and . . . fun besides. Oh, and how's Kathleen?"

"Karen's fine, sir." The publisher often got Will's wife's name wrong.

"Good, good. We'll talk."

When Will Shafer got back to his desk, an assistant city editor was waiting for him. Shafer could tell from his face that there was trouble.

"What's up, Gene?"

"Will, we've got a factual error in this morning's install-ment of the housing series. We say that a company pleaded guilty five years ago . . ."

Dear God, Will thought. "And?"

"The company pleaded no contest. Their lawyer called."

"All right." Shafer let out a long, slow breath of relief. "That's not insignificant, but it's not fatal either."

"No. It's just wrong. The reporter feels bad about it."

"So do I. All right. Send me a memo for the official files, okay? I'll talk to her later."

"Sure, Will."

Will thought he saw several sets of eyes looking at him. Other people were waiting for the opportunity to bring him their problems. Which would instantly become *his* prob-lems. He needed a respite.

He picked up the phone and dialed. The voice on the other end was familiar; Will knew the words by heart: "Hello, and thank you for calling Dial-a-Prayer. You know, the Bible tells us . . ."

Dr. Hopkins puffed sympathetically on his pipe, creating languid curls of blue smoke. "Not such a great day at work, Will. All things considered."

"I love your understatement. This golf thing is too much. He thinks of me as his personal aide."

"And that makes you angry?"

"Jesus Christ, yes!"

"Good. That's a healthy response."

"It makes me feel like I'm wasting my life. This golf tournament thing will eat up more and more of my time. Details, petty shit—Jesus!" He had to stop; a vein in his forehead was pulsing with anger.

"Let me put a bookmark in here, Will. Our time is almost up, and it's a good place to pause anyway." The psychiatrist relit his pipe. "In no way do I make light of your difficulties at work, Will. But—and listen now, because I'll say this as many times as I have to, until it sinks in—if you had more self-esteem, more sense of your own inner power, you'd much, much better at dealing with these troubles."

Will Shafer nodded his agreement, though the pain in his forehead was still there.

"I can't wave a wand and make Lyle Glanford less of a jerk, Will. But I can help you find the strength in yourself to do what's appropriate."

"That might be tough."

"It *will* be tough. And it won't come overnight. You'll have to do the work; I can provide some insight. And support." The doctor paused, his eyes turning serious and laser bright. Then he said gently, "Eventually we'll talk about your guilt."

"Guilt?"

"Guilt. We'll get to it, Will. We'll find what you're burying, or choosing to forget."

"How do you know I feel guilt?"

The doctor just smiled wisely.

"What if I'm afraid to go there?" Will said.

"One step at a time, Will. I'll see you next week."

Eight

▲▲▲

The next morning, Will Shafer knocked on the half-open door to Lyle Glanford, Jr.'s, office. The publisher's son looked up from his cluttered desk, smiled, and waved him in.

"Morning," Will said.

"Good morning, Will. Bet I know why you're here so early. Breaking ninety?"

"Yes. Right."

"Hell of an idea, Will. Don't you think? And a hell of a slogan, too. Don't you agree?"

"Well, it's catchy in a way, I guess."

"It sucks, Will."

"Pardon?"

"I said, it sucks. You and I have known each other long enough, we don't have to bullshit each other."

Will chuckled. "I gotta say, I was taken off guard by the publisher yesterday when he dumped it all on me." He could feel himself relaxing.

"You and me both, Will. I'm only his son, and not incidentally the vice president of the Gazette Publishing Company, whatever the hell that means. I'll tell you what it means: it

77

means I have to do some things I don't like. You want coffee, Will? I mean decent coffee, instead of that terrible stuff you brew in your office."

"Sure. Why not."

Lyle Glanford, Jr., pressed a buzzer under his desk, mumbled something into it.

"Lucky for you I'm an early riser, Will. Maybe I can get enough of this shit squared away to take a lot of load off you."

"I could live with that."

"Really? You mean running a paper in a decaying industrial town and trying to keep the bankers and bishop and candlestick makers happy and do your job at the same time . . . you mean that keeps you busy, fella?"

"Most days, yes."

"I bet. Thanks, Gladys."

Lyle was right; the coffee was better than the stuff Will Shafer brewed for himself.

"Can I be frank, Will?"

"Sure."

"We have something in common on this thing, Will. I mean, the publisher says he wants something, and we have to do it. Even if it isn't our cup of tea. Or coffee."

Shafer didn't know what to say, so he nodded.

"Of course, my old man would say I never found out what my cup of tea is, Will. But that's my problem." Lyle Glanford, Jr., smiled self-deprecatingly. "Anyhow, I'm going to help you on this thing."

"Thanks, Lyle. I can use it. I appreciate it."

"Hey, I owe you. Seems to me I can recall your doing me some favors."

"Well, everybody needs a favor sometime."

"Sure is the truth."

The desk phone buzzed.

"Gladys," Lyle Glanford said, "I really do want the calls held. . . . Oh. In that case . . ."

The publisher's son put his hand over the phone and whispered to Will: "It's my ex-wife calling."

Will stood up to leave, but Lyle waved vigorously, good-naturedly, for him to stay.

"Michelle? How are you?" Lyle said into the phone. "Okay. . . . Sure. . . . All right, you can do that, but ideally those would be rolled over. . . . Oh, I see. I see what you mean. Listen, let me get back to you, okay? Good . . . good. . . . You, too. Bye."

Will was embarrassed as Lyle hung up and shook his head. "How's Karen, Will?"

"Fine."

"You're a lucky man, Will. Let me tell you, if there's a hell on earth, it's a divorce. Hey, I say that, and I've been divorced a couple of years already. Ah, you don't need to hear this shit. I guess marriage wasn't my cup of tea."

Will Shafer saw the pain on the face and was touched by compassion for the man sipping coffee across from him. "Who's to say what the right brew is, Lyle?"

Lyle nodded and smiled. "That's a nice thing to say, Will. I appreciate it. Anyhow, so you can get back to editing this goddamn newspaper, let me give you a rundown."

For the next hour, they discussed plans for the *Gazette*'s ninetieth reunion and the golf tournament that would cap it. Lyle Glanford, Jr., led the conversation, and Will was impressed at what he had already done in terms of planning. Lyle's ideas about whom to invite and what to serve them, what companies to hire for food and decorations, which people to tap for committees and why—they all made more sense than Will had thought they might. And Lyle had planned for emergencies ranging from rain to possible strikes in the catering business.

"Terrific, Lyle," Will said at last, meaning it.

"Hey! Maybe I've found my niche, Will. Party organizer! What the hell, a sense of humor helps me hold on to my sanity."

Lyle laughed, and Will chuckled with him, even though he couldn't help feeling sorry for the publisher's son. "Lyle, you must have put a lot of hours in on this."

"I won't deny it, Will. But if we're gonna do it, I want it to be right."

"I have to admit, when I talked to the publisher, I had the idea we were starting from ground zero. I had no idea you—"

"Will, I could win a Nobel for perfecting cold fusion, and the old man wouldn't . . . Never mind. When he mentioned this damn reunion thing to me, I knew he'd drag you into it. I know what a job running this damn paper is, and I know you're gonna be plenty busy regardless. Least I can do . . ."

"Lyle, you've done a lot. I appreciate it."

"Don't thank me yet, Will. Not until it's over. But I'll help all I can. Hey, maybe we'll even have some fun. What about the staff? How do you think they'll react to writing anniversary stories?"

"Oh, I guess . . ."

"Yeah, they'll piss and moan. Complain about writing puff pieces to make advertisers and the Chamber of Commerce feel good. But they'll quiet down when they have some booze and good food. The golfers among them will probably enjoy a chance to play at the country club. Don't you think?"

"Yeah. Probably. It's a good course."

"By Bessemer standards. Don't bullshit me, Will. We've known each other too long."

Will laughed. "Actually, it isn't a bad course."

"Hey, Will, the important thing is getting the clubhouse remodeled in time. I'm leaving that up to the old man. Stay in touch."

"I will."

"I mean it. We might even have some fun."

Nine

▲ ▲ ▲

The young woman's face was full of pain and terror. She knelt next to the log, cowering in anticipation of the ax. The top buttons of her flannel camping shirt had been ripped off, and ugly red scratches ran from her exposed shoulder down to her cleavage.

The ax head hovered, poised for the death blow.

"You're going to die!" the man with the ax shouted.

"No! Please!" the woman said.

"You're going to die, bitch."

"No!"

"Beg me, bitch!"

"No! Please!"

The echoes of the shouts died away, as did the last of the camera clicks.

"Okay, everybody. That's it," Walter Striker said. Then, to the young woman, "Good work, Janet. You'll get your check in a few days."

The man who had been holding the ax had set it down. Now he helped the young woman to her feet.

"Thanks," she said, wiping the painted scratches off her skin with a tissue and rebuttoning her shirt.

"Can I give you a lift?"

"That's okay, thanks. I've got a ride. Bye, everybody."

"Bye, Janet. Thanks again," Walt Striker said.

A young man in dungarees and T-shirt appeared, picked up the plastic log and the ax, and took them back to the prop room. When he returned, he would haul away the green-and-brown canvas that had simulated a wooded background. Then he would sweep up the real twigs, leaves, and pine needles that had been strewn about for authenticity.

"Good, everybody!" Walt Striker said. "On time and on budget. Nice work, Grant."

"Thanks." Grant Siebert shook the hand of the editor of *Sleuth*. The crime magazine had just closed its September issue, whose cover article (based, more or less, on a real case) was entitled "Lunatic Lumberjack."

"Stop for a beer?" Walt Striker said. The editor was short, balding, dumpling shaped, amusing and easily amused—good company at a bar.

"Can't tonight," Grant said. "There're some things I have to do." That was not exactly true. But the photography session, as usual, had left him feeling slightly unclean.

When he walked out of the building in midtown Manhattan, he was glad to see that it had rained. It was early evening. The walk to his apartment was a long way, but he welcomed the exercise, even though he had to walk through a dirty part of town.

The rain had given the air a just-rinsed feel that he found pleasant, especially since New York had been unusually muggy for so early in the summer. Still, the odors of whiskey and urine clung to the West Side like skin.

Grant tried to ignore the smells as he walked down Seventh Avenue. Cops patrolled the sidewalks in groups of two or three, their pale blue shirts looking a bit crisper than usual in the cooler air.

"Hi, want some company?" The prostitute was eighteen or nineteen, hair in dirty strands. She was pale and bird thin and had scabs on her face. And arms.

"No thanks."

Near the subway entrance at Forty-second and Seventh, a black man winked at him. "Pretty girl? Pretty girl?"

Grant ignored him and walked on.

"Smoke? Smoke?" Another offer from the shadows.

As he approached Penn Station, between Thirty-first and Thirty-third, he saw the usual collection of beggars and the homeless. Sometimes he gave them quarters, but he was not in the mood tonight.

Just north of Penn Station, he saw a woman a little over five feet tall, dragging her worldly possessions in two soggy shopping bags, one in each hand. Her hair was dirty gray; she might have been forty, or sixty. She had got wet in the rain, but the rain had had no cleansing effect. Instead, it had only smeared the woman's grime and filth throughout her dress. Then the woman hiked up her dress to reveal soiled undergarments and horrid, strawberry-red skin sores.

Grant was past her now. The scream in his heart had died in his throat. God Almighty, he thought. God Almighty.

"Homeless Vietnam veteran here. Won't you please help."

"No, get away from me," Grant heard himself say. "Get the fuck away from me."

I should have taken the subway, he thought.

He walked faster. He felt guilty about snapping at the Vietnam beggar and vowed to make up for it. There would be plenty of opportunity: the beggar had been in front of Penn Station for months.

He let himself into his apartment building. Down the narrow pink corridor he went until he reached the elevator, which he summoned with another key. The elevator lurched its way to the fourth floor, where he emerged into a narrow blue hallway that usually smelled of fried foods. He got to his apartment door without seeing anyone, which was fine with him, and let himself in. After turning on the lights, he locked the dead bolt and fixed the door chain.

The entrance door to his apartment led directly into a

narrow kitchen, which was windowless but white and clean. It was large enough for a refrigerator, a small stove, a sink, some counter space, and a few cupboards.

A door from the kitchen led to a small living room. It had a window that afforded a view of the street, a sofa and one easy chair, a small coffee table, and a larger dining-room-size table where, in a straight-back chair, he did his writing.

His word processor and printer rested on the table, and Grant felt better when he saw the several fresh sheets of paper he had turned out that morning. He had done his writing for the day, and he could relax for the evening without feeling guilty.

Which is just what he wanted to do. He went into his tiny bedroom, hung his tie in the tiny closet, and looked at the telephone answering machine on the night table next to his bed. The machine was blinking.

Never mind; after his walk down Seventh Avenue, he was not in the mood for surprises. He would leave the machine on so he didn't have to answer the phone.

The phone itself had a long cord so he could have it in the living room, or even the kitchen, if he chose. At night, he always took it into the bedroom. His building was safe, but New York was New York, and he wanted the phone handy if he opened his eyes to the dark and heard a strange noise.

He got a beer, took off his shoes, and lay down on the sofa. From where he lay, he did not have to move his head to see the television set nestled in the bookcase. Maybe a ball game tonight, he thought. Something mindless . . .

A single ring came from the phone, then the loud click from the bedroom as the answering machine kicked in. For a moment he wondered if he should answer; suppose it's an important call. Suppose someone wants to buy my manuscript.

Screw it. The beer tasted so good he finished it in several gulps, got up, and fetched another. This one he would savor a bit longer. Maybe . . .

He hadn't got back to the sofa when the phone gave

another ring. This time, his sense of urgency took over, and he picked up the receiver.

"Just a minute, I'll be right with you," he said over the sound of his own recorded message. "Hello?"

"Yes, Mr. Siebert, I thought I saw you come in, but I got your recording just a minute ago, so I decided to try again."

"Hello, Mrs. Bowe." He had recognized the landlady's voice at once.

"Yes, well, it is that time again, and we can't let you—"

"I'll leave the check in the office tomorrow. Okay? Have a nice evening."

He decided to check the rest of his messages before lying down again.

"Mr. Siebert, this is Jerome Saltzman from the credit department of Barney's. We'd like to talk to you at your earliest convenience—"

"Check'll be in the mail tomorrow, dick brain."

"Grant? Is this Grant Siebert's residence? Grant, this is a voice you haven't heard for a while, or even thought of, probably. It's Will Shafer from the *Bessemer Gazette*. Remember? It's been a long time. Listen, I need to talk to you, I really do. Please call me at the office, okay? Call collect. Here's my number . . ."

Will Shafer was right: Grant had not thought of him in years. What could Will Shafer possibly want? He's coming to New York for a Broadway show, and he wants a cheap place to stay. Naw. He wants a job in New York and he wants me for a reference? Even less likely.

He lay back down on the sofa with an I'll-be-damned feeling. His eyes fell on a book that stood on the shelf next to the TV: *The Kingdom and the Power,* the book about the *Times* that he had been given in Bessemer as a going-away present.

Grant had seen items in *Editor & Publisher* magazine about Will Shafer's promotions over the years. He snorted ruefully into his beer. Good for Will Shafer, he thought. Little duck, little pond. Hey, have I done any better?

He had not been back to Bessemer since he left the *Gazette*. Sometimes he had wondered what it would be like to go back, but he had never wondered enough to do it. And there were things he had left buried there.

Grant thought back, to how frightened he had been when he first arrived in New York. He wondered if things would have been different for him if his first few days had gone better. He had felt like a small-town boy.

God, he had been a naive jerk. He had walked past the entrance of the *New York Times* twice, trying to appear nonchalant, before going inside. The neighborhood hadn't smelled so bad then; that he remembered. He had even managed to get to the main newsroom on the third floor, where he had used up all his guts just approaching the receptionist and asking to be pointed toward the metropolitan editors.

He had found a subaltern editor willing to talk to him for a few minutes, although the editor did so with a puzzled look that seemed to say, "How did this guy get in here?"

The Timesman had talked about Grant's need to get "a bit more experience" and had wished him well. Then the editor had excused himself, offered Grant a dismissive handshake, and suggested that he "drop by personnel" and fill out an application. And he had, though it was a silly, futile gesture.

Still smarting from humiliation, he had managed to get an appointment with a wire service's first or second assistant bureau chief in New York. The meeting had been in the early afternoon, and to Grant's surprise his interviewer smelled of beer. Too late it had occurred to Grant that he should have made an effort to keep his contempt from showing.

"Suppose we had something for you," the man had said. "What would you like to do for us?"

"Go to Vietnam," Grant had immediately said.

"Old story. And we have experts there who've followed it from the start. Takes a new guy six months just to cultivate sources."

"'Cultivate sources'?" Grant said. "That's part of the problem. Reporters have the wrong sources over there. And the same ones."

The interviewer might have had a beery lunch, but he could sure as hell focus his eyes, which gleamed with annoyance. "Well, we can't all go to Vietnam and win Pulitzers," he said.

Grant had wanted to say something snotty, the way he had sometimes replied to the assistant city editors at the *Gazette,* but he couldn't. This was a job interview, after all.

The interviewer had asked him why he left Bessemer with no job lined up in New York.

"I just needed a change," Grant replied.

The gleam in the interviewer's eyes had changed, Grant remembered later, from anger to mischief. "How much were you making when you left the *Gazette?*"

Embarrassed, but with his heart rising in anticipation, Grant told him.

The man shook his head slowly and frowned. "Well, you could never live on that in New York. Even if we had something for you." And then he swiveled in his chair, showing Grant his back.

It was a while before Grant could laugh about it.

He tried other papers, some magazines in the city. Then he tried the publishing houses and met more discouragement. Just when he was running out of cash and good dress shirts, he had landed at Sleuth Inc., publisher of pulp true-crime magazines. An overweight, rumpled man—Walt Striker—who smelled of hair oil and cigars had liked something Grant had said (or perhaps had just taken pity on him) and offered him a job.

The second beer was empty already. Coming back from the kitchen with his third, Grant Siebert opened the living room window to let in the rain breeze and the city noises. He heard a siren a few blocks away. Someone else hurt or dying or cut to pieces in New York City.

Grant had been so grateful to get the job at Sleuth Inc. that he had thrown himself into it. Amazing how much a person could accomplish, could endure, when his pride didn't get in the way.

He had worked his way up to copy editor, sometimes rewriting the gore tales that came in from stringers all over the country. He had showed a real knack (he was ashamed to think how much of a knack) for editing stories about suffering and murder. What the hell, the salary wasn't great, but it paid the rent. Grant's hours were flexible enough to leave him time to write.

Will Shafer. If there was anyone in the solar system he had not expected to hear from, it was him. Oh, it must be that he was coming to New York—some kind of editors' conference?—and wanted someone to show him around the city. Sure.

Maybe if I show him around, he'll buy me a big lunch, Grant thought. He relaxed on the sofa, letting the breeze caress the top of his head.

Next morning, halfway through his second cup of coffee, he called Will Shafer collect.

"Grant! It's been a long time. Good to hear your voice."

"Same here, Will. How's everything with you?" Not that I care a lot, he thought.

"Not bad. I'm keeping busy."

"Me, too." Siebert remembered that Will Shafer was married, but he didn't really want to get into much personal stuff.

"I bet you're busy," Shafer said. "You're doing magazine work?"

"Right. An outfit called *Sleuth*. True-crime stuff."

"I see. And I've seen your byline in the *New York Times*."

"I've sold them a few free-lance articles. A book review, a suburban feature."

"I see. Have you ever thought of working there full-time?"

"A long time ago I did. I didn't get hired."

"I see. Doing any other writing?"

"Yep. No books published yet. A few articles."

"That's great." Pause. "Grant, the reason I called . . ."

At last, Grant thought. He had made up his mind to lie; he would tell Will Shafer he was going to be out of town when Shafer came to New York.

". . . I'm getting in touch with some *Gazette* alumni. We want to have a reunion this summer."

Grant could hardly believe what he was hearing.

"Do you think you could make it, Grant?"

"I don't know."

"It's the *Gazette*'s ninetieth birthday. The publisher, well, I'm sure he wonders if he'll be around ten years from now, so he decided to have a shindig this year."

"A shindig?"

"Here's the story, Grant. This whole deal is partly self-promotion, okay? I mean, we're going to sing 'Happy Birthday' to ourselves and put out a special section. You know, how the *Gazette* and Bessemer have grown together. You follow?"

"I follow." But why me?

"Off the record, a lot of it is Chamber of Commerce–type bullshit. You know Lyle Glanford. Anyhow, for part of it I'm trying to assemble some of the old staffers for a reunion gig. A big dinner, I mean. I've tracked down some people who went on to become lawyers, politicians. Oh, I even found a couple of people who stayed in our field." Chuckle. "There's Charlie Buck. Remember him? Anyhow, he's an assistant managing editor in Milwaukee—"

Why me? Grant thought.

"—and then there's you, Grant. Are you interested?"

"But why me?"

"Why not? You went from Bessemer to New York, for crying out loud. How many other people ever went from the *Gazette* to New York?"

"I don't know. Not offhand."

"That's what I mean. Look, Grant, let me level all the way. The publisher is counting on me to have a big turnout of old *Gazette* hands, so I'm calling in all the favors I can. I know you and I weren't real buddy-buddy, but that's okay. We had different agendas back then. What say?"

"Damn. I just don't know."

"That's honest enough." Chuckle. "If it helps, part of this thing is a golf outing."

"Golf?" He hadn't held a golf club in a long time.

"The golf is all tied in with the Chamber of Commerce bullshit. Showing off the remodeled country club and all that. But at least it's a chance to play at the country club and have some fun. What do you say?"

"I don't know. I thought I left Bessemer behind for good."

"The publisher's picking up the dinner and party tab. Greens fees and caddies, each player pays. Sound okay?"

"I don't know. I just don't know."

"I hear you, Grant. Quite a bolt out of the blue, huh?" Chuckle. "If you come, I'll see we're paired up for golf, if that's okay. Listen, I gotta go. Think about it and let me know."

He poured himself another cup of coffee, berating himself for not saying no right away. The last thing he needed was a trip to Bessemer for anything, let alone to play golf with Will Shafer.

So why hadn't he just told Will Shafer that? Why?

He went to the closet, reached into a corner, and dragged out the long-unused golf bag, brushing jackets and coats out of the way. He took out a long iron, held it in his left hand, waggled the club. Strange, it felt so strange. It had been so long since he had swung a golf club.

"Goddammit!"

In a burst of anger that surprised him with its force, he swung the club as hard as he could into a sofa cushion.

Ten

▲▲▲

Will Shafer hung up and let out a deep breath; talking to Grant Siebert had not been too much of an ordeal, especially compared to the talk he had just had with the publisher, although Grant had seemed a bit aloof. Some things never change, Shafer thought.

Will hoped Grant would come. It wasn't that he liked him that much; it was just that Will hadn't had many positive responses to the reunion invitation. Charlie Buck from Milwaukee had said yes, probably because he was coming back to Bessemer anyway for his father's eightieth birthday.

Well, Shafer thought, we'll just have to fill up the tables with people who left the *Gazette* but stayed in Bessemer. There's plenty of them, Will thought ruefully. The publisher won't know the difference with a few martinis in him.

His secretary approached. "Do you want to see Jenifer Hurley now?" she asked.

"Give me five minutes, okay? Then fetch her. I need to sweep out my mental cobwebs."

Jenifer Hurley was the reporter whose mistake had appeared the day before in the housing series. Will Shafer could see her profile as she sat at her desk some fifty feet away. She was making a big project out of scanning the paper and eating a muffin.

Trying to be nonchalant, Shafer thought. Is she scared about what I'm going to say to her? Or is she psyching herself so she won't show her contempt for me? Both?

Will Shafer wondered if Jenifer Hurley was contemptuous of him. It was the nature of most young reporters to feel that way about high-ranking editors, especially if a reporter had the extra cutting edge that sometimes defined talent.

And Jenifer Hurley had talent, probably as much as any reporter he had known. Intelligence, drive, curiosity—she had all of those in abundance. More: she had a certain shrewdness, an alertness that seldom strayed into cynicism and never into naïveté. Will Shafer knew that because he had seen a lot of her unedited copy. Jenifer Hurley was a graceful writer whose prose was almost never elephantine or bumpy. Yes, she had gifts that could not be taught. What he hoped to teach her was a little patience.

Should he talk to her in his private office, set a few yards off the newsroom? Yes. He picked up his phone, buzzed, and instructed his secretary. "Marie, wait another few minutes, then send her in."

Will's office was cluttered, cramped really, with plaques and pictures on the walls and a picture on the desk of his wife, Karen, kneeling in the backyard with her arms around their young son and daughter. The view from the single window was gray: the wall of the *Gazette* printing plant right across the alley and if he stretched his neck, a parking lot.

Will Shafer poured himself coffee from the pot in the corner, knowing from the pot's weight that there was plenty of coffee for Jenifer Hurley. He would offer her some to put her at ease.

"Knock knock," Jenifer Hurley said in the doorway.

"Hi, Jenifer. Come on in and sit down."

In the two or three seconds it took Jenifer Hurley to pass in front of his desk and settle herself in the chair, Will Shafer admired her athletic body, her wide, smooth face framed by crow-black hair, her glorious youth. She wore no makeup and didn't need it: the ice-blue eyes that shone with intelligence and character (not to mention a trace of arrogance) were jewels enough.

She looked at him, her head slightly cocked, smiled slightly with closed lips, and waited.

"Would you like a cup of coffee? I'm having one."

"No . . . well, yeah, thanks. That sounds good."

Will got up, found a clean cup at the corner table, then saw that there was no powdered milk.

"Just black is fine," Jenifer Hurley said.

He set the coffee down on the edge of his desk right in front of her. He thought she looked absolutely gorgeous in her tomato-red sweater and faded blue jeans. What would she think of him if she knew he was seeing a psychiatrist? That she made him wish he were young again and could ask her to go out with him? Would she?

Looking at her made him feel at once protective, so much so that he wanted to put his arm across her shoulders, and sad. Because he felt that Jenifer Hurley, were she and he to suddenly, magically, be the same age instead of two decades apart, would not give him the time of day. Might laugh at him.

"Pretty bad coffee, isn't it?" Will Shafer said.

"I've had worse."

Where? the executive editor wondered. With whom? His place or yours? Do you talk to your boyfriend about me?

"Jenifer, I had an unpleasant chat with the publisher this morning. He's an early riser, you know."

"No, I didn't."

Will saw that she was holding tight to her composure, saw, too, the vulnerability in her eyes.

"Yeah, he is. Sometimes I wish he wasn't. He took some flak from his friends over the error in your story." How much to tell her? As much as I can. "Jenifer, the publisher wanted me to convey to you the importance of accuracy in a sensitive story like this, and he wanted me to assure him, frankly, that I still had faith in your reporting."

"And?"

Doing her best to sound defiant, Will thought. Good for her.

"So, Jenifer, I hereby convey to you the importance of accuracy in a sensitive story. And as for your reporting—"

His phone buzzed. "Excuse me, Will, Charlie Stark on line one from the composing room. He says it's urgent."

Will Shafer frowned, picked up the phone, and braced himself.

"Will, there's a problem, a bad problem, in the Sunday travel section." The voice on the other end was frantic. "The preprint is rolling right now."

In the background, Will heard the presses, like trains in the distance. That meant he had to find out *now* what the problem was, decide in two seconds what to do about it, then take the heat from the publisher later—no matter which way he decided. If he stopped the presses, it would cost money. If he didn't, another mistake would be added to the *Gazette*'s ever-burgeoning collection.

"Tell me in a few words, Charlie. Just tell me."

"A name's wrong. In that feature piece about Mrs. Wright's trip to China. The name of one of the people is spelled one way in the story and another way in the picture caption. One of them is wrong."

Good, Charlie. Using your common sense.

"And that's it?" Will Shafer asked. "That's it? Charlie, just find out which spelling is correct. Then write a correction and send it to the city desk for the main section of Sunday's paper, so we can run the correction the same day the story's in. Okay? Tell the city desk I said so."

"That's your final decision?"

"Of course—" Will Shafer stopped to put a clamp on his anger. "That's my decision, Charlie. Talk to you later."

He hung up, looked again at Jenifer Hurley. "Never a dull moment," he said. "Where were we?"

"I guess you have to make a lot of decisions like that."

Ah, he thought. A hint of respect in her voice. "Goes with the territory. Okay, so tell me how the mistake happened."

Nothing in her explanation surprised him. She had been so busy addressing subtle points raised by the *Gazette*'s lawyers and, to a lesser degree, the editors that she had stumbled on something much more straightforward. She knew the difference between a guilty plea and a no contest plea, and she had screwed up.

She was sorry, and her face showed it.

The executive editor nodded, sipped his coffee, thought about what he would say. "Look, Jenifer, it doesn't get any easier than this. You're how old?"

"Twenty-four."

My God, he thought. "Twenty-four. Well, if you go to a bigger paper, or one of the networks, it won't get easier. And you're plenty good enough so that you'll get that chance. Sooner than you think, maybe."

He paused, looked into her deep, intelligent eyes. He would do this right.

"With your ability, you'll be given the more challenging assignments no matter where you go. The kind of sensitive assignments that mean lots of second-guessing from editors and lawyers. Okay so far?"

"Okay."

Jenifer Hurley, if I could guide you and protect you, I would. "A relatively minor mistake can detract from a terrific piece of reporting. Are you familiar with the Watergate scandal?"

She smiled ingenuously. "Sort of. I mean, I've read a couple of the books about it, but at the time it happened I was in kindergarten or first grade, or something."

Lord, he thought, I am old. "Two guys from the *Washington Post* did a wonderful reporting job. But along the way, they made one bad mistake, about what someone had or had not told a grand jury. Anyhow, the point is, that mistake hurt them, diminished their effectiveness for a while. Uh . . ." I must sound pedantic, must not be getting through.

"And I have to watch that tendency in myself."

"Yes, I think so. I mean, when you get near the finish line . . ." Listen to myself, he thought.

"I understand. I just have to sit my fanny down and nail all the facts cold. Every last one."

"Right." Should he tell her more? Yes. "With a story like this, the publisher is apt to be hesitant about going ahead because some of the people that surface in the story are going to be friends of his. That's true of a lot of publishers, maybe most. That's the way the world is. So it's just that much more important to have the documentation in your hands. And use it correctly. Then, if a publisher is worried, you have the truth on your side. It makes the fight easier. And you still won't win every round."

"I understand."

Did she? How much more should he say? "Anything in my little lecture that you want to ask me about?"

"No. Thank you for being so understanding."

"My job. I'm treating you as you deserve to be treated, based on your overall reporting. Which is excellent."

"Thank you."

"So write a correction. No apology, just a correction. Two or three paragraphs, whatever you need. And instead of running it on the Local Page, we'll tuck it into the jump of your next housing story, as a box."

"All right. Thank you."

"Go and sin no more. And keep up the good work."

Then she was gone. Will Shafer spun around in his chair and looked out the window, blinking hard. He finished his coffee slowly.

An hour or so later, when he was at his desk on the news floor, a middle-level editor approached. He was frowning and holding a copy of that day's paper folded open to a particular page.

Trouble, Will Shafer knew.

"Will, take a minute to read this three-paragraph story where my thumb is."

The executive editor read. It was a seemingly routine item from the police blotter, about a car smacking a tree the night before. But the driver was identified as Jacob Frank, and Shafer figured he had to be attorney Jacob Frank, for years Bessemer's William Kunstler, an advocate of left-of-center causes and defendants and a frequent critic of the police.

"This is who I think it is?" Will said.

"Right. The problem—"

"Wait a second." Shafer cut him off; he wanted to react as a reader might, without any input on what might be wrong with the story. "Okay. The last paragraph quotes the cops, or one cop, as saying there's gonna be an investigation for possible drunk-driving charges, and that the front seat of the car was 'littered with empty beer cans.'"

"Right, Will. That's, well, accurate in a way, but—"

"What's this 'accurate in a way' shit?" Shafer felt his arm hairs rising in anger and alarm. "Wait, before you tell me, let me ask. Shouldn't we have waited until DWI charges were filed before mentioning that angle?"

"Yes, Will, but there aren't any DWI charges." The subordinate editor's face was sad and pale.

"Hit me with it," Shafer said.

"Jacob Frank just took the curve too fast and brushed a tree. That's all, bad driving. He was cold sober. He called this morning to complain. He was furious. Says we can check his story with the cops. I did, and he's right, and we're wrong."

"Then what's this about the front seat 'littered with empty beer cans'?"

"The front seat was littered with beer cans because he was on his way to buy some beer and—"

"And he was just taking his empties back."

"That's it."

"Even as you and I do."

"Yes."

"Jesus Christ Almighty. So we said something true but totally misleading and unfair."

The other editor nodded his head sadly.

"Ed Sperl?" Shafer demanded.

"Ed Sperl."

"Oh, for God's sake. He knows better—" Shafer stopped. It was not that Ed Sperl didn't know any better; on the contrary, he had probably known exactly what he was doing. The cops had used him, probably with his enthusiastic cooperation, to embarrass a lawyer whom they considered a pain in the ass.

"Sperl filed the story at the end of the day yesterday," the subordinate editor said. "It just sort of got sent through . . . you know . . ."

"Yeah, I know. Untouched by human minds." Will closed his eyes, felt his head starting to ache.

"Something wrong, Will?" Ed Sperl said. He was standing close enough for Shafer to smell the peppermint that was supposed to conceal the odor of the previous night's beers.

"Plenty. In my office."

Shafer went in and sat down. So did Sperl, without being invited.

"Bad story today," Shafer said. "That item about Jacob Frank. Just plain unfair. Why, Ed?"

"Jeez, Will, I'm sorry. It's easy to see in hindsight, I guess. And I should have. The cop on the scene went too far with what he told me. I let my guard down. The cop's been around a long time—"

"Probably since the antiwar protests," Shafer said. He wanted to say more, but he bit his words off. He wanted to call Ed Sperl a liar, say that he knew he hadn't let his guard down at all, that he had done what he intended, and that it was unconscionable. Say it, the executive editor told himself. Say it.

Sperl canted his head slightly, as if in mock contrition, but his eyes were cold. Measuring me, Shafer thought.

No, Will could not say what he meant. He could reprimand Ed Sperl, could write a note to put in his personnel file. But he could not tell Ed Sperl that he had the integrity of a reptile, because he couldn't prove it.

"I'll try to see that it doesn't happen again," Sperl said. "Learn from my mistakes, and all that."

And all that, Shafer thought. He studied the man sitting across from him. In a way, Ed Sperl was a throwback, the kind of reporter who had been far more common thirty or forty years before: twice divorced, hard drinking, deeply cynical, way too friendly with the police.

More than that. Ed Sperl had a totally thick hide; it was not so much that he suppressed his emotions, Shafer thought, as that he had none. No, that wasn't quite true. He felt excitement, from going to homicide scenes, studying accident pictures, perhaps from reading supposedly secret grand jury testimony from rape victims.

Sometimes Ed Sperl reminded him of a shark—ruthless, primitive, predatory. The image fit: just as the shark had not changed much over the years, so had Ed Sperl not changed much. He had always been slightly overweight from drinking, slightly red faced, and he had a crew cut.

He was dangerous. Sometimes Will Shafer wondered how much Sperl knew about him.

"Okay, Will?"

"What?" Shafer had drifted away for a moment.

"I said, I'll talk to the cop who gave me the bum steer, and I'll see that it doesn't happen again."

What's the use, Shafer thought.

"Should I call Frank and say I'm sorry?" Sperl said.

"No. I will."

"Okay. But I'll tell the police chief his patrolmen have to be more careful what they say. I have to see the chief this afternoon about some tickets his men have been laying on the *Gazette*."

Ah, yes. The editor got the message, a little reminder that the *Gazette* usually got lenient treatment when its delivery trucks sped through city streets or double-parked. And that Ed Sperl was the publisher's conduit to the police brass. Yes, that was a big part of Ed Sperl's power. Will Shafer also suspected Sperl might have fixed up some tickets accumulated by the publisher's family.

"Anything else, Will?"

"No. That's it. I don't want this kind of thing to happen again."

Ed Sperl was out of the office before Will finished his sentence.

Will swiveled around in his chair and stared out the window for a long time. He did not blink.

"I'm out here."

Will Shafer heard Karen's voice from the redwood porch deck; his wife had heard him come in the front door. He set his briefcase on a chair and draped his suitcoat over it.

"Hi," she said as he slid open the screen between the dining room and deck.

"'Lo."

"Long day, huh?"

"Is it that obvious? Hey, nice." He had spotted the tray on the table; it held bottles of gin and tonic water, glasses, a dish of lime wedges, and a bucket of ice. Behind the table was a covered grill that gave off wisps of smoke. Barbecued chicken.

"Hi, Daddy." His ten-year-old son, Brendan, waved at him from the round above-ground pool at the end of the yard. The boy smiled beneath his diving mask.

"Hi, sport. Where's your sister?"

"Hi, Daddy."

"There she is, " Will said, affecting a father's gaiety. "Hi, Cass."

But the nine-year-old, wearing a snorkel as well as a mask, was submerged already, literally swimming circles around her older brother. The girl had inherited her mother's physical grace, the boy his father's awkwardness. Ah, well, they were both intelligent.

Karen handed him a gin and tonic, and he kissed her on the cheek, hoping she did not detect his lack of enthusiasm. A silly hope, he realized.

"Tell me about your day if you want," she said, sitting in a folding chair a few feet from the grill.

Will Shafer sat down in the chair's twin and told her about his conversation with Grant Siebert, whom she had never met, and about Ed Sperl's despicable behavior.

"Can Jacob Frank sue?" Karen asked.

"Hmmmm. Well, he could, but he probably won't. One, since he's a lawyer, he knows as well as anyone that he'd have to prove actual malice to collect, since he's a public figure, and malice is awfully hard to prove. More to the point, it probably wouldn't be worth the hassle—"

They were interrupted by loud splashing and screams from the pool. Karen sprang to her feet. "Brendan, don't you dare do that!" she shouted.

"Ma, he pushed my head under."

"She kicked me first."

"Liar."

More splashes and louder screaming.

"Listen, both of you," Karen Shafer began. "That kind of behavior is going to come to a screeching halt right now."

Will Shafer swallowed gin, chewed ice and lime pulp, and studied his wife. She was a handsome woman, and summer was a good season for her: she looked her best with her skin medium tanned, looked good in the white slacks and terry-cloth blouse she had on now. She looked good with her sunglasses in place, looked good with the sunglasses propped up to rest pertly on her black hair so her hazel eyes could flash in the sun.

Karen had a habit of propping up her sunglasses when she was angry, and she had just done it so she could get the kids in line. "Last chance!" she shouted toward the pool.

The splashing subsided, turned almost sulky.

"So, this reunion thing is going to be a pain for you."

"Oh, for sure. The response is underwhelming. Charlie Buck says he'll come, but I think that's only because his father is having a birthday. And Grant Siebert wasn't enthusiastic."

"Do you have any help?"

"I do, actually. Young Lyle is pitching in."

Suddenly, loud splashing and screaming from the pool.

"Okay, that's it!" Karen said. She was on her feet and off the porch deck in two seconds flat, striding decisively toward the end of the yard.

Will used the opportunity to sneak another jigger of gin into his glass, topping it off with just a little tonic.

"Mom!"

Will Shafer felt duty bound to do something. He stood. "You two straighten up right now," he said. "I mean, right now."

His wife already had the situation under control. She was as good with the children as she was with everything else.

They were far, far from wealthy, but they were comfortable financially. Their house had four bedrooms, one of which was a study; a big kitchen, good-sized dining room, wood-burning fireplace in the living room, a basement that did not leak, a porch deck, a small pool for the kids. They had a big front yard and a backyard that offered much more than views of other backyards. From their porch deck, in fact, they could see a sliver of Lake Erie, off in the distance across the tops of the trees in the park several blocks away.

Brendan and Cass were walking up the yard now, their diving masks still in place, both pouting.

The wet feet of the children stomped up onto the porch deck. Under their mother's prodding, the boy and girl dried their hair, ears, and feet, then draped the towels around them before sliding back the screen and going inside. Their mother followed, doling out instructions.

In a few minutes, Will Shafer knew, his wife would come

back to the porch deck, sit down across from him again, and chat some more.

"Honey!" Karen's deep, resonant voice came from way inside the house. "Check on the chicken, okay?"

"Right." He took the lid off the grill, turned the chicken breasts. On the shelf attached to the grill was a bowl containing Karen's special barbecue mixture: store-bought sauce combined with a dash of honey and a little yogurt. Will Shafer painted the breasts with the stuff, knowing that in a little while the chicken would be golden glazed and delicious, the outside crisp and the inside moist with the juices sealed in by the honey and yogurt.

She was one of the most competent people he had ever known. She moved surely, gracefully, in the world of wives, the wives of merchants and manufacturers and bankers and doctors who made up the dwindling social elite of Bessemer. And she was equally at ease with the shrinking cadre of traditional women who stayed home and tended the home and with the growing legions of ambitious, even driven women who worked outside the home. She was gracious, too, with those women who worked not for a sense of self-fulfillment but simply because they had to so their fatherless children could eat and have clothes to wear to school.

Karen had always been a strong person, as well as a kind one, and she had a gift for sharing her strength with those who needed it most. Like her husband, Will thought.

When she was still Karen Manning, she had majored in sociology and earned a master's degree in social work. After their marriage, she had worked for several social agencies. She still wrote articles for sociological journals, especially on teenage pregnancy. Of all the social problems, she had written again and again, that was the saddest and most destructive, because it perpetuated just about every other problem one could think of.

Karen Shafer was occasionally sought by high school

guidance counselors on how to prevent teen pregnancies, and how best to deal with them once they occurred.

All in all, Will Shafer knew as he swallowed his drink and snuck another half jigger of gin into his glass, one of the most confident, competent people he had ever known. And one of the kindest.

Lord, she had seen something in him.

As he felt the gin glow start to take effect and tried to savor the sweet smell of lawns and the fragrance of the chicken, he thought (not for the first time, or the hundredth) that she was much more sure of her universe, her *self*, than he was about himself.

He belonged to the country club, belonged to a couple of other social clubs, because the publisher wanted him to and so took care of the dues. But that did not make him feel comfortable with these men, who were cut from a different cloth than he.

Karen had told him many times over the years that his lack of self-esteem was a treatable condition, not something in his chromosomes, and that counseling might help him. Might help him personally, might help him professionally— might even help him in the bedroom, she had said at last.

The psychiatrist had told him to take things one step at a time, one day at a time. Well, that seemed like good advice, especially since his days were going to be quite full enough, planning for the *Gazette*'s reunion.

"Breaking ninety," Will Shafer hissed into his melting gin ice. He chuckled.

His golf game had deteriorated in recent years from lack of practice. He had gotten less joy out of golf than he had long before. Maybe that was because he was often expected to play with people at the club, people who probably wouldn't look at him if he wasn't editor of the *Gazette*.

Or was there another reason? He felt a pain in his head, blinked hard. Too much gin? Too many memories? Too much forgetting, or trying to forget?

What had the doctor said? We'll get there, Will. We'll get to where the guilt is. . . .

Karen had urged him, prodded him, to see the psychiatrist. Would she be able to live with the results? Would he?

He heard her slide open the screen; she was coming back to the porch. He would do his best to enjoy the evening, would do his best to share with her. But he would not tell her how protective he had felt toward Jenifer Hurley, how sure he had felt that she was making more of her youth than he had of his.

No, he would keep that grief for himself.

Eleven

▲▲▲

As she jogged along the road across from a reservoir, she did not mind the occasional whistles from teenage boys in passing cars. Sometimes Marlee West even waved to them and grinned.

She did not jog fast, she did not jog particularly far—just a couple of miles at a time. But she jogged enough to keep her weight down, not to mention her blood pressure and tension.

Marlee jogged almost every day; it had to be a mighty heavy rain to stop her. If the weather did get really bad, especially in the winter, if the pavement was slippery as glass, she went to the health spa.

Now, fifty yards from her cottage, Marlee slowed to a walk. She had read that tapering off from a jog to a walk, instead of just standing around or slumping into a chair, was healthy because it kept the blood from pooling in the legs, thus preventing muscle aches.

Walking those last yards, Marlee savored the Saturday-morning sun on her face and exulted in the sweat that was washing the poison out of her system. Not that she had that many poisons: she was careful about her drinking, careful what she ate. Not too much fat or red meat, only occasional pizza or ice cream. No smoking. (She could hardly believe she had ever dabbled in marijuana; just the thought of putting smoke, any smoke, in her system was sickening. Well, that was long ago.)

Yet not so long ago. Maybe coming to grips with that paradox was what getting old—no, *older*—was all about.

Oh, heavy thoughts, Marlee. She laughed aloud, and her outcry was answered at once by a bark from her Airedale terrier, who had been sunning himself in his backyard pen.

"Okay, Nigel! Good boy. Mommie's gonna make breakfast, honey."

Marlee was seldom preoccupied with getting older, but she was having a party tonight, and some of the guests would be much younger than she was. Well, she hoped they would mix well. If not, too bad.

It was really a party for herself: she had recently won a statewide press award (five hundred dollars and a plaque) for "especially sensitive and perceptive commentary on social issues over a number of years," and she wanted to celebrate.

She had simply been writing what she thought needed writing about—often women who were doing new things (or traditional things) in a world that was changing too fast.

She had been delighted to win the award; it was the reminder that she had been writing "over a number of years" that had bothered her for a moment. But only for a moment.

"Hi, Nigel. Oh, slurp, slurp." She knelt next to the gate, letting the dog lick her ear through the wire.

The guest mix would be a risk, but she knew it was one worth taking. She had had lots of safe parties and dinners and had been to many—the kind where the guests are mostly of the same age and mind-set.

Tonight's party would be different. Maybe the guests would gather in little knots—people from the same age, sharing the same snotty biases. So big deal, the party might be a bore. She was not afraid of that. But if it worked, it could be a lot of fun, could even make the newsroom a happier place.

"C'mon in, Nigel. I'm gonna cook you an egg today."

It could very well be, with the right mixture of food and drink, and if she herself could be the catalyst—it just might be that the party would work. The older staff people might find things to like in the younger ones, might remind themselves that they had been like that once. The younger ones might begin to discover that their elders were not so different from them, in some ways.

"Here you go, Nigel."

She wondered, sometimes, why she saw things so much more clearly than other people did.

The Airedale gulped down his microwaved egg, then munched the rest of his food. Nigel was a wonderful watchdog, wonderful companion. Seventy pounds of courage and love wrapped in a muscular tan-and-black frame. Marlee would always have a dog, whether she lived alone or hooked up with somebody.

There had been men in her life. Whether too many or not enough she couldn't say. Anyhow, there had never been a long-term one.

Was that because she was a feminist? Could be, but that was what she was, and that was that. It could be that men in Bessemer were more off-put by a feminist than big-city men were. And Marlee's column on women's issues left no room for anyone in the world to doubt where she stood. And the award was a good reminder that she was reaching people.

She took her orange juice and cereal to the back porch and sat in the sun while Nigel did his postbreakfast airing and sniffing. Had she forgotten anything? She thought not. She would push as much furniture as possible against the walls to create open space. Maybe the party would spill onto the back porch. That would be good; people feel at ease in the dark, on a porch. And it would keep smoke from collecting in the rooms.

How many smokers were there? She tried to count. Not

many, thank goodness. What would she do if someone lit up a joint? No, that wasn't likely, not with Will Shafer coming. She wondered if anyone would start an argument with the executive editor. Well, he could hold his own.

She had come to like and respect Will Shafer over the years. He had treated her just fine, professionally and personally. He had told her to take a week off, with pay, after the death of her mother two years before. He had understood her burden, had known it was ten times greater because her mother's death came less than a year after her father's.

And as an editor, Will Shafer had backed her all the way—or ninety-nine percent, which was all a columnist could expect from an editor.

She had plenty of beer, plenty of wine, plenty of soft drinks. She had chips and dips, fruit and other munchies, and she already knew where she would lay it out.

She had placed charcoal in the grill, and she would light it an hour or so into the party, after things got going. The grill sat on the grass, a few feet from the porch. Good: it was obviously not going to rain tonight, so the hot dogs could cook down there in the yard. That way, there would be no charcoal smoke hanging under the porch roof.

"Nigel, boy, if you're a good fella you might get some treats tonight. That's right, boy, company's coming."

Marlee went inside, poured a cup of coffee, and took it upstairs. She undressed and stepped into the shower, pausing to study her body in the full-length mirror on the bathroom door.

Not bad, she told herself: a couple of freckles and moles here and there, but the jogging had really trimmed her. She smiled at how her body looked; good, hard muscle was just as attractive on a woman as it was on a man.

The water felt good as it rinsed away the poisons that the jogging had sweated out of her.

She had plenty of music to play, sounds that would go over

easy or make a lot of noise, depending on how things were going.

She had also dug out her shoebox full of old photographs from *Gazette* picnics, Christmas parties, farewell parties, along with several of the tape recordings from back when. There were dozens of pictures, a dozen or so tapes. Looking at the pictures ahead of time had made her feel nostalgic: many had been taken by Arnie Schwartz, for a long time the *Gazette*'s chief photographer—in fact, the paper's only photographer for many years. How many years had he been dead? Ten at least, Marlee thought.

Marlee had decided to spread the pictures on a table, along with the tapes and her recorder. That way, people could look and listen, or they could choose not to. It was no big deal.

One thing she saw in the pictures (besides her lost youth) was that newspaper people of yesteryear had been more eager to have a good time. God, so many of them were so . . . serious nowadays.

If there was one thing that could break the ice at a party (besides the right mix of people and a little booze), it was looking at old pictures. It was invariably fun for the people who were in the pictures, and it was often fun for those who weren't. Old pictures could narrow the gap of years in an instant. Okay, part of it was selective amnesia, but so was happiness itself.

Will and Karen Shafer were the first to arrive. So like him, Marlee thought; always dependable.

"Marlee, hi. Thanks for having us. And congratulations again."

"Amen, Marlee. Richly deserved."

"Thanks and double thanks," Marlee said. And to Karen, "And I'll never forget how generous you've been with what you know."

Marlee thought Will was as awkward as ever at kissing. He wore dress slacks and a blazer, even though Marlee had specified informal dress, and Marlee glimpsed a tie folded in his inside coat pocket just in case. What a tight ass, she thought.

"You've done some decorating since we were here last," Karen Shafer said.

"Yup. A little paint here and there."

"And the rocks," Will said. "Those rocks are, uh, nice."

"Thanks," Marlee said, not bothering to tell Will that the rocks had been around awhile and that he had commented on them before. Every six months or so, Marlee spotted a rock, at the beach or in the country, whose shape or color or both appealed to her. If she liked the rock, she brought it home. She had several rocks, most fist-sized or a little bigger, sitting on tables, shelves, and bookcases.

"Here's someone else," Karen Shafer said.

"Ah," Marlee said. "It's Ed Sperl. C'mon in, Ed!"

Ed Sperl wore wrinkled khakis, a loud sport shirt, and an insolent expression. Marlee didn't like him all that much, but he was often good at parties: he liked to drink, and he knew a lot of juicy stories from the police beat. That alone made him good company for the younger reporters.

But right now, there was an awkward moment. Will and Ed were trying to look congenial when everyone knew they didn't like each other. Will, especially, looked embarrassed as he chatted with Ed Sperl. Both men paused and smiled as Marlee brought them beer; Karen Shafer said she would pour herself some white wine and soda in a few minutes.

"Cheers," Marlee said, sipping her wine.

God, it was funny. Will looked as if his jaw had been wired for electricity, so that he could smile by pressing a button.

Marlee was relieved—as much for Will Shafer as herself—when she saw a couple more guests park out front. Yes, she could feel the momentum of the party.

Marlee had had several glasses of wine by the time she went to light the charcoal. She was happy. It was a warm night, and some of the guests were standing around on the porch, as she had hoped they would. So far, no sloppy drunks, big arguments, or broken furniture.

She loved the sounds of a party, the sounds she was hearing now: voices and laughter from the porch, a muffled din from inside the house.

"Marlee, does your dog like light or regular beer?"

"Don't you dare!" She chuckled, but anyone who offered her dog beer would never be invited to her place again.

"Marlee."

Behind her, a soft, diffident voice.

"Lyle, hi! I'm so glad you could make it."

"Me, too. And thanks for making the *Gazette* look good."

Lyle Glanford, Jr., hugged her gently, kissed her awkwardly. God, weren't any men at the paper easy around women?

"I was starting to think you weren't gonna show up," Marlee said.

"Oh, you know. This reunion thing, Breaking Ninety, is . . ."

"Breaking a lot of people's chops."

"Yes! That's sure as hell true." The publisher's son, a handsome man with his father's best physical features, laughed, and Marlee congratulated herself on putting him at ease.

"What are you drinking?"

"Well, nothing yet. Beer, maybe."

"C'mon," Marlee said, putting her hand on his shoulder and steering him back toward the porch. "I've got a whole tub full of cold ones. Hey, up there on the porch! Reach in and get a beer for Lyle."

"Boo."

"No top brass allowed."

But the insults from the dark porch were good-natured, and the publisher's son laughed again.

Marlee was proud as well as happy. She was probably the only person at the *Gazette* who could have a party like this, inviting everyone from the greenest cub reporter to the publisher's son, and get it to work. She could do it because she could kid the publisher's son in front of the rank and file, and vice versa. And she could do *that* because she was able to see them as people.

Oops, Marlee. Don't get big headed just because you've had a few drinks. Just relax and enjoy your own party.

"Thanks," Lyle Glanford, Jr., said, ripping the tab off a can of beer.

The only person Marlee would never think of inviting to a party was the publisher himself. He just never mixed with the regulars. But Lyle junior was all right. He had bounced around all the departments at the *Gazette;* his father had seen to that, wanting him to learn every phase of the operation. He had not shown himself to be brilliant, but he was far from the dolt that some of the younger reporters made him out to be. It was not his fault that he was the publisher's son.

Besides, Lyle had always been nice to Marlee. A couple of years back, just after his divorce, she had even thought he would ask her out. Or maybe that had been wishful thinking.

The guests had eaten nearly all the hot dogs. Some of the dog lovers in the crowd had thrown tidbits to Nigel, who acted as if he could stand a party every day.

Marlee switched from wine to beer and glided from room to room, looking out at the porch every so often to make sure no one gave Nigel any beer.

". . . your first dose of Bessemer winter is going to be an eye-opener, I promise."

"Yeah, well, I used to live up near Plattsburgh."

"Then you'll be right at home here."

"For sure some people have left Bessemer because of the winters."

"Storms here are the stuff of legend . . ."

That reminded Marlee: crammed down in her shoebox of old pictures were several of mountainous snowdrifts and a couple from the ice storm of—what?—twenty years before that had shut off power across the city. She nudged through the crowd, opened the closet door, got out the picture box again, went back to the dining room table.

"Hey, everybody!" Marlee said over the din.

"Message from Marlee! Shut up, everyone."

"All right," Marlee said. "All right. I'll keep this short, and you can go back to drinking, or whatever else consenting adults do."

Scattered laughter.

"Some of you old people might like these pictures," Marlee said. "Maybe you new folks, too. Give you a notion of what you're in for if you stay in Bessemer."

A few people crowded closer, started picking through the pictures. Marlee listened to the chatter:

"Look at that, for God's sake. Snow up to the streetlights."

"For the longest time, the Chamber of Commerce pressured the *Gazette* not to run snow pictures on page one. The merchants figured it would discourage shoppers."

"You're kidding!"

"I am like hell. Wait till you've been here awhile."

"Not so loud . . . there's Shafer."

"So what?"

"Ah, Shafer's a decent guy. For an editor."

That exchange among some younger reporters pleased Marlee. They're seeing good old Will as human, she thought. "Listen, you folks," she said. "If you want to hear some voices from the past, you can play the tapes from old parties. You old farts might hear your own voices. You young snots might like hearing how your elders used to sound. Just keep the volume down to a roar, okay?"

"Hard-core porn!" someone shouted.

"Better," someone said.

Marlee went back to the porch, where several guests were still drinking, and fished another beer out of the tub. She would make it last awhile.

"Good party, Marlee."

"I'm glad," she said. Damn, she was more tired than she'd

thought. It was hard work, throwing a party. Worth it, but hard work just the same. She drifted over to the dark corner of the porch and sat in an old wicker chair. She was close to the dog's pen and right next to an open window.

The door between the porch and kitchen opened and closed, and Marlee suddenly realized she was alone. Good. She felt like resting for a moment.

"Hi, Nigel."

She could make out the dog's shape, down there in the dark. She saw the tail wagging.

Marlee listened to the chatter around the table:

"Now when the hell was that?"

"Jeez, look at that snow. Okay, that guy's wearing plaid double knits, right? So must have been, what, '73 or '74?"

"Don't forget, the styles come to Bessemer a couple of years later."

"That's for damn sure."

"Will you look at this! Like silver spaghetti covering the whole world."

"That's from the famous ice storm."

Quietly sipping beer in the dark, Marlee enjoyed the conversation; the very innocuousness of it meant people were relaxed and having a good time. She heard clicks as someone turned on her tape recorder, then whirring noises for fast-forward and reverse.

A flat, metallic voice rose from the tape: ". . . *the friends I had here in Bessemer, you people, and I want you to know . . .*"

"You remember," a listener said. "That's Charlie Buck. Got out while the getting was good and made a name for himself."

Listening in the dark, Marlee thought, I sure as hell didn't. Well, so what?

"I like the pictures, but who gives a shit about this?" a voice said as another tape started to play.

So turn it off, asshole, Marlee thought to herself. No one's making you listen to anything.

"My old man has a tape recording of a fart contest."

"Oh, I've heard that! It's a stitch. Some English bunch made it."

"They just put the tape recorder under the city desk after the editors had had lunch."

"You foul-mouth bastard."

Marlee heard the recorder whir, click to a stop. Then long-ago yet still familiar noises rose from the tape spools. Sounds of tables and chairs bumping and beer glasses crashing to the floor.

"Damn," a listener said, "what the hell is that?"

"A party for . . . Grant Siebert, the label says."

"Must have been '73 or '74, I bet."

"No, no, before. I betcha he left . . ."

"Left before the Attica prison thing. I know for sure he wasn't around for that, and the riot was in September of '71."

Marlee sat up, turned, and looked through the window at the cluster of people in the living room. Her heart beat a little faster.

"I betcha it was . . ."

"It was the winter of the ice storm. Remember?"

"Sure. Or maybe the spring right after."

"What the hell's an ice storm?"

"Okay, who's the weather expert here?"

Marlee heard someone trying to explain what an ice storm was.

"Yeah, but when we say 'ice storm' around here, we mean *the* ice storm," someone said.

"I lost a hundred bucks' worth of frozen meat."

"Power was out for—what? Three days? Four?"

"At least."

Suddenly, Marlee's mood changed. Instead of wanting to be alone, she wanted to be part of the reminiscences. She got up from her chair and went inside.

Several people in her age group were listening with slightly embarrassed smiles and nostalgia-bright eyes. Several younger people were laughing appreciatively. Marlee wondered how she looked.

"Damn, listen to that."

"Humor unalloyed by compassion or taste."

"Who was this party for?"

"Grant Siebert. Went to New York and . . ."

"This is him, right here in the middle. The good-looking guy with the wise-ass expression. And right here is . . ."

"Is he coming back?"

"I haven't heard. Not that I care."

"I hope he learned a little humility if nothing else."

"Shh. Listen to this."

Those close to the recorder could hear fairly well; those farther away were having trouble, or maybe didn't care.

"*. . . heard his putter was out of his bag, if you know what I mean. . . .*"

Maybe it wasn't such a great idea to play the tapes, Marlee thought. "That wasn't supposed to be on there," she said. Damn; so far, it had been a very clean party.

Marlee saw Jenifer Hurley at the edge of the knot of listeners, her face wrinkled in concentration.

"What's all that stuff about the priest and the golf club?" Jenifer asked.

"Big, big murder back then," someone said.

"She's too young to remember."

"I'm not from Bessemer anyhow," Jenifer Hurley said.

"A priest was found battered to death in a basement. With a golf club. They never solved it."

"Probably a fag deal," Ed Sperl said.

Nice, Ed, Marlee thought. You know damn well some of my guests are gay.

"Hell of a case . . ."

"Marlee? Can we talk for a second?"

Will Shafer was standing next to her.

"Sure, Will. Come on over to the corner." She led him to a momentarily quiet spot near the kitchen and tried to tune out the party babble: ". . . right about the time of the ice storm . . . dead for quite a few days before they found him . . ."

"Marlee, can I ask you a favor? As a friend?"

"Sure, Will. What?"

"Could you, would you be willing to call Grant Siebert in New York and ask him to come to the reunion?"

"Me? Why me, I mean . . ." Marlee was stunned. She felt her face flush and hoped it didn't show too much.

"Marlee, we don't exactly have a stampede for the reunion. I'm batting almost zero with the out-of-towners. The publisher . . ."

"The publisher is gonna want at least a couple of big-city types," Marlee said. "I understand."

"Marlee, you have a knack, a social knack. I'd really appreciate it."

"Oh . . . sure. Soon, right?"

"Please. And thanks."

Marlee smiled and nodded. She had to be alone. She went to the porch, back to the wicker chair in the dark corner. Yes, her heart was beating faster; there was no doubt about it. Grant Siebert . . .

She looked over her shoulder through the window. Ed Sperl was standing at the table, flipping through the pictures. As Marlee watched, he pressed the buttons on the recorder. His face was full of concentration, or was he just trying to see straight after all the beer he'd had? She had never considered him sentimental.

I hope he doesn't screw up the recorder, she thought. But she was too preoccupied to dwell on it.

The door opened, and Will walked onto the porch. "Marlee, thanks for a fine evening. We're going to be going. And thanks again for, you know."

"Sure, Will. Really glad you came."

Marlee followed Will back inside, saw that a few other people were gravitating toward the front door. She wasn't sorry: she was suddenly quite tired, more burdened with emotion than she had been in a long while.

After seeing out Will and his wife, Marlee went to the kitchen to get some ice water. She walked past Ed Sperl, who was still standing next to the table, sorting through the pictures.

"Bye, Marlee. A good time," someone said.

"Glad I came, Marlee."

Marlee kept her smile. "Really glad you could make it. . . . Thanks for coming. . . . My dog appreciates the leftovers."

Just a few people left now, and Marlee hoped she wouldn't have to shoo them out. Ed Sperl was still at the table, flipping through pictures. He was holding a beer. I hope it's almost empty, Marlee thought, because I'm almost running on empty.

"Night, Marlee. Night, Ed."

Sperl put down the pictures, looked around him, seemed surprised that he was almost alone.

"Thanks for coming, Ed," Marlee said. "The younger crowd really appreciated your war stories."

"My pleasure," Sperl said. "It's fun, going down memory lane. You never know what you'll run into."

With that, Sperl winked, waved good-bye, and walked more or less steadily to the front door.

Alone at last, Marlee thought. It had been a good party; now she was glad it was over. She went back to the dark porch and sat down.

Twelve

▲▲▲

Grant's muscles still felt warm from his workout at the Y. He checked his mail, throwing out most of it, and tossed his gym bag in the corner. He got a beer, checking his answering machine: blinking light but no messages.

He lay down on the sofa, shook off his shoes, felt himself relax.

The phone rang.

Shit.

"Hello?"

"Yeah, I'm trying to reach Grant Siebert." Man's voice, long distance.

"You got him."

"You won't guess who this is."

"You're right."

"I tried to call you a couple times earlier, but all I got was your goddamn machine."

"Well, you got me now, so who the hell are you?"

Wise-ass laughter. "Glad to see you haven't mellowed, Grant. It's Ed Sperl. From the *Gazette*. Remember?"

"Sure. Yeah, hi." He had not liked Ed Sperl way back then

and hadn't thought of him in years, even after the call from Will Shafer about the reunion.

More wise-ass laughter. "You don't sound so glad to hear from me."

Okay, Grant thought. I can play this game. "Why should I be? We haven't talked in God knows how long."

"You're right. Sometimes it's good to renew old ties."

"Is that what we're doing?"

Chuckle. "Sort of. I'm calling about the reunion, Grant. I guess Will Shafer talked to you already."

The reunion, of course. "Yeah, I talked to Will."

"He was hoping you'd come back."

"I know. The thing is, I haven't been back for twenty years almost. I don't know . . ."

"I hear you. Poor Will's afraid they'll hold the reunion in a phone booth if he doesn't get a better turnout than he has so far."

"Did he tell you to call me?"

Chuckle. "Shit, no. He may get someone else to do that."

Grant remembered the feeling Ed Sperl had always given him. Something about him, some snakelike quality, had always made him uneasy.

"Look, Ed, I told Will I'd think about it."

"I know. Just in case you do come back, I'm collecting little capsule histories for a reunion program. You know, whatever happened to so-and-so. That kind of stuff. I just need to know in a couple dozen words what you've been doing with your life. You went to Notre Dame, right?"

"Yeah."

"You know who's a big Notre Dame fan, is Will Shafer."

"I didn't know that."

"He is. See, he went to Saint Jerome's right here in Bessemer. Word is, he really wanted to go to Notre Dame. Couldn't 'cause his father was sick and all that."

Sperl had a cynical, bored-sounding drawl that got under Grant's skin. "You know a lot," Grant said. "Is this going to take long? Like I said, I'm probably not even coming."

"You should think about that, Grant. Country club's being redone, food's not bad from what I hear. Golf course is pretty good by local standards. You still play?"

"Not really. I never got into the game much around New York."

"Hmmm. But you used to play in Bessemer?"

"A few times I did. That was a long time ago."

"With anyone in particular?"

"No. I'd just go by myself to a public course and get paired with someone."

"Hmmm. I've always heard you meet interesting people playing golf. Did you find that?"

"Mostly I met other golfers."

Chuckle. "When was the last time you swung a club in anger?" Sperl's voice had changed.

"The last time I played? I don't know. Why?"

"Just wondering. Just wondering."

"Anything else you need to ask me? I've got some things I need to get done."

"You married?"

"No."

"Good man! Smart man, I can tell you from experience. So you do magazine work, I hear?"

"Yeah. I'm an editor at *Sleuth*. We do—"

"Hey, hot shit! True-crime stuff. I know all about your outfit. Used to string for 'em."

"Is that right?"

"Funny, I just never saw you on the masthead."

"I'm not on it. Listen, Ed—"

"Just a couple more questions, Grant."

"Listen, Ed, hold on while I go to the john."

"Take your time. *Gazette*'s paying for the call."

In the bathroom, Grant splashed cold water on his face and tried to stop his knees from shaking. Ed Sperl had a knack for asking questions that seemed dull, wooden, even stupid, yet they left him feeling vulnerable.

"I'm back."

"So, Grant, you doing any writing? I remember when you left, you were hoping to set the world on fire."

"It's not burning yet. But I am writing, yes."

"What kinda stuff? You been published?"

"Fiction and nonfiction both. I've been published in a couple of the magazines. Last year in *Cosmopolitan* I had an article on a woman who's a homicide detective."

"Okay, how's this sound? 'Grant Siebert, a Notre Dame graduate and promising young reporter at the *Gazette* in the early 1970s, lives in New York, where he is a free-lance writer and an editor for a true-crime magazine.' You buy that?"

"Sure." Say something friendly and get out of this conversation, Grant told himself. "The *Gazette* treat you all right?"

"Mostly. Will's a pain in the ass sometimes. Publisher keeps him busy. And young Lyle, you remember him. He's coming into his own more. Discovering his place in the world and all that. Old man lets him change the light bulbs."

"Good." Grant didn't like the way Sperl talked in terms of everyone's weaknesses. What would Sperl say about him?

"Hey, I almost forgot. There was a big party at Marlee West's place not long ago. Remember her? I always figured she had the hots for you. Anyhow, she had a bunch of old tapes from farewell parties. We played the one from yours. Remember?"

"Sure."

"Ever listen to it?"

Ed Sperl's voice had a tone Grant didn't like at all. What is it with him? Grant thought. "I don't think so. I don't remember."

"Funny as hell to listen to some of that old shit. Your voice is there, all right. Funny the stuff people say when their guards are down."

"Yeah, well, we were drunk probably. Not to mention a lot younger."

"Ain't it the truth. We were all younger. The tape of your party, in particular, stirred up a lot of old memories. Know what I mean?"

"No, I don't."

"You ever listen to it?"

"No." Hadn't he told him that already?

"You should. Brings back old memories."

"Anything else you need from me, Ed?"

"No, not right now. But think about the reunion. We can talk about old times."

"I'll think about it. Okay?"

"Good hearing your voice again, Grant. I'll be talking to you."

"So long," Grant said, hanging up.

Talking to Ed Sperl had been like having a scab pulled off slowly. Maybe, Grant thought, it's because he has a better nose for the jugular than I ever did, even in the days when I was a journalist with a future.

Screw it. He ripped the tab off another can of beer. What had Sperl said to get under his skin?

"Goddamn him."

I would have been smart to skip my own farewell party. I should have, Grant thought. I should have left town quietly and never—

Grant was startled to feel something cold and wet on his pantleg. Oh, he had squeezed the can too hard, and some of the beer had splashed out.

Grant drained the beer, crushed the empty can in his hand, tossed it at the bookcase. The can knocked down one of his books on psychology and personality improvement.

Grant got another beer. Maybe he could force himself to write tonight, at least for a little while. That usually got rid of some of the anger.

He thought of the farewell-party tape. What had Ed Sperl found so interesting about it? What would I hear if I played it? The sounds of friends? No.

Should I have stayed in Bessemer, got married, had a couple of kids, cut the grass every week? The people are nicer. Some of them might have liked me, if I'd given them the chance. If I hadn't been running away.

Thirteen

▲▲▲

Walt Striker had called a staff meeting at *Sleuth* for ten o'clock. Grant had got up early enough to have breakfast and still walk to the magazine.

The phone rang. Grant hoped it was Walt, calling to tell him the meeting had been postponed. That way, Grant would have an extra half-hour or so to write.

"Hello."

"Is this Grant?"

Woman's voice, vaguely familiar, but long distance.

"Speaking."

"Grant, this is Marlee West. From the *Gazette*. Do you remember me?"

God. "Sure. How are you?"

"I'm just fine. I'm calling from Bessemer to twist your arm, hoping you'll come to the reunion."

"Hmmm. Well, that's honest enough."

"I know Ed and Will spoke to you already. To be really frank, Will asked me if I would call, too."

"How come I'm so important?"

Laughter; she has a nice laugh, Grant thought.

"I think Will is worried it'll be a tiny turnout. There's a few other people on my list to contact. I thought I'd start with you."

"Hmmm. Well, how are you, first of all?"

"Oh, good. Mostly. I have my own column now. Women's issues, although those issues aren't just limited to women. . . . Oops, never mind the soapbox. And you, you're . . . ?"

"Like I told Ed, I work for a true-crime magazine and I write."

"You like New York?"

"Oh, boy. Yes and no. All things considered, I'm glad I'm here. Where else can you get a good pastrami sandwich for ten bucks?"

"Uh, right." Laughter. "I have to admit, Bessemer doesn't have that much to offer. You've never been back?"

"No."

"Maybe now's the time. It could be a lot of fun. Find out what happened to everybody, whether they struck it rich or not."

"I know I didn't."

"Me neither. Anyhow, I'm trying to lure you with visions of nostalgia and friends and all that good stuff. Is that subtle enough?"

"Sure. Whoopie."

"Same old Grant," Marlee said, laughing. "Really, it could be a good chance to, you know, relive old times. If you want to."

If I want to, Grant thought.

"A bunch of us were doing that at a little get-together I had not long ago. Looking at some old pictures. Some of them old, old. Remember your farewell party? We played the tape of it."

"How can I forget. I think I got drunk."

"Didn't we all? Not to mention whacked-out on pot. At least I was. I don't do that anymore. So long ago, all that stuff. The voices sounded kind of scratchy."

"Uh, yeah. Ed said he heard my voice."

"Oh, yes. He's an odd duck, Ed is, but he can be entertaining, especially for the young reporters. He's got a great memory for old happenings, and he's a good storyteller. When he's sober."

"Hmmm."

"Grant, will you come?"

"Damn, I really hadn't . . ."

"Don't say no. Think about it."

Now Grant was anxious to hang up. "Okay. That much I promise. Listen, I have to go now."

After he hung up, every nerve end in his body seemed to jangle. "Son of a bitch," he said. "Son of a *bitch!*"

He sat down, tried to replay the conversation in his mind, told himself that none of it mattered, it was so long ago.

"Son of a bitch." Reliving old times. Jesus.

Now he would have to take the subway or risk being late for Walt Striker's meeting. But as long as he wasn't walking, he had a little time to spare.

God, can I really be feeling this? Nostalgia?

On the shelf in his bedroom closet was an old shoebox crammed with junk he never used but hadn't been able to throw out. He took it down, pulled out the pictures from his farewell party. There he was, a lot younger.

He picked up the tape from his party, got his recorder out of the bottom drawer of his dresser. What would he remember if he heard it? How would he feel?

The next morning, he was on a Long Island Rail Road train heading to Douglaston, Queens, where there was a golf range. He felt self-conscious, slumped in his seat and cradling a three wood and a couple of medium irons, and he was glad the train wasn't crowded.

The train went over the Cross Island Parkway, and the conductor called out the Douglaston stop. Off to the left lay a stretch of marsh grass leading to the end of Little Neck Bay. Grant saw ducks and gulls close in and farther out, white sails on blue water. Maybe it would be worth it, to his spirit, to take a train out to the Island once in a while.

Off to the right, he saw the driving range. The end of it, a dirt field where the longest hitters reached, was only a few yards from the tracks. But there was heavy fencing all around, and he realized he would have to walk quite a distance through the streets of Douglaston to get to the range entrance. Well, he picked a good day. Sunny but not too hot. At least he wouldn't be soaked with sweat when he was done.

He paid six dollars, then held a wire-mesh basket under a machine that disgorged several dozen scruffy, red-striped balls.

Only a fraction of the stalls were occupied; there were young men in T-shirts and cutoff jeans, a few older men. Grant Siebert went down the line until he was thirty feet or so away from anyone else. The sun felt good on his arms.

What should he try first? He teed a ball on the rubber nipple and picked up the three wood. His feet felt strange, his legs and back felt strange, his hands felt mittened and clumsy. But if he just kept his eye on the ball, could he go wrong?

Yes. He swung with the three wood and missed the ball completely. He was disgusted and amused at the same time. He swung again and hit the ball at a wild angle, sending it cracking into the side of the stall.

He was glad no one looked.

Grant saw a train heading toward the city, knew that another would be along in a half hour. He could make it easily . . . .

He put the three wood down and picked up a five iron. Years before, a good golfer had told him a five iron was the perfect club for a rusty player. He teed up another ball, waggled the club. Then he swung, topping the ball and sending it straight and low for a hundred yards.

The next shot with the five iron went a respectable

distance. Encouraged, he decided to try hitting iron shots off the artificial-grass pad instead of from the rubber nipple. With his first swing, he rammed the clubhead into the mat, several inches behind the ball and so hard that he felt a ping in his shoulder.

Disgusted again, he dropped the club, looked to the sky, and rubbed his arms. Maybe the sun would loosen his muscles.

"Beautiful day."

Grant was startled; he hadn't been aware of anyone approaching. He turned to see a young blond man of medium height. Dark glasses, big forearms, carrying several empty baskets.

"Yeah, it is," Grant said.

"Been a while, huh?"

"Right again."

"Sell you a lesson?"

"A lesson?"

"Name's Doug Barnes. I'm the pro here."

"Grant Siebert."

From the handshake, Grant could tell that Doug Barnes was as strong as he looked.

"May I?" Doug Barnes said, picking up the five iron.

"Be my guest."

"Tell you what. I'll hit a few and give you a few minutes of free advice. If you think I can help you, we can set up a time for a regular lesson."

"Okay."

"Now, when you get set up over the ball . . ."

Grant stood back several feet and watched. From years before he remembered: it was a beautiful thing, the way a truly fine golfer poises himself, looking steady and flexible all at once, a coiled spring of great strength.

The pro brought the club down and through in a slow, smooth arc, sweeping the ball off the mat and sending it high, straight, and far. Again and again, the pro hit, making minor adjustments to his swing and telling Grant about them (even though Grant had been unable to spot any flaws). There was, at most, ten yards' difference between the pro's best and worst shots, and none was off center by more than a few degrees.

It had been a long time since Grant Siebert had seen anyone swing a golf club as well.

"Now, here's what I saw you doing," Doug Barnes said. And he shifted his feet, his hands, his head, this way and that, telling Grant what kind of bad shot would follow, then making just that kind of shot happen.

"What do you think?" the pro said.

"I think it's a pleasure to watch you."

"Hey, it's what I do. But can I help *you?*"

"Probably. Yes."

"Tomorrow then?"

"I have to work. But I can go in late if I want."

"See you at ten. Thirty bucks for a half hour."

"Okay."

"Good. Now just hit the rest of those balls and concentrate on the basics."

Riding the train back to the city a little later, Grant found himself thinking about the tips the pro had given him. They had worked: even though Grant had a long way to go to get his game back, he had improved as the practice session went on. Toward the end, he had started to make good contact. With a few lessons and some practice . . .

He laughed, loud enough so a few of the other passengers looked. He had to laugh: here he was, getting hooked on the game again. Getting hooked on this damn game.

Back at his apartment, he was glad when there were no phone messages. He wanted no distractions as he opened a can of beer and poked among the old books on the back shelf of the closet.

There it was: Ben Hogan's book. Some golfers thought it was the best book ever written on the game. Could this be?

Grant felt his blood catch fire with the thought of . . . golf. It was true: golf made a person's problems seem lighter.

He laughed, splashing half a mouthful of beer onto his chest.

The recorder holding the tape from his farewell party was still on the table. Did he want to listen to it again? No, not now at least. He wanted to look through the Ben Hogan book.

▲ ▲ ▲

Fourteen

▲▲▲

Marlee awoke in the middle of the night to the sound of barking in the backyard pen.

"Oh, Nigel, you jerk. What am I going to do with you?" she said to her pillow.

The neighbors had been pretty patient. Nigel did not wake them up that often, and some of the kids from the block liked to come by to say hello to the Airedale once in a while.

Nigel barked again. Marlee had to admit he really had a super bark, deep throated and majestic, as though it were coming from far down a canyon.

"What is it, Nigel? Raccoon? Squirrel? Or you just barking at the moon?"

The dog liked to sleep outside on summer nights, and that was just fine with Marlee. She never worried about anyone's breaking in at the front of the house, but she was careful about the rear. She had had thick metal screens put on the inside of the windowpanes. Still, a burglar could sneak onto the back porch, especially if he thought no one was home, and force a window or the door to the kitchen with a crowbar and not worry too much about being seen. She had a dead bolt on the kitchen door, but you never knew.

Again Nigel barked, this time more fiercely. Then he gave his little bark-chirp, as though he was puzzled. Then another good bark. Had a squirrel wandered into his pen? Marlee hoped not; Nigel was a gentle dog, but he was an Airedale, after all, and it would be first nature for him to grab an animal.

"Hush, Nigel," Marlee whispered to her pillow. She was almost asleep.

Again the bark, yanking her back from half-sleep.

"Oh, Nig—"

Marlee had started to get up. Now she put her head back on to the pillow, slowly. She wasn't sure, but she thought she had heard the porch creaking.

She let her head sink into the pillow and lay still. Marlee tried to breathe with quiet little gulps so she could hear. But for the longest time (no, it couldn't have been more than a few seconds) she could hear nothing but the echo of her heart.

Slowly, she pushed back the terror. She continued to lie absolutely still, and after a while the soft sounds of the night reasserted themselves. Sweet sounds, Marlee had always found them: gentle teasing sounds of trees and crickets.

The porch creaked.

Marlee was seized again by the terror, worse this time because there was no denying what she had heard. She lay petrified; the fear was a beast in her chest, ready to scream.

She must not panic, must not panic, must not panic.

Nigel! Marlee could not hear the Airedale now. Had he (they? *They!*) done something to Nigel, the sweetest, most wonderful dog that God ever made?

Marlee remembered a column she had written, about how women could defend themselves from muggers and rapists. She had talked to policewomen and psychologists and women who had fought off attackers, and she had distilled their collective message into two words: *Don't panic.*

In her heart of hearts, Marlee had been disdainful of the

women who had been victims. She had thought of them as weaker, less good. Now she was one with them in terror.

At last, the echo of her heartbeat died away. Marlee strained again to hear noises from outside.

Nothing.

Long moments passed. She kept her head on the pillow, leaving only one ear exposed. She knew she would hear better if she raised her head, but she was afraid to. Marlee imagined that if she raised her head and looked toward the bedroom door, she would see someone standing there. She knew she had locked the door—she always did when she went to bed, and she relocked it whenever she got up in the middle of the night to go to the bathroom—but she could not convince herself that she was alone in her bedroom. Just the thought that someone might be standing near, watching her, filled her with terror. She knew that if she did raise her head, and someone really was there, she would go mad and scream forever.

Any moment she would feel a cold hand on her shoulder . . .

Stop it, stop it, stop it, Marlee!

At last, she convinced herself that if she looked, there would be no one there. Slowly she raised her head and turned to look toward the door.

Nothing.

She listened as hard as she could; her very skin seemed to be alert.

Nigel! Barking again! Oh, he was all right. He was.

All right. Can't just lie here, Marlee thought. She swung her legs out of bed, feet landing softly on the carpet, and knelt next to the open window. She kept her head beneath the sill as she listened with all her might.

Nigel barked again, the funny kind of bark he sometimes made when he didn't know whether to be playful or not. Raccoon, maybe. Yes, the coons sometimes made Nigel react that way. Marlee listened for clangs from the garbage cans. Any other night she would be annoyed to hear those sounds, because they would mean the raccoons were into the garbage. Now, she would welcome a clang; it would dissolve her fear in an instant.

Nothing.

Nigel again, not so much a bark this time as an inquisitive chortle. Oh, God, Nigel, I wish you were here next to me.

Marlee shifted her position under the window. She tried to think, but her mind was racing too fast, too fast, like her heart. Should she dial 911? Do it, Marlee! Pick up the phone. That's why you have a phone dial that glows in the dark, for God's sake! It must be behind the lamp. . . .

No glow, no glow, just darkness. Oh! She had left the phone plugged into the living-room jack. To get to it, she would have to go out there, into the dark. He might be there! There might be more than one!

This can't be happening to me, can't, can't . . .

Could she jam a chair under the bedroom door? She had thought occasionally how quick, how easy that would be. Now, as she trembled in the fear-filled dark, it seemed a hopeless task.

She thought of the exercise dumbbells, the set of five-pounders she often played with after jogging. They were on the floor next to the dresser. They could smash a man's hand if he tried to come in the bedroom window. Her fingers found the dumbbells, but her sweat made them slippery to the touch. They were useless; she could never . . .

Should she scream? If she did, Nigel would bark his head off so that whoever was out there—if there was somebody—would almost certainly run away. Unless he . . .

Marlee told herself that any moment she would hear the clang of the garbage-can lid hitting the ground. Instead, she thought she heard a rustle on the grass a few feet from her window.

This had never happened to her before; she had never been awakened in the middle of the night by a prowler. Now she understood the fear.

The rustle again, just outside. Please, God; let it be an animal.

Nigel growled and barked. I love you, Nigel.

Marlee fumbled with a dumbbell. God, don't let it come to that. Please.

Another bark, medium fierce, then the annoyed and inquisitive chortle.

Silence outside. Oh, it must just have been an animal. Must have, must have.

Marlee listened as hard as she could. Would she be able to tell an animal noise from a human sound?

Maybe she had imagined the creak on the porch. Or maybe it had just been a raccoon. They were known to be very bold in the suburbs, getting into garbage cans. In the country, they even snuck into kitchens sometimes. Marlee had had to put ammonia in her cans to keep them away from chicken scraps in the garbage.

All right, all right. Get it together, Marlee. Probably an animal. Probably.

In the dark, she tiptoed to where she knew the straight chair was, against a wall near the door. She fumbled with the chair, her sweaty hands slipping on the wood, but she managed to wedge it under the doorknob with very little noise.

She was relieved, but only for a moment. Because she heard the rustling again outside her window, and this time there was no doubt.

Feet. A man's feet.

He was just under the window now. Oh, God. The dumbbell shook in her hand. She could never . . .

She heard a metallic click, recognized it at once as the sound of a small stepladder's legs being locked into place. Her stepladder! He had found it on the porch, where she kept it lying against the railing. Oh, God, how could she have been such a fool. He had taken her own ladder and—

Marlee heard the scrape of a foot on the ladder step. Her earlier fear had been nothing compared to what she felt now.

Another foot scrape, louder.

Nigel barked, menacingly. He barked as loud as he ever had, so that Marlee could hear nothing else. Oh, Nigel, I love you so much; if you were only—

Get out, Marlee. Get out of the room, just get out of the room.

She raced to the door, stubbing her toe on one of the bed casters. She grasped the chair, but it wouldn't move, wouldn't move. Trapped in her room, trapped.

The phone rang in the living room. Marlee thought her heart would leap from her chest, thought a scream would fly from her throat.

Marlee tugged as hard as she could at the chair; it came loose with a crack of wood. She opened the door, stumbled into the terrifying dark of her own house. There, the glow of the phone. She could see it through her tears.

Ring, ring.

She picked up the phone, slumped to the floor as she picked up the receiver.

"Marlee, I hate to complain but—" The voice belonged to her neighbor, Mrs. Wemple.

"Prowler!" she shrieked. "Police! Prowler! Call the police . . . Oh, please . . ."

Marlee was bone tired; she hoped the coffee, bagel, and orange she had bought at the take-out place across the street from the *Gazette* would perk her up.

Good, the newsroom wasn't crowded yet. She wasn't in the mood to socialize. But she was glad Will Shafer was in.

"Morning, Marlee," the executive editor said, looking up from his desk. "Are you okay? You look exhausted."

"I'm mostly okay, and I am exhausted. Listen, Will, I need a favor. Two favors, actually."

"Shoot."

"I want to sub my column for tomorrow."

"Damn, Marlee, that'll mean killing a page. How vital is it?"

"Very." Marlee looked into Will Shafer's eyes; tell him, she thought. "I had a prowler at my place last night, and I want to write about it. I can have the column done before noon. Promise."

"A prowler? Are you okay?"

"Tired is all. Please, Will."

The editor frowned. He looks tired, too, Marlee thought. She remembered hearing that Will's wife was out of town for a few days at some sociology conference; kids must be a handful for him.

Marlee knew that killing a page at the last minute was no small thing; it cost money. She couldn't blame Will Shafer if he said no.

"You got it, Marlee. I'll tell the foreman."

"Thanks," she said.

"What's the other favor?"

"Could I use your office? So I can write without anyone hanging around me?"

Where to begin? From the heart, Marlee told herself. Slowly she began to type on Will Shafer's computer:

"I want to share something with you. I claim no special wisdom as I type this, even though I know something now that I didn't know only hours ago.

"I am more tired than I ever was before, yet I feel more alive.

"It is only a few hours since a prowler came by my house just as I was falling asleep. There are no words to tell you the terror I felt when I heard the sounds on my porch and outside my bedroom window."

Marlee paused, staring at the green glow of the computer screen. How safe she was now, in the quiet privacy of Will Shafer's office with the door locked. He had even said she could help herself to the coffee. She could smell the aroma from the coffeepot. Will was famous for making coffee that wasn't very good.

How safe she felt now, not just because she was among

her friends and colleagues, but because of all that had happened after the prowler came.

Write it, Marlee. Just get it down. You're on deadline. Remember?

And she did write, stripping her soul almost naked. She wrote of the contrition she felt for not having understood the depths of fear a woman might have, and how her experience had changed her forever—for the better, she hoped.

She told how easy it was to panic, how after screaming into the phone she had not had the composure to dial the police herself, but had relied on her neighbor to do it. And the neighbor had: Mrs. Wemple, who was close to seventy and old-fashioned, and Marlee had never sought her company because she was so old-fashioned.

Oops, no. Marlee was mixing thoughts with writing. No, she wouldn't write all that. Just say a neighbor woman, Marlee thought.

She wrote of how she had sobbed on her bedroom floor, lying there curled like a child, even after hearing the stepladder clatter to the ground and hearing the quick rustle of feet as the prowler fled, and hearing the great dog Nigel barking in fury.

She wrote of hearing the siren, of how quickly the police car was out front—even in her fear she knew the police had been quick—and how the spotlight from the police car had searched the corners of the yard, how the light had shone off the stepladder when, at last, she gathered the courage to look out the window.

She wrote how grateful she was to the police, who told her they were just doing their job. She recalled how she had criticized the police before, for not being sensitive enough with rape victims and women who had been beaten by their husbands. Now, she wrote, she was grateful with all her heart.

She didn't write about how sexy the younger cop was, how good he had made her feel when he comforted her, and how he had hit it off immediately with her Airedale. Hmmm, Marlee thought. Maybe I should call to thank him again.

And then she was done writing, or almost done. How to finish?

"People do care," she typed.

She sent her column electronically to the appropriate computer directory, then dialed the editor who normally handled it. "My sub's in, Ellie. I'm in Will's office if you need me."

Marlee sipped her coffee and munched on the bagel. She peeled the orange and ate it slowly, segment by segment. God, she was tired.

She hoped her column made sense. No, she knew it made sense. She hoped it wasn't too . . . too . . .

The phone rang. "Marlee, this is wonderful," her editor, Ellie, said. "Why don't you go home and rest."

"Thanks. I will."

She hung up, sat at Will Shafer's desk, finished her small breakfast.

Only one more thing to do.

Marlee cried.

Fifteen

▲ ▲ ▲

His feet were cold. He hadn't bothered to step into his slippers after waking up because he had to check on the noise. It was an irregular *thud, thud* coming from another room.

There it was again. He wished that he had taken the time to put on his slippers. The rest of him was cold, too, especially his back and shoulders. The night had turned chilly, really chilly for summer. He wished he had his robe.

What could it be, that noise? Nothing, he told himself, but it still made him uneasy. He looked out a window. All was black and still; it was the deepest part of the night, a long time to go before the first hints of the devil-routing dawn.

He heard the noise again. It was coming from below. He stood in the dark, telling himself not to be afraid, but it was no use.

Should he turn on a light? No. At least in the dark he was invisible, too.

Thud, thud, thud. The noise was louder now; there was no doubt it was coming from one floor down. A rat? There had never been rats before.

His feet were colder; so were his back and shoulders.

Should he go back for his slippers and robe after all? No, the noise had not only awakened him, it had drawn him near the door in the kitchen, the one he almost never opened.

He was standing at the door now. Too late to go back for his slippers and robe. Oh. A sliver of yellow under the door. A light on behind the door. He could not remember when he had last opened the door.

The noise again. He had to find out, even though he was afraid. He opened the door wide. There were stairs leading down. There was nothing at the bottom except bare basement concrete bathed in light. But the noise was louder now with the door open. Yes, it was coming from down there, from somewhere out of view.

And something else, another noise. A scuffing noise, from feet somewhere down there, scuffing feet on the concrete. Then a *thud, thud*. More scuffing, louder, like feet going in a frantic circle.

Standing at the top of the stairs, he was both bewildered and terrified.

The phone. His cold feet moved to the wall, and his trembling hands found the phone in the dark. He held the receiver to his ear, heard the dial tone.

His fingers were thick and numb. He could not find the right numbers. He held the phone in his hand and tiptoed back toward the open door. The scuffing seemed louder than ever; it must be coming from the foot of the stairs. Now he heard the *thud, thud* louder than ever. Something was banging against the basement steps, near the bottom.

He tiptoed the last few steps and stood at the top of the stairs, looking down into the light.

The priest was there, trying desperately to shake the golf club out of his head. Only the top of the priest's head was visible, the pulp and bloody hair showering red drops this way and that as the priest shook his head. The priest's feet scuffed on the concrete floor. Oh, the priest could not stand up for long, that was it.

Watching from the top of the stairs, he felt his eyes fill up with tears. The priest was suffering, had been in terrible pain all this time.

He wanted to tell the priest he was sorry. He cried out to the priest, and the scuffing and head-shaking stopped. The priest raised his head, the end of the golf club catching for a moment on the side of the staircase.

The priest had only one eye. Part of the mouth was still there, the shreds of lip hanging down, but the rest of the face was pounded meat. The eye was sad, as though the priest had been crying, but it was angry, too.

The scuffing started again; the priest was trying to come up the stairs. . . .

Watching from the top of the stairs, he screamed as loud as he could.

His foot lashed out and struck the side of the table by his bed. He screamed again, into the darkness, then groped for the light. Finally he found it.

He looked toward the window; the shade had slipped, and the ring on the end of the cord was dancing in the stream of air, bouncing off the air conditioner. *Thud, thud, thud.*

In his sleep, he had flung off the sheet. The cold from the air conditioner had flowed over his back and feet. His throat was raw from screaming.

He lay there, trembling. Tears ran down his cheeks. Was it good that he was alone this night?

Only a dream, and not the first dream about the night of the ice storm. So long ago. The other thing was not a dream: someone knew. After all this time, someone knew.

He stood on trembling legs, walked to the window. He turned down the air conditioner, and the cord stopped dancing. He peeked behind the shade.

Still deep in the night, hours to go before the devil-routing dawn.

Someone knew.

Sixteen

▲▲▲

Grant Siebert was late for lunch with Lorraine Pierce. He had remembered their date during his golf lesson.

"You been away?" Doug Barnes had said. "Haven't seen you in a few days."

"Things I had to do," Grant said, just before he hit an iron straight and far.

"Good follow-through," Doug Barnes said. "You taking steroids for lunch or what?"

"Holy shit," Grant said. "Lunch."

He trotted part of the way to the Douglaston station. Perspiring freely on the train, he tried to figure how he could get to the restaurant without being more than twenty minutes late.

If he took the subway directly from Penn Station to within a couple of blocks of the restaurant, he would be sweatier than ever and inadequately dressed, even though he might be almost on time. If first he took the subway downtown to his apartment and showered and changed clothes, he would be a half hour late. No, forty minutes at least.

So he went to his apartment, called the restaurant, and

left a message. Then he sponged off his chest and back while he was standing in front of the air conditioner, slapped on deodorant and shaving lotion, put on a clean shirt.

He got to the restaurant feeling not too fresh, his nerves on edge. And twenty-five minutes late. She's pissed, he thought as he caught her half-wave and half-smile from the corner table.

"Sorry," he said, bumping the table as he sat down.

"'Sokay," she said. "Hassle at the magazine?"

Should he lie? "No. I was . . . I was taking a golf lesson. Out in Douglaston."

"That explains why you look kind of sweaty."

Ah, nice dart, Lorraine. Bull's-eye. She was still smiling, but the points of her teeth showed more and her eyes were hard.

"Well, anyhow, I'm sorry."

"'Sokay. Why don't you order us some drinks. I'll have another vodka with Perrier chaser."

He did order drinks, from a waiter who seemed to sniff disapprovingly at him. He felt both guilty and annoyed, not quite clean and totally out of place amid the sparkling silverware and immaculate white linen. The lunch was off to a terrible start. Maybe a few gulps of alcohol would lift him to a mood that could still turn things around.

"I didn't know you played golf."

"I haven't for a long time."

"And you're taking it up again?"

"Golf kind of stays with you. Stays in your blood."

He was more conscious than ever of Lorraine Pierce's clipped, direct style of conversation. He imagined that it helped make her an effective lawyer. Early on, he had found it appealing. Now, at least today, it seemed much less so.

"Why right now?" she said. "Why take up golf again now?"

He was saved, for the moment, by the arrival of the drinks.

"To good health," he said, touching her glass with his and filling his throat with gin and tonic.

"So are you planning a golf vacation or something?"

"Uh, not so much a vacation as a reunion, actually."

"Reunion? Where?"

"In Bessemer. At the paper I used to work for."

"Really? What's the occasion?"

"The paper's throwing itself a birthday party."

"But where does the golf come in?"

"Part of the reunion is a golf tournament."

Lorraine shrugged and frowned. He finished his drink and signaled for another. Lorraine was barely into hers.

They ordered gazpacho and the Caesar salad for two.

"I never wanted to try golf," she said. "I need something I can throw myself into more. Like single-handing a sailboat."

"Mmmm." He was starting to feel the gin, but he was afraid the buzz wouldn't help.

"I'm kind of surprised you're going to Bessemer," she went on. "I know you worked there, but I never hear you talk about it. Have you ever been back?"

"No."

"Not once?"

"I said no."

"Hey, excuse me."

"No, my fault. I'm sorry." Things were getting out of hand.

"It's okay," Lorraine said. "I was just curious why you're going back now."

Because my memory's been jogged, Grant thought. "I don't know. The time just seemed right."

"But the time isn't right to go to Lake George?"

"Lake George?"

"You don't remember. Obviously."

"No. I guess not." The lunch wasn't getting any better.

"A while back we talked about going to my mother's cottage for a long weekend. The first chance we got. To get to know each other better."

"We will, only—"

"No, we won't. Because . . . When is the reunion?"

"Um, late July, early August."

"So you see? There's the chance, and you've made other plans. And we've never even . . ."

"Now wait. Let's think about—"

The arrival of the gazpacho gave him a reprieve. Could he turn things around? Did he want to?

They started to eat their soup in silence. Grant glanced at the round, white face across from him. Lorraine Pierce's best features were her black hair and dark eyes. When she put on weight, or when she was angry, her face seemed rounder than ever, her eyes shrank from squinting, and her lips looked thin from pursing.

Yes, Grant thought. She's angry.

"Let's start over," he said.

"So what's to start over?"

Oh, he knew that tone. The situation had skidded even further than he had thought. It might not be salvageable; he was starting to think so, and his gin mood seemed to be going in the direction of the skid.

"I meant—"

"Excuse me," she said. "Just excuse me."

Lorraine stood up abruptly. Grant saw that her lawyer's control was holding back an outburst of anger or tears or both.

"Ladies' room," she muttered as she left the table, brushing the tablecloth with her hip.

Grant gulped the rest of his gin, then shook the ice cubes. The waiter came.

"One more," Grant said.

"And the lady?"

"She's taking a recess."

Grant was not displeased with his wit, though the waiter didn't seem to get it. Oh, of course; the waiter didn't know . . .

"She's a lawyer," Grant said. But the waiter was gone, and the explanation hung in the air like a bubble.

He had met her at a party given by a journalistic society for reporters and lawyers. Walt Striker, who didn't really fit into either of those categories but who knew lots of people who did, had been invited and had taken Grant along. Lorraine Pierce had laughed at some of Grant's imitations, had seemed to enjoy talking to him, even though she didn't approve of the magazine he worked for. They had had several dates.

As he sat in the restaurant, he tried to remember why he had liked her—and tried to imagine why she had liked him.

Lorraine returned, brushing the tablecloth again with her hip. She smells better than I do, he thought.

"Don't get up," she said, taking her seat.

By now, Grant was darkly amused, as well as sorry. He saw that Lorraine had applied fresh makeup around her eyes, which were still squinty. She was spearing bits of Caesar salad with her fork and thrusting them into her thin-lipped mouth.

Unless he wanted a total shambles, he had to say something. "I would like to start over. I would."

"The point I was making, the point—if you're going to this reunion, there goes the summer. Don't you see?"

"No."

"Jesus, Grant," she hissed. "The weekend we're talking about takes us into August. Before you know it, it's Labor Day."

"And the summer has gone bye-bye." Oops, wrong thing to say.

She paused in mid-spear-stroke. Almost like a cobra waiting to strike, Grant thought. But she spoke with a control he found remarkable. "So, you do understand, at least."

He did, and was suddenly washed by a wave of contrition. "Look, if we can just . . ." He could still turn things around, he could!. "Look, I can get another weekend. I can. I'll just—"

"Even if you do . . . Oh, goddammit!" She set her fork down on the plate with an angry, ladylike little clink, shook her head slowly from side to side, and flashed a mirthless smile that seemed to say, Why am I bothering?

"I'm sorry, Lorraine. I am. I know I was thoughtless."

"Yes, you were. Where have you been the last few days? Out of town? I called and—"

"I, uh, I had things to do. Writing. I was writing."

"Wonderful. I applaud your dedication. But now this reunion. The point is, you put a higher priority on this reunion than on what we talked about. A reunion in a city you haven't visited in twenty years, for God's sake."

"That's the whole point of reunions," he heard himself say.

There, that had done it.

Lorraine opened her purse, threw two crisp twenty-dollar bills onto the table, added a ten as an afterthought, and stood up. "I left enough for you to drink some more, too," she said.

And she was gone. Oops, not quite. Here she was back again.

"Grant, you have a real cruel streak. Sometimes I think there's something perverse and violent in you, and not just because of where you work. God only knows where it comes from."

"Yep, God does."

"Do you?"

Should he tell her?

"You know, Grant, there's this thing in you. Whenever you're especially nasty, like right now, you push it as far as you can. Beyond, in fact. And then you're always so sorry, aren't you?"

"Yes."

"You know the men who are always sorry? Drunks and wife beaters. And they always do it again."

"I don't have a wife."

"And maybe you never will. I don't need this shit, Grant."

Now she was gone, for good. No, here she was again. "Unless you face it, Grant, you're going to be a really unhappy guy all your life, suffering from contaminated relationships."

"Hmmm."

"Or maybe you're afraid to face whatever it is."

That wounded him. "Maybe you should go," he said.

This time she had.

The waiter came by just then and reached for her salad dish.

"Leave it," Grant said.

The waiter retreated, and Grant reached across the table and slid Lorraine's salad bowl toward his own. He began to eat, not knowing if he felt sad, relieved, or both. Even before the lunch, he and Lorraine hadn't been in synch with each other. Now it was dead, had to be.

"Care for anything else, sir?"

The waiter had an imperious manner, and Grant was tempted to tell him to fuck off, but his drink was empty and Grant was thirsty. "Light beer. Any kind that's cold."

Grant realized (too late, ah, too late) that he had been very hungry. Now he ate ravenously, washing down the bites with the slaking beer. Grant thought the waiter gave him a sideways glance when he signaled soon for another, but a new bottle appeared on the table—along with the check. A hint?

He buttered a roll and chewed it slowly, trying to fight off the sadness by embracing the emptiness. He ate another roll and finished the beer. Time to go.

Grant stood up, steadying himself on the edge of the table, and walked across the carpet toward the exit. He was surprised that the other tables were empty.

"Thank you, sir. Good day." The waiter stood near the door.

Grant nodded, then went out into the sunshine. It was warm, dazzling bright. He fished in his jacket pocket for sunglasses, put them on.

He walked home, trying not to feel sad. Maybe he should

call Lorraine and leave an apology—or farewell—on her
answering machine when he knew she wouldn't be in.

Around Penn Station, beggars drifted close to him like
filthy bugs. Grant ignored them.

There were no messages on his answering machine, and
he was thankful for that. He just wanted to nap. Leaving the
answering machine on, he lay down on the sofa. At once, he
felt sleep coming on. He welcomed it.

He opened his eyes to the gray light. Just getting to be dawn,
he thought. Grant was thirsty and a little stiff from having
slept on the sofa. He got up and went to the window. The
city was stirring. He heard a street-washing machine below,
smelled the fresh smell of water and clean pavement.

Had the fight with Lorraine been as bad as it seemed?
Yes, he could tell from the feeling in his stomach that it had
been.

He went into the bathroom and peeled off his clothes. He
started to step into the shower, changed his mind, and
walked, naked, to the kitchen. He started the coffee brew-
ing so it would be done by the end of his shower.

Long after the shampoo was rinsed from his hair he let the
water run down his chest, down his throat. He toweled
himself, combing his wet hair straight back, put on a robe,
and went barefoot to the kitchen. The coffee smelled good.
Grant poured a cup and went back to the window. On the
sidewalk on the other side, a man and a woman hugged each
other. A taxi stopped in front of the apartments across the
way. A young woman carrying a duffel bag came out of the
building and said something to the cabdriver. Then a young
man came out, kissed the woman tenderly, saw her into the
cab.

I could love you people, Grant thought. He wished there
were more mornings like this. There are, he corrected
himself. You just sleep through them. Or see them before
you go to bed.

He poured more coffee, took a pitcher of orange juice and

a glass to the table where his computer lay. He shifted the computer so he could sit facing the window and the pure morning.

He wrote. He had been away from the words too long, so he had to get caught up again in their rhythm, had to get over the doubt and anger, which flowed from a bottomless reservoir.

He despised the part of him that was so self-centered, the writer part. But whenever he strayed too far from the autobiographical, he thought his prose became bloodless.

During one pause, he thought of his parents. He would call them. Maybe he would go see them. And Bessemer. He could not undo things, but perhaps he need not be haunted forever. Yes, it was time for him to go back.

He wrote until the sun was high and hot in a blue-gray haze.

Seventeen

▲ ▲ ▲

Grant ran off his checklist. Yes, he had all the clothes, toiletries, and other things he needed to visit his parents for a couple of days. He hoped he had the right state of mind.

He had called his parents in a rush of good feeling and hope, emotions that began to fade halfway through the conversation, but by then it was too late. He had committed himself to meeting them at their summer cottage.

He had borrowed Walt Striker's car. Now Grant was about ready to take the subway uptown to pick up the car and get out of the city. But something was bothering him, so he sat down and made a phone call. He hoped for an answer, yet feared it.

"Lila Burlson speaking."

He felt weak in the knees. "Hello. This is Grant Siebert. Sorry to bother you, but I'm going out of town for the weekend, and I was just wondering if you have any indication about what I sent you."

Lila Burlson was an agent he had heard about at the magazine, through Walt Striker, and she had agreed to read

153

his partial manuscript. He had mailed her a copy several days ago.

"Hi. Yes, well, I've been reading it. I see from your letter that you've had some nonfiction published."

"Yes."

"And you work for *Sleuth*. 'Death Trap Baited With Sex' and all that. Walt Striker said he liked you."

"Really?" Then how come your voice is dripping with contempt, Grant thought.

"Yes, really. Do you like working with Walt?"

"Mostly. I mean, I like Walt. As for the work . . ." Grant hesitated; if he betrayed contempt for what he did, she would pick up on it. "Most of what I do is editing. I only write that kind of stuff occasionally. It's good practice in scene-setting and dialogue. I don't pretend—"

"Never mind. I used to wonder about anyone who was into that stuff. You don't have any dark secrets, do you?"

"Maybe." The question was startling, but the teasing quality in her voice gave him hope.

"Well, whatever. As for your manuscript, I said I wasn't finished."

"Hmmm." Please, he thought.

"I can see that you threw yourself into it. And I do mean your *self*."

"It is, it is autobiographical to an extent, but it isn't—"

"I mean, you explore a lot of interesting themes. The elusive nature of happiness, parental love, being true to one's self. Some of your writing is quite sensitive and good. And there are some powerful undercurrents of anger. I mean, very vivid stuff, a lot of it."

"Thanks." His heart wanted to fly out of his chest.

"But I honestly can't commit myself to it as an agent. You see . . ."

The words knocked the wind out of him. Lila Burlson had seemed like a good prospect: young, independent, just starting out. Now he listened to her explain why she didn't like his work well enough to try to sell it: too self-conscious, too much introspection, not enough interaction.

"So," Grant said finally, "you think it sucks."

"I didn't say that. I only know I can't represent it at this time. Sorry I can't tell you something better."

"Okay. I understand. I appreciate your time." His face burned; he could not keep the tremble out of his voice.

"So, I'll send it back to you with my thanks for offering it."

"Thanks for reading."

He made it through the good-bye pleasantries, barely. He stepped away from the phone, afraid that he would smash it if he didn't.

"Son of a bitch. Son of a *bitch!*"

He slammed the side of his foot into the front of the refrigerator, heard something topple inside. Good: let it go rotten.

He swung the back of his hand at the stack of dirty dishes, sending a glass crashing into the wall at the cost of a little pain where his knuckles came together.

He sat down, deeply sad and ashamed. The load of emotions pressed down on his shoulders. Would it have been better if he had left without calling, then found the returned manuscript waiting for him when he got back? Would she have returned it by then? Did it matter?

He didn't know. He could think about it on the subway, and think about it some more on the drive to his parents' cottage. And think about it when he got back and saw the broken glass.

It was nearing dusk as he negotiated the final quarter-mile down the evergreen-lined dirt road. As he got out of the car, he could see the orange glow on the porch from his father's pipe.

"Evening," his father said cheerfully, as a colonel would address a private.

"Hi."

"Heavy traffic?"

"About normal."

"Figured you'd be here earlier. Take the Thruway?"

"No. Route Seventeen."

"Thruway's faster."

"Scenery's not as good."

"You missed a great sunset over the lake."

Jesus, Grant thought. He has to argue from word one. "Well, I'm here now. How are you?"

"Keepin' busy. Finally closed the Lawrence deal . . ."

Grant filtered out much of what his father said. The names, dates, figures of real estate deals in Syracuse and Rochester meant nothing to him, yet his father never tired of talking about them.

"Your mother's inside. You'll want to get cleaned up for dinner before long. You can get a beer for yourself."

As Grant opened the screen door and went inside, he realized without surprise that he and his father had not shaken hands. They had not seen each other in many weeks.

"Grant, honey!"

"Hi, mom."

His mother smelled of powder and sherry.

"Your dad is really glad you could come this time."

"I can tell he is."

"Oh, he is. He is!"

Grant patted his mother on the shoulder, eased his way past her, and took a beer out of the refrigerator.

"He's going to talk to you about a trip," his mother whispered. She was smiling conspiratorially.

"A trip?" Alarm bells in his head.

"Shhh. He'll hear."

Grant tried to keep his face neutral. He took a big swig of beer and was glad he had spotted a dozen or more cans chilled and waiting.

His mother announced with forced merriness that dinner was ready. The news was a relief to Grant, who had been sitting on the porch with his father in an awkward silence broken occasionally by banalities.

"How's things at the magazine?" his father said as they came inside.

"About the same. Okay."

"Do any more exploring?" That was his father's code for looking for a more respectable job.

"No. Been too busy."

His father frowned in what Grant was sure was disappointment.

"You're still writing, I take it?"

"Yep. Still writing." Beautiful, Grant thought. The one time he shows some interest, or pretends to, I don't want to talk about it.

But his father dependably reverted to form and showed no sign of pursuing the subject. "You said dinner was ready, lady."

"Yes, indeed, Mr. Siebert. Coming up."

It was his father's habit to call his mother "lady" instead of her name, Barbara, or some diminutive. Though he feigned affection, his tone was unmistakably domineering.

"Why don't you see if your mother needs help."

"No! I'm fine, really."

Too late, Grant drew back from the frantic tone in her voice. He had already started into the kitchen, so he saw her sneaking a gulp of sherry as she stirred the raisin sauce. He pretended not to notice, just as he had long ago pretended not to notice the bruises on her thin arms and narrow shoulders.

"That's not your car, is it?" his father asked.

"No. Borrowed it from a guy I work with."

"Sounds like it needs a tune-up."

"I'll tell him."

Grant's mother walked in (a little unsteadily, he thought) with a platter that held a steaming ham. "Now everybody just sit," she said. "Everything's under control."

She really wants it to be, Grant thought.

"I can use a beer," his father said.

"Coming up," Grant said, gently halting his mother and steering her toward her chair. "I'll get it," he said quietly.

Grant got a can of beer for his father and one for himself and sat down. He wished he was hungrier, because his mother had gone to some trouble. Ham with raisin sauce was one of his father's favorite dinners.

"So," his father said, "you think that school of yours is gonna have a decent team this fall?"

"They should. Got the whole offensive line back. As for the defense—"

"Plenty of speed, too, right? Those colored sprinters are all back, too, right?"

"Most of them, yeah. We should be all right."

"Better than all right, seems to me."

"Maybe. Yeah. Better than all right." Sometimes Grant could feel, or at least pretend, enthusiasm when he and his father talked about Notre Dame football. Not this time.

"They won all their games last year, didn't they?" his mother said.

"No," Grant said. "They lost to—"

"Don't you remember?" his father said. "They lost their opener at Purdue on a shit call by the referee. Then Miami beat 'em. We watched on TV, for crying out loud."

"I just forgot," his mother said.

"It's okay, Mom," Grant said. "The people in China didn't even know about it."

His mother tried to smile gamely but couldn't quite make it.

Grant studied his father. His hairline had never receded, and his hair had gone from black to steely gray. His face was tanned, unlined, and the glasses only made him look more formidable and intelligent. Grant could see why his mother had been attracted to him, and why other women were.

"So," his father said, "you're planning on going to a game in November."

His mother's foot nudged Grant's leg under the table in an unmistakable signal.

"I was, I was thinking . . ."

"The Penn State game, your mother tells me."

Grant felt adrift. "Well, I mean, I haven't exactly got it all planned."

"You need to plan three, four months ahead if you expect to get a motel room."

"I know. I've been to games at Notre Dame." That puny retort went right past his father.

"There's lots more alumni now than there were a few years ago, don't forget. How were you going to go?"

Grant's head was spinning. He had not even made up his mind to go to a football game; he had only mentioned to his mother a few weeks back that he might like to do it soon. Now his father was reviewing, dissecting, and dismissing plans Grant hadn't even made. Of course: his mother had taken part of their conversation and gone way beyond it, used it to shore up her shaky dream vision of a family.

"Hey," his father said, "are you in there somewhere? I said, how were you going to go?"

"Oh, well. If I went, I guess I'd fly."

"You take care of the motel reservations," his father decreed. "Start in South Bend, work out from there, get a decent place as close as you can to the campus. You can take the train up to Albany. We'll meet you there and drive. Figure on making it to Ohio that Thursday, rest of the way Friday."

Grant would need another beer, soon.

"Any problems?" his father demanded.

"Well, I'll most likely just be able to order two tickets."

His mother laughed, much too merrily. "Oh, I don't care about the game. I'll walk around the campus while you two are in the stadium."

"All set, then," his father said.

And then Grant's father reached over and playfully

punched him on the shoulder with such affection that Grant felt turned inside out with guilt.

"How much time off can you get?" his father said.

"A few days, I guess. Enough to go there and back."

"Take an extra couple of days off and we can make the start of deer season."

"Deer season?" His father had taken him hunting when Grant was a boy, too young to carry a gun himself. Grant had loved the boom of his father's gun, had dreamed about growing up and having his own gun. Then one day his father shot a rabbit, and the animal flopped pitifully, showering its blood onto the snow before dying. Grant had waited until he was alone in bed that night before crying.

"I can get an extra gun, no problem," his father said. "We could hunt—"

"I'm just not interested," Grant said.

"You didn't let me finish."

"Fred," his mother said, "maybe Grant just doesn't want—"

"He won't know if he likes deer hunting if he never tries it, is what I'm saying." Now his father sounded both domineering and wounded—a combination that had over the years made him almost invincible.

"Fred, maybe it would be cramming too much into a few days to try to go hunting. Maybe, maybe . . ."

His mother's voice seemed to slip on the sherry; she was straining to hold things together.

Grant had an inspiration: "I would probably have trouble getting more time off. I don't think I told you, but I'm going to a reunion in Bessemer."

"What kind of reunion?" his father said.

"The *Gazette*'s celebrating its ninetieth birthday. They called a bunch of people who used to work there and invited them back."

"That should be very nice," his mother said. Yes, the sherry had her in its sweet embrace.

"All right, then," his father announced. "We'll just make it a football weekend. But I still don't understand why you don't try deer hunting."

Grant shrugged, poked ham onto his fork, and worked on his beer while his father talked on.

After dinner, Grant's father went into his study to look at real estate papers. His mother suggested that Grant go sit on the porch. He took a fresh beer and did just that, leaving his mother alone in the kitchen with the dishes and her wine.

He sat in the dark, listening to the soft noises from the trees and the lake. "God," he said to the dark, "can't I even talk to my parents without getting trapped?" No, God. Don't answer.

He heard his mother moving about the kitchen, hoped desperately that she was not drinking more than she had been, hoped that his father's temper was no worse.

We relate to one another like magnets, he thought: always clinging or driving each other away. Never in between.

Deer hunting. Of course. His father wanted to take him deer hunting because they wouldn't have to talk. His father used a pickup truck for hunting trips, and the truck had a tape deck. Classical music (heavy on brass and drums) during the drive, then hunt. Once in the woods, they would be many yards apart and couldn't talk even if they wanted to. Beautiful: he has my company, getting God knows what out of it, and doesn't have to talk. If he's lucky, he gets to kill.

Going to Notre Dame was a little different. When his father went there with him (it had been a few years since the last time), he was able to make grand pronouncements, about football, about politics, about higher education, the fifty-five-mile-an-hour speed limit.

Ah, Grant thought, you're not so different from him. Here you sit on the porch; you wouldn't dream of going into his den to talk, would you? No.

At least at Notre Dame, Grant could feel a sense of forgiveness, from the grass and leaves, from the cold stones of the Grotto. If he could get away from his parents for a few minutes, Grant would go to the Grotto.

The Holy Mother would get an earful.

Grant opened his eyes to the darkness. Something had awakened him.

Of course. He heard the sounds from his parents' bedroom.

First he heard his father's voice: ". . . sick and tired . . . fill yourself with wine every goddamn night . . ."

Then a pillow being pounded, and his mother's voice: ". . . best I can. You've never even tried to help . . ."

". . . anyone help you if you drink a jug of sherry . . ."

". . . wasn't until you broke your vows that I started . . ."

". . . keep my vows when my wife pukes up her wine every other night . . ."

". . . dirty liar . . ."

Ah, she's crying now, Grant thought.

". . . sick and tired of cleaning up after you . . ."

". . . dirty liar . . . dirty liar . . ."

Grant listened intently, as he had done as a child. Some of his earliest memories had been of the night sounds. At first, he had pressed his hands to his ears as hard as he could, had shut his eyes as hard as he could—as if shutting his eyes could protect him from the *sounds!*

Year by year, Grant's reaction to the sounds had changed: he had listened, with horror but intently. Gradually, the horror had blended with fascination. That had continued into adolescence, when his hormones combined with the noises and left him feeling—what?

He dare not think too deeply on that. But he knew he liked it better when the sounds of his father slapping his mother were followed by those that meant her fingernails were raking his face.

This night, in the cottage by the lake, Grant listened as intently as he could. It had been a long time since he had spent a night with his parents. Would there be slapping and scratching tonight? No, the sounds were dying down now.

Grant slept.

Grant spent part of the next day watching a baseball game and trying not to notice the pouches under his mother's eyes. His father worked in his office part of the day (Grant could hear him on the phone) and emerged every so often to grab some leftover ham.

Late in the afternoon, his father suggested a walk—just the two of them, his mother was napping—and Grant had no reason to say no.

"You're heading back to New York tomorrow?" his father said.

"That's my plan." He already knows that, Grant thought. They were walking the perimeter of Red Fox Lake; the path beneath their feet was soft with brown pine needles.

"Glad you could come."

Grant said nothing.

"Things all right with you?" his father said.

"Yeah, mostly."

Grant studied the lake, tried to concentrate on the sights of fish ripples and loons and reflections. But he saw his father's profile (good, strong face, made even more handsome by the gray) and saw in his eyes that there was something he was waiting to say.

"Uh, last night. I don't know if you happened to hear . . ."

"I heard."

"Your mother hasn't been herself."

Yes, she has, Grant thought.

"She's worried," his father went on. "I, uh, I've had some tests. Had some bleeding, you know? Could be just hemorrhoids. Still . . ."

Grant was startled; this was new. "When will you find out something?"

"Soon, maybe. First batch of tests didn't turn up anything.

So they did some more. Actually, it wasn't just the bleeding. I haven't felt so great, you know?"

Grant said nothing.

"Anyhow," his father went on, "that's why the Notre Dame trip is important to me. In addition to the fact that I like to go to the place, in the back of my mind there's . . . you know."

Grant was embarrassed and guilty. He wanted nothing close to intimacy with his father.

"You're right," his father said, "right to go to Bessemer. It's a good idea, touching base with old friends, old times."

Out on the lake, a fish jumped and a loon bobbed.

"Anyhow, I didn't mean last night to discourage you from going to Bessemer."

"You didn't. I've been planning to go."

"What made you decide?"

Grant shrugged. He would wait out the silence no matter how long it took.

"So what's on your agenda for tonight?" his father said finally.

"I don't know. Thought I'd drive over near Horning. Find a quiet tavern."

"Watch out. Lots of cops out, looking for people to pull over. These country cops, looking for young guys . . ."

"I'm not so young anymore."

"That's right, you're not." A chuckle. "I forget that sometimes, because if you're not that young, it means . . ."

"I'll watch out."

"You, uh, seeing anyone at the moment?"

"Now and then."

"Mmmm. I used to play the field myself." His father chuckled.

You still did after you got married, Grant thought. And then he wondered how he would feel if his father died soon. Would he be relieved? What would happen to his mother?

"Oh, one thing," his father said. He had stopped to look across the lake and was making a big project out of lighting his pipe. "It's good that you studied history in college. Looking back, I might have pressured you too much to study business. A man sticks to what he knows. I know business, so I figured you should study it, too. Anyhow, you studied what you wanted, so I guess things turned out okay."

"I guess." Grant knew his father wanted him to say more. They turned and started back to the cottage.

"Never mind the deer hunting, that's okay," his father said, his voice again distant and commanding. "If you do get more time, you might want to come up early. In case it snows or something."

Grant said nothing. The moment had passed, and he was both sad and relieved. And he was glad his father did not suggest going over to Horning with him. He had to go alone.

Eighteen

▲▲▲

Marlee thought that all funeral homes smelled the same. The suffocating fragrance of flowers engulfed her the moment she stepped inside and unbuttoned her raincoat.

"Hello, how are you today," the man from the funeral home said.

"Just fine, thanks."

"Here. Allow me."

The man was tall and gray and had a lot of practice being somber. He spoke in hushed tones and positioned himself gracefully behind Marlee to help with her coat.

"We're sure getting our share of rain, aren't we?" the man said.

"And then some. I'm—"

"You're Marlee West," the funeral director said. "I recognize you from your picture. My wife is a faithful reader."

Marlee was about to say she was flattered, but he gave her no time. "Your friend is in the end room," the man said consolingly.

"Thanks. I'll visit the ladies' room first." She didn't need him to tell her where it was; she had paid her respects to other dead people here.

Marlee felt relieved to be in the bathroom: for once, the smells of soap and antiseptic were better than the scent of flowers.

She ran cold water, wetted a paper towel, dabbed at her cheeks. After drying her face, she combed her rain-moist hair and applied lipstick around the rough spot on her lip.

Ready, she thought.

Coming up the stairs, she saw a couple of *Gazette* people walking toward the end room. She was just as glad they hadn't seen her.

The news of the death had shaken her. It was not that she had had any deep fondness for him, but that he had suddenly . . . ceased to exist. He had been a vital presence, and now he wasn't.

Died, Marlee thought. He died.

She wondered what had gone through his mind just before he . . . died.

Marlee still had not decided whether to attend the funeral. Maybe she would. The *Gazette* was a family, after all. Sort of.

She thought of these things as she walked down the thickly carpeted main hall, past other rooms with bodies in coffins, rooms that smelled of old women's rouge and old men's stale clothes and . . . flowers.

And then she was at the door to the end room. For goodness' sake, she thought as she read the sign over the door. I never knew that was his first name.

EDMUND SPERL, the sign read.

Marlee entered and at the far end of the room saw the waxlike body of Ed Sperl, plumped snugly in a casket lined with pale blue. He wore a dark blue suit. She glanced only a moment at his face, enough to see that his cheeks and nose had been touched up, so that the effects of the drinking were not as obvious.

People stood in knots, shifting their feet awkwardly.

There was Will Shafer, and there Lyle Glanford, Jr. Lyle had doubtless been assigned the funeral duty by his father. Small knots of people stood a few feet away from the body, and seemingly as far away from each other as they could get. Separate sets of relatives from his two failed marriages. With one group stood a boy in his early teens; he wore gray trousers that were too short and a blue blazer that fit badly around the neck. He looked more sulky than sad.

Ed's son, Marlee thought. She wondered what the boy had been told, and she pitied him.

Marlee couldn't deal with the body scene quite yet, so she turned her back to the coffin and slowly added her name to the book of mourners.

She avoided looking directly at the body, sidling up instead to Will and Lyle.

"Hi," she whispered to both.

"Marlee," Will said quietly.

"Hi, Marlee."

Marlee thought Will Shafer looked as ill at ease as she had ever seen him. Did he feel like a hypocrite? Marlee wondered. It was generally known that Will couldn't stand Ed, personally or professionally. He just has to be here, Marlee thought. He's the editor.

Lyle, too, looked uncomfortable. Resentment at being assigned funeral duty.

Now for the hard part, Marlee thought. She steeled herself and tried to fix a smile without catching her lip.

"I'm Marlee West," she said to a plump woman flanked by two thick-set men. Her brothers, Marlee saw.

"I'm Olga," the woman said. She had been crying.

Marlee held on to her smile and let the words of the woman and her brothers fly past her ears like birds, never lighting. Because of the way Ed Sperl had died, the words embodied more than the usual funeral-home banalities and pleasantries.

". . . still don't know what happened . . ."

". . . probably never know why . . ."

". . . don't care what they say. He was a good man . . ."

"I'm really sorry," Marlee said. What else could she say? Or want to say?

Ed's son, meanwhile, was standing self-consciously, just outside the orbit of his mother, Olga, who did not think to rein him in for an introduction. That was okay with Marlee: despite her pity for him, she wasn't eager to have a brittle exchange with an awkward teenage boy.

Marlee extricated herself from the first knot of people and slid over to the second.

"My name is Marlee West. I worked with Ed at the *Gazette.*"

"Hi! I'm Gail, Ed's ex-wife. Jeez, I love your column."

"Thank you."

It was clear to Marlee why Ed Sperl had left Olga for Gail. The second wife was voluptuous, though far slimmer than Olga, and sensual.

"Damn, he was a pip, God rest his soul," Gail said. "Even after we split, we was good friends. God, he loved life so. That's why I can't figure . . ." Gail's eyes welled with tears, and she shook her head.

"I'm sorry for your loss," Marlee said.

She backed away from Gail, turned toward the coffin, and took a step forward. She had already decided not to kneel at the prayer rail, so she just bowed her head slightly as she studied the waxlike figure that had been Ed Sperl. The funeral home had done a good job of concealing the head wound, she thought.

Marlee prayed:

Hi, Ed. I don't know if you can hear me, or how much good I'm doing standing here. We didn't always see eye to eye, but . . . but . . .

Ed, a party was always a little more lively when you were around. Hey, don't I know it. You were at my party not all that long ago, and I remember you drank your share. More than your share, in fact, but the younger reporters got a kick out of you. Thanks for coming, Ed. And it's okay, that dumb remark you made about gay people.

I'm trying not to be a hypocrite, Ed. It's not that we were ever so super close or anything. But you know that. Still, it bothered me a lot—a knife in my heart, Ed, really—when Carol Berman called me the other day and asked me, all breathless, if I'd heard . . .

Ed, I'm sorry you didn't live a longer life. I hope the life you did live suited you all right. Hey, just the fact that you aren't here anymore, and that I feel bad about it as I stand here, that means your life counted for something. Counted for a lot, maybe. To some people, I'm sure it did. Am I saying that right?

Ed, that's all I can say. Except I wish you hadn't died and . . . and . . .

Good luck and so long, Ed.

Marlee turned away and found herself looking at Will Shafer. She smiled and felt her lip catching.

"How's Karen?" Marlee said.

"Fine. Just fine. She stopped in earlier. Just briefly. Had to take the kids . . ."

Marlee nodded without really listening to Will Shafer. She did not like being in the presence of death. But she was curious. "Can we talk for a minute?"

"Sure thing," Will Shafer said.

Marlee thought Will had just put on his business-at-the-office face, one of his several uncomfortable faces. She followed him as he tiptoed past the flower arrangements (the largest by far was from the Police Benevolent Association, with those from the *Gazette* and the Newspaper Guild second and third) into an adjoining room lined with sofas and chairs.

Will seemed to be aiming for a sofa close to the door to the coffin room, but Marlee wanted them to be alone, so she walked to a corner as far away as she could get from the mourners.

She and Shafer sat in chairs, facing each other at right angles.

"Relax, Will. I'm not going to ask for a raise."

The executive editor chuckled, nervously. No good, Marlee thought. He's super tight-ass today. He'd rather be anyplace but here, because everyone knew his dislike for Ed, and Will can't separate himself enough emotionally. I've got my own problems.

"The obit for Ed was awfully nice," Marlee said.

"Flattering even. Practically dictated by the publisher's office."

"I don't know what to make of the gossip I hear. Can you tell me, Will?"

Will Shafer frowned gravely. "What I know is kind of sparse, Marlee. State trooper found him in his car the other morning, early. Car was behind a Dumpster in the rear of a tavern. Little roadhouse way down near Horning. Shot in the head. His gun was on the seat."

"And there's no doubt it was his gun?"

"Oh, no, none. I knew he carried one. He had a permit."

"So they're certain it was a suicide?"

Will shrugged. "I don't know if they've made it official yet, but sure, that's what the police think."

"No note?"

Shafer shook his head no.

"And what was he doing way over near Horning?"

"Who knows? It's a pretty drive, I can tell you that. Well, you know. And we both know Ed spread himself around pretty good when it came to taverns and women."

"But why, I mean, why no note? And why drive all that way? It's like . . ." Marlee didn't finish her thought: that Ed Sperl might have been going to meet someone.

Marlee thought Will Shafer looked uneasy. "You know," he said, "it's hard to predict with people who drink to excess. They're apt to do most anything."

The Duke of Platitudes, Marlee thought as she looked at her editor. But in one sense he was right: Marlee had seen

Ed Sperl drunk enough times for her to think it might have affected his mind.

Something occurred to her. "What about the reunion? I bet Ed wasn't finished writing the program."

"That's right. I may have to do some of it myself. And the publisher wants me to write a little tribute to Ed."

"Oh, dear . . ." Marlee pitied Will Shafer in that moment. She knew he would have to rewrite it three or four times until it sounded as cloying as the publisher wanted it. God, was it worth it to be the editor?

"So," Will said, rising and looking back toward the coffin. "That's about it. I really don't know any more. You coming to the funeral?"

"I don't know. I mean, maybe. You?"

Will chuckled, darkly. "I guess I'd better," the executive editor said. "The publisher handled most of the arrangements because, you know, Ed's two ex-wives couldn't cope that well and so on. And he volunteered me to be a pallbearer."

"Oh." Marlee was embarrassed for Will.

"I guess I should go back in," he said.

Marlee put her hand comfortingly on his shoulder, and that seemed to stop him in his tracks. He half-turned to her.

"You know, Marlee," Will said, "people like Ed, they use up a lot of the goodwill that other people have. They just use it up. And then they wonder why—"

That was it; Will bit off his thought and was gone without another word. Marlee thought he had come as close as he ever had to revealing his true feelings.

Instead of going back into the room with the coffin, Marlee went through a door that led down a side set of stairs, toward the rest rooms. Instead of going to the bathroom, she used the main stairs to come back up into the main corridor. She saw a couple of people from the *Gazette* and managed to nod and smile. Then she fetched her coat and went out to the rain.

* * *

The gravel of the cemetery path glistened, and Marlee walked slowly, so she wouldn't twist an ankle. The breeze threatened to turn her umbrella inside out as it splashed rain in her face.

In the end, she wasn't sure why she had gone to the funeral. Not out of love for the deceased, certainly. Maybe she had gone because she hadn't been in a church for a while.

Oh, Marlee, don't be silly. Hymns and prayers and candles will only take you so far. To heaven, maybe? No, I don't want to think about that yet.

There: maybe that was why she had come. Someday *she* would be lying in a metal box, next to a gash in the earth, as Ed Sperl was now, and someone would be standing over her. If she was lucky, the words uttered next to her grave might ring clear and bright in the sunshine. She would like it if birds sang in the background.

Or maybe the words would be tumbled in the wind, punctuated by the rain splattering on the tent.

" . . .the body of thy servant, Edmund Sperl, O Lord . . ."

The priest was young—liberal and tolerant, Marlee figured from his brief, compassionate sermon. The kind of man who would have worn long hair and sideburns and been an antiwar protester in the days of Marlee's long-ago youth. The priest had been in grade school then.

The pallbearers had had a rough haul: a couple of times, carrying the coffin up a tiny rise, there had been a real danger that someone's feet would slip in the mud. They had managed all right, as it turned out, and now they stood solemnly by the pit that would soon welcome the Lord's servant, Ed Sperl.

Will Shafer looked wet, miserable, and—what? Who could tell with him. . . . Lyle junior seemed to be trying consciously to keep his face blank, as if the emptiness of his expression would show how little he cared for the man whose body he had just borne. The other bearers were the brothers of Olga and a stranger Marlee didn't recognize. Maybe a cop friend of Ed's, she thought.

Finally it was over, the flower petals tossed by Ed's kin sticking to the glistening metal of the coffin. The people walked away from the grave, some more sad than others, going their separate ways.

Marlee had tried to catch Will's glance at the graveside, but he had kept his eyes to the ground. Did he feel too much like a hypocrite, and did he think the people from the *Gazette* would have contempt for him, just because he was a pallbearer and everyone knew he didn't like Ed?

Oh, Will, it's all right, for crying out loud. Think of it as doing a dead man a favor. We understand.

She saw Will heading toward his car, so much in a hurry that he left the gravel path for a shortcut across the slippery grass.

"Will!" she called after him. But her call was lost in the sound of cars starting up, and in the same wind and rain that had tumbled the words of the priest.

"Will!"

Too late. She saw him get into a car—his own car, she realized. Ah, he had been so eager to get away from the funeral business that instead of riding back to the funeral home in the limo with the other pallbearers, he had had his wife pick him up.

For such a tight-ass guy, Will could be such an odd duck. Especially when something was bothering him.

Nineteen

▲ ▲ ▲

Will Shafer lay next to his sleeping wife. He was happy, more happy than he had been in a long time. The sex had been good tonight, for both of them. Yes, he was starting to understand what Dr. Hopkins had meant when he told him to relax and "let it happen." This night he had, and it had worked.

I love you, he whispered into the dark toward his sweetly snoring Karen. I do love you. God, it was good to have her home. It was so lonesome when she was gone, even for a couple of days.

He could make out her snores over the air conditioner. Tears came into his eyes, and for a moment he was overwhelmed by a desire to put his arms around her shoulders and hug her and bury his face in her hair. But that would wake her, and she deserved to sleep.

The feeling passed, and he propped up the pillow on the headboard, sitting up a little. He could see her shape in the dark. I love you, he whispered again.

What had Dr. Hopkins said about the therapy? Like peeling away the skin of an onion. Strip away a layer and there's another beneath and another and another, until—

And Will remembered his reply: "It feels more like being skinned alive."

From down the hall he heard a soft cry, then a muffled moan, then innocent snoring. His son had had a nightmare, awakened for a moment, then realized where he was—safe in his own bed—and fallen happily back to sleep. How lucky he was.

How lucky I am, Will Shafer thought. Thank you, God, if you're listening.

Now Will realized he was more wide-awake than he had been a few minutes before. At least if he lost sleep this night it would not be to anger and sorrow and . . . guilt.

Will got up, put on his robe and slippers, tiptoed down the hall to the kitchen. He turned on the low light over the sink, poured a small glass of milk. Then he had another thought. He tiptoed into the dark dining room and took the bottle from the cabinet. Just the thing for the middle of the night: a glass of milk laced with brandy.

He turned off the light over the sink, slid open the door to the deck, went outside. Light from the half-moon shimmered on the water in the pool, and crickets sang contentedly in the grass. Any man could be happy with this, he thought as he sipped his drink.

He had been spending a tremendous amount of energy suppressing a memory—that was what the doctor had told him. It was amnesia, of a sort, but the doctor had said that when he faced whatever it was, he would find that it had been there all along. Then his headaches (and some of his other problems) would probably stop.

Will felt a headache coming on right now. He would still finish the milk and brandy; he needed to sleep.

The crickets were so happy in the grass. Probably because I haven't cut it in a while, Will thought. No, it hasn't been all that long; it's just grown so much in the rain. For a while there, it was raining every day, from the time Ed Sperl—

He felt a throb of pain in his temples. No more brandy and

milk. He went inside, poured the contents of the glass into the sink, went to the bathroom, and swallowed two aspirins and tiptoed back to bed.

"What's new, Will?" Dr. Hopkins puffed on his pipe and crossed his legs.

"Nothing much."

Dr. Hopkins puffed and stared at him through the smoke. Waiting, Will thought.

"Actually, that's not quite true," Will said. "Karen and I made it last night, and it was all right."

"Ah." The doctor sucked on his pipe and nodded pleasantly. Still waiting. Finally, he said, "How is work, Will?"

"Couldn't be better." Will laughed bitterly.

"I'm glad." Puff, puff. Smile. "But I have the feeling— correct me if I'm wrong—that you're still not sharing everything with me."

"Oh? Really?"

"Really. Do you want to share anything about last night, Will?"

Will waited for the pain in his temples to subside. "We made it—nothing unusual—and it was . . . okay."

"Did you fantasize at all?"

"Damn it. I knew you'd ask that. Yes."

"Ah. Was it . . . ?"

"Yes, yes. Okay? I fantasized about that lovely young creature in my office. Okay. Jesus, you'll have me feeling like a junior high kid."

"That might not be all bad, Will. Do you care to tell me . . ."

"I fantasized that I made this lovely young woman happy, which I probably couldn't do in real life."

"You don't know that."

"Don't I? And that she, that she enjoyed being with me. Okay? Let's go on to something else."

"You weren't able to sleep afterward? Many people sleep quite well. What did you do?"

"I got up and mixed a little brandy and milk and went out on the porch deck."

"And what did you think about?"

"I thought . . . I looked at the moon, the way the light reflected on the kids' pool, and I . . ."

The doctor puffed, puffed. Finally he spoke, softly. "Listen to yourself, Will. You're holding back. Tell me one thing you thought of on the porch deck. Just one."

"I . . . There were things I felt lucky about. Karen, the kids, the house. All of it. But there was something else. I was—" More suddenly than ever, the pain stabbed into his temples, like huge, strong fingers squeezing through the bone into the tissue beneath.

Will closed his eyes and rubbed his forehead, praying for the throbs to subside. When he opened his eyes, a paper cup full of water had materialized on Dr. Hopkins's desk. Next to it lay a tissue on which rested two aspirins. Will swallowed the aspirins gratefully and drank the water.

"It's powerful, Will. Whatever it is."

"Is it possible that I'm just going insane?"

"I dislike that term, even when it's used in a forensic sense. But no, I don't think so. You're blocking something, that's for sure. I have a hunch you're bumping right up close to it sometimes."

"Maybe it's not just one thing."

"Ah. There's an interesting thought, Will. Let's talk—"

"I was a pallbearer a few days ago."

"Really? Relative or close friend?"

"Neither. I couldn't stand the son of a bitch. God rest his soul." Will laughed and laughed and laughed. Self-disgust contaminated his mirth, but he went on and on, tears flowing down his cheeks. He wiped his face with his handkerchief and saw that the doctor was studying him intently.

"How did you wind up being a pallbearer for someone you dislike, Will?"

"The usual way. Publisher thought it would be nice. The deceased worked at the paper."

"Well, then. We both know why it bothered you. It has to do with control of your own life. Remember how angry you were about getting stuck with the reunion planning? So now you're forced, more or less, to carry the body of a man you disliked."

"No!" Will hissed with a sudden fury that flung spittle from his lips and startled the doctor as well as himself. "I didn't dislike Ed Sperl. Okay? I *hated* him, more than I can possibly tell you. I hated the dirty cocksucker."

Will's temples throbbed anew with pain so intense he thought he might vomit. His throat was sore from his hissing. He felt degraded by his outburst.

"It's all right, Will," the doctor said gently. "You can say anything you want in here. That's the rule."

Will Shafer nodded. His eyes were closed, not just against the pain but against scalding tears.

"Was there something about this man's death, Will? Something that bothered you more than it might have ordinarily?"

"Maybe." Will was trying not to cry, but it was no use. "He was shot. Down near Horning. Looked like a suicide."

"Is there anyth.ng else about it, any . . . ?"

"I can't stay on this subject. You have to wait a minute."

Dr. Hopkins kept a box of tissues on his desk. Early in his therapy, Will had secretly been disdainful of anyone who might reach for them. Now he grabbed tissue after tissue, pressed them against his welling eyes and across his tear-swollen cheeks. He was beyond shame.

"I know it's hard, Will. Believe me, I know."

Will blew his nose, wiped his eyes a last time. The pain in his temples was subsiding. He had routed his demon—or retreated from it. "I don't want my wife to see me like this. She would never be like this, sniveling and weak, crying like a baby."

"We, all of us, have our moments of utter, childlike despair. All of us. She continues to be supportive, your wife?"

"Yeah, she's a trooper. Jesus, this hurts!"

"There's nothing tougher, I know. The allusion to skin has

come up in some of our talks. I have a good friend, a doctor who's one of the best people in the Northeast at treating burn victims. As many times as he's seen it, he's never gotten used to the pain patients go through when their dead skin has to be cut and washed away. The pain is part of the healing. Last time, we talked a bit about your parents, particularly your father."

Father. For a moment, his temples throbbed again. "Sometimes I miss my father, and sometimes I think it wouldn't have made any difference if he'd lived."

"You told me you still feel sorrow on his behalf, now and then."

"Sorrow? Yes. Anger, too. I lost a chance. . . . Here we go again."

And so Will plowed the same ground, finding old stones and new nuggets. He had dreamed of going to Notre Dame; instead, he stayed in Bessemer and went to Saint Jerome's because it was what he could afford.

He was a long time letting go of Notre Dame. He wanted to go there if he had to wait on tables and sweep floors. But Saint Jerome's was what he could afford, with the scholarship from the *Gazette*. And because his mother needed money, he did indeed wait on tables and sweep floors.

"I grew up thinking dumb Catholic boys stayed in Bessemer and went to Saint Jerome's, and the smart ones went to Notre Dame. A snob. Me! Now I'm not even much of a Catholic."

"Everyone is a snob about something, Will."

"I wanted to go to Notre Dame; I'd daydreamed about it since I was a kid. And my father wanted me to, even though we couldn't afford it. . . . Here's something: there's a guy coming back for this reunion, someone I haven't seen in twenty-odd years, and I resent him. Because he went to Notre Dame and I didn't."

"It's so clear, Will, that your having to stay home left a big mark on you, in ways you don't even know yet."

"I remember his farewell party, when he was going off on

an adventure. I remember thinking, after the party he was going home to pack. I was going home to pack, too, but only to go to a training seminar the *Gazette* was sending me on. He was leaving for good, but I was coming back. You see?"

"Control and self-esteem, Will."

"Maybe I just like to feel sorry for myself."

"There's a lot more to your pain than self-pity, Will. I think there's a terrible reservoir of guilt that we have to tap. Some of your pain comes from punishing yourself."

"For what?"

Dr. Hopkins tapped the bowl of his pipe on the ashtray. "You'll have to tell me that, Will. When you're ready."

Twenty

▲▲▲

Ed Sperl's first wife was sitting in a booth near the back of the little diner a half-block from the *Gazette*. Marlee spotted her right away and smiled a greeting.

Marlee joked for a moment with the grillman (once a month, no more than that, she ordered his pancakes, the best she had had anywhere). Then she went down the aisle to meet Olga.

"Hi," Olga said. "Thanks for coming."

"No problem. Been waiting long?"

"Ten minutes is all."

The waitress came by. Marlee ordered two coffees and for herself, a tuna-fish sandwich. She guessed from Olga's face that she was looking for the cheapest thing on the menu.

"I can recommend any of the sandwiches," Marlee said. "And the soup is always good. Get whatever you like. My treat."

"Oh, thanks, but I couldn't . . ."

"The *Gazette*'s paying for this," Marlee lied. "Get what you want."

Olga smiled her gratitude, then ordered a large bowl of

soup as well as a sandwich. Marlee wondered if Ed Sperl's first wife was genuinely poor and despite her plumpness, not eating well.

"How can I help you?" Marlee said, glad now that she had agreed to see this sad, fat, awkward woman.

"I don't know how to say this right. It's just that, I mean, when I called you last night . . ."

The coffee arrived. Marlee hoped Olga would use the interruption to get her thoughts together.

"Go ahead," Marlee said.

"Do you ever, like, investigate things? I mean, do you as a journalist ever look into things involving insurance and stuff like that?"

"Gee, Olga, it's tough for me to answer yes or no without more specifics." Of course, Marlee thought, watching Olga rehearse her words; I should have known.

Marlee got several letters a month from women newly widowed or divorced who were baffled by insurance policies because their husbands hadn't bothered to keep them informed or (much sadder) hadn't bothered to keep up the premium payments. Usually, Marlee answered the queries by postcard, giving terse advice on where to go for help. Occasionally, a reader's problem would be interesting enough for Marlee to devote part of a column to it. But Marlee had learned to be cautious about committing herself to meeting with people on their problems; if she said yes to everyone, it would use up all her time.

"What I mean—well, the way Ed died and all is probably gonna affect how much money—" Olga's eyes welled with tears. "I'm sorry. I'm so sorry."

"It's okay. Take your time."

"It's just . . . You see, when they said, you know, that he killed himself, someone from the benefits office at the *Gazette,* she told me there might be a problem on the insurance. And I *know* there'll be a hassle on another policy Ed had. . . . Oh, this is so awful."

"It's okay. So Ed had you as a beneficiary even after you split up?"

"It was written into the divorce. Partly for our son's sake." Olga gulped, blinked hard, and seemed to gather her strength. "Bottom line is, the suicide ruling could lower the benefits. Cancel them, even, especially the policy with the private company."

"I see." But Marlee didn't exactly.

"The lady in the benefits office at the *Gazette,* she said the publisher might do something on a personal basis, in view of Ed's long years of service and all. She said something financial on a personal basis, but—" The tears came again, and Olga blew her nose.

Seeing the unpretty, grief-stricken face across from her, and noticing now that Olga's clothes looked shabby and unlaundered, Marlee was filled with pity. If she could help this person just by listening, that was fine with her. She wished she could do more. "Take your time and eat your lunch," Marlee said, as soothingly as she could. "If you like dessert, they have terrific apple pie here."

Again, Olga seemed to gather her strength. "I was hoping you could talk to someone. About the insurance. Maybe write an article."

"Gee, Olga. What could I say exactly? I mean—"

"I thought you might have some influence. I'm not ashamed to ask. I can't afford to be ashamed."

"You mean influence with the insurance people?" Marlee was only slightly offended; she was sure Olga was too unsophisticated to know that she was asking her to do something unethical.

"Could you? Maybe if you just said you were going to write something, you wouldn't have to actually—"

"No. I can't. No way. Even if I had any influence in a situation like this—and I don't, believe me—I couldn't."

"Okay. I just had to ask. I hope I didn't, you know . . ."

"No. No. I hope you understand."

Olga ate quietly, and Marlee said nothing for a while. The

double burden of compassion and powerlessness to help the poor soul across from her was spoiling her lunch.

"He talked of us maybe getting back together, Ed did," Olga said at last.

"I didn't know that."

"Yep, he did. Thing is, after he left me to go with that whore, I never totally lost the feeling for him. He didn't for me either. You know?"

"Mmmm." Marlee felt a blend of pity and disgust; it was hard for her to imagine how a woman could have so little self-esteem that she would continue to care for a man who had left her for someone else.

"He was a character. We were really talking about getting back together. He was getting tired of her, you know. The whore, I mean. He said he was due to come into some money and we'd be set, once we got back together."

"Ah." Marlee didn't want to hear more of this; it was too sordid and depressing. She watched Olga dive into the apple pie.

Olga's eyes brightened. "Did you, um, like Ed? I mean, were you friends?"

God, what a question. "Well, he was a guest at my last party. But we didn't travel in the same circles. And I never—"

"Oh, no. I didn't mean that." A smile, almost a chuckle, from Olga.

"They did a nice write-up on him," Olga said.

"The obituary? Yes, it was nice."

"A good send-off. Ed would have liked it."

Marlee smiled as sweetly as she could without feeling like a hypocrite: she had almost gagged reading Ed Sperl's obituary. Most newspapers, including the *Gazette,* had a habit when burying one of their own of running a much bigger and more laudatory obit than the dead person deserved. That had certainly been true with Ed Sperl; the obit had made him sound like Edward R. Murrow, H. L. Mencken, and Gay Talese rolled into one person.

Marlee had her own epitaph for Ed Sperl: here lies a drinker and a chaser, a dinosaur who slept with cops and couldn't quite redeem himself by telling good cop stories and entertaining cub reporters at parties.

"Maybe you could write something," Olga said. "In your column."

"Huh?" Marlee was more stunned than if a piece of ceiling plaster had fallen onto the table.

"If you could say something about, about how he loved life and all. Even a little mention. I'd really appreciate it."

Marlee was tuning out Olga's words and despite her lingering compassion, starting to tune out Olga herself. What in God's name is this woman thinking of? Marlee thought. I know she's naive about newspaperdom, but goddammit, if she reads my column at all, she has to know it's *mine*.

". . . even just a little something, it might be enough to make people ask if he really killed himself. You know?"

"I'm sorry. What? My mind wandered for a moment."

"I was saying, if you could just write a little something about what a live wire Ed was—you mentioned he was at your last party—and how he loved life so much. It might help."

"Help? Help what?"

"Help with the insurance. If you sort of hinted, personal-like, that you think maybe Ed didn't kill himself. One of my brothers, he used to sell insurance, and he said the insurance company might not want to fight it if there was a story in the newspaper that maybe Ed didn't commit suicide."

I thought I was here so this woman could lean on my shoulder, Marlee thought. I'm the naive one.

"No," Marlee said. "I can't do that. I just can't."

"I already talked to the police, down in Horning, and they . . ."

Again, Marlee was trying not to listen. "No. I'm truly sorry for your grief, but I can't help. Not like that."

Olga sighed. For a moment, Marlee was afraid her lunch

guest would start to cry again, but it seemed she was out of tears for now.

"Okay then," Olga said. "I had to try. Thanks for the lunch. I hope I didn't take too much of your time."

"Not at all. I'm sorry I can't do more. Lunch is the least I, the *Gazette*, can do." But Marlee was glad Olga was getting ready to leave.

"He was something, Ed was. Some nights, I lay in bed thinking . . . Never mind. I bet a woman like you must think I'm a fool, giving a damn about a man who did what Ed did."

"Olga, I try not to judge how people should live."

"I guess one reason I don't want to think he killed himself is that, if he did, what's it say about me? I mean, he wasn't gonna come back." Here came the tears again.

Marlee bowed her head. However disingenuous Olga was, she was suffering. When Marlee looked up, Olga was getting to her feet.

"Was Ed unhappy at work, that you know of?"

"I almost never talked to Ed about work. Our jobs were so different."

"I keep thinking, why would he do what he did? I guess I don't want to believe."

"I'm really sorry, Olga."

"Thank you. You know, maybe my brother was right, the one who used to sell insurance. He said Ed drank so much he was a beer-brain, and a beer-brain is apt to do anything. Anyhow, thanks for the lunch."

"You're welcome."

"I do like your column. I'm sure you help a lot of women."

Marlee nodded in appreciation, then listened to Olga's heavy, graceless feet going toward the door.

Tonight, Marlee would jog and take a slow, hot bath. Then she would turn on the phone machine to keep the world out, lie in bed with Nigel next to her, and sip some wine—as much wine as she felt like.

Twenty-one

▲ ▲ ▲

The publisher had made the suggestion with a smile, had even affected a breezy manner after knocking on the door to Will's office and sticking his head in: "How about driving out to the country club and seeing how the remodeling is coming?"

The invitation was a command, no matter how pleasantly conveyed, and before Will could guess how far behind he would be on his work, he was sitting in the publisher's air-conditioned Lincoln.

"Beautiful day, eh?"

"Sure is," Will said.

Actually, it was on the muggy side, but the air-conditioning shielded the publisher from the weather, just as (or so Will imagined) the tinted glass shielded him from the decay that was slowly spreading out from the city's center.

"Do you mind a little detour?" the publisher said, almost shyly.

"Course not." What else was Will to say?

The publisher took a sharp turn down a side street, then another turn, then another. Now he steered his Lincoln up a street lined with rotting houses and overflowing garbage cans. Men and women sat on front steps, sweating idly in the summer heat, their brown faces staring with curiosity and resentment at the passing car.

The publisher slowed the Lincoln almost to a stop. "See that house, Will?" The publisher pointed to a sagging, three-story, wooden building that hadn't been painted in years. "That was my father's house, Will. I spent my childhood there. A long time ago." The publisher's voice had dropped to a sad hush.

"Ah."

"Yep. Right there in that side yard I used to throw sticks for my dog to fetch. Part collie, part shepherd. A mutt, really. Lived to be thirteen."

Will's annoyance had evaporated; he was touched that the publisher had shared part of his past with him.

"Sort of sad, what's happened to Bessemer. Don't you think, Will?"

"Yes."

"Maybe we can help turn things around, Will. I hope so. The city needs it. Its people need it."

"Yes." Maybe I've been judging him too harshly all this time, Will thought.

"'Cause if we don't turn things around, Will, if we don't attract new jobs, new vigor, there'll be hell to pay."

"The fire next time."

"What? Well, whatever. Things can't go on like this, Will. We need new business and industry."

"I agree, sir." And he did, although he didn't dare say that Bessemer also needed more leadership and generosity from some of the businessmen and industrialists who were already there.

"I look at these people, Will, and it just . . . It makes me sad and sick."

"I know the feeling, Lyle." He was moved by the publisher's nostalgia and social conscience.

"Yep, Will, it makes me sad. If jobs aren't found for these people, if they aren't put to work, the drug-and-welfare mess is gonna grow and grow. And pretty soon we'll see people like this on *our* streets."

It was a twenty-minute drive out of the city to the country club. On the way, they passed the reservoir and old stone houses that many decades before had been homes for the steel and coal and shipping millionaires and the bankers who had made Bessemer what it was, good and bad. Those millionaires were long dead (though their descendants were still the community's aristocracy), and some of the mansions had become private schools or nursing homes.

A few of the mansions remained in the families that had built them. And the biggest mansion of all, on the biggest estate grounds of all, had become the Bessemer Country Club. Long ago, it had belonged to Andrew Carnegie, who used it as a summer getaway for hunting, fishing, and riding. The steel tycoon's wealthy guests had ridden in their horse-drawn carriages up the tree-lined, serpentine drive that the publisher's Lincoln now negotiated.

The publisher parked in the shade of a huge tree, near several trucks that bore insignias of contracting, plastering, and plumbing companies.

"I love it out here, Will. Don't you?"

"It is lovely."

That much was true. The gray-stone mansion stood like a fortress, as it was in a sense—against time and social change. It had once been the estate's main house; now it housed the country club's formal dining room, a first-floor bar and grill overlooking the golf course, lockers and offices.

Down a steep slope, off to one side, was a long, narrow building that had once been the stable area. Now it housed grass-cutters and rollers and other greenskeeping machinery. In front of the building, facing a grassy area separated from the eighteenth fairway by out-of-bounds stakes, was a driving range.

Off to the other side of the main building was a small structure that had once been servants' quarters. Now it was the golf pro's shop. In front of it was the starter's shed and the first tee.

"Let's see what's what, Will."

As he walked with the publisher across the gravel parking lot where horses had once been cooled, Will heard cheerful shouts and splashes from the swimming pool behind the building. For a moment, he glimpsed the cool cobalt water, savored the tanned limbs of slender women and the joy of their children.

Will knew that the publisher had pressured the city and county for tax breaks on the country club property, so that the club could more easily afford to see to the comforts of the dwindling ranks of the wealthy. And Will knew in his heart that the children he had seen on the city street not a half hour before were no less worthy.

"Hurry up, Will," the publisher said. "Getting hot in the sun."

The building was full of the sounds of hammers and power saws and smells of plaster and paint.

"We've been promised it'll all be done on time, so say a prayer," the publisher shouted into Will's ear.

Will nodded; it was easy to pretend that the grimace he made from the noise was really a smile.

The publisher put his hand on Will's elbow and steered him toward the bar. The noise there was lower.

A half dozen men knelt on the floor, their work clothes wet from sweat as they pulled up moldy old carpet and the tacks beneath.

"This is long overdue, Will. We've waited too long to spruce up the old place."

Will wondered what the publisher had in mind when he said "we." Will belonged to the club (though only because he was editor of the *Gazette*), but he didn't come to it that often. He had never felt comfortable here.

"The new carpet'll be a royal blue, Will. Krause tells me it's the best he has."

"Hmmm." Emil Krause owned The Carpet Prince of

Bessemer, the biggest rug and carpet seller in three counties, belonged to various boards and committees, and got his name in the *Gazette* a lot.

A tall, well-muscled man in denim work clothes approached, his mouth twisted into a half-smile, half-sneer. Will recognized him and was on guard instantly.

"Hey, Arkie! Long time no see." The publisher shook hands warmly with Archangelo Grisanti, contractor, civic mover, Knights of Columbus leader. And pain in the ass, Will would have added.

"Hi, Lyle. Good to see you. Hello, Will."

"Arkie, good to see you," Will said cordially.

"Say, that Hurley gal of yours is causing me a lot of grief," Grisanti said.

"How's that, Arkie?" Will said.

"'How's that . . .'" Archangelo Grisanti laughed and punched Will on the shoulder, playfully but almost hard enough to leave a bruise. "I'm just waiting for her next mistake," Grisanti said. "That last one was a beaut."

"We ran a correction," Will said. "Beyond that—"

"If you feel wronged, our door is always open," the publisher said. "That was my father's policy, and it's mine. You know you can call Will, Arkie. We recognize how misunderstandings can—"

"Excuse me, sir," Will said. He had been pushed onto a tightrope; he couldn't go back, couldn't stumble, couldn't lose his nerve no matter what. "We need to be clear here. Jenifer made a mistake, but overall her stories have been fair and—"

"That's a matter of opinion," Grisanti said.

"Fair and above board," Will pressed on. "And your company, Arkie, doesn't come out too bad."

"Then why do I keep getting mentioned?"

"Will, maybe he has a point," the publisher said.

Goddamn you, Lyle, Will thought. "You keep getting mentioned, Arkie, because the contracts do show a pattern.

No, not a criminal pattern, we've never said that, but a political pattern."

It was bad enough to be on a tightrope, bad enough to have Archangelo Grisanti eager for him to stumble. Having the publisher watching and listening made it worse. Go on, Will told himself. No choice. Go on. "Look, Arkie, I know you pretty well," Will said. "You know me. Okay? You got a beef, you call me. I always have spare time. Just ask Lyle."

The publisher and Grisanti both chuckled.

"You can talk to me, Arkie," Will continued in his best man-to-man style. "But I can't pull the rug out from under one of my reporters." Pause to breathe before taking the biggest step of all. "Lyle wouldn't let me do that even if I wanted to."

Archangelo Grisanti looked at Will, then at the publisher, then back to Will.

Yes, Will thought. I've won for now. I've won a reprieve.

"All right, goddammit," Grisanti said. "I've blown off my steam for now. The *Gazette*'s been pretty good to me, mostly. What the hell . . ."

"You've been good to us, Arkie," the publisher said.

"I'll drink to that," Will said.

"Tell me," Grisanti said, leaning conspiratorially toward both his listeners. "Will, does your attitude have anything to do with the fact that the Hurley gal has one of the nicest set of tits in the city?"

The publisher guffawed and slapped Archangelo Grisanti on the shoulder.

Goddamn you, Will thought. Goddamn you a million times, Lyle.

"I knew you'd understand *that*, Arkie," Will said, punching Grisanti's shoulder as hard as Grisanti had punched his. "But she's still the best goddamn reporter in town."

"Especially now that Ed Sperl's gone," Grisanti said. "Damn shame."

"Yes," Will said, wondering how many tickets Sperl had fixed for Grisanti's drivers.

"Well, look, time's wasting. Arkie, why don't you show us around," Lyle Glanford said.

"Let me catch up," Will said. "I need to check out the plumbing."

"We'll be on the second floor," Grisanti said, leading the publisher away.

The men's room was one floor down. Will found the stairs behind a temporary partition of sawhorses and canvas. Yes, it had been a long time since he had been to the club. Everything seemed strange.

The light near the bottom of the stairs was dim. Will held on to the railing. He caught a smell of mold. Damp. It was damp in the basement.

He paused in the gloom at the bottom of the stairs. More partitions on either side of him. Dim light. He could barely see. He felt dizzy. The ancient basement had a smell that seemed familiar.

Will thought he heard humming sounds from far away. Then he heard hammering sounds, far away. No, the hammering was closer now, closer. *Whack, whack, whack.*

Where was the bathroom? Where? The light was so dim. Will felt hot and short of breath. Straight ahead, into a dark passage, the only way that wasn't blocked off. The passageway smelled of ancient mold and decay. He felt afraid, as though lost in a nightmare.

Near the end of the short, dark passage Will found a door. He turned the knob. Open. Yes, the gurgle of plumbing and a stink that almost made him faint. The bathroom, no doubt about it. It seemed so different. But the smell, the smell . . .

He held his breath against the stench as he used the urinal that he could barely see. Then he rushed out into the gloom.

Will leaned his back against a cold wall, cleared his eyes, breathed deep despite the smell. From far away, the sound carrying through the walls, he heard humming and hammering. Closer! There was a hammer noise that was closer. *Whack, whack, whack.*

Have to get out, have to get out, back to light and fresh air. . . .

Which way? There, canvas hanging, wooden sawhorses, behind the canvas more dark. Canvas smells of damp and rot; the touch of the canvas felt slimy on his sweaty arm.

Here, down here, Will thought. Dark hall, but smell not as bad. *Whack, whack, whack.* Hammering noises all around him now, the noise filling his ears.

Whack, whack, whack!

Will wanted to scream like a child. Light and air. Need light and air.

Light! Under a door just ahead of him. Push on the door. Nothing. Find the doorknob, twist hard. Push with both arms, then harder with a shoulder. Push!

The door burst open, and Will stumbled out, into the sunlight. He had come out of the basement onto a concrete apron near the driving range. Several players were hitting balls.

Whack, whack, whack.

"Buddy, you must be lost." The young man who came toward Will wore a golf shirt and visored cap with the club insignia.

"I was just, I was just using the john."

"Basement's supposed to be closed off. Someone shoulda told you. Use the john next to the pro shop."

Will nodded, then walked around the outside of the main building, up a terrace, back to the main door he had entered with the publisher a short time before.

Just before he went inside, he wiped his face with his handkerchief. The cloth came away from his skin soaking wet.

The light in the study was on. Karen looked up from the computer. "Article idea for a journal," she said. "Thought I might get to it when the reunion's behind us."

"It can't come too soon."

"Longer day than usual."

"Publisher didn't think I had enough to do, so he took me out to see the club."

"Oh? The renovations are going all right?"

"Yes. The paint should be dry, and we can be pretty sure no chunks of plaster will fall onto the roast beef."

"I left a couple of hot dogs on the grill for you. Kids are over at . . ."

But he had already nodded and turned away. He took a beer from the refrigerator, slid open the door to the porch, and found the wieners still warm over the slowly dying coals. She had left buns, ketchup, and mustard on the porch table.

He sat in a deck chair and took off his shoes. He was more tired than he had been in a long time.

He heard the porch door slide open.

"You don't have to stop your work just because I'm home," he said.

"No. And you can be alone if you want. Shall I go back inside?"

"No. I'm sorry. No."

She pulled a chair next to his and sat down. "Anything you want to tell me about?"

What could he say? At the country club, I got pissed at a crooked dago contractor who tried to shaft me with the publisher and then made a lewd remark about a high-breasted young reporter for whom I have an overwhelming attraction.

"Anything?" she pressed.

And then I got lost in the dark basement and was terrified out of my mind because I guess I was thinking of something long ago that I can't face.

"Then maybe I should go back inside."

No! He put his hand on her forearm. She sat down, and he took her hand.

"After this reunion is over, we are going to take a vacation," she said. "The publisher is not going to stop us, and he'll just have to find someone else to do the extra fifteen or twenty hours a week he takes for granted from you."

"A vacation? A real one?"

"Somewhere with water and sand."

"The kids?"

"We'll leave them with my mother, at least for part of the time. She loves them, especially Cass. I haven't worked out all the details yet, but we'll do it."

She's been thinking about this a lot, he thought. He squeezed her arm, feeling sorrow and guilt wash over his love.

He finished his beer and squeezed the empty can. She reached over and took it out of his hand. "I'll get you another. I'll join you, in fact."

While she was gone, he saw sheet lightning, far away over the lake.

"I saw that flash through the window," she said, handing him a beer. "Feels like it could rain. The tomatoes could use it."

"So could the fairways."

"You haven't played this year, have you?"

"No. I have to practice. Dr. Hopkins said I should try to have fun."

"There you are. Here's to fun." She touched her beer to his.

"I know I've been a load," he said. "I'll try to be more . . . more . . ."

"Just be what you are. You're Will Shafer. I didn't marry you, didn't go out with you in the first place all those years ago, because you were handsome or flashy. You're not. But you are good and decent."

"I'll get better for you."

"No. Get better for us, if you want to. Most of all, get better for you."

"I will. The doctor says the road I'm on goes only one way. I wish I knew where it led."

"Never mind. Just get there. Meantime, we have a reservoir we can draw on. It's deep."

But not bottomless, he thought.

"I can carry some of your load," his wife said.

"You have. You are."

"But you have to let me."

"I know." But he knew he could never share his feelings about Jenifer Hurley. And he had not told his wife about the terror in the basement.

Twenty-two

▲ ▲ ▲

Marlee found police head-
quarters a comforting place in an odd sort of way. The
building was dirty-brown brick flecked with streaks of
pigeon droppings and had been that way as long as she could
remember. The inside had a smell she recognized instantly:
a blend of tobacco smoke, burnt coffee grounds, and years of
varnish and dust.

Marlee had got a call from Detective Jean Gilman the day
after her column about the prowler. Could she come down to
headquarters for a chat? Marlee had said yes. But now her
guard was up; she had enough commitments, personal and
professional.

The detective emerged from behind swinging doors. "Hi.
Thanks for coming," she said.

"My pleasure." Marlee shook hands and studied the some-
what square face framed by short brown hair.

"Let's go back here." Gilman led the way back through the
doors into a dark corridor and then to a small, cluttered
office.

"Can I get you coffee?"

"Sure, black is fine," Marlee said. Gilman had motioned for her to sit in a cushioned chair.

Gilman set a steaming mug on the desk next to Marlee and sat in the chair behind the desk.

Marlee blew on the coffee, sipped, waited.

"I read your column all the time. I think you do a wonderful job."

"Thank you."

"You reach a lot of women, I'm sure."

"I hope so." Marlee studied the detective: dark sweater, little makeup, pretty but (deliberately) not too pretty.

"I found the column on your experience with the prowler really moving."

"It was from the heart, believe me."

"I know this may sound sexist, in a reverse sort of way, but I think most men are really incapable of understanding how vulnerable a woman is. Do you agree?"

Marlee sipped, thought it over. She didn't really want a heavy discussion. "I think men, decent men, understand. Intellectually, they do. They just may not be able to know how it *feels* to be a woman in a vulnerable situation."

"Yes, good distinction."

"Men don't worry about being raped."

"Not unless they're prison punks."

"I suppose."

"Okay, I asked you to come by for a reason. A favor, actually."

"I figured."

Smile met smile head-on.

"Yes, well. I've been doing some work lately with rape victims. We've always had, as I'm sure you know, a hard time getting them to testify. Even in this day and age."

"I know that." Marlee let her go on for a minute or so before saying, "Maybe you should tell me what you want from me."

"Frankly, we're looking for a little publicity. We thought your column, that is if you think it's worth it . . ."

"Oh. A column about what you're doing?"

"That, and maybe some input from you. From having read you, I figure you'd encourage victims to help us."

Marlee thought about it. Gilman was taking things right to the edge, saying she didn't want to presume and then doing just that. Although anyone who'd read her column could figure where she stood, so maybe Gilman had a right to presume. "I can't promise anything now, but I might be interested," Marlee said at last.

"Fine. I figured that. You'll think about it, at least?"

"Yes, I will. I almost never promise anything right away, you understand. Sometimes I have to bounce something off the editor. Plus I'm careful at first."

"You have to have a little skepticism. I know."

Gilman smiled—a good smile, Marlee thought.

"Yes, well. If you do say yes, you might be able to sit in on some of the sessions. If the women say okay. Which I think they might."

"I wouldn't use names, of course." Marlee wondered if Gilman had already made some promises she wasn't telling her about. That's okay, Marlee thought. I don't mind being used if I get a good column out of it, and if I *know* I'm being used.

"Oh, I forgot to mention, one of our male detectives takes part."

"A man? Talking to women about that?"

"Yes. Not all the women want to talk to him, but some are willing. And the husbands find him reassuring."

"He must be a special guy."

"Judge for yourself. I'll introduce you."

Marlee followed Gilman back down the hall, toward the swinging doors, and into an office the size of a janitor's closet.

A man was sitting at the desk and talking into the phone. Thick, neat salt-and-pepper hair, trim mustache, lean face with hard angles. He wore a crisp white shirt that showed off his broad shoulders.

Handsome, Marlee thought.

The man said good-bye into the phone and stood up. "Ed Delaney," he said, offering a hand and a smile.

"Marlee West."

"Jean filled you in?"

"Yes. I said I'd think it over."

"I hope you say yes. Listen, it's good meeting you, but I have to run."

"Cutting out early?" Gilman joked.

"Got a date," Delaney said. "With a ten-year-old who's sick in bed. The joys of single-parenting. Oh, Marlee, that column about the prowler was wonderful."

"Thank you." He's got a kid and he's divorced, Marlee thought. "I guess I should be going."

Gilman walked Marlee toward the swinging doors. "You know," the detective said, "we approached Ed Sperl about this and got nowhere."

"Oh, wrong guy! Ed wasn't that kind of reporter. Or man."

"I guess not. The new fellow from the *Gazette*, the young fellow, is a little easier. More sensitive than Ed."

"That's easy. Ed wasn't sensitive."

"Yes, well. You knew him much better than I did."

"I'm not so sure." For a moment, Marlee thought of telling her about the lunch with Olga. But not wanting to share too much too soon she canceled the thought.

"Awful, what happened with Ed," Gilman said. "No matter what kind of guy he was."

"Yes."

"With all I've seen being a cop, maybe because of it, I still find suicide heartbreaking. Had he been depressed?"

"No. No, I don't think so. He had a couple of broken marriages, and he drank too much. But that was how he was."

"I knew he was a drinker," Gilman said. "Couple of times when he came around, I could smell the mints he was sucking on to cover up the beer from the night before. He took up half a morning of our time on something and didn't give anything back."

"He took up your time on what?"

"Some old thing he was researching." Gilman and Marlee were just outside the swinging doors.

"What old thing?"

"Something from way back. Actually, he was talking to Ed Delaney. But since Delaney and I usually work as partners, he was really taking up my time, too."

"Was it a case Ed Delaney had worked on?"

"Something he had a connection with way back when he was a patrolman."

Marlee sifted that: she knew Ed Sperl had been most comfortable with the real hard-bitten, old-line detectives. Ed Delaney didn't seem like that type at all.

"Anyhow, thanks for your time, Marlee. Talk to you soon."

As she walked to her car, Marlee thought about the puzzling bit of information about Ed Sperl. Memory snippets from the lunch with Olga intruded, along with recollections of Ed Sperl at her party. Then she remembered how Ed had looked in the coffin.

God, it was so depressing, all of it.

She started her car; it coughed a couple of times. Great, Marlee, you still need a tune-up. That's another thing for your list. But first, go home and jog about three miles and maybe you'll feel better.

Twenty-three

▲ ▲ ▲

Grant was working on his shoulder turn, trying to get his whole upper body, not just his arms, into the swing. It was hard work, a whole new body habit to learn, but Doug Barnes had promised him it would be worth it.

Halfway through his second big bucket of golf balls, Grant knew Doug Barnes had been right. Driver, four wood, five iron—whatever club Grant used, he got more distance and straighter shots if he remembered the shoulder turn.

He imagined that the Bessemer Country Club course must be a pretty good one. Even in Bessemer, it figured that a country club would have a better course than the public layouts. He hoped so. Maybe the golf would be the best part of the trip.

He had other things he wanted to do in Bessemer. Thinking about all that made him nervous, even angry, and he swung too hard on his next shot, topping the ball and sending it an anemic forty yards.

"Shame on you, Grant," Doug Barnes said. "That's your worst swing of the morning."

"I know."

Conscious that Doug was standing nearby, Grant teed up another ball, took a deep breath, and swung as slowly as he could.

"Yes!" Doug Barnes said. "Good shoulders, good weight transfer. You hit that halfway to Little Neck Bay."

"Damn straight," Grant said, thrilled.

"You swung a minute ago like your boss was lying there on the mat, holding the ball in his mouth."

"That's a nice thought."

Doug Barnes laughed. "Stop in the pro shop before you leave, okay?"

"Okay." Grant hurried through the rest of the bucket.

"So when are you leaving for Bessemer?" Doug Barnes asked.

"Couple of weeks."

"Never been there. I hear it's a friendly town. Tough winters, though."

"Yeah, they are."

Grant waited silently while the pro rang up a sale.

"Listen," Barnes said when they were alone in the shop, "it's none of my business, but, you know, I thought you might need some golf clothes to take with you."

"Uh, yeah. I guess. I was gonna buy some."

"So I thought I might be able to help you out here."

"Oh." Grant felt his face flush. He had been postponing buying golf clothes because he was far from up on style and shy about asking advice.

"I know what you're thinking," Doug Barnes said in his friendliest way. "You think the prices here have to be higher than in a cut-rate shop."

"Well . . ."

"You're exactly right, they are, because we're not primarily a clothing shop. But look at this." Doug Barnes bent low under the counter, stood up, and held out three brand-new, folded golf jerseys. One was white, the other yellow, the third sky blue.

"Pretty," Grant said, meaning it.

"These'll fit you fine. And I have slacks to match. What are you, a thirty-six, thirty-seven waist and, what, a thirty-three inseam?"

"On the nose."

"Then you're in luck. We normally sell stuff like this at half price, because each of these garments has a flaw. Here, see this bad stitch . . . ?"

"Right. I see it. Barely."

"Half price just because of that. But for you, two-thirds off. Can't beat that anywhere, Grant. All cotton. You like cotton?"

"Sure."

"Me, too. It wrinkles more, but it keeps you cooler. And so what if it wrinkles a little. Two-thirds off. Interested?"

"I guess. I mean, sure." But he was puzzled. "How come two-thirds off?"

Doug Barnes smiled. "You've spent a lot on lessons and balls. Besides, I'm the pro here and I like you. I like your determination."

The golf pro reached across the counter and put a hand affectionately on Grant Siebert's bicep. Grant recoiled slightly, but Doug Barnes seemed not to notice.

"If you've got time, why not try them on," Barnes said.

"Uh, okay. Where . . . ?"

"Dressing room's there in the corner."

Grant put on the sky-blue jersey and matching slacks; he felt self-conscious when he emerged from the dressing room and was relieved that no one besides Barnes was in the shop.

"Hey, you look like a golfer anyhow," Barnes said.

Barnes stood next to him and felt the waistband of Grant's slacks with the tip of his finger. Then he tugged gently at the back of his collar. Grant stiffened.

"Don't worry," Barnes said, chuckling. "I'm not gay. I used to work in a men's shop."

"Never can tell." Grant had tried to sound light, but he knew he had failed, and he felt his face burning.

"Ain't that the truth. So you're all set, Grant. These fit you okay, and the others are identical. So you're in business."

"Can I pay with a credit card?"

"Whatever you like. If you're in a hurry today, you can catch me next time."

Grant went to the dressing room and changed back to his regular clothes, thankful that he would not have to wait the extra few minutes for Doug Barnes to ring up the charge on his credit card. He was still smarting from embarrassment. The golf clothes were better than he could have found at the price anywhere else, but he felt somehow unworthy of them. He had wondered—only for a moment, but still he had wondered—if Doug Barnes was making a pass at him. Now he felt ashamed for having suspected that.

When Grant came out of the dressing room, Doug Barnes was talking to one of the most beautiful women Grant had ever seen.

"Grant, I'd like you to meet my fiancée . . ."

The name passed right over his head. He heard himself say, "I'm Grant," as he grasped the soft, fragrant hand. Blond, green eyes, tan skin, perfect teeth, gracious smile.

"Nice to know you, Grant. You're a golfer, I take it?"

"Linda's a teaching pro at a club in Westchester," Barnes said.

"Ah." Grant caught her name the second time around. "Well, I'm not much of a player. I'm kind of getting back to it."

"He's lying," Barnes said. "Good, powerful swing. It'll be like clockwork if he keeps at it. Here's your duds." Doug Barnes handed him a bag. "What say to a beer sometime soon, Grant?"

"Sounds good. Gotta catch a train now. So long."

Clutching the bag of clothes, Grant burst through the door to the outside, brushing past someone on his way in.

"Grant! Your clubs." Doug Barnes stood in the door,

holding the two woods and the iron. Grant did an about-face, faked a casual, self-deprecating grin, and took the clubs.

"Next week," Barnes said.

"Right." Grant hurried away, toward his train.

Twenty-four

▲ ▲ ▲

Will Shafer heard the soft knock on his office door, looked up, and felt his heart leap. Jenifer Hurley smiled through the glass as Will beckoned her to come in.

"Got a couple minutes?" she said.

"For you, sure. Have a seat."

"I bet you're snowed under, having to worry about the reunion as well as the paper."

"Yeah, it's a bit much. It gets closer every day. At least I've had some help, from Marlee and others, including Lyle." Will looked into her eyes (could there be any in the universe more luminous?) and waited.

"I, I'm not sure how to begin."

No, Will thought. Don't tell me you're leaving the paper. Please.

"Maybe I should start with a question," she said finally. "Was—that is, if you can tell me—was Ed Sperl working on something just before he died? An investigation of some kind?"

"No. Not that I knew, anyhow."

"And you would have known? I'm sorry, I didn't mean to sound dumb."

"That's okay. Yes, I would have known. At least I would have known if the paper had committed itself to something."

Jenifer Hurley frowned, her eyes no less luminous, no less beautiful in shrewdness.

"Why do you ask, Jenifer?"

"It's just . . . I was over at the Public Records Building, a few weeks ago almost, and I ran into Ed."

"Ah. This would have been not long before he died."

"Just a few days." Jenifer Hurley seemed to shiver. "I haven't known that many people who have died."

"You get more practice as you get older. I don't know if you get used to it." How young you are, he thought.

"Anyhow, I ran into Ed. And it was kind of strange."

"How so? Police headquarters is right across the street. There's even a basement connection."

Jenifer Hurley shook her head, telling him respectfully but definitely that he didn't know what he was talking about. "That connection was closed last year, when they put up some partitions to create more storage room. See, when they installed the computers in the records building and at police headquarters, they took a lot of old file cabinets and stuck them in the basement."

"Ah. I see you're more up-to-date than I am."

"I became pretty familiar with what was stored in this place and that by researching old real estate documents."

"That was a terrific story this morning, by the way."

"Thanks. So I saw Ed, and I asked him what he was doing."

"And?"

"He mumbled some bullshit answer about old crime statistics. He was being evasive."

"Mmmm. What do you think he was doing?"

"He was *not* researching old crime statistics, that's for sure. I know, because I've cultivated some of the clerks in records, and I know my way around. There aren't any old crime stats in the area where I saw Ed. And even if there had been, I still wouldn't have believed him."

"No?"

"No. Ed wasn't that . . . serious, as a reporter. He was—God, I know he's dead, but it's the plain damn truth—he was an old-fashioned police reporter. No more than that."

"So what do you think he was looking for?"

"I don't know. I thought you might. I do know what kind of records are kept where I saw Ed."

"What?"

"Case folders on crimes from before 1980, when the police department started switching to computerized records."

"Ah. Are these folders on crimes that are solved or unsolved?"

"Both. The solved ones, at least the major crimes, have pretty thick folders. They contain not only the police paperwork but all the court stuff, from indictment to conviction to appeals. The ones from the late sixties and beyond get real thick because the Miranda ruling affected them. . . . I'm sorry. I'm running on."

"That's all right." Jenifer, Jenifer, he thought. What a natural you are. The endless curiosity, the way you make connections. I wish I could protect you always. . . .

"As for the old folders on unsolved cases, a lot of data on the medium-range crimes—thefts and burglaries and such—is being transferred to computer discs. The data is kept mainly for insurance purposes, in case the crimes are ever solved. In other words, there're fewer and fewer old folders down there as the months go by. And more and more, the folders that are there are on old homicides. Complete with pictures and all. The kind of stuff that's not so readily transferred to computer discs."

"I see."

"So that logically leaves old homicides as the kind of stuff Ed was snooping in. Doesn't it?"

"But maybe someone is just coming up for parole, and Ed—"

Jenifer Hurley smiled patiently and shook her head. "I already checked with the appeals bureau in the district attorney's office. That's where a reporter would go for something like that. And that's really a court story, as opposed to a police story, isn't it? Way out of Ed's domain."

"Yes, I guess it would have been. So what do you think?"

"I don't know what to think. I thought you might, you know . . ."

"I don't know. Haven't a clue."

"Hmmm."

How lovely she is, Will thought. How lovely in her cleverness and intelligence. Her frown, her eyes gleaming as she concentrates.

"You know," Jenifer said, "not just anybody can roam around back where Ed was. In the old police cases, I mean. That stuff's not like deeds and assessments. It's not public record. So Ed had to pull some strings."

"He had the strings. Ed had the strings." Will Shafer wanted to say more. Go ahead, he prodded himself; forget you're the executive editor; be indiscreet. "Jenifer, I do know this much: Ed had a lot of angles, and played them. He had a set of ethics that belonged on the junk heap of journalism."

She was looking straight into his eyes, with a curiosity and—yes!—a respect, respect for his frankness, a respect he had longed to see. Go on, Will told himself. Go on.

"It's the truth," Will said. "The truth doesn't change just because he's dead. God rest his soul, if you believe in that, but Ed was, Ed used what he knew to hurt people." Will felt dizzy, as though he were going way beyond where he ever had before. "A police reporter in a town this size, he's bound to know things, have the power to hurt." Stop, Will told himself. Stop! "Anyhow, he's dead. I'm sorry for his family, or families. Whatever."

"I do know what you mean. I know about what he did to Jacob Frank. 'Car littered with empty beer cans,' for God's sake." Jenifer Hurley shook her head in disgust; she was sharing her feelings with him!

"Yes. That was inexcusable. And there were other things." Now Will could go no further.

"Will," Jenifer began slowly. "I want to ask something I have no right to ask."

She was sharing her innermost thought with him! "Go ahead and ask."

"Is there any, you know, inside story about how Ed died? I mean, I saw him not many days before. I mean, why would he do that?"

"Kill himself? Who can ever know why someone kills himself? Ed was . . ." Come on, Will. You know the term they use on the South Side, down near the steel plant: a beer-brain. "Ed was a man who drank more than he should. Sometimes a lot more."

"I know that. Still, I don't know." Jenifer Hurley frowned, shook her head, shrugged. "I don't know."

"Shot to death with his own gun, Jenifer."

"I know. I know. And we still have no idea what he was snooping for down in records."

"No."

"Okay," she said. "Thanks for your time."

"You're welcome. And be careful, Jenifer."

"Be careful?"

"Don't, don't get hurt. I know you're a hungry reporter, but do be careful. This is a small town in some ways."

"I will. Thanks again."

"My pleasure. Go and sin no more."

Then she was gone, leaving Will Shafer alone with his memories and his yearnings and his worries.

Twenty-five

▲▲▲

Marlee was on her way to meet Jean Gilman and Ed Delaney at the YWCA building for a session with rape victims and their husbands. As usual, she was about ten minutes late and feeling harried. Purse, notebook, extra pens, enough money. All set, she thought as she got into her car.

The car would not start. The engine did not even turn over.

"Oh, damn. Why is this happening to me?"

Again she turned the key. Nothing.

"Son of a bitch!" Now she was angry at herself as well as her old car. Jumper cables! One of her neighbors had a set of jumper cables.

Oh, Marlee, suppose it isn't the battery. All right, all right. Got to get a ride.

Marlee fished in her purse for Jean Gilman's home number, found it, went back inside, punched the digits, and counted the rings. One, two, three.

"Hello?"

"Jean, thank goodness. It's Marlee and my car won't start. If I call a cab, I'm bound to be late. Could you pick me up?"

"I've got a better idea. Ed Delaney lives closer to you. If he's left already, I'll get in touch with him by radio. If you don't hear back from me in five minutes, he's your ride."

Marlee hung up, sat down, caught herself smiling.

A car honked outside.

"I'm really leaving now, Nigel. Be a good boy."

Ed Delaney got out and opened the car door for her.

"Oh, thank you. I feel like such a jerk. I knew the damn car was overdue for the garage. Was this out of your way?"

"Not at all. Glad you decided to come along tonight."

"And I'm glad for the ride."

Good, Marlee thought. She could tell from the smell of the car that Ed Delaney wasn't a smoker.

"Do you have a good mechanic?" Delaney said.

"No. I mean, I did, but he sold out. I got through the winter okay, but you know." Marlee thought she was babbling like a high school freshman on a date

"If you'd like, I can call my former brother-in-law. Runs a garage over on Forest. Topflight mechanic."

"Really? It's no trouble?"

"Of course not. He's busy, but I can get you in fast."

"That's, that's very nice. Thank you."

"I'll call him tomorrow and get back to you. Name's Rick. Very nice guy, easy to talk to. And he's honest."

Marlee thought about that. The feminist in her was bothered that Ed Delaney should be on such good terms with his former brother-in-law. How did Delaney's ex-wife feel about that?

"So," Marlee said, "you've managed to stay in touch with her family?"

"Oh, yes. We get along just fine."

Yes, Marlee felt a feminist resentment. But she had accepted a ride from Delaney, after all, and had to be pleasant. "How's the sick ten-year-old?"

"A lot better, thanks. A little rest in bed, a little TLC."

"What's her name?"

"Laura. She's a super kid, really. It's a tough load for a ten-year-old, not having a mom around."

"I imagine." Now she was curious as well as resentful. Did she dare ask him personal questions? Maybe he would dislike her for it. Or would it be worse if she disliked him for his answers?

They rode mostly in silence for the next twenty minutes. When they were a block from the YWCA building, Marlee said, "Is she alone tonight? Your daughter, I mean?"

"Baby-sitter from down the block."

Delaney expertly parallel-parked across the street from the Y building.

"Does Laura see her mother regularly?"

Delaney looked startled, then he smiled softly. "I'm sorry, I thought you knew. I'm not divorced. My wife died a few years ago."

"Oh, dear. I deserve to feel really stupid, and I do."

"Not at all. I shouldn't have taken for granted that you knew."

"No. No. I'm the one who took something for granted. I really . . ." Marlee had to stop; her voice was about to break, and she could feel her upper lip catching on her teeth. This was going to be a terrible evening.

When she emerged from the YWCA three and a half hours later, Marlee was exhausted. She had listened to three women who had been raped, then had listened to the three husbands. The women had been in a small room with Jean Gilman, the men in a small room with Ed Delaney.

That's the way these women wanted the evening to be, Gilman said. They would talk to a female detective, but not to a male detective, and they would only talk at all if their husbands were separate. That way, the women could say what they truly felt.

Fine, Gilman had said. That's how the women want it, that's how it will be.

"I don't mind telling you, the arrangement made things

tough for me," Marlee told Delaney in the car afterward. "Having to dash from room to room, afraid to miss something in one place and feeling the need to be in the other place."

"I thought you were terrific. You managed to act like a reporter and be compassionate at the same time. A neat trick."

"Well, thank's very much."

"I mean it. I heard that the women liked the way you listened to them, to their feelings. And the men respected you, too."

"How could you tell that?"

"The way their shoulders were hunched up. They were paying attention."

"I thought modern cops were supposed to be scientific. What's this stuff about their eyes and shoulders?"

"My dad, he was a cop. God rest his soul. He always told me to trust my gut feeling. Intuition, whatever you want to call it."

Marlee liked Ed Delaney. She decided to try to erase totally any lingering damage from earlier. "If you can tell what people are feeling," she said, "then you know how bad I feel for my mistake about your wife."

"Forget it. I thought you knew, that's all." Delaney let several seconds go by. "Actually, if you want to get on my good side, you can let me buy you a beer."

Marlee thought Ed Delaney was manly without being macho. She resolved to be careful with her emotions, but there was no denying she liked his company.

"This is a good feeling," Delaney said. "I don't get a chance to stop at a tavern that often."

They had a corner table just big enough for a potted candle, an ashtray, a pitcher of beer, and a basket of peanuts. They used the ashtray for the peanut shells. Several men at the bar were watching a baseball game on television. With the attention focused elsewhere and the darkness of the corner, Delaney and Marlee had an oasis of privacy.

"I only do this once in a while," Marlee said. "Like a lot of people, I indulged more in my youth. Long ago."

"Hey, don't say that. We're about the same age. But it is hard for me to believe that Laura's ten already."

"Was, was your wife sick long?"

"A couple of years. Uterine cancer. For a long time, after she got sick and, and later, I had this 'why me?' feeling. Even though I knew Anne was the one who had the right to feel that way."

"So did you."

A sad smile lit his face for a moment and was gone.

"It must have been very hard."

"Very hard, yes. I can't tell you how hard. Thing is, she always had good health habits. Aw, hell."

"Sometimes I think we're all sitting ducks."

"How about you? You look like you're in shape. You swim? Jog?"

"I jog a little. I watch my diet, don't do peanuts and beer too often."

"Me neither. I used to put away a lot more beer than I do now."

"Really?"

"My name's Delaney and I'm a cop. Remember?"

"I remember. That's why I won't admit that I used to do pot."

"Good. Don't admit it. If you did, I'd have to bust you. Along with half the guys in my academy class."

"Really?"

"Okay, probably not half. But more than a few. Things were different when I was in the academy. God, twenty years ago. Sometimes it seems like yesterday I was a patrolman."

"Oh, that reminds me. Jean Gilman said Ed Sperl was bugging you about an old case just before he died. Something you worked on years ago."

"He was a pain in the ass. A couple of older detectives liked him, but I never did."

"No?"

"No. The guys who liked him were the kind of cops who used to crack the heads of students and talk about crime in the black neighborhood as 'bongos and banjos.'"

"Hmmm. Yes, Ed fit in with people like that. But what was he bugging you about?"

"He said he needed information on an old murder for a feature story."

"Really?" Marlee thought that odd. The *Gazette* normally didn't like stories like that. "What was the case?"

"Something that happened when I was a rookie. Remember that priest that got whacked in that house over near the Ambrose Parkway? It would have been in January of '71, because I was just starting out."

"I remember. Ed made a couple of rotten jokes about it, including one at my party. Which didn't go over so good with me because a couple of my guests were gay."

Ed Delaney jerked his head; his eyebrows shot up. "There were indications that that priest had engaged in homosexual activity. That wasn't publicized."

"Well, Ed Sperl certainly had some good sources."

"Yeah, sure. But it was the kind of thing cops were supposed to keep quiet about if they didn't want to get shitcanned."

"Was there some kind of directive to that effect?"

A collective cheer went up from the bar as a baseball player in Boston hit a home run.

Delaney snorted. "No. The way I got the message was like, oh, like getting spun around real fast in a revolving door. And when you're done spinning, you're supposed to forget what you've seen and heard. You know?"

"I guess so. Things like that happen in newspaper offices sometimes."

"All I know is, the day I saw the body I was called to the

captain's office and told to erase my memory. Those weren't the exact words, but that was the message."

"Wait! You actually saw the body?"

"I was the first cop there. Never forget it. Some old Irish priest had come by to check on this young priest, who was supposed to have gone on vacation and was overdue to return. Turned out the young priest had never left. He'd been dead in the basement awhile."

"I remember. How horrible."

"Golf club sticking out of his head. You don't want to hear the rest, believe me. But his pants were partly undone and there were definite signs of, you know."

"I can guess. But what about the hush order?"

"Here, let me top off your glass. The detective captain, guy name of Ray McNulty, told me to keep my trap shut. 'This is a Catholic town,' he said. Now what's that tell you?"

"I don't know. I've covered the police beat, but it's not my strong point."

"The diocese wanted it hushed up. The bishop had enough trouble back then with priests who were protesting Vietnam or running off to get married."

"The bishop?"

"Sure. 'This is a Catholic town.' People at the diocese were probably just as glad the case was never solved, 'cause then it all would have come out."

Marlee sipped her beer, tossed a peanut shell at the ashtray, sifted her thoughts. "Something's still not right. Just because part of the story was hushed up back then, that's no reason for Ed to try to snoop around again all these years later. He wasn't that dedicated as a journalist."

"You'd know that better than I, Marlee."

"And wouldn't it still be tough to pry information loose, with a lid on?"

"Maybe. But we're talking twenty years here. The guys who were the department honchos then are long gone. For that matter, there's been a lot of changes at the diocese."

Something's still off, Marlee thought. "How much did you tell Ed Sperl about what you saw that day?"

"Not a hell of a lot. I was pretty vague, in fact. I've told you more than I told him."

"Oh. Why?"

"I like you better. You're a better person."

"Thanks. I think." Marlee smiled, felt her face flush for a moment.

Ed Delaney took a big gulp of beer. "I guess you could say I even lied a little to Sperl, in the sense that I held back on the homosexual angle."

"But in reality there was no doubt?"

"None."

"So what was Ed Sperl looking for?"

"Damned if I know. I told him if he wanted more info, he'd have to go to the old case files down in the basement."

"And did he?"

"I don't know. He'd have needed permission from someone in brass, someone with a key. Which I'd guess he could have gotten."

"Odd."

"One thing, he kept asking me about the golf club sticking out of the priest's head. Some guys get off on that stuff, I guess."

"How awful. Who would care about such terrible stuff?"

A roar went up from the bar at another home run.

"Getting a little noisy in here," Delaney said. "Actually, it's time for me to get going."

Delaney walked Marlee to the door. They told each other how much they'd enjoyed each other's company, shook hands, and said good-night.

Nice, Marlee thought when she was inside. He's nice.

"Hello, Nigel. Hello, boy. Kiss, kiss."

The Airedale climbed off the sofa, greeted her with sleepy eyes and wagging tail.

"Did you guard the house, boy? Good fella."

Marlee put on her pajamas, fetched some ice water, went to her bedroom.

"Come on up, Nigel."

The dog climbed onto the bed with her. She had had the dog in her room at night since the prowler.

Marlee was tired, but she felt good-tired. Tomorrow, she would arrange to get her car fixed, take a cab to work, maybe do a rough draft of a column.

Marlee had been glad that Grant Siebert was coming to Bessemer, but she was thinking now about Ed Delaney. Ed Delaney, with a daughter in his life and a wife in his memory. One thing at a time, Marlee.

She finished her ice water, set the alarm a half hour later than normal, turned out the light. She was drowsy almost at once, but while she could still think, she suddenly wondered if Ed Sperl had been doing a story for Grant Siebert's magazine. Maybe that would explain things.

But Marlee hoped that wasn't true; the whole business seemed sordid, even though that was the kind of thing Grant Siebert did for a living. Maybe she could call Grant and find out if Ed was doing something for him. Sure, she had an excuse: she would say something about the reunion.

Then another half-formed thought about Ed Sperl crept unbidden into her consciousness. Something, something, something. A memory. But before she could bring it into focus, she fell into slumber, her snores blending with those of the dog lying next to her.

Next morning at the *Gazette,* Marlee called Grant Siebert in New York. It took her a while to work up the courage, and she had to swallow butterflies when he answered. Trying to ease into the conversation, Marlee asked him if he was looking forward to coming back to Bessemer. Grant said he was.

By the way, Marlee asked, was Ed Sperl doing some article for your magazine about an old crime in Bessemer? Grant paused, and Marlee thought his voice had a different tone when he replied that no, Ed Sperl hadn't been doing anything for *Sleuth.*

"What was the case?" Grant asked.

"About twenty years ago a priest was beaten to death with a golf club. It was never solved."

"Then we wouldn't have any use for it. We only do articles about cases in which there's been a conviction or guilty plea."

"Oh, of course. I guess I should have known that."

"I'm curious why you thought he might have been doing something for us."

"Oh, well, I happened to find out he was rooting around in old files. Even talking to a cop who saw the body."

"I don't know anything about that, Marlee. I remember the case, but only vaguely."

"I see." A creepy feeling came over Marlee. "Grant, you heard about Ed, didn't you? You know what happened?"

"Yep. My folks saw a small item in the Albany paper. I guess he died not long after I talked to him."

"Probably, yes."

"I really wasn't very friendly with him. I guess I should be sorry he's dead."

Marlee wondered if Grant was really as callous as he sounded. She hoped not. "He was at a party of mine recently, so I really felt . . . funny after he, you know."

"Yes, he mentioned your party."

From his voice, Marlee could almost see Grant stiffening up. All right, time to say good-bye. "I, uh, hope we get a chance to chat when you're here, Grant."

"Me, too."

"Good. We'll probably discover we're not the same stupid jerks we were back then, you know."

"Could be. So long."

As she hung up, a memory light flickered in a corner of Marlee's mind. Then it was gone.

"Marlee, have you seen this?"

Jenifer Hurley was standing by Marlee's desk, holding a piece of pink paper.

"It just went up on the bulletin board," Jenifer said. "The publisher is springing for a party at his spread. For the reunion."

"Oh, great. Sit down a minute." Marlee liked and respected Jenifer Hurley, envied her youth and gave her occasional advice on how to avoid the treacherous shoals of male chauvinism at the *Gazette*.

Marlee read the pink paper: the publisher was hosting a brunch at his house on the Sunday morning of the reunion, the day after the golf tournament.

"Have you been there?" Jenifer asked.

"A few times. It's quite a big house, I assure you. The publisher will have a big tent in the backyard with about six thousand dollars' worth of food and booze, probably a band."

"Wow!"

"And Lyle junior may jump in the pool. If he does, his father will laugh even though he'll be embarrassed."

"Embarrassed?"

"Oh, yes. The publisher is at heart, shall we say, a formal man. Stuffy, in other words. It embarrasses him that his son is divorced and bounced around a few schools."

"Silly."

"Silly is right. And he's got to feel a little sad about the reunion turnout. I hear on the grapevine that there aren't many out-of-towners coming back. So a lot of people who used to work here but didn't leave Bessemer are having their arms twisted. Along with some public relations people and Chamber of Commerce types who never worked here at all."

"Their arms aren't the only ones being twisted. I had to do a little puff piece for the reunion program. Lyle junior asked me in a nice way, but he wasn't really asking, if you know what I mean."

"Alas, Jenifer, that kind of bullshit goes on at most papers."

"I guess. I heard some of the old cranks on the copy desk complaining about having to edit stuff for the reunion program along with the regular stories."

"More bullshit." Marlee chuckled, then thought of something. "Excuse me a minute." She stood up, looked toward the copy desk a couple of hundred feet away to see who was there. Then she sat down and dialed.

"Copy desk. Weir speaking."

"Gil, is it true what I heard? That you guys are a bunch of old cranks?"

Jenifer Hurley blushed, lowered her head to make herself invisible.

"Marlee! What's up, dollface?" said the voice on the phone.

"Never mind the 'dollface,' you old fart. How are you?"

"Not bad, doll. What's up?"

"You folks have been handling a bunch of stuff for the reunion program, I hear."

"That's right, doll. Some of it's so bad, it even turns me off. And I've seen everything."

"I know. Have you seen anything written by Ed Sperl?"

"Sure, doll. What do you need to know?"

"Was he doing something for the program about old crimes? Or a particular old crime?"

"For the reunion program? Lord, no, doll. That wouldn't make sense even for this place."

"No, I guess not."

"Hold on, doll. I have a list of the pieces for the program. Just hold on."

While Marlee waited, she looked at Jenifer Hurley. Jenifer's eyes were bright pools, her face taut with concentration.

"Marlee," Gil Weir said, "Ed did several things for the program, but nothing like you mentioned. He did a Chamber of Commerce puff piece and another puff about how the city is wooing high-tech business to take the place of steel. Plus a couple of little bios: Charlie Buck, Grant Siebert—you remember them."

"Okay, Gil. You're sure that's it?"

Marlee could see that Jenifer was impatient for her to hang up.

"Sure I'm sure, doll," Gil Weir said. "I have the complete list of reunion stories right in front of me. From Will Shafer himself. And I know there's nothing else coming, 'cause the programs are being printed tomorrow."

"Thanks, Gil."

"Don't bother to read the stuff, doll, unless you've got insomnia. They killed what would have been the best thing in the program."

"Oh, what?"

"Ed Sperl wanted to do a cute little piece about what people were doing on the night of the ice storm. The Chamber is gonna sell T-shirts with the slogan 'I Survived the Great Ice Storm.' Trying to market the town's bad weather instead of fighting the image."

"Well, who killed the story?"

"Will Shafer and the publisher, I hear. Will said stories like that were trite. You ask me, it could have been a nice read. Remember all those babies who were born exactly nine months after the big New York blackout in the sixties?"

"I remember."

"I hear Will and the publisher didn't want Ed going around and asking people how they were spending their time that night. Who knows? Maybe a lot of people were in strange beds."

"Could be. Thanks again Gil." Marlee hung up.

"Why did you ask that about Ed Sperl?" Jenifer asked.

"I just had a reason to be curious. Why?"

"I don't mean to pry. Yes, I do. Please, tell me why you asked that. Then I have something to tell you."

"Oh. Okay. I was talking to a cop last night, a guy I met through my column, and he mentioned that Ed Sperl had been bugging him about an old case, one the cop happened to have been in on years ago."

"What case?"

"It was twenty years ago. A priest was killed in the basement of a house."

"Go on, go on, go on."

"Easy, girl. So I asked my cop acquaintance why Ed wanted to know about it."

"And he said?"

"For an article. Ed Sperl was supposedly doing research for an article."

"Now isn't that interesting. Because he wasn't doing it for the reunion program, obviously."

"No."

"And he wasn't doing it for the *Gazette.*"

"Oh? How do you know that?"

"Will Shafer told me."

"Oh. How did you happen to ask him?"

"Because a couple of weeks ago, when I was in the basement of the records building, I ran into Ed. I asked him why he was there, and he gave me some bullshit answer about looking up old crime statistics."

"Oh, Ed didn't give a damn about stories like that," Marlee snorted.

"Of course not. And there are no crime stats where he was burrowing."

"Well, for sure Ed was interested in the case of that priest. And I even thought he might have been doing it for one of those pulp crime magazines. So I called Grant Siebert in New York—you don't know him, he used to work here and he's coming back for the reunion, and he's an editor for a true-crime publication—but Grant said Ed wasn't doing anything for him."

"What made you call this guy Grant?"

Marlee felt herself blushing and hoped it didn't show. "I know Ed talked to him earlier, about the reunion, and I thought . . . I don't know what I thought. Maybe that Ed had worked out a deal with him."

"This is all very strange," Jenifer said. "I heard you say something about something being killed. What was that?"

Marlee told her.

Jenifer sniffed derisively and said, "That sounds like Will. He's so uptight on stories like that."

Marlee thought for a moment. She didn't want an argument with Jenifer, but she had to defend the editor. "Will's judgment is usually on the mark. Really. I can remember newspapers doing stories about a bunch of babies being born nine months after a power failure or a big blizzard or something that kept people marooned. Sometimes, the statistics turned out to be not quite accurate. And Will's right: the story's been done before."

Jenifer frowned and said, "Hmmph."

Marlee remembered something she hadn't told Jenifer. "I had lunch with Ed's ex-wife, right after the funeral. His first ex. She said they were going to get back together."

"Ha!"

"And that Ed was coming into some money. That's what she said."

"Could he have been doing a book?"

"I doubt it, Jenifer. A book takes discipline, and I just can't see Ed doing that."

"No, especially since he was half-drunk or hung over all the time. Jeez, Marlee, I saw how much he put away at your party."

The party. Yes, something about the party had been blinking in the back of Marlee's head. Now she knew what it was: how Ed Sperl had stood at the table, listening to old tapes, going through old pictures. As if he really cared.

Oh! The string of sick jokes about the death of that priest. On the tape from Grant's farewell party.

"Are you okay, Marlee? You look . . ."

"I'm okay, I think. We have to sort some things out. God, this is all so strange."

"Isn't it, though?"

"And all of a sudden Ed's dead by his own hand."

"Bullshit," Jenifer said.

"What?"

"Trust me, Marlee. Ed didn't kill himself."

"Why do you say that?"

"I'm just an amateur psychologist, Marlee. But Ed didn't seem depressed to me. A red-nosed drinker and a bum, yes. But not depressed. I'm not sure he was deep enough to be depressed."

Marlee shook her head. "It does seem odd. Let's assume Olga was telling me the truth, that Ed had said he was going to come into some money. That doesn't sound like someone planning to kill himself, does it? Heck, Jenifer. He was shot with his own gun. He must have done it."

"No. I think I have good instincts. All my instincts say he didn't."

"Have you told anyone?"

"No. What can I say? That my instincts tell me something? Who can I say that to?"

Marlee thought for a moment. "There may be someone. Listen, what time are you getting out of here today?"

"Fourish."

"Look, my car's been towed to a garage for some work, so I need a ride home. Okay? And there's something we should listen to."

Twenty-six

▲▲▲

Jenifer Hurley had a red Toyota that she drove a little too fast. In the ride to Marlee's house, they talked about Marlee's car and Jenifer's car and whether it was better to buy new or used. Marlee knew Jenifer was getting ready to ask her something.

Finally Jenifer said, "You've known Will Shafer a long time."

"Longer than I want to remember."

"What do you think of him?"

"As a person or as a newspaperman?"

"Either. Or both."

"Oh, boy. Kind of stiff, but decent. He had a hard time, when he was younger. Folks were poor. Only way he went to college was on a *Gazette* scholarship. That helps explain why he's a lifer at the *Gazette*—like I am, I suppose. As an editor, he's the same way: good, decent, kind of stiff."

Jenifer said nothing.

"What made you ask?" Marlee said.

"It's just that, I don't know, I've had this feeling. When I'm with him sometimes, he seems like he's somewhere else. Like something's tearing him apart, you know?"

"Hmmm. Maybe he's not the same around me. Or I'm so used to him I don't notice. Bottom line, he's management but he's fair. You remember where my house is?"

"Yep. I met Will Shafer's wife at your place. At the party."

"Karen. Very smart woman, very lovely person. It says something good about Will that he's married to her."

As soon as Marlee got out of the car, she was greeted by barking.

They went inside. Nigel said hello with slurps and tail-wagging, and Marlee apologized to Jenifer for the dog's indiscreet sniffing. Then Marlee put the dog out, poured two glasses of chilled white wine, and got out her tape recorder.

"Remember I said I wanted to listen to something? It's the recording from Grant Siebert's farewell party. From twenty years ago."

"God, I was still in Mickey Mouse pajamas. I already heard it, you know. At your party."

"Yes, I do know. And what I remember is Ed Sperl looking at pictures and fiddling with the tape recorder. See, I was sitting on the porch, looking through that window right there, and I saw him. He was right about where you're standing now."

"There were a bunch of pictures and tapes that night."

"Yes, but the tape from Grant Siebert's party had the stuff about the priest. The window was open, and I could hear. People around the table were talking, and when they talked about Grant, my ears perked up." Marlee stopped, felt her face get warm. "Anyhow, I didn't know there was anything on here that meant much, but let's listen."

"Do you think Ed Sperl might have been gay?" Jenifer said.

"My God, what a thing to ask. Why?"

"Hey, why not? Stranger things have happened."

"But Ed was married . . ."

"Twice."

"And he fathered a child."

Jenifer chuckled, a trifle patronizingly. "So what? Maybe

the fact he bailed out of two marriages should tell us something."

Marlee let a long gulp of wine cool her throat as she thought that over. "He was always making crude remarks about gay people. Remember, at my party?"

Jenifer shrugged, raised her eyebrows. "Could have been a smoke screen. I mean, anymore I'm never surprised when someone is gay. And look at how he died: shot in his own car, in a parking lot of a tavern way the hell away from here."

"Oh, you think he might have been meeting someone way over near Horning because he didn't want to be seen with him here?"

"I'm saying it's possible. Suppose he was gay. That would explain a lot, wouldn't it?"

"Well, it could, although I don't know about the money angle. And you said you didn't think he killed himself."

"Lovers' quarrel maybe?" Jenifer shrugged. "I'm not saying I have it all worked out yet."

"Let's listen to the tape."

"You could donate that recorder to the Smithsonian."

"It still works."

Marlee pressed the play button:

" . . .elected to leave Bessemer for a larger city on the Hudson, are here in the bosom of your friends—"

"He hasn't any!"

"Shhh."

"—to drink, make merry and get some cheap gifts . . ."

"Not cheap . . ."

Marlee and Jenifer sipped wine, and Marlee refilled their glasses as the tape played.

"It sounds like you people were stoned out of your minds," Jenifer said.

"Oh, we were. Or a lot of us were."

"In closing, Grant, what else can we say, except break a leg and . . ."

"That wasn't a bad send-off," Jenifer said.

"No, especially considering how snotty Grant was to some

people," Marlee said. "I think young newspaper people were different then. Any excuse for a party."

"And this is what Ed Sperl was so interested in?"

"Oh, no. A little later there's a lot of foul talk about that priest. Listen."

The tape spun on; sometimes Marlee could not tell which sounds were voices and whispers and furniture bumping from twenty years before and which were electronic hissings from the recorder itself:

"*. . . time on the city desk, you tell me. I heard a dark rumor at headquarters, on deep background, that the priest wasn't just golfing down there, if you get my drift.*"

"*So? You're the one who's supposed to have the terrific police sources.*"

"That was Ed Sperl needling Will Shafer," Marlee said. "They didn't like each other even back then."

"*. . . work on your personality, Ed.*"

"*Could it have been a fag deal?*"

"*Oh, yuk!*"

"That's my friend Carol Berman, that last voice," Marlee said. "The other voices right there I'm not sure of. Now, all this stuff about homosexuality was never publicized."

"But some reporters knew, obviously. Or Ed Sperl did."

They listened again:

"*You bastard.*"

"*The guy's dead, for God's sake.*"

"*They held a mass of the resurrection, but it didn't work.*"

"Old joke," Jenifer said.

"Yes, it was old even then."

Bump, bump of tables and chairs.

"*Betcha whoever did it is long gone.*"

"*Still hacking away.*"

"*You sick bastard.*"

"*. . . yuk . . .*"

More mutterings and bumping.

"*. . . a double mortal sin.*"

"*. . . Two for the price of one.*"

The laughter was far away and fading. "No doubt about it," Marlee said. "A little alcohol makes a farewell party seem like more fun than it is. Pot helps, too."

"I just can't see you doing pot."

"I don't anymore."

"How many of these tapes do you have?"

"Damn, I don't know. Mostly I recorded them for the people who were leaving, you know?"

"A nice thing to do."

"Like most souvenirs from farewell parties, the tapes probably got put away somewhere and forgotten. A lot of people were leaving the *Gazette* back then. Lots of parties, lots of tapes."

"But Ed was interested in this tape, you said."

"So, should we play it again?"

"All right."

But Marlee was suddenly reluctant. Hearing the tape had left her depressed, as though it didn't matter whether one left Bessemer or stayed, because life could be pointless after a while if one was alone too much.

Marlee was glad when the phone rang. "Go ahead and listen," she told Jenifer. "I've heard enough." Rather than pick up the phone in the kitchen, Marlee went into her bedroom.

"Hi, Marlee. Ed Delaney here. I just called to see how you made out with your car."

"Oh, hi! They took it away this morning. Your friend Rick was real nice and gave me a break on the towing charge. Says the car'll be ready tomorrow."

"Good. You can rely on whatever he says. So how are you doing otherwise?"

"Fine. I've been listening to a twenty-year-old tape recording. Oh, it's of a farewell party at which Ed Sperl made some filthy jokes about that priest."

"You told me he made some bad jokes at a party you threw not that long ago."

"He sure did."

"Marlee, this is totally off the record, okay? I told you I thought the diocese was just as glad we didn't solve that case. I've always wondered if it was another priest that did it."

"My God. Could that be?"

"Sure it could."

Another thought—more like a bad marriage of two thoughts—came to Marlee. "Is there any chance at all that Ed Sperl didn't kill himself?"

"I haven't heard any suspicions otherwise. Why?"

"Because the person who's been listening to the tape with me, another reporter, she thought maybe Ed didn't."

"And what's her reasoning?"

"She, it's not reasoning exactly. It's her instincts."

There was a pause, and when Ed Delaney's voice came back, he sounded annoyed. "Marlee, the ruling was suicide. That's what the medical examiner over in Horning found."

"I know. I know."

"I hear the 'but' in your voice."

"Could you check? Unofficially, I mean?"

"I suppose I could make a call or two. Tell me what you're thinking."

"One of his ex-wives called me one day, and I bought her lunch. She said she and Ed were going to get back together, and that he was going to come into some money."

"From where?"

"God knows. But that doesn't sound like someone who was about to kill himself. Does it?"

"I don't know. What else are you thinking?"

"Could he have been gay?"

"Almost nothing surprises me anymore," Delaney said. "I know what you're driving at. Proving anything would be more than a long shot."

"You wouldn't necessarily have to prove . . ." Shit, Marlee thought. Hooked again. Now he's going to think you're a jerk, and he'll be right.

"What are we talking about here, Marlee?" Delaney's voice was all cop now.

"If you checked, it might help Ed's ex-wife." Deep breath, then get it all out at once. "She might collect more on some insurance if there was some doubt raised about whether it was a suicide."

"Oh, boy. I didn't hear you say that, Marlee. Because if I had, it wouldn't be kosher for me to investigate anything. I'm supposed to be in the business of gathering facts, evidence sometimes, and never mind who it hurts. Or helps."

"I know. I know." Marlee felt a pang of contrition.

"I'd be walking real close to the line if I did what you suggest, assuming I'd heard what you just said."

"Yes. I know. I'm sorry."

"Sorry for what? I told you, I didn't hear you."

"Oh."

"I'll let you know what I find out."

"Thank you. Oh, thank you."

Marlee was smiling as she hung up. She was startled to see Jenifer standing in the doorway.

"I just wanted to know if I should let your dog in," Jenifer said. "He was whining."

"I'll get him. How much did you hear just now?"

"Enough to figure it out. Maybe he'll find something." But Jenifer was frowning.

"What's wrong?" Marlee said.

"Whether or not Ed Sperl's ex-wife makes out with the insurance isn't really the point. Is it?"

"Well, no, but if we . . ."

"Call me a hard-ass if you like, and I know you're more experienced than I am. But a reporter's supposed to go after a story for the sake of getting at the truth."

"Yes, and suppose it's true that Ed Sperl didn't—"

"If things were turned around, you wouldn't feel the same way. Would you, Marlee? If the ruling was that Ed Sperl died in an accident, or someone killed him, you wouldn't be pressing some cop's buttons to find out it was a suicide. Would you?"

"No, of course not. But that wouldn't help anyone, it would only hurt." But Marlee knew Jenifer had got it right.

"Okay," Jenifer said. "Maybe your cop friend will find something out regardless."

"I hope so. He might be able to tell us something about Ed's death."

Jenifer nodded agreement, but the disapproval shone in her eyes.

"Shit," Marlee said. "I know I should be more hard-boiled sometimes. Less involved emotionally."

Jenifer shrugged. "Maybe he'll find something."

Marlee managed a smile, but her eyes were hot. She knew the bond between Jenifer and her had been spoiled.

"I have to be going," Jenifer said.

"Thanks for the ride."

"Anytime. Let me know what your friend finds out, okay?"

"Sure." She walked Jenifer to the front door. "I think he's a good cop," Marlee said through the screen. "He goes by his instincts, too."

But Jenifer was halfway down the walk, and Marlee couldn't tell whether she had heard her.

Nigel barked.

"Shut up, you stupid Airedale!"

Marlee poured herself a glass of wine, drank half of it in a gulp.

Wise up, Marlee. Make up your mind what you are.

Twenty-seven

▲▲▲

Sometimes his daughter's intelligence could be a problem. It had taken all of his tact and cajoling to get her to stay in her room with her crayons and be happy about it.

"How come I can't go out and play?" Laura had asked.

"'Cause you're just getting over being sick," Ed Delaney had said.

"Why do I have to go to my room if I haven't been bad?"

"'Cause your old man has to do some work on the phone."

"How come you don't do that at work?"

Ed Delaney didn't have a good answer for his ten-year-old, or himself. Now, with Laura in her room, he got the number and dialed.

"Horning police, Sergeant Dibble speaking."

"Sarge, this is Detective Ed Delaney from up in Bessemer, shield number four-one-six. Could I talk to one of your detectives?"

Delaney got switched through with no trouble. He wasn't surprised that the detective who answered was familiar with the case of Sperl, Edmund, apparent suicide. The Horning police department wasn't that big.

Delaney kept it casual for a few minutes, letting the other guy talk, getting a sense of how trusting and trustworthy he might be. Then Ed Delaney got to the point: "I'd appreciate it if we could go unofficial and just talk cop to cop from here on."

The next morning, Ed Delaney sent Laura to her room again to play with crayons after promising to rent a movie for her to watch on the VCR that evening. Next he sat down with his third cup of coffee, called headquarters, and told Jean Gilman he'd be a little late. Then he dialed the Fraternal Order of Police, intending to get the latest whereabouts and phone number of retired Detective Captain Raymond McNulty.

Before anyone answered, Delaney's instincts kicked in and he hung up. He didn't want that many people to know he was calling Ray McNulty.

Delaney thought he remembered the name of the Florida Gulf Coast town where McNulty had gone in retirement. After trying the wrong area code the first time around and shooing Laura back into her room once, he got the number and dialed.

"Hello." The hoarse voice hadn't changed.

"Captain, this is Ed Delaney calling from Bessemer. How the hell are you?"

"Eddie! Don't you know I'm not a captain anymore? God, it's been a long time. Has the snow melted up there yet?"

"It's July, for God's sake. We do have summers here."

"Yeah, short ones. How's all the good people?"

"We're busy as hell. Trying to do more with less. You know."

"It was ever thus. Jean Gilman turned out to be a decent partner, I guess. Keeps her cool pretty well for a woman?"

"She's fine, fine. Good cop." McNulty would never change, Delaney thought. He had an incurable prejudice against female cops.

"And that sweet little girl of yours, how's she?"

"Laura's fine, fine. She keeps me busy."

"Don't they always."

Ray McNulty talked for a couple of minutes about his job as security manager at a large trailer park for retired people, and how, unlike Bessemer, they didn't have too many problems with "Third World types." Then he told Ed Delaney about his wife's back problems and his own arthritis, and how glad they were not to have to shovel snow anymore.

Finally Delaney said, "Ray, remember how every so often we used to have one of those little chats that never even happened?"

"Sure, Eddie." McNulty's voice had turned cold serious.

"This is one of those chats."

"Whatever it is can be between you and me and the God of Irishmen, Eddie. You know that."

"This is about that priest in the basement with the golf club sticking out of his head."

Ray McNulty exhaled with a long, low whistle. "God in heaven, Ed Delaney. What's your interest in that after all these years?"

"That *Gazette* guy, Ed Sperl, was bugging me about it just before he died. Oh, did you know about that?"

"Yep. My daughter sends me the Bessemer paper every so often. A straight shooter, Ed Sperl. Too bad."

Delaney couldn't have disagreed more about Ed Sperl, but he wasn't about to say so. He told McNulty about Sperl's reawakened interest in the slain priest, but he glossed over the details of Sperl's apparent suicide. And he didn't say a word about having asked a Horning detective to copy the file on Sperl's death, including the pictures, and send it via Express Mail to him at his home instead of headquarters.

"I learned a lot from you, Ray. About keeping my ass from being bitten off by the sharks in the department, about being a good detective."

"You always had what it took, Eddie. If you'd played politics better, you'd be captain now. But you're like your father, God rest his soul. You don't always go along. What did you call to ask me?"

"When the priest got killed, who told you to lay off?"

"Ah, me." There was another long, low whistle, and when McNulty's voice came back, it was shaky. "You're sure you want to ask me that?"

"I'm sure. I remember you said, 'This is a Catholic town.' Who?"

"It was Chief Potenza who gave me the word, Eddie. Real clever he was, giving me the word in such a way that he couldn't be blamed and I couldn't miss the message. Sly dago, that's how he got to be chief, God rest his soul."

"'This is a Catholic town,' you said. Did that mean Potenza got the word from the diocese?"

"You figure it out, Eddie. Back then, we had Chief Potenza and Bishop Ciccarelli. The bishop was worried about the image of the diocese, and the chief was worried about going to heaven."

"That would explain a lot, wouldn't it?"

"Yep. We both remember how that priest looked, Eddie. Didn't take a genius to figure it out. Who knows, maybe it was all for the better. We probably wouldn't have caught the guy anyhow. At least the priest's family didn't have to see the corpse dragged through the mud, the way it worked out."

"The family was from out of town. Somewhere in Pennsylvania, I think. Did they have money?"

"I never got deep enough into the case to find out, Eddie. I always figured maybe. Money talks in the church, too."

"I know. I know."

"Let it be, Eddie. That's my advice."

"Hmmm."

"Every so often, maybe once or twice in a cop's career, something comes along that's just too dangerous to get close to, for one reason or another. That priest with the golf club in his brains was the thing in my career."

"I'll watch out."

"Do that. Call me again when you want to talk about fishing and sunshine."

"Thanks, Ray. Thanks for talking to me."

"Thanks for what, Eddie? We never talked." And with that, retired Detective Captain Raymond McNulty hung up.

Delaney waited until Jean Gilman was out of the office before dialing the *Gazette*.

"Marlee West speaking."

"Hi. It's Ed Delaney."

"Ed, hi. Listen, I'm sorry but I just can't make the counseling session tonight. The reunion starts tomorrow and I have to take my dog to the vet, and I've just got too much to do."

"What's wrong with him?"

"I don't know, but he hasn't been eating, and I can tell from the look on his face that he's sick."

"I hope it's nothing serious."

"Me, too. I'm getting out of here a little early to go to the doctor."

"Do you need a ride?"

"No. I have my car back, and it's running fine, thanks to Rick."

"So, you're going home and then right to the vet?"

"As soon as I can."

"Why don't I meet you at your place and drive you."

"Oh. That's real nice, but I can manage."

"I wanted to talk to you about Ed Sperl. I have some new stuff."

"Oh. Okay. I'm leaving in about ten minutes."

"See you at your place."

Ed Delaney stopped in front of Marlee West's house. He put the Express Mail envelope from the Horning police under the driver's seat, then got out and stood by the car.

He had half-expected to hear Marlee's dog barking. When he didn't, he found himself worrying. The thought of Marlee heartbroken made him sad, and that realization startled him. Now that he thought of it, he could have arranged to meet Marlee later in the evening, instead of driving her and her dog to the veterinarian.

It was a pleasant July, soon-to-be-August afternoon. Warm, not oppressive. On a whim, he stepped onto Marlee's front yard, plucked a few blades of grass, sniffed the green smell, and tossed them away.

He saw an old woman standing on the porch next door, looking at him suspiciously.

"How are you today?" Delaney said.

Delaney wasn't sure if the woman nodded, but he was sure she was uneasy.

Marlee drove up. "Hi, Ed. Hi, Mrs. Wemple."

At last, the old woman on the porch smiled broadly and waved.

"She's the one who called the police the night of the prowler," Marlee said.

"She was giving me a suspicious eye."

"I kept Nigel inside today, in case it got too hot. Stupid Nigel, I don't know why the hell he has to do this."

They went inside.

"Nigel! There you are, baby."

The Airedale shuffled toward Marlee and glanced without much interest at Ed. Delaney didn't know much about dogs, but he could tell from the animal's eyes that it was hurting.

On the way to the vet, Delaney didn't even mention Ed Sperl. It was obvious that, for the moment, Marlee cared only for the dog in the backseat. After Marlee told him the vet's address and nearest cross street, Ed told her to relax, that he knew the way ("I used to drive a patrol car, remember?"), and that he would even turn on his siren if it looked as if there was an emergency. Then Ed wondered if he was caring too much about this heart-on-her-sleeve woman and her dog.

The veterinarian told Marlee he didn't know what was wrong, but that Nigel was in no immediate danger. The vet said he would keep Nigel overnight and do some tests in the morning if Nigel didn't perk up.

"Do you want me to tell you what I found out about Ed Sperl?" Delaney said on the ride back to Marlee's.

"Oh, yes. I can think better now."

"Under my seat, I have the complete file from the Horning police, which I'll go over with you when we get to your place. It includes the pictures."

"No thanks, I don't want to look at the pictures. But what . . ."

"His gun was approximately where you'd expect it to be. There were no other fresh bruises or injuries indicating a struggle. No drugs in his system, only alcohol. Plenty of that."

"So it does look . . ."

"There was no note, but I can tell you from experience that that doesn't mean much. What else? . . . There was quite a bit of blood in the car, indicating that that's where death occurred."

"Did anyone see him before he died?"

"The Horning police interviewed the bartenders who were working that night. One remembered serving Sperl earlier in the evening. Remembered he had several drinks."

"Then what?"

"And that's it, almost. Next thing anyone knows about Ed Sperl, he's found dead in the car the next morning. Nothing solid pointing to anything but suicide."

"So no one heard a shot, obviously."

"No. But that doesn't necessarily mean anything. The car was in a far corner of the lot, about as far from the tavern as it could be. Ed's gun was a .32 revolver. That's a nice medium gun, and it doesn't make a loud noise."

"Come in. Let me offer you a glass of wine. Or a beer."

Ed Delaney sat in an easy chair and went over the details. He kept the photographs—Ed Sperl with his eyes open and death-glazed in the car, Ed Sperl lying naked on a metal autopsy table—in the envelope. Marlee sat on the sofa, sipping wine, her feet up on the table. Ed thought she looked tired.

"So that's it," Marlee said finally. "I hope this didn't take up too much of your time."

"That's all right. It's my time to do what I want."

"And there's nothing to indicate he didn't kill himself?"

"Nothing that can be put in any kind of official way," Delaney said carefully. "You can't always put your feelings in a report."

"What?"

"My gut feeling is that something might be wrong with this. Ed Sperl had more than twice the legal amount of alcohol in his blood, assuming he had tried to drive. But the bartender doesn't remember serving him anywhere near that."

Delaney paused, saw from Marlee's face that she knew he had more to tell.

"Another thing," Delaney went on. "When Ed was done at the bar, he went to a corner table and talked to a guy for a little while."

"Well, what about that other guy?"

"No description. The other bartender—not the one who served Sperl at the bar—thinks that the guy with Sperl bought a couple of six-packs just before he and Sperl left around the same time. He wasn't sure they left together, and he very definitely couldn't provide a description of the other guy."

"All right. You said your gut tells you something's wrong about Ed's death. Tell me why you feel that."

"It's, it's too pat in some ways, and in others . . . Okay, Ed Sperl is sitting in his car, which just happens to be in the farthest, darkest part of the lot, and he gets stinking drunk. There's empty beer cans in the car, in a paper bag."

"The six-packs the other guy bought?"

Delaney shrugged. "So let's say Sperl gets real drunk, and he decides to shoot himself, but he wants his car to be neat, so he puts the cans in a bag. I'm not sure about that."

"Well, was he too drunk to shoot himself?"

Delaney chuckled without mirth. "I've seen DWI cases in which someone's blood alcohol level is so high you'd swear he couldn't crawl, much less get into a car. So we'd have to say he could shoot himself."

"But why would he, all of a sudden?"

Delaney shrugged again. "Another thing is the gun in his hand. In the pictures it doesn't look quite right to me. It's hard to explain exactly. I've seen my share of gun suicides. None of the ones I've seen were holding their guns the way Sperl was. Do I think it was too loose in his hand, or too tight? I don't know. I don't know."

"Could someone have put it in his hand?"

"I think that's possible. Possible. And what about this other guy? What became of him? Suppose Sperl was meeting someone for some reason he was ashamed of. Or nervous about."

"Oh. Could Ed have been gay? Would that . . ."

"Nothing surprises me, not anymore. But Sperl *was* with someone, at least for a while. The other guy must have come in a different car, right? Unless he got a ride to the tavern with Sperl or someone else, then got a ride away from the tavern with someone after walking out of the place with Sperl."

"Riddles, riddles. And I told you, when he was at my party he was real interested in old pictures and the tape from a long-ago farewell party with jokes about that priest."

"Play it for me."

Marlee got the recorder and put it on a table in front of Ed. "The tape's in it. You know how to work it, I suppose."

Delaney nodded and pressed play:

"*. . . to aid in your quest for glory . . .*"

Ed pressed fast-forward.

"*. . . whoever did it is long gone.*"

"*Still hacking away.*"

"*You sick . . .*"

Marlee felt embarrassed, not so much by the vulgarity as

by the drunken foolishness. "All that bumping was from people banging into the tables and chairs," she said. "Some of them were, you know."

"Yep, I know. Been that way myself."

Ed listened awhile longer, turned off the recorder.

"So?" Marlee said.

"Nothing, Marlee. No secrets."

"But you do find something strange in all this."

"Let's say some things that bother me. Loose ends. Hey, I just said 'loose ends,' but before I said it was all too pat. See, I don't know what I think."

"But what about the tape, and those old pictures? There was something that Ed was interested in."

"I don't know, Marlee."

Delaney finished his beer and debated with himself whether to tell Marlee about his talk with Ray McNulty. No: that would be a breach of confidence.

Marlee was staring intently at the envelope holding the file on Sperl's death.

"Ed, you had this sent to your home instead of headquarters. Why?"

"Things have a way of getting lost at headquarters."

But the flint in Marlee's eyes told Delaney that the lie was inadequate.

"Ed, you felt something was wrong even *before* you got the file, didn't you?"

"I had my doubts."

"Come on, Ed. I'm not a big investigative reporter, but I'm not a fool either."

"I never thought you were. Marlee, I can't tell you any more. Not right now."

"There is something. I know it."

"Marlee, I'll tell you this much. This is a Catholic town. That's what a good cop told me a long time ago. I think there were people who never wanted that priest killer tracked down. The trail would have been too dirty."

"Who wouldn't have wanted it solved? Someone in the church?"

"Maybe the victim's family had money, influence, and didn't want their beloved son disgraced as well as dead. Now I've really said enough. Don't press me, okay?"

"Okay. But if there was a cover-up years ago, that's just plain wrong. And what could it have to do with Ed's death?"

"Maybe nothing. Or maybe Sperl was gay and ran into the same guy who killed the priest."

"But Ed used to make bad jokes about gays."

"So what? Could have been just a cover for his own act."

"But that would be an almost unbelievable coincidence, wouldn't it, if Ed ran into the same guy who killed the priest?"

"Coincidence, yes. Unbelievable? Like I said, nothing surprises me anymore. And even though this is a Catholic town, it isn't that big a town."

"What happens now?"

"What happens is, I'll do some more discreet poking around. And I'll share what I find with you. Off the record. Okay?"

"Okay."

"Now I have to go."

"A lot's happening at once," Marlee said, walking Delaney to the door. "Ed Sperl. Nigel getting sick. The reunion starts tomorrow. I don't feel like celebrating anything."

Ten minutes later, Marlee did feel like celebrating: the veterinarian called to say that the mighty dog Nigel had passed two large pieces of plastic, probably from a child's beach bucket. Yes, Marlee said, that made sense. It was not the first time toys had blown onto her property from a couple of yards down. She thought she recalled having seen such a bucket yesterday, in fact, but had never got around to picking it up.

The veterinarian said Nigel should stay in the hospital over the weekend, just in case there was any damage to his bowels, but that he would almost certainly be all right.

The news about Nigel made Marlee feel lighter. A two-mile run up around the reservoir and back made her feel lighter still. As she was cooling down, she thought through what Delaney had said.

This is a Catholic town. Maybe the victim's family had money and influence. God, wouldn't it be something if Ed Sperl had got involved in something too big for him—something far bigger than the traffic tickets he had helped people fix?

On an impulse, Marlee picked up the phone and dialed the *Gazette's* library. "Rachel? This is Marlee. I'm calling from home. I hope it's not too much trouble, but I need you to look up something from the microfilm."

Marlee gave the library assistant her request and got a return call fifteen minutes later. After listening as the library worker read the first big story about the 1971 killing, Marlee thanked Rachel profusely. Then, before she could talk herself out of it, she dialed long-distance information for Sharon, Pennsylvania.

There was only one listing under the name she was interested in. After the second ring a woman answered. From the sound of the "hello" Marlee figured her to be in her sixties or seventies.

"Hello, my name is Marlee West and I'm calling from Bessemer, New York."

"Yes?"

Marlee thought the woman sounded puzzled and nervous. "I'm trying to reach the family of a Father John Barrow, who, um, died in Bessemer some years ago. Do I have the right family?"

"Oh! Who? I, I'm going to call my husband."

Marlee held her breath, strained to hear the anxious, muffled exchange on the other end. I have the right family, Marlee thought. No doubt about that. Don't hang up. Don't, don't, don't.

"Who did you say you were?" A man's voice, loud, challenging. Marlee repeated her introduction word for word.

"Why are you calling us?" His voice was still loud, but there was something else. Sorrow, Marlee thought.

"Sir, I've lived in Bessemer all my life, and I know about your son, how he died."

"Why are you calling us? Just who are you?"

Anger as well as sorrow in the voice, Marlee thought. She knew what she had to say, even if the man hung up. "Sir, I'm with the *Bessemer Gazette.* I didn't write about your son's death at the time, but—"

"Why are you calling now, for the love of God?"

The man's voice had broken. Marlee felt sorry for him, but at the same time she was monitoring her impressions: the man and his wife were not sophisticated, and therefore likely not rich or influential.

"Sir, please hear me out. I promise I'll try not to add to your grief."

"You're wasting your breath with your kind words. I heard them all twenty years ago. They were no good then either."

"Sir, do you know any reason why your son's death would not have been investigated thoroughly? Any reason at all?"

"What kind of a crazy goddamn question is that? And why in God's name—"

"Mr. Barrow, something about your son's case may be coming to light after all these years."

"What does that mean?"

"Sir, was your son a homosexual?"

Marlee held her breath as the silence of heartbreak filled the moment.

"What if he was?" the old man said finally, quietly. "That made him no less in God's eyes, did it? Did it?"

"No, sir. It didn't."

"You have no right to put that in the paper now, after—"

"Mr. Barrow, please. I'm not writing a story. I have, I mean, I'm calling because I have reason to think your son's death was not investigated very well. On purpose. Please don't hang up. Please try to trust me."

Twenty-eight

▲ ▲ ▲

A couple of hours later, Marlee drove down a well-lighted tree-lined street, stopping when she saw a porch light.

Ed Delaney was waiting for her on the front steps.

"Thanks for making time to see me," Marlee said.

"That's okay. I'm just sorry you had to come over here. There was just no way I could get a sitter."

He led her in to a narrow screened-in porch that ran the width of the house, sat her down on a rocking wooden bench with cushions, and excused himself. While he was gone, Marlee wondered what it would be like to sit on a porch with a man every night in the summer, listening to the crickets, or the rain falling through the leaves. She wondered if there was any man in Bessemer she could be happy with.

Delaney returned with two cans of beer and handed her one. "Cheers," he said. "Now tell me what couldn't wait."

"You said it might have been the church that hushed the investigation when that priest was killed. Or that he might have come from an influential family that squelched it."

"'This is a Catholic town,' is what I said. That's—"

251

"I understand that," Marlee interrupted. "But it wasn't his family that hushed things up."

"How do you know?"

"Because I talked to his father tonight." Marlee said that in a rush, not quite keeping the tremble out of her voice.

She told him how she had slowly broken down Thaddeus Barrow's suspicions, got him to talk about his son, John. His only son. Yes, he had known his son was a homosexual, had found out about it just before his son was done with his seminary studies—although once he did find out, some other questions were answered. Such as why the adolescent John Barrow had spent so much time at the golf range, hanging around with an assistant pro about whom, Thaddeus Barrow learned much later, there had been whispers.

What surprised Thaddeus Barrow and his wife was how few questions the Bessemer police asked them, and how the whole thing "just seemed to have died down" when the Barrows called the Bessemer police.

"Ed, the parents weren't trying to hush anything."

Delaney's silence in the dark told her to go on.

"They believe their son is waiting for them in heaven. And they wanted his killer caught. They even considered hiring a private detective to come to Bessemer and hunt for him."

"Why didn't they?"

"Thaddeus Barrow was a steelworker, and he hurt himself real bad at work. Bad enough that he took a long disability, or whatever. He was a long time getting better, and by the time he was better the steel business was sick, and there wasn't any work for him."

"How did you find out all that about these people?"

Marlee thought for a moment. "I listened to them, and I didn't try to bullshit. And I suppose Thaddeus Barrow could sense . . ."

"That you felt sorry for him."

"Yes. Ed, these are salt-of-the-earth people. Simple people. Not rich, not sophisticated, not influential. They didn't want their son's case forgotten. Just the opposite."

Marlee had finished her beer, and she waited for Delaney to say something. The seconds went by, the silence broken only by the soft night noises heard through the porch screens. "Ed?" Marlee said at last.

"What?"

"What's going to happen?"

"To be honest, probably nothing."

"How . . . ?"

"Think a minute. There's two deaths twenty years apart, one in Bessemer and the other way over in Horning, in a different county. On the surface, there's nothing tying them together."

"I don't agree."

"Hear me out. Sure, Ed Sperl was bugging me about a killing that took place in '71, when I was a rookie, and we know he wanted to peek at the old file."

"And he was fascinated with the tape that had people talking about the priest."

"Fine. And so what? Sperl getting shot in his car that way bothered me. I told you that. But there's nothing I could tell a prosecutor over in Horning."

"No?"

"No! My hunch isn't enough. For a prosecutor or grand jury, I mean."

"Well, did you tell the Horning police about your hunch?"

"Not in so many words, no."

"Ed, what does that mean?"

"It means I was already sticking my neck out getting the Horning cops to send that file to me at my home. That's irregular, to put it mildly."

"But you thought it was important enough that you did it. And how could it hurt you?"

"Trust me, it could. If the brass heard through the grapevine that I was poking into something way out of my jurisdiction . . ."

Marlee was stung—disappointed in Ed Delaney, angry at herself for having believed he would help.

"Marlee, someone wanted that priest buried, quietly and forever. I've seen what can happen to cops who cross the wrong people, in or out of the department. And I'll tell you something else."

"What?"

"Your newspaper's never been any help when good cops have gotten bum deals, from politicians and God knows who."

"I don't make newspaper policy. All right. I think I should go."

"Look, when you first bugged me about Sperl it was because of that woman—Olga? —so she could maybe collect some insurance, right?"

"Only partly, Ed. Only partly."

"Partly. Let me tell you, that's not a good enough reason for an investigation."

"You said you'd poke around and share what you found."

"I will, quietly."

Then Marlee understood. "What's different now is that I've actually done something, talked to the priest's father. It was easy for you to talk about digging into this or that when it was only hypothetical. Now that I've *done* something, you're scared. That's the truth, isn't it? That's what this is all about."

Delaney was silent for a long moment. "The truth?" he said wearily. "The truth is, this is a Catholic town. An even bigger truth is that I've got a kid asleep in the house, and she looks to me for everything."

"Good night, Ed."

Marlee held it together until she was outside, in the sweet darkness. Then she started seeing the glow of the street-lights through tears of fury.

"I'll keep my ears open, Marlee. I promise."

Marlee didn't answer.

After Marlee West's car pulled away, Ed Delaney went back into the house, tiptoeing so as not to wake his daughter, and got another beer. He took it back to the porch, where he drank slowly, wishing he had done a lot of things in his life differently.

When she got home, she poured herself a tall glass of wine and drank half of it in one gulp. Missing Nigel, she said a silent prayer for him. Stupid Airedale; doesn't even know enough not to eat plastic.

She was still angry and frustrated, but feeling less annoyed with Ed Delaney. He was on the mark when he said the *Gazette* had never done anything to help cops who got a bum deal. The police department was shot through with politics; after every mayoral election there were dozens of promotions and demotions and transfers, nearly all based on who had campaigned for whom and which constituencies— Polish, Italian, German, Irish, black, Jewish, Hispanic, some combination—the new mayor had to pay back. Marlee knew that. She also knew the *Gazette* winked at some lawbreaking, especially sports betting in the steel plants and prostitution, and that the *Gazette* had cozy arrangements with the police about parking spots for reporters and photographers and (much more important) the paper's delivery trucks.

Marlee finished the rest of her wine and set the glass down with an angry clack. Okay, Ed Delaney. Touché. But there's still something very wrong with what happened to Ed Sperl.

Marlee called the *Gazette* and got Jenifer Hurley's home number from the night operator.

"She just left a few minutes ago, Marlee. Give her a while to get home."

"Wow. She was really working late."

"I walked by the library and saw her doing some research."

"Thanks, Mildred. She never quits, does she?"

Marlee waited fifteen minutes, dialed Jenifer Hurley's number, and got an answer on the second ring. Then she laid out what Delaney had told her, what she had learned from talking to Thaddeus Barrow, and how Delaney had pulled back from his earlier enthusiasm.

"Is that all you got?" Jenifer said.

"All? Goddammit, Jenifer, I practically . . ." Marlee heard Jenifer laughing and realized the joke. "You bitch."

"Seriously, I'm impressed. What prompted you to call that old man, and how did you get so much out of him?"

"Curiosity and compassion, in that order. And after our little friction earlier, I had something to prove."

"Not anymore, you don't. I wish I had as much to report. I spent a lot of hours tonight going over Ed Sperl's old clip files."

"Why?"

"I don't have enough hobbies. And I thought there might be a clue to . . . whatever. If there is, I missed it. Marlee?"

"What?"

"You're sure this Delaney guy is straight? I don't mean straight sexually, I mean—"

"I know. Yes, I think so. Yes." It had not occurred to Marlee that Delaney might not be honest.

"You said he seemed to be pulling back, is why I ask."

"I know." Marlee had not told Jenifer about Delaney's having had the Horning police send the file on Ed Sperl to his home; she thought that would be a breach of confidence. "Jenifer, I know you're more skeptical than I am, and I know that trait serves you well. But I do have reason to be sure Delaney's not covering up anything himself."

"All right."

Marlee wondered if Jenifer meant that. "And he's right about the *Gazette* and how it's never come to the rescue of any cops who got shafted for political reasons, Jenifer. I've been around the *Gazette* a long time." Much longer than you have, Marlee thought.

"And you've lived in Bessemer all your life, which means you know at least as well as I do how a few people at the top of the social structure run the town."

"I sure do."

"And somebody's covering up something. Somebody's been covering up for a lot of years. If not the family of that priest, then, I don't know, maybe someone close to the bishop."

Marlee was silent for a moment. What Jenifer was suggesting sounded fantastic to her, yet she could not dismiss it. She knew Bessemer too well—and she knew that Jenifer Hurley had instincts that were as good as those of any reporter who had passed through the *Gazette*.

"Ed Delaney said he'd keep his ears open, Jenifer. I believe him."

"Fine, but we need more than that."

"For what?"

"To break this thing, of course. I'm as hungry for this as I've ever been for anything. It's a great, great story. I know it."

Marlee didn't know what to say, or how to feel. The kind of investigating that Jenifer was talking about went way beyond newspaper reporting—or at least way beyond the kind of reporting Marlee was good at. And there was something else: "Jenifer, you know damn well the *Gazette*'s never going to print anything like that if the diocese doesn't want it printed. Not unless somebody is actually arrested or indicted and the paper can't ignore it."

"First things first. I'm going to do a little poking."

"How?"

Jenifer chuckled. "I've been going out with an assistant district attorney. You know how those people are chosen, from the political clubhouses. They're privy to a lot of stuff, and sometimes they're willing to talk. My friend is from a large Italian family: cousins in the steel plants, in the school district, at city hall, you name it. I can get him to talk a little."

"You're sure?"

Jenifer chuckled. "I'm sure. He's nuts about me."

"Oh."

"You don't approve?"

"I didn't say that."

"You didn't have to. I'm certainly not going to go *that* far for a story, but I'll use whatever I can. Besides, he likes my company."

"I wasn't making a judgment," Marlee said. "At least I was trying not to. You have to do what you have to do."

"Right. Hey, Marlee, I'm young and hungry. What can I tell you? I'm only gonna be young and hungry for a little while. The *Gazette*'s got lots of people who wish they'd had more spark way back when."

Marlee wondered if Jenifer included her in that legion. "We'll talk some more, Jenifer. Right now, I'm going to get some sleep."

"Okay. You did good, Marlee. I mean it."

"Thanks. We'll talk some more after the reunion."

"You know who must have some unbelievable stories to tell, if he only would? Will Shafer."

"What makes you say that?"

"Because in his job he must know a lot of things that the *Gazette* has covered up. Or finessed. Too bad he's so damn discreet. Maybe if he gets to drinking at the reunion he'll open up."

"Not Will. Good night, Jenifer."

Bone tired, Marlee locked the door to her room and flopped down on the bed. After a quick prayer for Nigel, she fell into a deep slumber.

Twenty-nine

▲ ▲ ▲

THE *GAZETTE* MARKS **90** YEARS
WITH A REUNION AND A TRIBUTE
TO THE GREAT CITY OF BESSEMER

The Gazette Company, publisher of the *Bessemer Gazette* since the newspaper's beginnings, marks its 90th birthday this weekend with a reunion of former staff members, a series of social events and a celebration of the city's industrial heritage.

Lyle Glanford, publisher of the *Gazette*, has dubbed the celebration "Breaking Ninety," a reference not just to the birthday but to the golf tournament at the Bessemer Country Club that will be a central part of the festivities . . .

"We want to show the world, as we remind ourselves, that we are part of a postindustrial Renaissance," Glanford said.

"There are those who say that big steel is finished. Well, we know that the great men who built the steel industry in Bessemer had strong hearts as well as strong shoulders. So do their children and grandchildren . . .

What total horseshit, he thought, wadding the newspaper in disgust and tossing it into the wastebasket. Some things never change. And now it was here—the event he had mostly dreaded but could hardly avoid.

How fitting that the memories and the ghosts should be summoned because of a reunion. What was it the advice columnist had written years before? "Regret is the cancer of life." True enough. But the regret was there, part of his life, and might always be.

Sometimes, even though it made his head throb, he would replay the string of events. The decisions that were trivial in themselves, but whose sum had meant blood and death.

If he had not gone out that long-ago night of the ice storm . . . but he had.

If he had chosen a cheap workingmen's saloon down near the steel plants . . . but he had gone to a place where he could feed off others' happiness.

If he had not liked the priest's company . . .

His head throbbed. That last thought was silly; one didn't choose to like someone's company, for God's sake. One didn't choose to be drawn to someone.

All right.

If he had not followed the priest that night to the house . . . but he had.

If he had drunk less beer that night, maybe he would only have pushed the priest away instead of . . .

If he had stopped after hitting the priest once . . . but he had hit him again and again until, until . . .

If he had called the police right away—God, if only—it would all be long behind him now, no matter what. But he had fled into the icy night.

If he had just kept quiet at the farewell party . . . but no, he had to make his jokes. His harmless little jokes!

All right, all right, all right. Please, God, just let me get through this.

It was almost time to leave for the reunion.

* * *

Marlee parked in the ramp under the Bessemer Hotel and took the elevator to the main floor. She thought of the night so many years before when she had come to the hotel with a tall, awkward boy for her high school prom. Then as now she had had butterflies, although then they had been due to adolescent shyness. Now?

Emerging from the elevator, Marlee immediately saw the results of remodeling. It had been a long time since she had had occasion to go to the Bessemer Hotel, and the chandelier, carpeting, and paint were all new. But they could not hide the underlying tackiness. It was not just the water stains already visible on the new paint high up in the dim ceiling corners, or the tired-looking, poorly dressed old men who sat on sofas way off to the side—permanent hotel residents who paid a weekly rate.

Those sights were part of it, but only part. Beneath it all was the sense that the hotel—and outside, Bessemer, her hometown—was decaying. Dying?

No, not dying. Dying ends. Decay can go on and on. The hotel (and the country club, and the golf course) had been given a face-lift, in large part because the publisher had wanted it. He had probably thrown in some of his own money. But a face-lift was only a face-lift.

Enough, Marlee thought. I can't change the world. I have enough trouble with my life.

Her day had actually gone well: the vet had called to say that Nigel was improving, that there didn't seem to be any damage to his intestinal tract, and that he could probably come home in the next day or two. Stupid dog, she thought. But she smiled.

Marlee ducked into the ladies' room, saw the same face she had fussed over not a half hour before at home, decided that the face and her pale blue dress looked pretty good.

Out again, onto the main floor, to the big open staircase that led to the Ingot Ballroom of her prom memory. Large tables flanked the staircase; one table held T-shirts (red,

blue, yellow, black) with the words *I Survived the Ice Storm.*
The other table held stacks of reunion programs. Marlee
was not interested in looking at the program right now; she
knew there would be extras in her office.

She went up the stairs, walked in to the music and the low
babble of conversation. She was not too early. Some *Gazette*
people and some Chamber of Commerce types were standing around, talking over drinks, waiting for the alcohol to
loosen them up.

She would get herself a drink, try to have a good time.

"Hi, Will. Hi, Karen." On her way to the bar, Marlee
passed the executive editor and his wife. Karen Shafer
looked so . . . together, Marlee thought. She always did,
much more so than Will, although he was handsome in a new
seersucker jacket that went beautifully with his shirt and
tie. Karen must have advised him on his clothes, Marlee
thought.

A small, dark-skinned bartender in a white coat served
her a vodka tonic. Marlee looked around the room, filling up
now with more Chamber types, some *Gazette* people, and
here and there, someone who had worked at the paper and
left. Oh, there was Charlie Buck over in a corner. He had
gained weight, but he looked prosperous. She would say
hello to him when she got a chance, maybe chat for a minute
or two.

Marlee sipped the vodka, studied the faces, flashed half-
smiles at some of the faces that met hers. God, this is
awkward, she thought. Just like my high school reunion.

In the center of the room stood a long table banked high
with beds of ice on which lay hills of shrimp and sliced
turkey, ham and beef. Nearby, there were melon balls and
cheese cubes pierced by brightly colored toothpicks.

"Nice spread, huh?"

Marlee turned to see her friend Carol Berman. "Oh, hi!
Now I have someone I can talk to without worrying about
what I say."

"I didn't think you ever did. To tell you the truth, I wasn't that hot on coming here, but both Lyles did some gentle arm-twisting, if you know what I mean."

"I know what you mean."

After watching Carol pile food onto a plate, Marlee felt hungry, so she speared some shrimp and melon. Yes, the food was good, and the vodka was giving her a pleasant glow.

"So, how are you?" Carol said.

"Okay. I have a minor health crisis with my dog, though."

"Oh, dear."

Carol was fond of Nigel and wanted to know about the Airedale's problems. When Marlee told her what had happened, Carol clucked sympathetically—then laughed. At first Marlee was offended, but the more she thought of it, the more it seemed funny to her. At least it was funny since it was going to turn out all right. Marlee laughed, too.

"Weren't you thinking of showing the dog once?" Carol said.

"Oh, that was a long time ago. Some dog groomer told me Nigel was a very handsome dog and might do well in shows. I put him in a couple of events, but nothing happened."

"Did they give him an IQ test? I mean, any dog that can't tell hamburger from plastic . . ."

"Oh, you bitch!"

The conversational group was breaking up, its members attaching to new groups. Marlee headed for the bar for another drink, picking up snippets of talk along the way.

". . . playing golf tomorrow . . ."

". . . early tee-off? How about you, Will?"

"I lucked out," Shafer said. "I don't have to tee off until almost noon."

Marlee wondered, not for the first time, whether she would like golf. Neither of her parents had played, so she had never taken it up. Maybe next summer . . .

Marlee got another vodka tonic, stepped away from the bar, looked around the room. She saw Lyle Glanford, Sr., holding forth with several businessmen and a few people who had worked at the *Gazette* years before. She recognized the president of the telephone company, the head of the power company, a builder named Archangelo Grisanti. Not for the first time she thought that Bessemer, especially if it was one's hometown, was so easy to cover as a journalist because the same people (usually men, a fact she resented) belonged to more than one sphere of influence. Maybe I do belong here, in this small town, she thought. Maybe . . .

"Marlee?"

She turned and looked into the face of Grant Siebert. "For goodness'," she stammered, almost dropping her glass as she transferred it to her left hand so she could greet him. "It's good to see you, good to see you."

"Same here." Grant was smiling.

"You look good."

"Thanks. You, too."

He really does, Marlee thought. Fuller face, trim mustache, thick hair. And yet a way about him that's—what? Defiant? Vulnerable? Both?

"Well, I'm glad you could come. I've been pressed into service as kind of a semiofficial part-time organizer, probably because I've been at the *Gazette* so long."

"I imagine it's been a lot of work."

"Oh, well, Will Shafer did a lot more. That's him over there, with his wife."

"I already said hello to Will."

"How are you anyway? Where are you staying?"

"Little motel on the edge of town. I wanted to be near the golf course instead of right in the city."

"Good idea. Did you drive?"

"No, I flew. Rented a car once I got here."

Marlee took a long gulp of her drink and was afraid the vodka wasn't helping her poise much. There was a nervous silence, and Marlee was relieved when Grant ended it.

"I'm not that sentimental," he said, "but I did enjoy circling over the city in the plane, seeing new things and trying to recognize things that were here when I was."

"God, so long ago now. I guess, I guess I haven't seen you since your farewell party."

"The party, right. At the . . . what was it?"

"The Silver Swine. It's changed a lot. Last I heard, someone was trying to make it go as a vegetarian restaurant. Quiche and yogurt and all that."

"Really? In this town?"

"In this town. Bessemer, city of broad shoulders and quiche."

Grant laughed, seemed to loosen a little. Marlee was starting to enjoy his company. Then she got an idea. "I think I remember you told me Ed Sperl hadn't written for you recently," she said carefully.

"Right. He used to string for us a long time ago. But I never dealt with him directly."

"Mmmm."

"Why?"

"Just that there might be something happening right here that would make a good story for your magazine," Marlee said.

"What's that?"

"Oh boy, where to begin. When we talked long distance a while ago, I told you about Ed Sperl's death, didn't I?"

"I already knew. I mean, my mother saw an obituary in the Albany paper. That's how I knew."

"Oh. Okay. Well, a lot's happened since then."

She told him as much as she could as concisely as she could without mentioning Jenifer Hurley by name. Marlee was deliberately vague about Ed Delaney's on-again, off-again interest. She figured Ed Delaney would be scared off but good if he found out she had told anyone else about his semiprivate investigation (halfhearted though it was), especially if the person she told worked for a true-crime magazine.

"Isn't that the darnedest, Grant?" Marlee said when she was finished.

"You could say that. What's it all mean, do you think?"

"Well, I have wondered—I guess I can say this, because he is dead, after all—but I've wondered if Ed Sperl was gay. That could explain a lot, couldn't it?"

"Uh, maybe. Tell me what you're thinking."

"That maybe, somehow, Ed bumped into the man who killed the priest. Now, that wouldn't seem all that farfetched if the priest was killed by someone who was gay, would it? I mean, it would narrow down the possibilities a lot. This is a small town in a lot of ways. And if you go back twenty years, being gay was something a lot more people kept secret."

"Suppose it wasn't a man. The killer."

"Oh." Marlee was stunned; she had not thought of the possibility of a woman.

"Think of it," Grant said. "How strong would a woman have to be? Do you play golf?"

"No."

"Oh, okay. If you did, you'd understand how much force a club generates even when the person swinging it is of very average strength. So say a woman hits him once, stuns him so he's helpless. She'd be able to finish the job with no resistance at all if she was of such a mind."

"You think so?"

Grant laughed in the old familiar, slightly smart-alecky way. "I shouldn't claim to be an expert, but I deal in stuff like this on my job. And sure, a woman swinging a golf club would have all the strength she'd need."

"God, that would be something."

"And you think, uh, you think there might have been a cover-up?" Grant said.

"Well, yes. Anything's possible." And I've said way too much already, Marlee thought.

"And if the killer was a woman . . ." Grant flashed a knowing, slightly wicked grin.

"That would be something," Marlee said.

"Wouldn't it? Believe me, if you stay close to this kind of stuff, it gets in your blood. There's a lure to it. Maybe I shouldn't say that, but it's the truth. Hey, you look a little pale."

"I feel pale." What he had just said had made her feel like a snake was crawling over her back.

"Well, let me get you another drink. I'm in need myself. Gin?"

"Vodka. And tonic."

The room was much more crowded now, noisier. The men and women around Marlee—some of them bumping her as they made their way to and from the bar and the buffet table—may as well have been painted clowns. She felt dizzy and nauseous from the image of a woman's battering a man's head in with a golf club. Could that be?

"Here you are, Marlee. I didn't mean to paint such a gory picture for you. Maybe I'm too used to this kind of thing."

"I hope not," she managed to say. This time, she took two big gulps from her drink. The vodka was like plasma.

"I have the idea that Ed Sperl was not well liked by some people," Grant said. "Hated, even. Being a police reporter in a town this size, he probably gave some people reason to hate him. This is a small town."

And a Catholic town, she thought. Marlee badly wanted to change the subject. "You're playing golf tomorrow?"

"Sure am." Grant made a face and shrugged. "My game is so rusty, I don't expect much. But as long as I was coming to Bessemer, I figured I might as well."

"I was, to tell you the truth, a little surprised when you accepted the invitation. I had the feeling when you left that you never wanted to see Bessemer again."

Again, Grant shrugged and produced a half-insolent smile. "I guess I just figured it was time, that's all. I mean, one visit every twenty years isn't bad."

"So, good luck and all that."

"Thanks. I'm playing with Will, of all people."

"Great."

Marlee was getting tired of standing in the same place. "I think I'll see who else is here. Talk to you later?"

"Sure."

Moving around, Marlee felt better. Talking to Grant had been momentarily exhilarating, then draining. Was it Grant himself, or what they had talked about? Both, probably.

On her way past the buffet table, she crossed paths with Will again.

"Thanks, Marlee," the editor said. "The publisher's having a good time and doesn't seem to notice who isn't here. So thanks for your extra work."

"I'm glad I could help, Will. You're the one who got stuck with so much."

"Anyhow, things are going pretty well. See?"

Will nodded in the direction of Lyle Glanford, Sr., sipping a cocktail and looking elegant in a summer suit that, Marlee was sure, he couldn't have bought in Bessemer. His silver-haired, ornamental wife stood next to him, smiling and shaking hands gingerly. Mrs. Glanford (was her name Veronica?) was always polite and supercilious and had a way of smiling as she looked right through people.

"I'm glad, Will. Grant says you're playing golf with him."

"Yeah. I just hope I don't hurt myself. Maybe if I drink enough, I'll have a nice easy swing. Oops, here comes Karen. Bye for now."

Marlee finished her drink (her third already?) and listened to a local singer's rendition of "John Henry Was a Steel-Driving Man." It didn't sound very good.

At one point, she saw Grant talking to Lyle Glanford, Jr. Yes, Lyle was having a good time; at least he was drinking a fair amount. As she watched, Lyle seemed to be listening intently to Grant, who seemed to enjoy the audience. Then Grant leaned slightly and said something to Lyle, who nodded sagely.

"Marlee, come and talk to me." Jenifer Hurley was standing next to her.

"Hi," Marlee said, glad for the younger woman's presence. "I didn't know if you'd come."

"Why not? Happy birthday, *Gazette*, and all that. Come on. Let's talk."

Jenifer headed for the least-crowded part of the room. The men she passed glanced appreciatively, and some did more than glance. Jenifer was stunning in a sleeveless yellow dress that flattered her curves and beautifully complemented her tanned arms and lustrous hair. She and Marlee went by Will, whose eyes shone for a moment with what Marlee thought was pure longing.

Finally, Marlee and Jenifer were off near a wall. No one was within ten feet of them.

"You were right about Ed Delaney," Jenifer said. "My prosecutor friend says he's as straight up-and-down as they come."

"Yeah, well, he's also backing off a little."

"Hmmm. Well, maybe we can turn him around again. Are you free tomorrow? During the day?"

"I guess so. Tomorrow night, I'm going to the country club."

"There's someone we want to talk to."

"About . . . ?"

"About what's been on our minds a lot. Trust me, we want to talk to him."

"Well, who is he, and how does he know us?"

"He doesn't know us. He's a cousin of my prosecutor friend, but that's absolutely between you and me."

"And he knows something, about Ed Sperl?"

Jenifer shrugged. "I told you my prosecutor friend belongs to a big, big family. I'll pick you up about ten."

"Jenifer, who is this guy?"

"I don't know. Honest. My prosecutor friend says he's 'straight up-and-down'—he likes that expression—and that we can trust him. We just have to make him trust us."

"Where are we seeing this guy?"

"I don't know yet. My friend has to set it up first."

"Do you think something will come of it?"

Jenifer's eyes (for an instant Marlee envied her for them) flashed with cold shrewdness. "Any information is better than none. And my feeling is yes."

Marlee felt both alert and competitive; she wanted badly to contribute something. "Maybe it wouldn't hurt if I called Olga again, just to pick her brain. One of Ed Sperl's ex-wives, the one who told me Ed was expecting some money."

Jenifer nodded. "Why not?" Then she smiled knowingly. "It's under your skin, isn't it? The story, I mean."

"You could say that." Marlee smiled back.

"Excellent. Now I'm going to circulate and have a drink or two and pretend I like some of these people before I go home."

Marlee felt alive. Just a short time ago she had felt half-sick and depressed; now it was as if she had been drinking black coffee instead of vodka. I'll be damned, she thought. I haven't lost it all as a reporter. I sure as hell haven't!

Marlee went to the bar again, ordered a weaker-than-usual drink and started on one last circle around the room. She chatted with businessmen and politicians and *Gazette* alumni, who seemed to be outnumbered. She remembered everyone who had worked for her paper and tried to be charming to everyone.

But her mind was somewhere else.

She encountered Will and his wife again, shook hands with Lyle Glanford, Sr., and his wife, giving her the same see-through stare she got.

She saw Jenifer Hurley again, in animated conversation with Archangelo Grisanti, the builder whom she had written about in a not-very-flattering way. The man obviously appreciated Jenifer's body even if he hadn't liked her stories. Marlee watched Jenifer deftly sidestep Grisanti's attempt to drape an arm over her shoulder. Marlee chuckled to herself as Grisanti seemed to have his arm around a crescent of air.

Still, Marlee's mind was somewhere else.

Halfway around the room, she again met Grant Siebert, who seemed to want her to linger. "We'll talk some more," he said. "Tomorrow night or at the brunch on Sunday. Or maybe, uh . . ."

"Sure, we will," Marlee said. In fact, talking to Grant some more was a pleasant thought.

But Marlee's mind was still somewhere else. She was glad when she completed her circle through the room, glad as she fled down the wide steps she had long ago ascended with prom-night nervousness, glad when she was in her car.

In her eagerness, she fumbled with her front-door key. Once inside her house, she gave a quick look around: everything seemed to be the same as when she had left. After the night of the prowler, she had never taken her security for granted.

Was it too late at night to call Olga? No, especially since she had extended herself on Olga's behalf.

She found Olga's number and dialed. The first time Marlee tried, she was sure she had punched a wrong number.

She tried again and got the same result.

Marlee paused, squinted again at the number, punched each digit crisply. She had not made a mistake; this time, there was no doubt.

"We're sorry," the recorded message said, "but the number you have reached has been disconnected."

Thirty

▲▲▲

Hearing Jenifer's car out front, Marlee took one last gulp of coffee, poured the rest down the sink, and raced outside.

"Where are we going?" Marlee asked.

"North Park. We're meeting this guy by a bench under a big tree near the duck pond."

Marlee was silent and nervous.

"It's okay," Jenifer said, sensing Marlee's unease. "My prosecutor friend is a straight up-and-down guy. He says it's safe."

Marlee filled her in about trying to call Olga the night before and finding that the number had been disconnected.

"Well, now," Jenifer said. "This gets more and more curious, doesn't it?"

"Yes. Indeed. Don't speed, okay?"

"I'll be careful. What do you think it means?"

"The Olga I know—although not that well, I admit—didn't seem like a woman with a lot of sophistication, self-esteem, you know."

"Not much in marketable skills?"

"Definitely not."

272

"Or marketable beauty?"

How heartless, Marlee thought. But true. "No."

"So maybe she just moved to a different neighborhood. Or stopped paying her phone bill. Ever think of that?"

Marlee allowed herself to feel smug—very smug. "This morning, I called the *Gazette* and got a library clerk to look up Olga's block in the street directory. I got half a dozen phone numbers of people who live within a few houses of her."

"Excellent! And?"

"I managed to reach four people. They all said Olga seems to have left for good. One had the idea that she'd gone to Arizona."

"Arizona! Sunbelt! Now that is interesting. I wonder if she left a forwarding address."

"Wonder no more. None of the neighbors knew of one. More to the point, the friendly post office didn't have one."

"Well, well, well. And this is the woman you were feeling sorry for. A funny time of year to go to Arizona, don't you think? Bessemer summers are pretty good, after all."

"Maybe she has family there?"

"Family? Marlee, I'm willing to bet she went to Arizona for one reason: it's far away."

"You think she was afraid?"

"You know the lady better than I do, Marlee, but it makes sense to me. She split because she was afraid, or because somebody paid her off."

"Or both. An offer she couldn't refuse. Damn."

Jenifer found a parking spot next to the cast-iron, spiked-top fence that ran around the perimeter of North Park.

"A glorious day, isn't it?" Jenifer said.

"Beautiful. Good for the reunion golfers. Almost makes me want to take up the game."

"Not me. I don't have the patience."

"You learn patience as you get older."

They walked down a sloping gravel path. Squirrels and

birds played in the grass around them, and the sun filtering through the trees cast ever-changing light patterns. Some of the trees still carried huge tar-covered scars from the ice storm that had torn off their limbs two decades before.

"There's the duck pond, and there's a bench under a big tree. That must be where."

"No one there," Marlee said.

"We're early."

It was not quite ten o'clock.

"Say, who is this guy anyhow?"

"Vito—he's the guy I've been seeing, the assistant DA—says it's a second cousin of his, or something. I told Vito about all that's happened, and he apparently talked to his cousin, and his cousin said he could tell us something."

"That sounds a trifle vague," Marlee said. Actually, it sounded worse than vague. Marlee didn't subscribe to stereotypes, but she still didn't like meeting a total stranger (who happened to be Italian) to discuss a crime.

"This man's name is Dean," Jenifer said.

"Dean something, or something Dean?"

Jenifer just shrugged.

"What do you know about him?"

Jenifer shrugged again.

Several joggers went by, singly and in pairs, men and women. At least it's broad daylight, Marlee thought.

She looked up the path they had just come down and saw a man walking toward them. Marlee sized him up in a hurry: medium height and build, loose-fitting casual pants, short-sleeve sport shirt, graying curly hair, tan skin, and dark glasses. Italian, she thought.

"Jenifer?"

Jenifer turned, saw.

The man came up to them, stopped, smiled without taking off his dark glasses. "You're Jenifer and Marlee?" he said.

"I'm Jenifer."

"I'm Marlee."

"And I'm Dean. Um, how much did Vito tell you about me?"

"Not much," Jenifer said. "Just that you're honest."

"'Straight up-and-down' is the operative phrase," Marlee said.

At that, the stranger laughed. His was a friendly laugh that showed bright teeth. "So's Vito. A good boy. Good man, I should say. I only see him a few times a year, but I love him dearly."

"He said you had some information," Jenifer said.

The stranger nodded—grimly now, the smile gone. "I can tell you a little, okay? I don't know how much it fits in with what you know, or if it helps you at all, but I'll tell you what I remember."

Marlee and Jenifer waited for him to speak. Instead, he walked slowly toward the duck pond only a few yards away. "Here, duckie, duckie, duckie!"

At that, the stranger took several pieces of bread from his pocket, broke them into small pieces, and tossed them into the water. The ducks had come to the water's edge as though welcoming an old friend, and they immediately stirred the pond with splashing and soft nibbling.

Marlee and Jenifer had followed the man, who now turned toward them. "I knew the man who was killed, John Barrow. I wasn't all that close to him, but I knew of him. I can tell you, because I know it for a fact, that there was, oh, a feeling among some in the Bessemer church hierarchy that there might be less suffering if the case were, oh, not pursued all that aggressively. But I know there were other people, high in the church, who loved John very much—loved him as a person—and very much wanted his killing solved. I know that definitely."

Marlee and Jenifer waited for the man called Dean to go on. Instead, he removed his glasses to reveal large dark eyes. Kind eyes, Marlee thought.

"We, I mean John's friends, waited for the detectives to come around and, you know, really question us at length.

About John's known contacts and so forth. But that never happened, despite the news accounts of the time, on television and in your newspaper, that 'all available police manpower' was being used. It wasn't.

"And I began to wonder if it might be just me. I was young then, didn't trust my perceptions all that much, so I talked with a much older man, one who knew the score. And I said to him, 'Am I wrong, or is John's death just being quietly swept under the rug, perhaps because he was homosexual?' And this older man, who as I said knew the score much better than I, said that indeed it was just being swept under the rug."

The man called Dean paused. Though he had total self-control, the pain on his face was obvious. It's so true, Marlee thought, so true that gay people have to endure so much more.

"As I said, the older man I talked to, he'd been around. He knew Bessemer inside out, had contacts at many levels, and he told me that the bishop himself was dismayed that more wasn't being done to find John's killer. This wise old man told me that the bishop was very hurt and disappointed all the rest of his life that more wasn't done by the police."

Marlee's memory circuits flashed right and left as she recalled her conversations with Ed Delaney, who had thought someone in the church had quashed the investigation.

"So," Jenifer began carefully, "you're saying you know it wasn't the church powers-that-be . . ."

"As surely as I know anything," the man said, "I know it wasn't the church."

My God, Marlee thought. "You're a priest," she said matter-of-factly.

The man nodded. "My name is Dino Morini. Some of my friends call me Dean for short, not because I dislike the name Dino."

"And you know . . . ," Jenifer began, before Dino Morini cut her off with a hand gesture.

"All I knew, as a young priest, a young man, was what I

heard from a much older and wiser man. A priest, Father Brendan Sullivan. He happened to be the one who discovered John's body."

The ducks had gone away, there were no joggers nearby, and Marlee and Jenifer waited in transfixed silence.

"He was a good and holy man, this Father Sullivan. Wise in the ways of the world, wise in the ways of the church, the ways of the diocese. To me, he was like . . ." Dino Morini smiled sadly at the unspoken thought. "So, that's about all I can tell you. Dear God, all these years later . . ."

"We appreciate your seeing us," Marlee said.

"Well, I don't know how much good I did you. At least, maybe I gave you a perspective. After twenty years, there aren't that many people who know much of the truth. And lies take on a life of their own, you know?"

"We know," Jenifer said.

"Look outside the church for the start of the cover-up," Dino Morini said. "If I were you, I'd look to the police. Now, I think I should be leaving. Use what I told you any way you can. Just treat our conversation in total confidence. Understood?"

"Of course, Father," Marlee said. "You can trust us."

"I know I can. And you," he said to Jenifer, "say hello to my cousin."

"I will. Thank you."

Father Dino Morini turned to go up the gravel path he'd come by. Pausing a moment, he looked at Marlee and smiled. "You were surprised when I said I'm a priest. You thought something else, at first."

"Well, I thought maybe . . ."

Father Dino Morini chuckled. "Emphatically not. When I took my vow of celibacy, I was forsaking something much better."

Riding back to her house, Marlee felt an electric excitement she hadn't experienced in a long time.

"You were great back there," Jenifer said. "You had him made as a priest before I did."

"Mmm. Well, we wouldn't even have met him if not for you."

"This feels very good, Marlee. Being on the hunt of something. And I don't think there's anyone I'd rather hunt with."

"Thanks. You know, I like doing my column, helping women and all that. But I'd forgotten how it feels to be digging, really digging for something."

"You're good at it. And I apologize for underestimating you."

Marlee looked at Jenifer's profile, so intelligent and strong as well as beautiful. For a moment, Marlee envied her youth. Then Marlee felt something close to love. "Jenifer, I should thank you for getting my juices flowing again."

Jenifer pulled up in front of Marlee's house. "We'll sit down early in the week and hash all of this out," Jenifer said. "Jeez, I've got a housing-authority story I have to do Monday. Never mind, I'll make time for this somehow."

"Do you have any idea what next?"

"Not really. It'll probably be good just to let it simmer."

"Maybe. Hey, do you want to come in for coffee?"

"No, thanks. I have some things to do. I guess I'll see you at the country club thing tonight?"

"Oh, you decided to go. Good. Oh, it could be fun."

"Maybe the only way I'll ever see the inside of the place. Should I pick you up?"

"No, thanks. My car's running fine. We should probably take separate cars, in fact, in case one of us has a better time than the other."

Once inside, Marlee lay down on her sofa and tried to unwind. Let things simmer over the weekend, Jenifer had said.

No. Marlee wasn't ready for that. She sat up, reached for the phone, and dialed.

"Ed, it's me. We're still friends mostly, aren't we?"

"Sure."

Marlee filled Delaney in on the meeting in the park. She couldn't give the priest's name, she said, but he had known the priest Ed had seen at the house where the killing took place. And she told him about Olga's disappearance.

Ed hardly said a word while Marlee talked. Finally, she was done. "Ed, what do you think?"

"I think I'm a cop, and I want to do some digging."

"Earlier, you were kind of—"

"I'm a cop, I said. A cop. We'll get together on this. Soon. In the meantime, do you have any plans?"

"Well, tonight there's the reunion banquet. And tomorrow there's the brunch at the publisher's house."

"We'll talk as soon as we can. Meantime, be careful."

Thirty-one

▲ ▲ ▲

Only a moment before, Grant Siebert had sent his first drive of the day a couple hundred yards down the fairway. He's been practicing, Will Shafer thought. For a moment, Will envied Grant's slacks and shirt, which he thought were more stylish than his own.

Will teed up nervously. He was too eager, and so he took his eyes off the ball at the last instant. He topped it, although he caught enough of it to send it a hundred fifty yards out.

"Not bad," Grant said.

Will and Grant stood together off to the side as Lyle junior teed up. Will thought the publisher's son looked tired and hung over. Lyle sliced, into the right rough but playable, and walked over to wait by Will and Grant. Then a pink-faced young banker who rounded out their foursome took a slow, smooth swing that propelled his ball two hundred fifty yards down the middle.

"Now we know how bankers spend their time," Lyle said.

Walking down the fairway, Will resolved to enjoy the game, the day, as much as he could.

Standing over the ball for his second shot, Will forced

himself to breathe deeply. This time, he caught the ball with the sweet spot of the three wood and sent it straight for the green.

By the time they paused for Grant's second shot, Will was standing on a little rise that offered a view of Lake Erie. There were purple clouds on the horizon. Storms could blow in quickly from the lake in high summer.

Marlee dozed. Too many conflicting sensations and emotions had jammed her brain circuits, and she was tired. She had lain down on the sofa planning to sort things out; instead, she had drifted into sleep. Once when her eyes popped open, she reached down, expecting to touch Nigel's tough, bristly back. Not there.

She turned her head slightly; out the window, a sun-filled sky. She could see a gently soughing tree.

Eyes closed again. The priest in the park had seemed like a good man. But how can we be sure he's telling the truth? Or maybe he's telling the truth as best he remembers, but his memory's no good. Or suppose he's not a priest. Oh, yes, he must be, because Jenifer's boyfriend sent us to him. But what about Jenifer's boyfriend, if that's what he is . . .

I'm doing this all wrong, she thought. I start out with a few simple questions, but then I ask questions about the questions, and all of a sudden I have ten times as many questions as I started with. And no answers.

Marlee gave up; she let herself drift away.

When she opened her eyes again, she saw that the sky had changed. Could she have slept that many hours? No. But the day had taken on a gray skin, and the trees were tossing harder; Marlee could hear them.

Far away, thunder rolled across the sky like barrels. It took her a moment to pick out the other sound, of someone at her door.

"If we start to get lightning, we don't want to be under any trees," Will said.

"Why not?" Grant said. "The way I'm playing, it might be a blessing."

"Only a game," Lyle said.

Will actually felt sorry for Grant, the man who had once been such an annoyance to him. After a good start, Grant had faltered, hitting some balls out of bounds, another into a pond, and making a lot of mistakes by trying too hard.

Will's own round had been mediocre, which was about what he had expected. He was having fun, all things considered, and was not disappointed. Lyle, too, was playing a so-so round, having bounced back from his hangover.

Only the banker was playing really well, and he didn't seem to be enjoying it all that much. When the first raindrops came, Will started to unbuckle the umbrella from the side of his golf bag.

"Never mind," Lyle said over the suddenly mounting wind. "Right down here."

Lyle led the way down a gravel path to a wooden shelter separated from the nearest patch of woods by a good hundred feet. The size of a small garage, the shelter had an overhanging roof and screened windows with shutters.

"I don't remember this being here," Will said.

"It's new," Lyle said. "My father's idea. He thought it would be good because this is the farthest point from the clubhouse."

The foursome ducked inside, leaned their bags along one wall, and sat on the wooden benches. Now the rain began to drum like pennies on the roof.

"Just a shower," Lyle said. "Almost like the tropics. In a half hour, we'll be back out there. Meanwhile, we can relax."

"Fine," Will said.

"How about you?" Lyle said, looking at Grant. "Are you having a good time?"

"So far. I wish I was playing better."

"You've got a decent swing," Lyle said. "You just need to loosen up."

"I'll try." Grant smiled, darkly.

"No, don't try. If you have to try to loosen up, you're not loose. Get it?"

"Now I do," Grant said coldly.

Will flinched at Grant's tone and saw Lyle narrow his eyes. But after a moment, Lyle broke into a grin. "Smart-ass New Yorker!" he said. "Tell me the truth: if you had it to do all over again, would you stay in Bessemer? Work for Will here?"

"Hard to say," Grant said. "I can't do it over."

"So what brings you back here?" the publisher's son asked.

Grant shrugged; Will thought he looked uneasy. "Just to renew old . . . acquaintances," Grant said evenly.

That made Lyle guffaw. Grant smiled, and the banker tried to smile.

"You haven't been back in twenty years. Since you said good-bye to this god-awful town. Am I right?"

"That's right."

To the banker, Lyle said, "You're too young to give a damn about reunions. How old are you, anyway?"

"Twenty-eight." The banker looked as if he wanted to be in another solar system.

"Well, you're a damn good golfer." With that, Lyle slapped the banker good-naturedly on the shoulder.

"Thank you." The banker managed a smile.

"Which makes me wonder how good you are with money if you're spending so much time on your golf," Lyle said.

Finally put at ease, the banker laughed.

"It's raining harder," Will said.

"I came prepared," Lyle said. He went over to his golf bag, unzipped the big pocket, and took out a paper bag. Lyle ripped off the top of the paper bag, scattering ice cubes onto the floor of the shelter, and smiled triumphantly as he displayed a gleaming six-pack of beer. "Who's gonna join me?"

"Glad to, Lyle," Will said. It was early in the day but what the hell.

"Sure," Grant said.

Lyle handed them each a beer, then turned to the banker. "I forgot your name."

"Jim Powell," the banker said.

"Well, Jim Powell, how about a beer?"

"It's a little early for me." Jim Powell smiled wanly as his three golfing companions drank beer. Will didn't want him to feel left out, so he said, "Where did you learn to play golf like that?"

"Been playing since I was a kid—" Powell began.

"Powell?" Lyle said. "Now I know where I heard that name. Your father is the dentist."

"Orthodontist, yes," Powell said. "That's him."

"So," Lyle said, "you played a lot of Wednesday afternoons with your father, I bet?"

"Yes. Still do."

"And probably played on your college team."

"At Cornell, yes."

"That's one school I never tried," Lyle said.

"Anyhow," Will said to Powell, "you have a game to envy."

"Amen," Grant said.

"Thank you," Powell said. "I enjoy it."

"You're lucky if you enjoy playing golf with your father," Lyle said. "I wish I could enjoy playing with mine."

Will saw something in Grant's eyes. It might have been anger, might have been understanding, might even have been sadness. Then it was gone.

It rained harder. Some drops splashed into the shelter. Powell got up and closed the windows partway.

"You're with Bessemer Trust," Lyle said.

"Yes, I am," Powell said.

"They tell you at the bank that golf is important?"

"Some people do use it for networking, yes."

Will braced himself for a snide remark from Lyle. He wished the young banker wouldn't make himself such an easy target.

"Networking," Lyle said as he hurled his empty beer can noisily into a corner and opened another beer with a spurt of foam. But Lyle's kindness had taken over, and he merely snorted mildly with disgust.

"Listen," Powell said. "I do believe the rain's letting up. I think I'll swing a club for a few minutes so I don't lose my groove."

"Rain or not, he's wet behind the ears," Lyle said when the banker was gone.

"He's young," Will said. "He's just trying to figure out how he fits in. Like we all had to do once."

"Like we all had to do," Lyle said wistfully.

"All of us," Will said. He looked again at Grant and thought he saw him nod.

The rain on the roof was much fainter now.

"How will we know whether to start playing again?" Grant said.

"They'll sound a siren from the clubhouse," Will said.

Lyle threw his second empty can noisily into the corner and stood up. "I need some air," he said. "Then I'm ready to tear this goddamn course apart."

"It's a good course," Grant said. "Very pretty."

"I agree," Lyle said. Picking up his golf bag, he lurched toward the door. Then he paused and looked straight at Will. "Tell you something you didn't know," he said coldly. "Arkie Grisanti built this little shelter 'cause he thought it would make my old man happy. No big deal, right? You know damn well Arkie is gonna want something in return. So be ready, and don't say I didn't warn you."

"Thanks," Will said. "I appreciate that." When Lyle had gone, Will looked at Grant and said, "Grisanti's a builder. The paper's had his feet to the fire on a couple of things, and he keeps trying to go over my head to the publisher."

"And the publisher's son was warning you?" Grant said incredulously.

"A decent guy, Lyle is. Publisher's son or not, he has it tough. Maybe *because* he's the publisher's son. I can't imagine the pressure he must feel sometimes."

"Some job you have," Grant said. "You must really have to watch your ass."

Will chuckled. "I just try to do it the best I can and only take the important baggage home with me. It pays to have a tough hide. I didn't, at first, but I've acquired more of one."

"I bet."

It was hard to tell now whether the drops on the roof were fresh rain or just water being stripped from the trees. From the distant clubhouse a siren sounded.

"I guess we can go chop up the grass again," Will said.

"Yep. Maybe the beer'll help my swing. I just hope Lyle doesn't fall over."

"He'll be okay."

They picked up their bags and went out. It was a short walk through the rain-cooled air to the next tee, where Lyle and the banker were staying a good distance apart as they took their warm-up swings.

"What made you come back?" Will said to Grant. "I was surprised, frankly."

Will thought he saw something in Grant's face, as though his guard had come up instantly.

"I just felt it was time, that's all," Grant said.

"Well, I hope you enjoy everything." Will saw the flecks of sand and mud on Grant's golf slacks, looked down, and saw similar stains on his own clothes. "At least we look like golfers," Will said.

"Yeah. Bad ones."

"Funny. Years ago, when you worked here, we never played together."

"No."

"If we had, we might even have liked each other," Will said. He saw Grant flinch, but he went on. "Stranger things have happened. As I remember, we kind of rubbed each other the wrong way back then."

"Yeah, I guess we did."

"Ever do an imitation of me?"

"No."

"Ever wish you'd stayed?" Will asked quietly.

"Hey, you guys!" Lyle shouted from down the path. "Let's go."

"Yeah," Grant said. "I suppose there've been times I wish I'd stayed."

"I can tell you there've been times I wish I hadn't," Will said. "Maybe we can compare notes before you go back."

"Okay. Sure."

They were at the next tee. Lyle was standing off to the side as Powell prepared to drive. The banker swung too hard, topped his ball, and barely sent it over a knoll a hundred yards out.

Lyle steadied himself enough to hit a decent, safe drive. Will followed, going a little to the right but playable. Then Grant hit his ball in the same direction, so they walked down the right side of the fairway together.

"The publisher treats Lyle like crap sometimes," Will said. "Of course, we can't choose our parents, can we?"

"No. Sure can't."

"I guess the trick is to see them as just people. Are yours still around? Alive, I mean."

"Yes."

"Mine are gone."

Grant felt uneasy. For some reason, Will Shafer seemed to want to empty his soul.

"Do you keep in touch with your folks?" Will said.

"Kind of. My folks and I are planning a football trip to Notre Dame this fall."

Grant was surprised when Will stopped dead in his tracks for a second.

"Ah, that must be great," Will said softly. "I used to envy you—still do—because you went there."

Grant was out of things to say for now.

"Yeah, I wanted to go there," Will said. Then he shook his head and resumed walking. "The rough's not too bad. Looks like I can use a four wood from that lie."

* * *

Marlee had been surprised when Ed Delaney knocked at her door. She let him in, apologized for being half-awake, sat him down, and made some coffee. They talked for a few minutes about the weather, how rain was blowing in off the lake and would probably screw up the golf tournament.

"Serves 'em right," Delaney said. "If I can't play at the country club, why should anyone else?"

"Shame on you," Marlee said. "There are some really nice people playing right now. One or two."

"I doubt it."

Marlee waited. It was up to Ed Delaney to speak next, because they both knew he had come for a purpose. Marlee was eager to tell him as much as she could about the meeting in the park, but first she would wait him out.

"Twenty years can go by awful fast," Delaney said.

"For people our age, yes."

"Reason I say that, all of a sudden I've got twenty years on the force. Means I can retire at half pay and start a new career, managing a security company or something like that, the way a lot of old cops do. Put it another way, as long as I work after twenty years, I'm working for half pay. In effect."

"Oh. It's hard to think of you as ready to retire."

"I've been fighting the whole idea. Part of me, maybe the best part, likes being a cop. But lately this thing we've been talking about . . . Damn it, I don't know how to put this."

As Marlee waited for him to go on, she noticed that the rain was letting up.

"Truth is," Delaney said, "if I'm enough of a cop that I'm not ready to retire, then I should still be enough of a cop that I don't back off. I've been reminding myself of that."

He paused, Marlee waited.

"What I said on the porch, how I was, that wasn't the cop in me," Delaney said. "Being a cop, a good cop, means doing what you have to do. Even if you risk pissing somebody off and getting busted to patrolman and walking a beat again."

"You mean . . . ?"

"I consider myself a good cop," Delaney said. "If there's something here, I'll find it. No matter what it takes. Or what it costs."

Marlee smiled. "That's so good to hear. You don't need to know all about my soul crisis, but I've had to do some thinking of my own. About hoping to find something and going after that part of it, or trying to learn the truth, no matter what it is."

"Heavy stuff," Delaney said, frowning in mock solemnity. Then his face went cold serious. "I went down to the old-records section and got out the file on the priest. Went through every scrap of paper there."

"Must have been a lot."

"No, that's the point. The pictures were there, from the crime scene and the autopsy, and there was my report as the first officer on the scene, and the medical examiner's report. I saw some notes filed by burglary-squad detectives, based on stuff their snitches told them. It was all worthless, of course. I mean the stuff from the burglary detectives."

"Worthless?"

"When I was in the basement where the body was, an old detective took me by the hand and gave me a little lesson. What it boiled down to was that it looked like a homosexual killing, not a burglary. Then things got turned around and the case was all of a sudden being treated as though it had started out as a break-in. There was even a note in the file that entry could have been gained through a basement window. But there was no sign of that. It was all bullshit."

"Why, for God's sake?"

"It was all for show. The most important thing of all, there was a memo there, about an interview with the bartender who'd called a few days after the body was discovered to say he might have seen the priest in this tavern around the time he was killed. The night of that big ice storm, as a matter of fact."

"Everyone remembers that storm, and where they were."

"That tip was never followed up, and that stinks, if you

think about it. This bartender had called because he thought he recognized the priest from a picture."

"But he wasn't sure?"

"There wasn't a real up-to-date picture. This was back before we had pictures on drivers' licenses, remember. And people were changing their hairstyles, growing mutton-chops and beards and all that."

"When whiskers came to Bessemer," Marlee said. "I'm sorry, go ahead."

Delaney leaned forward in his chair, his eyes more intense than Marlee had ever seen them. "See, the memo about the bartender made more sense than anything else. It was really promising. If the priest was gay, he might have been trolling the night he was killed."

"Right."

"But there was no follow-up. None. The thing from the bartender was the only good lead in there, the only one. And to not follow up on it flies in the face of good detective work. It's so basic."

"But if there was a cover-up, why wouldn't the memo about the bartender have simply disappeared?"

Delaney smiled shrewdly. "It's one thing to screw up an investigation with stupid police work. Happens all the time, even when it isn't meant to. But to destroy something already in the file, that's something much more dangerous. And that's assuming whoever was covering up had access to the file. So I can understand why the note about the bartender stayed there."

"And if Ed Sperl saw the file?"

"Which we're sure he did. If he saw what I did, he'd have the same reaction."

Delaney and Marlee stared at each other for a minute. Ed tapped his fingers on the table.

"We're thinking the same thing," Delaney said. "When Sperl saw that, he'd know there'd been a cover-up."

Marlee nodded, tried as hard as she could to be coldly

objective. "God rest his soul," she said. "Ed Sperl drank right here in my house, and I'm sorry he's dead."

"But?"

"At his worst, he was a bum. If he found out something about someone—some secret—he might try to exploit it."

"What they call blackmail. I thought of that."

"And that would explain the money he was expecting. We know he wasn't writing a story for the *Gazette,* or a book, about this case, and as far as I know, he wasn't writing for one of those pulpy true-crime magazines. They don't pay that much anyhow." Marlee stopped; she had just thought of Grant Siebert and wondered how much to believe him, or how much to believe anyone.

"Let's figure Sperl was a greedy son of a bitch who tried to squeeze someone," Delaney said. "Trouble is, the person he tried to squeeze had killed once."

"And maybe killed again, killed Ed Sperl."

Delaney shrugged. "I've heard that killing gets easier after the first time."

"You've never killed anyone?"

"No." Delaney looked troubled.

"What is it, Ed?"

"I've thought now and then if my daughter would look at me the same way if I ever killed anyone."

"She, she'd know that you had done what you had to do."

"Mmmm. But getting back to topic A, I know what you said about your talk with the priest's father in Pennsylvania. But I still think the diocese could squelch something better than anyone else."

"Ed, I have something to tell you."

She told him everything she could remember about the meeting with the priest. She said she couldn't reveal the priest's name because he'd asked her not to, and she spoke only in a general way about how she and Jenifer had been introduced to the priest in the park.

"I'll be damned," Delaney said when Marlee was finished.

"But you told me an old cop said, 'This is a Catholic town.' That's what you remember him saying."

"Sure. And it is. We both grew up here." Delaney's face darkened. "That can mean so many things. Maybe the killer was another priest, or someone local with a lot of church influence. Or maybe it's simpler than that. Every March on the nearest Sunday to St. Patrick's Day there's a big communion breakfast for Irish cops. Priests and cops, cops and priests. True harps all, and very much intertwined. You want to complicate things more, I know a couple of cops who've gone into the priesthood over the years. For that matter, a cop friend of mine spent some time in a seminary."

Marlee had an itch in her brain. "This is all fine, Ed. But why now? If Ed was trying to squeeze someone and got killed for it, why now? And why his sudden interest in the old case? . . . Of course."

Delaney smiled thinly and nodded. "Until his untimely death, Ed Sperl was a curator of all things bright and beautiful about the reunion. Right? Suppose he was gathering nuggets about how people survived the great ice storm, which we think was the same night the priest got whacked."

"God, you mean it might have been someone who worked at the *Gazette*!"

Delaney chuckled. "You were telling me how there's been a parade of people who've gone through the *Gazette* over the years. Some left town, some stayed in town. We're talking about a lot of people."

"Dozens. Dozens. I've been to farewell parties as many times as I've been to the beach, almost. And it isn't just ex-*Gazette* people who came back for the reunion. We started twisting the arms of other people."

"We?"

"The reunion organizers, of which I was one, unofficially. Because the publisher and his Chamber of Commerce friends wanted it, we called other people. Oh, hell, we called some people who had no connection with the *Gazette*, just because we didn't want our own birthday party to be too small."

"And those people were asked to say where they'd been the night of the ice storm?"

"I guess," Marlee said. "Depending on whether Ed Sperl wanted to ask them."

"So. Assume, just assume for a moment, that Ed Sperl was gay and knew the gay scene around Bessemer. I can tell you from the time I spent on vice that it was a pretty small scene, and a quiet one. Ed might have known of someone trolling the night of the storm, someone who was gay and in the closet."

"Ed might have known," Marlee agreed. "And he might have picked up on it if that person didn't want to talk about that night. No one in his right mind would say anything to draw attention to himself if he'd killed someone that night."

"No. But suppose somebody just refused to go along, refused to be a good sport and say where he was that night."

"That would draw more suspicion," Marlee agreed.

"Not a bad theory, yes?"

"Well, yes. But the pictures Ed was looking at that time in my place, and the tape with the jokes on it, how do they fit into all this?"

"I never said I had all the answers. Could I have some more coffee?"

"Oh, sure. I have some time before I have to get ready for the dinner at the country club." For a fleeting moment, Marlee wished Ed Delaney were going there with her; she wondered if it showed on her face.

"Those pictures Sperl was interested in, who took them?"

"Arnie Schwartz, the *Gazette*'s chief photographer for a long time. He used to take them just to be nice. He's dead now."

"God, isn't everybody. Do me a favor. Let me take those pictures with me, okay? I know I looked at them once, but what the hell. If Sperl was intent on them, maybe I should be, too."

"Sure, Ed. Be right back."

Marlee got her picture box from the corner of the closet in the hall. Then she glanced at the clock: almost three. If she called the vet right away, she might get one of the doctors or a nurse before they left for the weekend.

"Excuse me just for a minute, Ed," she said, handing Delaney the pictures. Then she went into her bedroom and dialed the veterinarian. A woman answered.

"It's Marlee West. I own that sick Airedale, Nigel. Just calling to be sure he's okay."

"Hi, this is Dr. Grimm. You betcha he is. He had a tiny bit of discomfort in his last bowel movement, but that's not abnormal. I'm not really concerned, but I would like to keep him until Monday, as I said."

"That's fine. Just give him a hug for me."

"Will do. I'll be checking on him tomorrow, too. Not to worry."

"Thanks. Bye."

When Marlee returned to the living room, Delaney was on his feet. "Have a good time tonight," he said.

"Oh, I'll try."

"I think there's a good chance that if the priest killer is still around, he'll keep a low profile."

"That would be good. I think. God, what a thing to live with."

"Maybe Ed Sperl wouldn't let him."

"Oh! What about his ex, Olga? Is she safe?"

Delaney frowned. "I was afraid you'd ask that. For now, probably. Maybe for good, if she stays far away. Thanks for the coffee."

Thirty-two

▲▲▲

Feeling uncharacteristically dapper in a pale blue seersucker suit Karen had picked out for him, Will walked across the parking lot of the Bessemer Country Club with his wife on his arm. The rain had rinsed the air, left it smelling like mint.

"Be sensible tonight," Karen said.

"That's my trouble. I'm always sensible."

"Yes, but you had some beer playing golf and you were singing in the shower. Remember?"

"Vaguely."

Will halted under a tree that hung over the lot and that offered the last measure of seclusion before they would go inside.

"What?" Karen said.

"This is almost over, this birthday nonsense. And there's still some summer left for us to sit on the deck and look at the lake. Do I sound like a fool?"

"Of course. How many beers *did* you have?"

"Just three, I think. One on the course while it rained. Then two more in the clubhouse, talking with Grant Siebert and some of the other guys."

295

"Then you had four all told, because you had one in the shower."

"Oh. Okay. But you should have seen Lyle. Didn't have much more than I did, but he was pretty close to plastered. And all day he was on the ass of this young banker."

"Shhh! Now don't forget to pace yourself, Will."

And then they were inside in the music and babble of the country club, with its new paint and new carpeting and reupholstered furniture.

"So," Will said. "Let's mingle."

"Okay, we'll mingle," Karen said. "Just don't mingle too much with the gin and tonic."

Will spotted Archangelo Grisanti. "Arkie! What did you shoot?"

"A ninety-two."

"Too bad, Arkie. You didn't even break ninety. Get it? Oh, and thanks for building that shelter over by the thirteenth. It kept me dry."

Karen and Will moved on, toward the bar at the end of the room.

"What was that all about?" Karen asked.

"Tell you later. Oops."

Will felt a warning pressure on his arm; Karen had spotted the publisher before Will had.

"Will," Lyle Glanford, Sr. said. "Isn't this grand?"

"Indeed, sir."

"The product of the work of a lot of good men—and women!"

Will saw Karen smile grudgingly at the forced gallantry laced with sexism.

"Did you have a good round, Will?"

"Well, Lyle, let's say I had fun."

"I have to confess I took a motor cart for the last few holes. Too bad about the rain interruption."

"Oh, I don't know. Lyle and I sat in the shelter over by thirteen and had some beer with Grant Siebert. You remember him; he worked for us in the early seventies."

"Yes. Well, I'll be seeing you later at the table, Will. Right now I'm trying to find my son."

Will noticed a tightness around the publisher's mouth that always indicated anger.

"Ah, me," Will whispered to Karen. "He's pissed at Lyle junior for something. I know it."

"Don't let yourself get stuck in any baby-sitting or mediation role," Karen said quietly.

Good advice, Will thought. He ordered a gin and tonic for himself and a white wine for Karen. "You have to admit, the place looks a lot better," he said.

"A lot better. Of course, there aren't that many people in Bessemer who can come here to see it, but who cares?"

"Pretty snooty attitude if you ask me. Hi, Marlee."

"Hi, Will. How are you Karen?"

"Hi, Marlee," Karen said.

"You look terrific."

"Oh, thanks."

"I just hope the food's good," Will said. "Hi, Grant. You look like you recovered from golf. You remember my wife, Karen."

"Sure. Hello." Grant smiled uncomfortably as he sipped a beer and sidled up next to Marlee.

"Hi, Grant," Karen said. "I understand you and Will had fun today."

"It was fun," Grant said. "You wouldn't know it to see me play, but I really did practice."

"Hey, you weren't that bad!" Will said. "Never mind the score. You hit a lot of good shots. We all did!"

"Will is feeling very expansive tonight," Karen said. "He's ready for another round of golf. And another round of something else."

"Why not?" Will said. Then he saw Lyle Glanford, Jr., approaching, drink in hand. "Hi, Lyle. This is it, buddy. We're all done. If the food is no good, they can't blame us."

"I got news for you," Lyle junior said. "My father can find ways to blame me for everything."

"Ah, you did a hell of a job. So did I. And you, Marlee. And Grant, thanks for coming all this way." Will touched Grant's glass with his own.

"Fine," Grant said. He smiled but did not let down his reserve.

The conversational group was held together for a few minutes by talk of who was sitting where. Will and Karen were sitting at the publisher's table, as were Lyle junior, a couple of other *Gazette* executives, and the head of the Chamber of Commerce. Marlee was sitting close by, with Jenifer, some other reporters and middle-level editors, and a businessman she didn't know.

"How about you, Grant?" Karen said.

"Table thirteen," Grant said. "I didn't recognize any of the names."

They talked for a few more minutes before the people in the group spun off and attached to other groups. Then Will and Karen were more or less alone.

"He's shy," Karen said.

"Who?" Will said.

"Your friend from New York. He's shy."

"Grant? I can't believe it. He always had an ego big enough to fill the whole newsroom. And he's not exactly my friend, although we did play golf."

"He could be your friend. And he is shy."

Will thought about that. Karen was usually on the mark.

The publisher's table was among the first to be served, and Will and Karen wound up with good pink cuts of beef. Lyle junior was on the other side of the table.

Will took only an occasional sip of Bordeaux during the meal.

"Old dad, this is a little bit of all right," Lyle junior said to his father, who answered his son with silence and a cold glint in his eye. "More than all right. Don't you agree, Will?"

"Sure," Will said.

The president of the Bessemer Chamber of Commerce

was at the dais now, looking serious and self-conscious. He tapped a spoon against a water glass, and a number of diners did the same to signal for quiet. Lyle junior also struck his water glass, so hard that Will thought it might break and shower water and glass all over the table.

"May I have . . . may I have your attention, please," the Chamber president said over the gradually receding noise. "Please, thank you. I know some of you haven't finished your meals, but we'd like to get started. We have some announcements to make and some awards to give out."

"Whoopee!" Lyle junior said.

Will turned his head toward his wife to hide his laugh.

"The sooner we're done with these formalities," the Chamber president said, "the sooner we can commence a night of dancing and . . ."

"Commence?" Lyle junior said. "Did he really say 'commence'?"

". . . of you have come a very long way to be here. You know, in my position I meet a lot of people, and I can tell you that even those who leave Bessemer always carry part of it with them . . ."

"In their lungs," Lyle junior said quietly. "And they still leave."

". . . happy to report that our prayers to the gods of golf were answered, so that we were able to complete all rounds despite the rain . . ."

Will looked around the room, nodding and smiling when he saw faces he knew.

". . . too many people, really, to thank by name, but a couple of people I do want to single out. Archangelo Grisanti, are you out there . . . ?"

Will spotted Marlee West, and they exchanged smiles. Then Will, quite by chance, found himself looking into the eyes of Jenifer Hurley, who was sitting right next to Marlee. Jenifer smiled at Will, who thought she had the most lovely teeth in the world. Jenifer, Will said to himself, that bastard

Arkie Grisanti said something crude about you, but I stuck it right back down his throat. . . .

"She's too young for you, Will," Karen whispered in his ear.

"Hmmm?" Will tried to pretend he didn't understand, but it was no good; his face was hot.

". . . and, of course, the publisher of the *Bessemer Gazette*, our great home-owned newspaper whose ninetieth birthday we are marking this summer . . . Lyle Glanford! Please stand, Lyle."

The publisher stood, to applause, and Will held his breath, praying that Lyle junior would not pick this, of all moments, to do something irreparably stupid. The applause and the moment faded peacefully, and the publisher sat down.

"I'm happy for you, Dad," Lyle junior said to his father, patting him respectfully on the back.

"Thanks, Son." The elder Glanford's patrician face softened a little.

". . . time to announce a few awards from the golf tournament . . ."

By now, a few diners were tiptoeing away from the tables. Will figured he, too, would head to the rest room soon, if only to stretch his legs.

Will saw Lyle junior get up, excuse himself quietly, and move toward the main corridor. On the way Lyle crossed paths with Grant Siebert, whose smile seemed strained. Together, they walked out of the dining room.

". . . low round of the day was turned in by Jim Powell of Bessemer Trust. Jim shot a seventy-seven, ladies and gentlemen, and let me tell you, that's not bad considering the rain delay . . ."

The banker, several tables away, smiled broadly. Will was happy for him, and happy that he could accept his honor without hazing from Lyle junior.

". . . oldest golfer was Warner Winters of Winters and Sons Appliance Store. Warner is seventy-nine years young, folks, and I wish I could tell you his score matched his age."

Laughter and applause.

"You didn't win anything?" Karen asked, a tease in her voice.

"Only if they give prizes for survival," Will said.

". . . how we appreciate those of you who did think enough of Bessemer to come back, and we do thank you. I can't name everybody, but I see Charlie Buck from Milwaukee, Grant Siebert from New York City . . ."

Will looked toward Grant's table; he wasn't back yet. Too bad.

". . . prize, it wouldn't be fair to award it on the basis of low score. Sorry, Jim Powell. So we had a drawing. Anyhow, our grand prize of a new set of Jack Nicklaus golf clubs goes to . . . Archangelo Grisanti!"

"Isn't that the man you spoke to on the way in?" Karen whispered to Will.

"Yep. Life is unfair."

". . . you'll just bear with me a little longer, folks, I am just about done. Honest. I would like at this time to pay tribute to members who are no longer with us . . ."

Will spotted a middle-aged woman dressed in a club uniform. She was threading her way through the tables, clearly looking for a certain table number, or a certain person. After a few moments, she headed straight for the table where Marlee sat. Will saw the woman bend over and say something into Marlee's ear.

Marlee's face went white. The woman went away, and Marlee leaned over to Jenifer, who put her hand on Marlee's arm and said something. Marlee smiled weakly, shook her head no, and stood up. Still pale and biting her lower lip, she walked to the exit.

I wonder what that's all about, Will thought.

I just never thought it would happen this soon, Marlee thought. By the time she went through the main door out to the cooling night, her eyes were filling with tears.

"Stupid, stupid, stupid," she said. She was cursing herself for giving her heart to a dog, cursing the dog for deciding tonight was a good night to die.

The Bessemer Animal Medical Center hadn't put it quite that way, but that was the meaning in the message the club attendant had delivered: "Your veterinarian says Nigel has taken a turn for the worse, and you should come as soon as you can."

The air outside the country club smelled faintly of cooked beef, and she could hear a microphone voice as she walked through the parking lot. She was parked near the end, and by the time she reached her car, she could smell the wet grass of the golf course.

Do I want him to wait to die, wait until I get there? Yes; yes, I do. Please, God, I want to be with him so he's not afraid.

Damn the doctors. You promised he'd be all right, Marlee thought. No, of course they hadn't promised. They never did. But they had said there was no reason to worry. Oh, Nigel.

The Animal Medical Center was way over on the other side of the city. Even taking the Ambrose Parkway, it was a good half-hour ride. Marlee drove right at the speed limit, deliberately putting all her concentration into handling the car. If she started sobbing over that stupid dog, she wouldn't be able to see.

Marlee took the exit too fast, cheated on a couple of lights, floored it the rest of the way to the animal hospital. The lot was empty except for a single car near the side entrance, which was lighted.

"Please," she said aloud. "Hang on, Nigel. I'm coming to say good-bye."

Marlee allowed herself one sob, got ahold of herself, and pressed the buzzer. She expected one of the doctors to appear. Instead, a white-haired security guard opened the door. "We're closed, miss," he said.

"I'm Marlee West, goddammit! You called me to say my dog is dying."

"Gee, miss, I don't know anything about that. Come in."

"Look, somebody from here called and said I should get over here right away because Nigel, my Airedale—"

"Nigel! Oh, hell of a nice dog. He was okay last I checked."

"Then who . . . ?"

"Was it a man or woman who called, because the duty doctor for emergencies tonight—"

"I don't know. I mean, the message was delivered to me at the country club."

The security guard looked puzzled.

"Can I sit down?" Marlee said.

"Miss, I think someone with a sick sense of humor just played a rotten joke on you."

"Do me a favor. Go check on my dog right now."

"Sure."

Marlee sat in the half-light by the guard's table. The man had been watching a small black-and-white TV set and drinking from a thermos of coffee.

She heard metallic noises of gates opening and closing. The sounds seemed farther away than they were. Then barking: a big dog, little dog, medium dog. Then the guard's voice, barely audible, making kindly "hush" sounds.

The guard returned. "Your dog couldn't be better, miss. I can take you back there to see for yourself, if you'd like."

For a moment, Marlee was tempted. "No, he'd just get all excited when he saw me and miserable if I didn't take him home."

"Rotten, dirty joke."

Marlee was thinking.

"My folks, they had an Airedale when I was a boy. Major, we called him. Saw him kill four rats in the blink of an eye once."

"Can I use your phone?" Marlee said.

Grant could not remember the last time he had been so afraid. He had desperately hoped to surprise her, catch her alone. Tonight might be his last chance, unless he hung around Bessemer another day or two. Well, maybe I should, he thought. Then, another inner voice said no, that was no good. He had planned things a certain way. It had taken all his determination to go this far; he couldn't change things.

He had had only a couple of drinks at the banquet, hadn't stayed for the dancing (who wanted to dance?), because he had to stay as calm as possible, do this thing right.

Grant was sitting in a car on the street where Marlee West lived. He was parked about a block away, on the opposite side of the street, in the shadow provided by a huge evergreen. The butterflies in his stomach made him feel like a teenager, only this nervousness was far worse. Well, he had committed himself. There was no turning back.

He had found Marlee's address easily enough, had driven around the block twice to be sure he was right, then had parked quietly under the tree. Was he ready? He didn't know.

He unwound the car window, breathed deep of the smell of lawns and trees on a summer night. Despite those smells, he could detect the scent of his own nervous perspiration. Would she be able to smell him before he—?

No, no, no. Don't think about that. God damn you anyhow. God *damn* you.

Grant wondered if the people in the darkened houses were more happy than he was. He thought they were. How could they not be? Sometimes he thought the whole world must be happier than he was. And why was that? Was it his fault he was carrying a bigger load of sorrow?

"Stop it," he hissed to himself. "Stop it. Okay?"

Okay, another inner voice answered, but tentatively.

Grant swallowed hard. He would do it, do what he had to do, finish business that had been bothering him for twenty years. He would find Marlee West alone and . . .

Why should the thought of it terrify him so? It shouldn't be that hard.

Over the years, he had tried to tell himself there was no

reason to be bothered by the pictures and the tape recording that reminded him of his days in Bessemer. But they had bothered him, reminded him of the unfinished business. He had been tempted time and again to throw out the pictures and tape, but he hadn't. Why? Maybe he wanted to be reminded.

And here he was, crouching in a car on a dark suburban street. Stalking Marlee West. Where the hell was she?

Headlights from behind? Grant sank as low as he could into the seat, praying he was invisible. Was the other car slowing down beside him? It seemed to be.

The light went away. Slowly, Grant raised his head. The car was just a little ahead of him, moving slowly. When it went under a streetlight, he saw the unmistakable shape of a shield over the license plate. Cop!

His heart beat wildly. Grant watched the car cruise slowly past Marlee's house, then turn a corner and disappear.

Grant's fingers trembled as he turned the ignition key. He drove slowly down the street, pausing in front of Marlee's house. Dark. Then he saw a light in the window of the house next door and, just before the light disappeared, the silhouette of a woman looking out at the street.

In a fresh rush of panic, Grant pushed the accelerator down. He cursed himself all the way back to the motel. He had left the business unfinished.

After Marlee turned the corner, she saw the car parked in her driveway, saw a man with a familiar shape standing on her neighbor's lighted porch.

Marlee parked in front of her house, recognized the man talking to Mrs. Wemple, felt tears of relief come to her eyes.

"Ed!" Without thinking about it, Marlee rushed across her lawn to Delaney and put her arms around him. Quietly, she began to cry.

"It's okay, Marlee. Everything's fine. You did the smart thing."

"But why you, Ed? I mean, when I called the police, I didn't mean for you to be bothered."

"I know, I know. I left instructions that I wanted to be called if you needed help."

"Oh. Thank you."

"My pleasure. Too many funny things have been happening."

"Mr. Delaney told me what happened, Marlee," Mrs. Wemple said. "You know, I'm a night person, and I've been kind of keeping an eye on your house ever since you had that prowler. And tonight, sure enough, I saw a strange car. If Mr. Delaney hadn't shown up when he did, I was all set to call the police."

"That's so nice, Mrs. Wemple. Thank you."

"You were smart, Marlee," Delaney said.

"Oh, I don't feel that smart. But when I got to the animal hospital and found the call was fake, I had to wonder. The guard said it was a rotten joke."

"I think it was more than that," Delaney said.

"You know," Mrs. Wemple said animatedly, "my sister-in-law's neighbor's house was burglarized while they were attending a funeral. Can you imagine such a thing! And she said the police told her about a family that went away for a weekend and came back to find their house empty! All the furniture gone! And they found out that a young boy who worked at a gas station down the street was working with the burglars. He would find out who was going on trips, because the people would bring their cars in for checkups."

"Let's go inside, Marlee."

"Thank you again, Mrs. Wemple. I'm your friend for life."

"Oh, you're so very welcome. We have to watch out for each other. One other thing, Officer?"

"Yes?"

"I don't know how much it helps you, but I think I got the first two letters on the license plate of the car I saw."

Marlee sat in the living room while Delaney went through the house, checking all the windows and doors.

"Everything looks fine," he said. "There'll be a patrol unit close by tonight, believe me. But I don't think you have to worry."

"I won't. Not now. This is so baffling."

"Baffling, yes. But think about it. Whoever did this—"

"Knew I had a sick dog at the vet. So if they could keep me away from the house for just a little while, they wouldn't have to worry about me or my dog. I know."

"More than that, Marlee. Whoever left that message for you at the club knew where you'd be."

"Well, God only knows how many people that includes. And not just people I work with. A whole bunch of people who came back for the *Gazette*'s anniversary heard me talking about my dog."

"So then we've got a whole load of people who could have left a message for you tonight. But see, there's probably only one person who'd have any reason to."

"Yes."

"You know what I'm going to say."

"Not exactly. But I know this craziness all started after Ed Sperl was here for my party that night. And then he got interested—and I got interested—in that old killing. And now he's dead. God, this is all so crazy."

"Strange, but not crazy. There's a reason as sure as we're sitting here. Ed Sperl knew something about the priest's death, or thought he did. Or was getting close. And he was real interested in old pictures and tapes."

"They're just pictures and tapes of people getting drunk or stoned, and giving other people fond farewells."

"No, think. They're more than that. If the killer from twenty years ago had a connection with the *Gazette* . . ."

"God in heaven, there's a clue of some kind in the pictures. Or on a tape. Or both."

"You tape-recorded all the farewell parties?"

"Well, most. At least for a while, till the routine got kind of old. After a while it seemed kind of silly."

"And how many of the tapes had stuff on them about the priest?"

"Well, Grant Siebert's, as I said. Maybe some others later. Oh, God. He's here. Grant. For the reunion."

"All right. Damn, the pictures you gave me are at my place. Look, why don't you invite me to the publisher's brunch tomorrow. As your guest. You can do that, right?"

"Oh. Sure I can. Spouses and friends welcome."

"Good. Maybe our guy will be there. Who knows? And I just want to get the feel of things."

"All right. Dress casually."

"Sure. We'll go, drink some of Glanford's Bloody Marys. And we'll listen to tapes and study pictures."

"My friend Jenifer will be there. She's a terrific young reporter who's been working with me on this."

"Well, okay. But I'm playing close to the vest with everyone but you."

"Ed, what about the license-plate number Mrs. Wemple saw?"

"With just those two letters, *RK*, it doesn't help much. There could be a hundred thousand cars . . . God, am I stupid."

"What?"

"Those are two letters for downstate cars, close to New York. Yep, it's worth a try."

"What is?"

"Think as hard as you can, then write down the names of people you know who used to work at the *Gazette* and moved to the New York area."

"To New York? There aren't that many who moved to New York. There's Grant Siebert, but he doesn't own a car, he told me."

"Then how'd he get here?"

"He flew. Oh, and he rented a car when he got here."

"All right. There's only so many car-rental places in Bessemer. Maybe he got one right at the airport."

"God, I don't want it to be him."

Delaney gave her a hard look.

"I know," Marlee said. "The truth is the truth, no matter what."

"I'm sure as hell not saying it's him, Marlee. Damned if I know. There could be a bunch of people who rented cars. I can do a check early in the morning before I pick you up."

"Fine. Don't eat much for breakfast. There'll be plenty of food."

"Good. Listen, it would be good if all your doors and windows were locked, even though there is going to be a police car nearby."

"All right."

Delaney said good-night. It was a long time before Marlee got to sleep.

Thirty-three

▲▲▲

What will you be looking for?" Marlee asked as Ed Delaney parked at the end of a row of cars in front of Lyle Glanford's mansion.

"Oh, I don't know." That was partly a lie: he would be looking for anyone who seemed to want to single out Marlee, or ask her too many questions about when she'd be home and when she wouldn't.

"I forgot there were houses like this," Delaney said.

"Yep. He's rich and we're not."

The Glanford mansion sat like a brick castle atop a huge, gently sloping lawn. Ed started counting the windows to guess the number of rooms but quickly gave up.

"I was inside once years ago for a Christmas party," Marlee said. "The house is even bigger than it looks from here."

The mansion was on a winding wooded road that, Delaney knew, was always well patrolled by the police. The other houses in the neighborhood were also large (though Delaney thought Glanford's was the biggest), and their owners came from Bessemer's old-money dynasties of steel, shipping, banking. The dynasties were aging (some would say decaying), but people in the houses still wielded influence and power—some more gracefully than others.

All of which made Delaney uncomfortable. Though he resisted it, he could not entirely shed the feeling that he didn't belong at any party given by someone rich enough to own such a house. And that kind of diffidence was incompatible with the instincts of a good cop.

Okay, he had shoved his feelings aside before; he would do it again.

They walked up a white-gravel driveway that ended at the entrance to a three-car garage and a sign that said FOLLOW THE WALK TO THE RIGHT AND AROUND THE CORNER. The sign was unnecessary because music and barbecue smells were in the air.

"Oh, well. It doesn't hurt to daydream once in a while," Delaney said. He surprised himself, letting down his guard. There was something about Marlee . . .

"I'm sorry I wasn't more help a while ago," she said.

"Nothing to be sorry for."

"I really did look hard at all the pictures from old parties. All I saw was a bunch of memories, some better than others."

"I know. I know."

"I promise to listen to the tapes again later. I just couldn't handle it this morning."

"On an empty stomach? I can't blame you."

"Well, did you find anything, anything at all, in the pictures and tapes?"

"No," Delaney said. "But a lot of detective work is going over the same ground again. Sometimes something that was there all along all of a sudden becomes clear. Sometimes."

Sometimes, Marlee thought.

They turned the last corner of the garage and came to a backyard half the size of a football field. It was flanked by tall evergreens, and at the far end was a white picket fence with a gate that, Marlee knew, led to a long set of steps going down to the beach. Above the picket fence was a clear, unobstructed view of Lake Erie, which glimmered in the late-morning sun.

Off to the left, near one row of evergreens, was a wooden stand where the white-coated musicians sat, playing tunes that had been popular in the forties and fifties. To the right, near the other row of evergreens, was a long orange tent.

Underneath, uniformed cooks tended grills and barbecue pits covered with sizzling wieners, sausage, and chicken. Beyond the large tent was another, only slightly smaller, with long tables covered with pitchers of tomato and orange juice and trays of limes, lemons, and cherries.

"Marlee! Welcome." The publisher had seen her and Ed and was walking toward them, smiling graciously. He wore white flannel pants and a pale blue sport shirt and looked at once casual and elegant.

"I'm happy to be here, Mr. Glanford. I'd like you to meet a friend, Ed Delaney."

"A pleasure, Mr. Delaney. Any friend of Marlee's is a friend of ours. Welcome!"

"Thank you, sir. I'm glad to be here."

"Well, then. Good. Make yourselves at home here. We certainly are fortunate with the weather, don't you think?"

"Yes, sir," Delaney said. "Not too hot." Got to stop saying "sir," Delaney told himself.

"Right. Good. You're among the early arrivals, so chow down and have fun."

"We will, Mr. Glanford. Thanks."

Delaney put food on his plate, leaving enough space to put a cup of black coffee in one corner so he could carry a Bloody Mary. Marlee got a smaller serving. Then they walked around the yard, which was already more crowded than when they'd arrived.

"Hi, folks," Marlee said to Will and Karen Shafer, who nodded and waved. Will was wearing dark glasses.

"Who's that?" Delaney said.

"The executive editor and his wife. Will Shafer's his name. Good guy."

"He been at the *Gazette* a long time?"

"Oh, yes. Longer than I have. Why?"

"Just curious. Was he at that party for what's his name way back then?"

"Grant Siebert's party. Yes, Will was there."

"You're sure?"

"Sure I'm sure. Some things you remember like they were yesterday. Will and I were talking at the bar together before Grant arrived. Will was there, absolutely."

"Mmmm."

The band struck up an old-fashioned arrangement of "Happy Days Are Here Again." Ed and Marlee were out near the end of the yard, looking toward the shimmering lake.

"Beautiful, isn't it?" she said.

"Yeah. Do you remember anything else about that party? Anyone there who didn't belong, who got unusually drunk or stoned and might have said or did something, something . . . I don't know. Something."

"Well, me." Marlee laughed. "I was stoned near the end."

"Other than you?"

"A lot of people were drunk and stoned. Ed, what about the license-plate check?"

"Inconclusive." Delaney was shading the truth. A check had shown that Grant Siebert had indeed rented a car at Bessemer Airport with a plate number beginning *RK*. But several other people had rented cars with those two letters.

And even if the car seen by Marlee's neighbor, Mrs. Wemple, was Grant Siebert's—so what? The location of the motel where Siebert was staying might—might—have made it logical for him to drive near Marlee's home.

And even if it was Siebert in the car, and even if he was hanging around Marlee's house, that wasn't illegal. There was nothing to arrest him on—nothing even to question him on.

Delaney and Marlee walked slowly back toward the house.

"What's behind those big bushes?" Delaney said.

"Patio and swimming pool. In the summer, Mr. Glanford and his wife sleep in the downstairs bedroom, which opens up right onto the pool area."

"Why the hell do they have a pool when they have their own private beach?"

Marlee laughed. "Because he's Lyle Glanford, and he inherited the only newspaper in town, and he's rich."

"You say they sleep in the room by the pool in the summer. What about the winter?"

"Their upstairs bedroom has a fireplace."

"Figures. Hey, who's that?"

"That's my reporter friend Jenifer Hurley. I'll introduce you. Hi, Jenifer."

"Hi, Marlee. Oh, hi."

"I'm Ed Delaney."

"Jenifer Hurley. Nice to meet you."

Marlee could tell that Ed was struck by the loveliness of Jenifer, who had on light green shorts and a yellow sleeveless top. She knows yellow is a good color for her, Marlee thought.

"Marlee, what happened to make you rush out like that last night?" Jenifer said.

"God, you wouldn't believe," Marlee said.

As Marlee told Jenifer about the bogus call and how she had rushed from the club to the veterinarian, Delaney took alternating sips of coffee and Bloody Mary and studied the crowd.

Delaney recognized some of the faces just from watching Bessemer television news: Chamber of Commerce people, banking people, redevelopment people, hospital trustees. The categories overlapped.

Oh, for God's sake: there was the mayor. Delaney felt an almost instinctive shiver of nervousness, for the mayor—any mayor—had the power to make life miserable for any cop. Delaney was glad he was wearing dark glasses. There was a good chance the mayor would stay only a little while and wouldn't recognize him. Not that Delaney was doing anything wrong by being at the Glanford brunch; it was just that, since he had never been good at department politics, he preferred to attract as little attention as possible from politicians.

Dozens of people were swarming over the lawn now, with more arriving by the minute. What's a party like this cost? Delaney wondered. Five thousand bucks? Ten?

Delaney counted several city councilmen, a few school board members, a captain in the Bessemer Coast Guard unit. Lyle Glanford, Sr., received them all graciously, with a broad smile if not a warm one. Also paying homage were the Episcopal bishop of Bessemer, a Catholic auxiliary bishop, a rabbi, a heart surgeon.

"What do you think?" Jenifer demanded of Delaney.

"Huh?"

"What do you think about what happened to Marlee last night?"

"We can't rule out a sick joke," Delaney said. "I mean, Marlee writes a feminist column, and there are a lot of male chauvinists left in Bessemer."

"Bullshit," Marlee said quietly.

"Amen," Jenifer said.

"Okay," Delaney said. "I agree. A joke is only a remote possibility. What I think is, somebody thinks you know something, Marlee. Or more accurately, thinks your old pictures and tape recordings are dangerous for some reason. Why is beyond me. So far."

A thought had been forming in Marlee's head; now it crystallized with chilling clarity. "The prowler. That was after my party."

"Yeah," Delaney said. "That occurred to me, too. Now this thing last night."

"Then it must be someone right in Bessemer," Marlee said.

"Not necessarily," Jenifer said. "Bessemer's got an airport and plenty of good roads in and out."

"Over there," Marlee whispered to Delaney. "Shaking hands with the publisher. That's Grant Siebert."

"Glad to be here, sir," Grant said.

"Our pleasure, Graham. Darling, this is Graham Siebert. He used to work for the newspaper."

"How do you do, Graham?"

"Fine, thanks. Lovely place here."

"Do you have family here, Graham?"

"No, sir. My father's in real estate and development and such. He mostly does business quite a bit east of here, over near Syracuse."

The patrician bearing of Lyle Glanford, Sr., and the see-through stare of his wife made Grant so uncomfortable that he didn't feel like correcting their pronunciation of his name. Besides, he was still angry at himself for having failed the night before.

"Say, Grant. How're you feeling this morning?" Lyle Glanford, Jr., said. "Better than I am, I hope."

"Not bad, all things considered."

"Care for a little hair of the dog? Bloody Mary?"

"That sounds good."

Delaney had deliberately separated himself from Marlee and Jenifer. He was sure they had things to say that they wouldn't say in front of him, and he wanted to be far enough away from Marlee to study people looking at her. He walked a few feet away, pretending to look out toward the lake. But behind his dark glasses, his eyes were darting this way and that. Grant Siebert seemed to be looking in the direction of Marlee and Jenifer. So did the editor—Will Shafer?—for that matter.

Delaney finished his food, got another Bloody Mary, tried to pick up snippets of conversation and arrange his thoughts at the same time. Somebody, something. What?

". . . should have seen Harry on the fourteenth. He put

three balls in the water. Brand new Titleists, they were. Plop, plop, plop . . ."

". . . you and me, I counted three shots he took just getting out of the sand, so don't tell me he had a six on that hole . . ."

". . . Arkie Grisanti, that son of a bitch, winds up with a new set of Nicklaus clubs. I coulda cried when they announced it . . ."

"Ed, do you want to just kind of walk around the yard some more. I hope you're not bored."

"Huh? Oh, no. I'm not bored. Yeah, let's walk around some more."

As they meandered around the great lawn, Ed Delaney was startled to find that he was holding Marlee's hand. He liked the feeling.

"Do you have any new thoughts?" she said.

"Yeah. I don't mean to alarm you, but I don't think you should be alone tonight."

Marlee stopped abruptly and stared at him.

"Think about it, Marlee. The prowler. Last night. If it is the pictures or something about one of your farewell tapes, whoever wants them will probably assume you still have them. Right?"

"Yes. It does me no good even if you have them for safekeeping, does it? All right, I'll pack a little bag and—"

"Why don't I just stay at your place tonight? Don't worry, I'm not making a come-on."

"I didn't think that. Besides, I'm a big girl. But what about your daughter?"

"She's got a slumber party at a friend's house. It's settled, then."

"Thanks, Ed. Do you think he, whoever, might . . ."

"Honestly? I don't know. Probably what's most likely to happen is . . . nothing. Then your paper's birthday party dissolves and everybody goes home."

"And we never find the answer." Which is maybe how it's supposed to be, Marlee thought.

They were out near the picket fence that lined the bluff overlooking the lake. Marlee thought she saw something on the horizon, and she took off her dark glasses to be sure. Yes, purple clouds way, way out there. It might be many hours, but more rain was coming.

"Listen, I wanted to apologize for yesterday."

"Nothing to apologize for," Grant said.

"You're being kind," Lyle Glanford, Jr. said. "I should remember I can't handle the booze the way I used to."

"Who the hell can?"

"Ain't that the truth." Lyle laughed. "Anyhow, I'm gonna find that banker fella and make amends. I think I was rude to him."

"He'll get over it."

"Listen, I'm really glad we played golf," Lyle said. "There's so much crap connected with having the last name Glanford that it's nice to be able to relate one-on-one without the bullshit. Know what I mean?"

"I think so."

"Here, let me get you a refill."

"I think I'll switch to gin and tonic."

"You got it. Coming up."

Grant liked Lyle, especially in contrast to the pompous Lyle senior. "You seem a little less, uh, formal than your father," Grant said.

Lyle junior guffawed. "My old man was born with spats on, for God's sake."

Grant laughed. "Is there any guy who doesn't have trouble getting along with his old man somewhere along the line?"

"Nope. Listen, I get down to New York fairly often. My old man sends me on errands. You and I'll get together. Yes?"

"Sounds good. Sure."

"Are you having a good time?" Karen Shafer said.

"Sure," Will said. "You?"

"Better than you, probably. You seem distracted."

"Oh, I am a little."

"Do you know why? And can you tell me?"

Yes and no, Will thought. "A letdown, maybe. I had a decent time last night, and I enjoyed the golf, all things considered. Something about golf always makes me . . . Hell, I don't know." There's a limit to what I can share with my wife, Will thought.

Then he reminded himself that he had a session with the psychiatrist scheduled for the next morning, early. The time was a change from his usual slot. The doctor was getting ready to go on vacation.

The crowd on the great lawn was starting to thin.

"Had enough?" Marlee said.

"Yep," Ed said. "I've had my fill of Bloody Marys, and I don't want to start drinking beer."

"Learn anything?"

"I don't know. Here comes your friend."

Jenifer Hurley drew the appreciative glances of the remaining men, including those in clerical garb, as she walked over to Marlee and Delaney.

"It was nice meeting you, Ed. We'll talk tomorrow, Marlee." Jenifer started to go, then turned and said, "Did you ever see such a concentration of power? I think anybody who's anybody was here today. Or at least sent someone."

Marlee and Ed stopped at his house. His daughter was at her friend's home already, and Ed stayed inside just long enough to retrieve Marlee's tapes, recorder, and pictures.

At her place, they watched television for a while and flipped through the Sunday paper. Marlee said no to listening to the tapes, said no to looking at the pictures again.

"They won't tell me anything, Ed."

Earlier than usual, she went to bed, feeling safe with a cop (not just any cop, she acknowledged to herself) in the house, looking forward to going back to work the next day. So much had happened: seeing Grant Siebert (she had hardly talked to him at the publisher's brunch) and wondering how he fit into her life, if he did; meeting the priest in the park; the dirty rotten trick about Nigel. Ah, Nigel. She would see him tomorrow.

Marlee slept.

Delaney quietly shifted the sofa around so that he could sleep with his head toward the back of the house. He didn't expect any intruders during the night—not with his and Marlee's cars out front—but he still placed his revolver on the floor where he could reach down and grasp it in an instant.

For a few minutes he studied the pictures Marlee had given him. No, nothing. They told him nothing. Of course not; he hadn't been there. Marlee had: there she was, looking a lot younger. And kind of pretty—not prettier, pretty.

There was something there, in the pictures and tapes, something that should have been harmless. What?

Delaney listened one more time to the tape with the dead-priest jokes. He kept the volume low, and he impatiently fast-forwarded. To hell with it; he had heard enough for tonight. If there was something there, it wasn't coming through.

He lay down, surprised at how tired he felt. He was glad he had gone to the publisher's place with Marlee; Ed Delaney, cop and true harp, getting a glimpse of how the rich and famous lived. Had it done any good to go there? Probably not. No one had come up to Marlee and asked her anything to arouse suspicion. Ah, maybe that meant whoever it was was a local and recognized him as a cop. Could that be?

Ed thought about that. Maybe that made sense. Bessemer was a small town in some ways.

Drowsy, he tried to replay the day in his mind: pause here, fast-forward there. For a moment, he thought there were words and images he wanted to dwell on. But he wasn't sure why, and before he could sort things out, he was in oblivion.

Thirty-four

▲▲▲

Dr. Hopkins smiled wisely through the aromatic cloud of pipe smoke. "So you survived the reunion and even managed to have some enjoyment."

"I did, yes."

"And now it's back to work on a rainy Monday morning." The doctor glanced at his open window. Raindrops hung like jewels on the evergreens just outside. "I appreciate your coming outside of your regular appointment hour, Will. It's true what they say about therapists—we do go away for August—and I thought it was essential that we talk today."

"Where are you going? For vacation?"

"Bird-watching, Will."

"I always figured you for a swinger." Will laughed.

Dr. Hopkins grinned. Then his expression turned serious. "So? What about this Jenifer? You mentioned how lovely she is. Why do you not think of her more in terms of, you know . . . ?"

"Yeah, I know. Actually, I have been. A little."

"Ah!"

"Ah, yourself." Now Will chuckled. "You're good, you know that. At getting me to loosen up."

321

The psychiatrist shrugged. "It's my job, Will."

"You know how I think of her? Sure, I imagine making love to her. But sometimes I just see myself putting my arms around her and hugging her. Or I put my arm across her shoulders and, and . . ."

"Protect her?"

"Yes! Is that crazy?"

"No. I think it says something good about you. And I think she reminds you of what you never had. What you were cheated out of, if you care to put it that way."

"Which is?"

"Youth." The psychiatrist paused and puffed. "The youth you never really had because of your family's troubles. Especially your father's."

"Oh, God."

"We may be close, Will. I think we are, close to facing what's been torturing you. Facing it and staring it down."

But Will already knew that, and just then he remembered the smell of a basement. He shuddered.

"What is it, Will?"

"Oh, Christ."

"Take your time."

Will closed his eyes, breathed as slowly and deeply as he could, waiting for the worst of the feeling to pass. He put his hands to his face. In the sweat of his palms, he smelled the basement smell.

"Take as long as you want, Will."

Will checked his watch. His session must be up. He was glad. He expected the doctor to say any moment that his time was up. Then the chill came into his soul again, and he put his hands to his face once more. There, on his sweat, was the smell of a basement, a smell of mold and something more. Something human. For a moment, Will thought he might faint.

"I know this is hard, Will. I do know."

"So tired. I am so goddamn tired. Everything is piled on top of me."

"You know, intuitively at least, that what's making you so tired is the tremendous energy you're spending to keep something buried. Something from the past."

"Christ, what new thing can I say? How many times are we going to plow the same ground?"

"Until we plow deep enough."

"Well, we can't do it today, can we? I must be taking up someone else's time by now."

"I didn't schedule anyone else this morning, Will. And I took the liberty of scheduling you for a double session. I think you're ready to go where we haven't gone yet."

"And where is that?"

"I think you know. Or part of you does. And I'll help steer you."

"Christ. I'm too tired to do any more today."

"Anything we say, anything you say here, is inviolate, Will. As inviolate as a confessional."

"You think I have a great sin to confess?"

"Your term, not mine. What made you tremble a few minutes ago? Can you tell me?"

Will remembered.

"Can you tell me, Will?"

"I smelled a basement." There. Will had opened the door a crack.

"A basement?"

"A basement, and a smell, from a long time ago."

Will watched Dr. Hopkins's face. For a moment, the psychiatrist seemed about to say something. Then he changed his mind.

"A basement," Will repeated. He took a deep, trembling breath. "If I go on . . ."

"What you say here is in absolute confidence, Will. Forever and ever."

"I was reminded recently at the country club, when I groped around in the dark in the basement."

The doctor's face showed curiosity and patience, indomitable patience.

Will could not go on just yet. He had to take a detour, even a short one. "I did tell you a lot already about my father, his troubles. Didn't I?"

"Yes."

"And I did, I thought I was, you know, correctly evaluating things as I was telling you, to tell you what was germane."

"That's enough, Will."

"Pardon?"

"That's enough of the impersonal, abstract words. Listen to yourself. No more bullshit, Will."

Will Shafer felt like a boy stripped naked.

"I think you're ready, Will. For whatever. Go on, please. And as you remember, tell me what you *feel*. And what you remember feeling in the past."

Will looked into the doctor's face. The doctor's eyes twinkled, as though he'd had an inspiration. "Will, did you ever play golf with your father?"

"Oh, once or twice. He wasn't, oh, he wasn't into the game much."

"Why do you suppose that was?"

"Who can say? Some people are, some aren't."

"I'm interested in your father. Tell me about when you played golf with him."

"Which time?"

"You choose, Will. You said there were only one or two occasions. Did you enjoy it?"

"I never really played that well back then. Or later, for that matter. I'm not—"

"Did you enjoy playing golf with your father?"

"I tried to. I mean . . ."

"Why couldn't you have a good time playing golf with your father, Will?"

"Well, hell. Even back then, the city courses were crummy. I mean, they just weren't as good as, as . . ."

"The country club course."

"Well, sure. Everything's relative, but . . ."

"The country club course was better, and you sometimes wished you could play there, Will."

"Yes. Sure."

"But you couldn't, because your father, your parents, didn't belong."

"Wait a minute! You make it sound like—"

With a commanding wave of his hand through the blue pipe smoke, the doctor silenced him. "Sometimes you wished your parents belonged to the club so you could play there. You wished their financial situation was better."

"Yes. Sure, I admit it."

"Normal adolescent desires, Will. We've already talked about the financial situation and how it helped to determine where you went to school. I'm interested now in how you felt toward your father. What kept you from enjoying his company when you played golf with him?"

Will closed his eyes. A memory was crawling out of his soul. "My father, he was strange in some ways."

"Were you ever ashamed of him?"

"Ashamed?" Will's face stung as though he'd been slapped. "I guess. Like most adolescents, there were times."

"Tell me about a time you were ashamed of him. Pick one time and tell me your feelings."

"Look, before I go on, I know that if my father were here, he'd be able to tell you plenty of things about me. Okay? Plenty of reasons for him to be ashamed of me." Will's voice had started to break; it sounded strange to him.

"He's not here, Will. Go on. Pick one time and tell me."

"One time. Okay. This is silly, but there was a time we were playing on a city course. No one wears fancy clothes to play on a city course, but my father—this is almost funny, I can remember thinking it was—he had these old suit pants that he wore to play golf. One time he was bending over to tee up his ball, and they actually started to split. You know? Okay, I guess to be honest I was, you know, ashamed."

"Because you thought your father was a jerk?"

"Don't! Don't you say that! He wasn't!" Hot tears welled behind Will's eyes. He thought, what's happening to me?

"You said you were ashamed of him, Will."

"Not all the time. I—oh, shit." Will rubbed at the corners of his eyes with a handkerchief.

"Go on, Will. Was there another time you want to tell me about?"

Will did remember another time, a funny time. Just thinking of it made him start to laugh. He cleared his throat to speak, but only laughter came out, so much laughter that the tears ran freely down his cheeks.

The doctor smiled softly, wisely, and waited.

"This really is funny," Will said. "I said I'd never played the country club course as a kid, a teenager."

"Yes."

"Not true. I played about three holes. With my father."

"Tell me about it."

Will stifled a laugh; if he laughed now, he would never get through the story. "One morning, I guess it was between my sophomore and junior years in high school, my father woke me up early. I mean *early*. Still dark. He said we were going out to the country club, that he had an invitation from the pro there."

"Ah."

"No, no, just listen to this." Will was on the edge of laughing or weeping, he didn't know which. "We got there in the half-light of dawn. We'd snuck out of the house, you know, so as not to wake up my mother, and I, I couldn't say no to him when he acted like that. All strange, like he needed me. I think, looking back on it, he used to lie awake at night, dreaming and yearning and . . . God only knows.

"And there we were. We parked at the far end of the lot. It was so early, there was no attendant there yet. So we took our clubs, real old clubs, only one set actually. He gave me some of his clubs, which I carried in a little cloth bag my mother had made for me. My mother had made a golf bag for me, sewn a little kit for me! And my father and I went over to the tenth tee.

"And there we were, all alone. It was a lovely morning, the dew and birds and all, but weird. My father had said we had an invitation to play, but I began to wonder about that when he reached into a trash can and fished out a used scorecard."

Will giggled as the tears flowed freely; the doctor nodded but did not smile.

"The card was from a twosome of the day before, so it had some empty spaces on it. That was going to be our scorecard, because we were sneaking onto the course."

To his astonishment, Will was laughing and crying at the same time. But he could sense an end to the laughter, while the tears might be from a bottomless well.

"Then what, Will?"

"So we teed up to play the tenth, a little downhill par three. My father was wearing the same old, funny suit pants because he didn't want to spend the money on golf slacks, or thought he couldn't, and my mother had stitched them up after they'd ripped."

Will's tears kept coming. What was happening to him?

"Go on with your story, Will."

"So we hit our balls on the tenth and went down the hill, finished up that hole, played eleven."

"Were you talking with your father as you played?"

"A little. Mostly we just swung at the ball. I couldn't always use the exact club I wanted. As I said, he had some in his bag and I had some in mine."

"You didn't have your own set of clubs because there wasn't enough money, Will?"

"I had a goddamn paper route for five years, and I bussed tables in restaurants, and I worked in the goddamn motel . . ."

"You did all that anyone could expect, Will. Please continue. Were you enjoying golf with him that morning?"

"Well, yeah. I was sort of getting a kick out of it. The world is beautiful that time of day in the summer. And I could sense, I felt he was glad for my company. You know?"

"He probably was."

"In fact, he probably thought up the whole thing while he was lying awake. He probably thought he wanted my company. Oh . . ." A gush of tears flooded his cheeks.

"Go on, Will. Take your time."

"A guy from the club came around to put the flags in the holes. We were there so early, the flags weren't even in the holes when we started." Will laughed and sobbed at the memory. "And the guy from the club drove up to us in his little tractor and he looked at us like we were nuts. 'What the hell are you guys doing here?' he said. 'You ain't members. Get the hell off the course.' So we left."

"And then?"

"We got back to our car. It was the clunkiest, rustiest goddamn car in the lot. By that time, there were some other cars there, Lincolns and Cadillacs and such. There were some golfers walking toward the first tee with their goddamn alligator and leather bags and fancy clothes. They looked at us like we were shit."

"Really?"

"At least I thought they did. Then here comes this guy from the clubhouse, one of the assistant pros or something. He said if we snuck on again, we'd be arrested. My father started to say something about having a membership application pending—which was a big lie—and the guy said bullshit, that we'd better stay away."

"And you were embarrassed?"

"Sure. People were watching. I still don't feel totally comfortable at the clubhouse all these years later."

"You're a member now."

"Sure, because I'm the editor of the *Gazette.*"

"You felt terribly ashamed, as a teenager."

"Sure. Wouldn't you?"

"Ashamed of your father, Will?"

Tears hot in his eyes. "He was always making up stuff, for God's sake. Pretending he was a real prosperous motel owner. I remember, after he got fired from the steel plant for acting like a big shot once too often, he said, 'I can run a motel as well as anyone.' He said that."

"And he couldn't."

"Of course not. It was a dumb idea to start with. Mortgaging the house again to put money down on the motel . . . The bank never should have lent him the money."

"You said earlier he could talk a real good game, Will. At least when he was in a 'high' mood. That's not uncommon in people like your father."

"My mother should have stopped him. What did she know? The person who made out in the deal was the old lady who sold him the motel."

"And your father struggled."

"They both did. My mother and father worked day and night. Motel never did make money. 'I can run a motel as well as anyone,' he said." The tears were letting up. Will's face felt puffy from crying.

"And when your father died, Will, your dream of going to Notre Dame evaporated. You were only able to go to Saint Jerome's because you got a scholarship to Saint Jerome's through the *Gazette*." The doctor knocked his pipe against the ashtray and set it down. "Tell me the rest, Will," Dr. Hopkins said gently. "Tell me the worst thing you remember."

"The worst thing? Oh, God. It was a hot summer day. We hadn't seen my father for, oh, a couple of hours. I was in the motel office, helping my mother with a couple of fix-up chores.

"My dad had been going to the rooms, putting in new sheets and towels. At that point he and my mother had let practically all the help go.

"There weren't that many rooms to do. That's why my mother and I were wondering what was taking him so long. Finally, there was a phone call. From some creditor, saying he absolutely had to talk to my father.

"So I went to find him. There was a concrete walkway that

ran along the front of the units. Down near the end I saw the cart. You know, with the towels and soap and sheets. So I figured he was in one of the rooms, cleaning. My dad, cleaning. Jesus, he didn't even clean very well."

Will stopped, waiting for a torrent of tears and sorrow to pass.

"I looked inside the rooms near the cart, and he wasn't there. And a feeling came over me. I remember the cicadas were chirping a mile a minute in the heat, and I said to myself, remember this moment, because this is a big moment in your life.

"I went to the end of the line of units. Around the corner, down below, there was a door to the basement room where all the supplies were stored. The door was closed.

"I stood in front of that door for a minute or so. I was afraid, and yet I was curious, too. I unlocked the door, and the light was on in the storeroom. The door on the far side of the room was open a little, and I could see that the light behind that door was on.

"That door led to another room—a basement, actually. Furnace, boiler, fuse boxes. And pipes, lots of pipes.

"I got over near that door and I saw a soda can on the nearest shelf. Root beer. My father always loved it. I'd seen him get a can of root beer out of the machine a little earlier. And behind the can were his glasses. He'd taken his glasses off.

"I stood next to the door and I said, 'Dad, are you in there?' In a normal voice. 'Dad, are you in there?'

"No answer. So I went right up to the door and stood there. 'Dad?' I said. 'Dad?' Nothing. I remember the smell. There was the basement smell and . . . something else.

"So I pushed the door open, and there he was. He'd stood on a stool, looped his belt around his neck and tied it to a pipe. I could see right away that he was dead. And I stood there, it seemed like the longest time, looking at him. I felt almost detached. Very calm. I remember thinking, 'My father is dead, and I must go tell my mother, and then we'll have to call the police and find out what to do.'

"So I left him hanging there, in the basement, and went back outside, into the hot August day. And I thought, looking at the cars going by on the road as if nothing had happened, it was just another day. Except that my father had killed himself."

Will paused, sobbed from deep in his soul.

Dr. Hopkins puffed. "A terrible weight for a teenager," he said softly. "For anyone. And there's more, isn't there, Will?"

"More?"

"Still more you want to tell me. You mentioned a smell."

"Oh, my God. God Almighty."

"You've come so far, Will. You're there now."

"The smell. I guess what must have happened is, he'd changed his mind, at least for a moment. There were scuff marks on the nearest wall, where he'd kicked. Maybe he was trying to . . . Oh, Jesus . . .

"One of his shoes was off, he'd thrashed so much for, for however long it took. And his pants had come loose, come partway down, with the kicking and his not having a belt on. And there was, there was—you know what can happen to a body at death. Well, it had. To him, to my father.

"And as I left the basement, I remember feeling ashamed of him again. He was my father, and he couldn't bear to live, he was so unhappy, and not only didn't I help him but I was ashamed of him. Ashamed of my dead father."

"And when you told your mother, what then?"

"She screamed, loud and high. I've never heard anything so bad. She ran out of the office, toward where my father was. She wasn't very athletic, my mother, and she always had a weight problem. To tell you truth, she looked funny as she ran." But at the memory, Will sobbed again.

"Go on, Will."

"She screamed again, so loud it echoed off the basement walls, when she saw him hanging. Oh, God. She never was, she never did recover from that. Never."

With that, Will put his head into his hands and cried like a child. He felt as if his heart were being ripped out. He didn't know how long he cried. When he was done, he looked at the doctor and blinked.

"Your father's suffering has been over for a long time, Will. Your mother's, too. It's time to let go of yours."

"I have felt so sad for so long."

"Guilt can be a cancer, Will. It has been for you. Your father was a very troubled man, a very sick man, judging from what you've told me. It's only conjecture, of course, but he might even have had a tough time getting adequate therapy today, let alone a few decades back."

"He didn't leave a note. I always thought the impulse might have come on him suddenly, while he was cleaning. He just felt buried by everything."

"That may be, Will, although in my experience most suicides aren't sudden."

"Sometimes when I've seen men playing golf with boys, I've wished, wished . . ."

"You've carried the load long enough, Will. Let it go. Your father was a proud man. He wouldn't want you to carry it, would he?"

"I guess not."

"You know he wouldn't. His suffering is over. He's at peace."

"At peace? A nice thought." Will felt lighter.

"Your father would be proud of you. You know he would."

"Yeah? Yeah. I guess he would." Will felt lighter still.

"Now, Will, our time really is up for today. I think we can really see daylight now. Just try not—"

"Try not to put a timetable on it. I won't. But the first chance I get, I'm going to watch a sunset from my porch deck. I'm going to drink a little gin and hold my wife's hand. The sunsets are beautiful this time of year. Maybe tonight, if the rain stops."

Thirty-five

▲ ▲ ▲

The warm rain made rainbow-colored puddles in the *Gazette*'s parking lot. Marlee wiped the steam from the inside of the windshield, searching for a space close enough to the door so she wouldn't get soaked. Damn, no luck. When she was almost at the end of the lot, down by a corner of the dock where papers were loaded onto delivery trucks, she spotted Lyle Glanford, Jr. He was standing at the edge of the dock, under the roof and out of the rain. He waved to her and signaled for her to open her window.

"Marlee, just drive up and park in the publisher's spot," Lyle shouted over the rain. "He's not coming in today. You'll get soaked otherwise."

"Oh, Lyle, you're a peach. Thanks."

Yep, she thought; there are good things about working at a place for a long time.

She saw the huge steel door of the bay opening. Then she backed out of the hissing rain onto the dry concrete where the publisher usually parked.

"Can't say we don't treat our people right," Lyle said.

"This is great. Thanks so much." Marlee hugged Lyle and

kissed him on the cheek. "Oh, can I get out of here later? I have to pick up my dog."

"Sure. Just press that button on the wall. If a guard's around, he'll do it for you."

Next to Marlee's car was Lyle junior's, and next to his were a couple of cars that Marlee recognized as belonging to other *Gazette* executives. Will Shafer had a reserved space, but he hadn't come in yet.

Marlee went in the main building through the back door, walked down several metal corridors that smelled of ink, grease, and newsprint, then took an elevator to the newsroom floor.

Jenifer was at her desk. She waved at Marlee and went back to her typing. Marlee checked her messages: Detective Jean Gilman had called; nothing urgent; please call back.

Marlee thought of Ed Delaney, who had stayed at her house when she left. He'd said he wanted to listen to the dead-priest tape one more time, look at pictures just once more. Just in case. Marlee thought of calling him, decided against it. She would call later.

She called the animal hospital: indeed, Nigel was ready to leave, as good as new. Since she didn't know exactly how long she'd be at work (especially if she and Jenifer talked things over), Marlee decided to use her lunch hour to pick up Nigel and drop him off at home.

Sitting at her desk, Marlee tried to separate her feelings: she liked Ed Delaney, though she wasn't sure exactly how she liked him, yet she was disappointed—hurt, really—that Grant Siebert had not talked to her more. Now why was that? He had been a snotty bastard back then, and he probably hadn't changed enough to make it worthwhile. Well, the hell with him. Marlee would make the day a good one, somehow: talking to Jenifer, picking up her dog, later a jog up by the reservoir and some wine.

What more could there be in life?

Her phone rang.

* * *

If he did not do it today, Grant Siebert thought as he drove slowly through the lashing rain, he might never. He had squandered his chances to corner her alone; now the easy chances were gone, and he would have to make his own opportunities.

He drove down Marlee's street, squinting to see through the rain. There, there was her house. Maybe she had not left for work, maybe . . .

Goddamn it! Not only was her car gone, but there was a strange car in her driveway. What the hell was she doing?

Easy, Grant told himself. Try to act like a big boy. You don't know whose car it is, and it's not your business anyhow. Son of a bitch.

He drove by, not quite sure where to go next. He had checked out of the motel, and his plane didn't leave until much later. Well, screw it. He would stay another day if he had to.

Spotting a phone booth, he pulled over. Son of a bitch, I should have brought a raincoat, he thought.

Heart beating fast, he fished coins out of his pocket, plunked them on the shelf under the phone. Do it now, he thought, before you talk yourself out of it. Do it, do it, you dirty coward. All these years . . .

He dialed.

"Marlee? It's Grant Siebert. Listen, I didn't get a chance to talk to you much. Uh, could I stop by and see you today before I fly back to New York?"

Ed Delaney had called his daughter's friend's house just to check. Yes, his daughter assured him, she had slept well (ha, Ed thought), and she would stay there most of the day if that was all right. Ed supposed that it was and made his daughter promise to call him at work later.

Marlee had left him a big pot of coffee, had told him what to switch on and off, then gone to work. Alone in the quiet of the house, he wondered if his daughter, Laura, would get along with Marlee if . . .

Slow down, Ed told himself.

Sipping his coffee, he walked to the window, looked at the rain pooling in the street, saw a few cars go by.

Yes, there was something in his head, a collection of impressions and recollections, some from a long time ago and some much more recent, that were trying to gel.

The recent things—what were they? Something he had heard while walking around the big lawn with Marlee. Something about golf clubs.

Ed felt weak in the knees. God Almighty, he thought. Can that be it?

The rain soaked Delaney's shoulders and matted his hair. He paid no attention.

Shielding Marlee's tape recorder and pictures under his coat, he rushed into the headquarters building. Jean Gilman was at her desk. "Some messages for you," she said.

"Anything from Marlee West?"

"No. I tried to call her once, about the next counseling session, but her line was busy. I'll—"

"Listen. This is important. If she calls, tell her I think I know . . . I know . . ."

"What?"

"I can't say any more right now. Tell her I've got something. Tell her not to go anywhere with anyone she doesn't know real well."

Jean Gilman chuckled. "Should I tell her not to take candy from strangers?"

"This is serious. I'll be gone for a while."

"Where?"

"Basement of the records building."

Still clutching the pictures and recorder under his dripping raincoat, he rushed off.

Delaney's feet squished in his shoes as he stood in front of the old metal filing cabinet. It's here, he thought. It's here, and it's been here all along. There's only a couple of people in the world who would have known, who would have cared, all these years later. One of them was Ed Sperl, and the other one killed a priest. And then he probably killed Sperl.

Delaney used his key, unlocked the cabinet, pulled the long drawer toward him. There was the file: "Barrow, John; 71; unsolved."

Delaney pulled out the file, thumbed through the photographs. After twenty years, they were no less horrible. They would never be any less horrible. He wiped his rain-wet fingers on his shirtfront, then picked through the papers.

Yes, there: in addition to the golf club embedded in the victim's skull, two other clubs were lying near the body, both from a new set; the rest of the set was found upstairs with the victim's luggage.

A new set of golf clubs.

Alone in the mildew smell of the records room, Delaney thought of that day in the house, after he'd seen the corpse. He remembered the detectives checking the priest's bedroom, how one of them had made a passing remark about the priest's new set of golf clubs.

Delaney put Marlee's recorder on top of the cabinet, pressed the play button:

"... quest for glory in the Holy City of New York, we ..."

Delaney pushed fast-forward.

"... mention it. The cops are keeping the pictures locked up tight."

"What a disappointment for you."

Voices of Ed Sperl and the younger Marlee, Delaney knew. He fast-forwarded again.

"... wasn't just golfing down there ..."

Fast-forward.

"... have been a fag deal?"

Fast-forward.

"Betcha whoever did it is long gone."

"Still hacking away."

"You sick bastard."

"... yuk ..."

"... awful thing ..."

"... a terrible thing ..."

"... to ruin a new set of clubs on a fag ..."

"You just committed a double mortal sin ..."

Delaney stopped, rewound briefly, stopped, pressed play again.

"... to ruin a new set of clubs ..."

Delaney pressed stop, stared at the recorder. "Who are you?" he whispered. "You knew the priest's golf clubs were new. Hardly anyone else in the world knew that, but you did. That's because you planted one of them in the priest's head."

He put Marlee's pictures on top of the cabinet, stared at the silly, careless, insolent, stoned faces from two decades before, squinted at the less-clear faces and parts of faces and shoulders and backs.

"You're in one of these pictures, aren't you?" Delaney whispered. "Maybe more than one. I don't know if you moved away or stayed at home, and I don't know how you look today, without your sideburns or beard or whatever you grew back then. But you're here, aren't you?"

Delaney locked the file back in the cabinet and ran back to his office. When he got there, Jean Gilman was gone. She had left no messages for him. Delaney dialed Marlee's number. After a few rings, the switchboard operator came on the line and said that Marlee was away from her desk.

"What do you think?" Jenifer said.

"Yes," Marlee said. "Yes. And I think we can work well together."

"So do I. Now all we have to do is get Will Shafer's approval. Should we go in together and ask him?"

Marlee thought. "First, let me talk to him alone. I think it's best if I pitch him on it first. I know he respects both of us, but he respects me in a different way, I think. Or feels easier with me. We go way back, Will and I."

"Okay. Whatever you say."

Marlee and Jenifer had talked at length in the coffee room off the main news floor. Jenifer had thought about it much of the night, she said, and after she and Marlee had reviewed every scrap of knowledge they had, Jenifer was determined. She and Marlee would go to Will Shafer and try to get his okay for a story about the unsolved slaying of the Reverend John Barrow.

Marlee had deferred to her younger colleague, for this kind of story was more her forte. Jenifer sat across from Marlee, both of their coffees long cold, and wrote down what they knew:

That a promising early clue in the slaying, namely the tip from the Silver Swine bartender, had never been followed up, contrary to established police procedure.

That commanders in the detective division at that time had encouraged investigators to look for burglary suspects, even though there were clear indications that the slaying had been sexually motivated.

That the parents of the victim were bitterly disappointed to this day that their son's killer had not been pursued more vigorously.

That at least one veteran police officer still on the Bessemer force had specific recollections about how the inquiry was sidetracked.

That a Bessemer priest who had known the victim had come forth to say that church leaders from that era, most of them now dead, had been disappointed that the case had not been pursued.

That the *Gazette*'s veteran police reporter, Ed Sperl, had died under suspicious circumstances after showing renewed interest in the case, and that a man seen drinking with Sperl on the night of his death had not been found.

That one of Sperl's ex-wives had apparently fled the state under puzzling circumstances.

"Now," Jenifer said, "I think we have a pretty good case for a story to take to Will Shafer. What's wrong, Marlee. I see something in your face."

Marlee was uneasy. "I'm having trouble sorting out what we can say from what we were told in confidence. I mean, by Father Dean and by Ed Delaney."

"I know where you're coming from, Marlee. I don't want to violate any confidences either, if I can help it."

If I can help it: those words bothered Marlee.

"Look," Jenifer pressed on, "just suppose we did a story that caused the investigation to be reopened, and they caught the killer. I'd say the story was worth it at almost any cost. Wouldn't you?"

"I guess."

"Listen, Marlee. No news sources have ever accused me of violating any confidences. They've called me a bitch and a whole lot worse, but no one ever said I broke my word. We start off with what we know, and we take that to an editor we hope we can trust—"

"We can trust Will."

"—and *then* we work on pinning down attribution and so on. If what Delaney told us would get him in trouble, we look for someone else to tell us the same thing. Same idea with Father Dean. If that doesn't work, we find a more subtle way to get the same point across. First things first: we clear it with the editor."

"Okay. I'll talk to him. Today, I hope."

"Excellent. After the first story runs, with any luck we'll start getting new tips. Then maybe some prosecutor trying to make a name for himself will say something for publication. Then the ball starts rolling."

"Funny. Back a little bit, when Ed Delaney seemed to be backing off, he said there wasn't enough to take to a prosecutor."

Jenifer smiled shrewdly. "Taking something to a prosecutor is one thing, especially if you're a cop and thinking in terms of evidence and covering your ass. If we can get backing, we can take something directly to the public."

"That sounds noble, almost."

"Just realistic. The newspaper is where the power all comes together. We'll talk some more. Right now, I have to get back to my housing story." Jenifer stood up to go.

"All right."

"What is it? You still look distracted. Cold feet?"

"No, it's personal. I'm not sure how much I should like Ed Delaney's company. And a little later, Grant Siebert is coming by to see me. Grant Siebert, of all people."

Jenifer sat down again. "He's the one whose party you taped. Why is he coming to see you?"

"I don't know. He was just going to stop by the paper and say hello before he goes back to New York, I guess."

"Hmmm. Be careful."

Jenifer got up and left. Marlee sipped cold coffee, wondering when her life would be predictable once more.

Back at her desk, Marlee found two messages, both saying that Ed Delaney had called. She dialed his number, got no answer, then dialed Jean Gilman's number. No answer.

Marlee looked over to the corner, saw Will Shafer's secretary but no Will behind the desk. Marlee dialed the secretary to see if the editor was in his private office.

"Not here yet, Marlee. Said he had some personal business to tend to this morning."

"Thanks, bye."

Marlee tried to plan the rest of her day: she had some work to do on her next column, and Jenifer would probably want to confer with her some more. Plus Marlee hoped to see Will Shafer at some point. And Grant was supposed to stop in; no telling how long that would take. . . .

So, Marlee figured, if I'm going to pick up Nigel, I should probably do it pretty soon. I'm not getting much done this morning anyhow. She called the animal hospital and said she'd be along to pick up the dog.

"Marlee, I heard what happened the other night," the

doctor said. "That's a vicious joke. Who would do such a thing?"

"Darned if I know."

"Anyhow, the little fella is fine and dandy. I'll give you something to put in his food for the next few days, but you should have no trouble."

"Good. I can live with that. I'll be there in a little while."

As she was about to leave, her phone rang. "Hi, Marlee. You wanted to talk to me?"

"Will, hi." Marlee turned, saw the editor smiling and waving from across the room as he held the phone to his ear. "I need to discuss a story idea with you. Today sometime, maybe?"

"Middle or late afternoon looks good, kiddo."

"Good, thanks." *Kiddo?* Will must be mellowing out, she thought.

On her way out, Marlee passed Jenifer, who was on the phone and taking notes. Jenifer nodded, moved her lips to mouth the words, "Talk to you later."

Marlee went through the back corridor, toward the loading dock. On the way, she exchanged greetings with a pressroom foreman and the head of the deliverers' union—overall-clad, grease-and-ink people many of the younger reporters didn't know or care about.

She pressed the button on the wall near her car, and the big metal bay door rumbled open. The rain had stopped, but there were still puddles in the street and across the way in the parking lot.

Marlee's car wouldn't start. At first, she thought it was just balky; perhaps she had driven too fast through a deep puddle and—what?—got the battery wet or some wires or something.

She tried the ignition again, and again and again. The car would not start. Not now, anyhow.

"Damn it. *Damn* it!"

Marlee was doubly disappointed: now was a bad time for

the car to fail, and she had thought Ed Delaney's brother-in-law was a good mechanic.

Should she go back upstairs and ask Jenifer if she could borrow her car? Or should she just try to get a cab?

Of all the times to be held up by flooding on the Ambrose Parkway. Delaney cursed, pounded his fist on the dashboard, radioed headquarters again. Finally he was patched through to Jean Gilman, who had been at a meeting. He asked her to try to reach Marlee and tell her to wait at the *Gazette* for him.

It's been there all along, Delaney thought. All along. It wasn't just a stupid joke from an old tape, or a couple of pictures from a long-ago party. It was the combination. Together, the tapes and pictures might show—did show— who had been at that party twenty years before, and who had made that crack about the priest's new golf clubs.

Delaney loathed the thought that Ed Sperl had picked up on the clue but that he himself had not. He tried not to think about it. When that proved impossible, he rationalized: Sperl had fastened onto details of cases as a hobby—a sick hobby at that. He had picked up the fact that the clubs were new, and that that little detail hadn't been given out to the public. Where had he learned that? From Ray McNulty? Maybe. It wasn't so much that Sperl had recognized the voice on the tape—he probably hadn't, at first—but that he had caught the remark about the new clubs. Then he had gone hunting for the owner of the voice.

"Son of a bitch!" Delaney threaded his car through the steaming puddles on the parkway, inching past stalled vehicles.

At that party twenty years ago, Sperl hadn't heard the remark about the clubs. He had only caught it at Marlee's recent party. Whoever had said it way back then had been fairly close to the recorder.

Delaney glanced down at the pictures on the seat. There! There was the goddamn recorder on the table, right in front of stony-eyed Marlee. Who was that dumb-looking guy holding a book and reading from a piece of paper? Delaney had no idea. And there was Grant what's his name, with a younger version of the wise-ass smirk Delaney had seen when he'd met him.

Delaney radioed in again, told headquarters to see to it that Grant Siebert did not get on a plane to leave Bessemer. Better yet, Delaney said, find Grant Siebert and hold him. For what? Delaney was asked. Find a reason, Delaney said. Again, he was patched through to Gilman. No, she had not been able to reach Marlee West.

He told himself to be calm, that the woman sitting next to him was no stranger and might even be called a friend. Surely he could be calm. Surely when they stopped at Marlee's house to leave off the dog he could find a chance to grab the tape and pictures. Or at least the tape. Later, she might wonder if he had taken it, but that was secondary. Above all, he must get the tape. It was by far the deadliest link with the all-but-forgotten sin of his youth. If he could wipe it out, no one else need know, ever. He had paid his penance a hundred thousand times.

"I'm really glad I ran into you," Marlee said. "I should probably take one of those night courses in auto mechanics so I'm not so helpless with cars."

"You work with your mind, not your hands. Remember?"

"Right. Are you sure you have time to do this?"

"Of course. Lucky I ran into you when I did."

"I'm so glad," Marlee said. "I was just going to try to borrow a car or get a cab."

"You might have had a tough time getting a cab, with the rain and all."

"I know."

They were heading across town on the Ambrose Parkway. He slowed down where there was flooding. God, it was so hard to stay calm; the harder one tried, the more nervous one got. Just like in golf.

Today might be the most important day in his life. If he could stay calm, pull it off, get the tape out of Marlee's house, there would be nothing in Bessemer that could tie him to the bloody corpse in the basement.

"You people were so lucky," Marlee said. "With the rain, I mean. It could have washed out the golf."

"Sure as hell could have. Maybe it should have, considering how I played. At least I didn't break any clubs."

Marlee chuckled. "People who play keep telling me to take it up, that it's a game that hooks you."

"Worse than that," he said. "It gets in your blood."

He wondered if getting the tape would stop the nightmares.

"Huh!" Marlee said.

"What?"

"I thought for a second I saw Ed Delaney going by in the other lane."

Delaney pulled into the *Gazette* parking lot, found a visitor's spot, cursed the slowness of the elevator. On the main news floor, a receptionist pointed him toward Marlee West's desk. "I don't see her around right now," the receptionist said. "Maybe someone close by can tell you where she is."

"Well, if she left the office, would she come by here?"

"Most likely, but there are other ways out."

"Terrific. Look, if you see her, make her wait. Okay?"

"Well, is she expecting you?"

Delaney flashed his badge. "It's very important." Then he saw a lovely young woman approaching him, realizing after a second or two who she was.

"I'm Jenifer. I met you—"

"Right. I'm trying to find Marlee. I think I have something on . . . Uh, can we talk somewhere?"

"Follow me."

Jenifer led Delaney to her desk, which for a moment at least offered some privacy. He flung his damp raincoat over a chair, put the tape recorder and pictures on Jenifer's desk.

"I know what you and Marlee have been working on," he said.

Delaney told Jenifer Hurley what was on the tape and in the pictures.

"My God," Jenifer said. "Wait till I tell her."

"Where the hell is she?"

"Hmmm. If she's not around, she might be picking up her dog. She mentioned something—"

"Can I use your phone?"

Delaney looked up the number for Bessemer Animal Medical Center and dialed. Marlee West had left a short time ago with her Airedale terrier, Nigel.

"Was she with anyone?" Delaney said into the phone.

"I think she was alone. At least she came in alone."

Delaney hung up. Then he dialed headquarters, gave a description of Marlee's car. "Stop the vehicle and hold for further orders." He gave Marlee's address and ordered that her house be watched: she would almost certainly drop off her dog there soon.

"My God," Jenifer said. "Do you think . . . ?"

"It's possible. Yes. We need to know who that voice is, need to know it right now."

"We can ask Will Shafer," Jenifer said. "I know he was there."

Jenifer led Delaney to the executive editor's desk. Will Shafer looked up over his reading glasses. His secretary started to say something.

"It's okay," Will said. "What is it, Jenifer?"

"Will—"

"We need you, and we need some privacy," Delaney said, holding up the recorder. "This is urgent."

"Come on."

Will led Jenifer and Delaney to his office and closed the door. "What's this about?" the editor said.

"A party," Delaney said. He put the recorder on Will's desk, found an outlet, plugged the recorder in. Then he put the pictures on the desk.

"Look at those," Will said softly, beginning to smile. "My gosh, that's a long time ago. There I am, and—"

"Listen," Delaney said. "We know this is the farewell party for Grant Siebert. That's him there. We need someone to figure out the other faces and—"

"Well, that's Marlee, of course. And Grant, and Charlie Buck, and some of Grant's hangers-on. Friends, I suppose I should say."

"Listen, damn it. There's a voice here, on this tape. We think it belongs to a face in one of these pictures. Now, you're going to listen to the tape and tell us who the voice belongs to."

"Whose voice?" Will said. "Do you have any idea who it is?"

Delaney resisted the impulse to say Grant Siebert. There was no telling what a defense lawyer could make of it later if he coaxed Shafer now. "You just listen," Delaney said, "and I'll tell you which voice we need to identify."

"What if I can't tell?"

"Don't say that. Just listen." Delaney pressed the play button.

"*. . . eat shit . . .*"

"I'm afraid that might be me," Shafer said sheepishly. "Letting my guard down after a few beers, taking out some resentment."

Delaney nodded.

"*. . . putter was out his bag, if you know . . .*"

"*You bastard.*"

"Mmmm. Charlie Buck, I think," Will said, blushing at the foul joke heard in Jenifer's presence. "Or no, maybe Ed Sperl. To tell the truth, I'm not sure."

"*Betcha whoever did it is long gone.*"

"*Still hacking away.*"

Will shrugged; Delaney signaled for him to listen closely.

"*. . . to ruin a new set of clubs on a fag . . .*"

Delaney pressed the stop button. "That last voice. Who is it?"

"There's something familiar," Will said. "I think there is.

You know, we're like a lot of papers our size. So many people pass through here on their way to wherever."

Delaney pressed rewind briefly, then the play button.

"*. . . to ruin a new set of clubs on a fag . . .*"

Will sat down, put his hands over his face as he concentrated. Then he looked at the pictures. "Are there any other photographs from that party?"

"I don't know. I think these are all the ones Marlee had."

Will frowned and picked up the phone. "Rachel, I need something right away. Go to the picture archives and pull Arnie Schwartz's shots from 1971. Or just get everything he developed in March or April of that year. Bring them to my office. Drop everything else, okay? Thanks."

Delaney looked at Will Shafer. "You've got to remember. Do you understand me?"

"I'm trying. It could be Grant Siebert. Could be, I say. I thought Arnie's pictures might help. He was the chief photographer back then. Used to take pictures at going-away parties."

"I know. Be sure now. Be sure." Though he said that, Delaney was filled with elation that Shafer seemed on the edge of identifying the voice as Grant Siebert's.

"Let me hear that again," Will said. He looked at Jenifer, saw the laser concentration in her eyes, felt silly as he realized he wanted to impress her by remembering.

"*. . . to ruin a new set of clubs on a fag . . .*"

Will leaned back in his chair. "I think, I think there's something I recognize. God, could that be? Right after that party—I'm trying to recall—I think that's when I went to Westchester for a management seminar. And I think he was there. His voice was different because he had an infected tooth or gum or something. He'd fallen on his face, slipped and fallen during the big ice storm, though he never said much about it until I asked him. His voice was different for a while."

"Who?" Delaney said quietly.

* * *

"I really appreciate this," Marlee said. She put her hand on his forearm and was surprised at the tension she felt in the muscle.

"It's okay."

"You're sure you have time?"

"I'm sure. Yes."

"I should have thought the doctor might give me a prescription to fill. It shouldn't take long."

Marlee went into the drugstore, leaving him alone in the car with the Airedale terrier. The dog bent over the seat, sniffed his ear curiously.

"Good fella. Good fella. Yes, I like dogs. I do."

The bright-eyed dog licked the back of his head, wagged his tail, sniffed his ear some more.

"Yes, yes. I love you, too, big fella."

He was not sorry for the delay; he figured Marlee would take a few minutes at her house to get the dog squared away. Maybe she'd have to give the dog a pill and put him outside. That would give him a chance to get the tape.

He closed his eyes and prayed. He did not want to kill anyone else.

"There's no doubt in your mind?" Delaney said.

"No. The more I listen, the more sure I am. We talked a lot that weekend, about everything from parents to Notre Dame football. And how his father wanted to keep him close to home."

The editor's phone rang. "Will, it's Rachel. I'm sorry, but we can't find Arnie's pictures from then. No negatives either."

"Thank you." Will hung up. "The pictures are gone," he said to Delaney. "I guess that's not surprising, is it?"

"No."

"But I'm pretty sure that's him," Will said. "See, right there. Just out of focus, over Grant's shoulder. Yep. That's Lyle."

"Dear God," Jenifer said. She sat down, her face quite white.

Delaney had to press it. "You're as sure as you can be that it's not Grant Siebert? Because we think he might have driven by Marlee's house . . ." Delaney stopped himself.

"He probably just wanted to talk to her," Jenifer said. "I know he was planning to come by and see her today before going back to New York."

"Why?" Delaney demanded.

"Because," Jenifer said impatiently, "he probably just wants to see her. Old times' sake. Or maybe he's sorry he never asked her out. How the hell do I know?"

"Shy," Will said quietly. "My wife thought Grant was shy."

"Is Lyle here in this building?" Delaney said.

"He was earlier." Will picked up the phone. "Hi, Gladys . . . Ah, he's not. Thanks." To Delaney, he said, "Lyle's not in his office."

"Is he in the building? Do we know that?"

"Well, I can call downstairs and see if his car is there. Oh, that's odd. Yes, it is odd."

"What is?"

"I came in late. When I parked my car, I saw Marlee's in the publisher's spot, of all places. Down next to the shipping bay. I thought it was strange, but I figured maybe Lyle knew his father was out today and told Marlee she could park there because of the rain."

Delaney was immediately suspicious. "Find out if his car is there," Delaney ordered.

Will called down to the security post near the loading dock. "Lyle's car is gone," he told Delaney. Then he said into the phone, "See if there's a car in the publisher's spot. . . . There is. All right."

"Well?" Delaney demanded.

"Marlee's car is still down there."

Delaney picked up the phone, dialed headquarters, told the dispatcher to forget about looking for Marlee's car and check for one belonging to Glanford, Lyle, Jr.

Just before he hung up, Delaney thought of something else to tell the dispatcher: "The car's probably got one of those VIP Friends of the Police shields on the license plate."

"Yes, it does," Will said.

"That's confirmed on the VIP shield," Delaney said into the phone. Then, to Will, "Take me down to Marlee's car."

Delaney followed the editor, who led him to an elevator, then through a maze of corridors. Delaney cursed himself for not detecting what Ed Sperl had picked up on the tape, even more for not figuring out sooner who could have squelched the homicide investigation twenty years before.

Delaney remembered what he had seen on the sprawling lawn at the publisher's brunch: politicians, church people, bankers, executives. It was at the newspaper where the power from all sources found a center.

"This way," Will said.

Delaney followed, through one last narrow corridor. He was surprised to realize that Jenifer Hurley was a couple of steps behind them.

Will opened a door onto the loading dock. The big metal doors were rumbling open one by one now, and the dock was full of engine sounds as *Gazette* trucks backed in to receive bundles of the early editions.

Jenifer rushed ahead, looked into Marlee's car. Nothing out of the ordinary. "Maybe she just took a cab," she said. "She was alone when she stopped at the animal hospital. Right?"

"They thought so," Delaney said. "They thought so."

"On second thought," Jenifer said, "it makes no sense that she'd take a cab. She's not afraid to drive in the rain, for God's sake. So why would she take a cab, unless her car wouldn't start?"

"Her car was just fixed," Delaney said. He reached into the car, pulled the hood-release lever, went around the front. He lifted the hood and saw a tangle of wire spaghetti. "She's with him," he said.

* * *

Marlee was relieved: they were almost to the turnoff to her street, and it was looking as if she'd get back to the *Gazette* in time to meet Grant. How would she handle that? Easy enough: sit down over a cup of coffee.

"I hope your father doesn't get mad at me for leaving my car in his spot," she said. "I'll get it out as soon as I can, even if I have to tow it."

"No problem. We can have someone look under the hood when we get back."

Marlee chuckled. "Talk about a company that takes care of its own."

"We do that, all right."

That reminded Marlee of something. Yes, Lyle might know, and an informal yet private setting seemed a perfect opportunity to bring it up. "Have you by any chance heard anything from Ed Sperl's first wife, Olga?"

Lyle paused before saying, "What makes you ask?"

Marlee was stung by his tone, at once rebuking and remote. She had not known Lyle to assert his management position that way before. "Never mind, it's none of my business."

"But you made it your business, didn't you? What makes you ask?"

Oh, this is all wrong, Marlee thought. She was embarrassed and upset and wanted only to change the subject. "I shouldn't have," she said. "I'm sorry."

"But you did. What made you ask?"

Okay, Marlee thought. I can be a little porky, too, if that's the mood you're in. "She came to me one day and hung all her problems out to dry on my line, that's all."

"Her biggest problem was that slimy bag of pus she used to sleep with. The late Ed Sperl."

A chill caressed Marlee's skin. She had never heard Lyle talk like that, had never heard his voice sound like that, with a hate that was almost palpable. She had never realized that Lyle was among those who loathed Ed Sperl—

Oh.

In an instant, Marlee understood and felt faint. The Lyle who was sitting next to her was not the Lyle she had known, or thought she had known.

"We do take care of our own," he went on. "Olga can stay in Arizona all her life."

Arizona. But of course: Lyle would know she had gone to Arizona. No doubt he had sent her there and made it worth her while.

Slowly, Marlee turned toward Lyle, who was staring straight ahead. She noticed the small smudge of grease on his forearm, knew at once how it had got there. She looked at his eyes—shiny, staring straight ahead, as though seeing something far away.

In the moment before terror filled her, she reflected quite clearly: Lyle is insane.

Lyle started to round the corner of Marlee's street, but he jammed on the brakes when he saw the two patrol cars a block away. Marlee saw the police cars, too. Somebody knows, she thought. Ed Delaney! That was him on the parkway, driving toward the *Gazette*. He knows it's Lyle!

She reached for the door handle, but Lyle was ahead of her, locking all the doors from the buttons on the driver's-side door. Besides, he had swung the car around with dizzying speed; even if she had been able to unlock the door, the centrifugal force would have stopped her from opening it. In no time, the car was back on the Ambrose Parkway.

"Lyle, please."

The puddles had shrunk, and he jammed the accelerator to the floor. Lyle was passing everything, missing some cars by less than a foot as he changed lanes with terrifying speed.

"Please, Lyle. I don't want to die. For God's sake."

Nigel growled, whimpered, emitted a quizzical chortle. Then he settled on a deep, threatening growl.

"Nigel, no. It's okay. For the love of God, Lyle . . ."

Marlee turned to look out the back, praying to see flashing red lights. There were none.

"Lyle, please. You don't have to . . . I mean, with your power you can fix—"

When Marlee realized what she had said, everything came into focus. Everything.

Lyle swung the car violently to the right. It nicked a guardrail as it hurtled down the next exit, swerving so suddenly that Marlee's dog tumbled onto the floor with a yelp.

"Nigel!"

Marlee grabbed the dog's leash; she would try to get out of the car, scratch Lyle's eyes if she had to, hope that Nigel would bite, but she would get out of the car, out of the car.

"I'm allowed to have this," Lyle said, proudly waving a silver revolver. "My daddy got it for me. It's real!"

Marlee was crying now, she could not help it. She recognized where they were: on a road that led past weed-strewn rail sidings to an abandoned industrial park. Was this where she would die? "We've been friends, Lyle."

"No."

"Yes! We were, Lyle. We were! Friends."

"I only had friends when people knew my last name. When I played make-believe, they weren't my friends."

"Oh, God."

Lyle pulled to the right, braked hard. The car skidded and stopped. "If you were my friend, you wouldn't have found out." Lyle's voice was breaking; to Marlee, it sounded like that of a heartbroken six-year-old. "If you were my friend, you wouldn't have played that tape at your party."

"I didn't mean to hurt you, Lyle. I didn't mean it."

"You did! You did! You think I don't know? I do know. I know what you and Jenifer were doing. I hear things. I have feelings, too."

"I know you do, Lyle."

"He made me go with him to my father's cottage, over near Horning. He made me promise to pay. I was afraid he'd tell on me."

"Oh, God."

"If it hadn't been for the tape you played, it would all still be a secret."

"It can still be a secret, Lyle. I swear to God. I'll give you the tape. Honest."

Lyle cackled, proud of his cleverness. "I'm not so dumb, you know. I'm not!"

"I know you're not, Lyle. Honest."

"Grant has the other tape. But he told me he'd be my friend, in New York. He'd give it to me. I betcha he would!"

Lyle's voice had slipped into a child's falsetto, all the more terrifying because the light had gone out of his eyes.

The dog yelped and barked between growls; now the Airedale's head was between Lyle and Marlee, its uncomprehending eyes wild with confusion.

Marlee prayed.

A siren, from far away. Was it coming this way?

"Please, Lyle."

"I want you to come with me." Lyle used the gun to point toward the door handle on Marlee's side; there was a click as Lyle pressed the unlock button.

"Lyle . . ."

"I want you to come with me."

Marlee got out, stood on the side of the road, her legs trembling, hardly able to support her. She could smell the weeds and mud. The siren was still far away.

Lyle had got out and come around the front to face her. "I want the doggie to come, too."

"Please, Lyle."

"Get the doggie."

Marlee opened the rear door. Before she could grab Nigel's leash, the dog was by her. No growl, no snarl, just a leap for Lyle's leg. Lyle shrieked as fangs sank into his calf.

"Nigel! No, Lyle. Please!"

Lyle's face had gone white with fear and pain, but he was still on his feet, and he still had his revolver. Nigel shook his head, the way Airedales do with their prey, and for a moment the jaws came loose. The dog lunged again, but

Lyle had moved back a few feet, and this time Marlee stepped on the leash, and the dog stopped short of Lyle's leg.

"See, Lyle. I am your friend. I didn't want him to hurt you."

Lyle's leg was bleeding freely under the torn trousers, and he was starting to cry. His face showed not anger but hurt feelings. "He hurt! He hurt!"

"He didn't mean to, Lyle. He didn't." Marlee was down on her knees, her right arm wrapped around the dog's shoulders, the left gripping the leash as hard as it could. "Nigel, *no!*" The dog thrashed and snarled, wanting only to go back to the skin and blood.

A siren? Yes, and coming this way, at last.

"He hurt," Lyle moaned. "He hurt."

"It can be all better, Lyle. It can be all better."

But Lyle's lips were turned down, and there were tears on his cheeks. The child felt betrayed and could not be consoled.

"Let your friends help, Lyle."

"You were mean," Lyle sobbed. "I wasn't mean to you. Dog was mean, too. Bit me."

"Oh, Lyle."

Marlee could see the police car now, a half mile away and closing.

Lyle was limping as he started into the high, wet weeds. Pouting and choking back a sob, he turned to look at Marlee. "He was a mean priest. He wanted me to touch him . . . down there! He did!"

Lyle turned and limped into the weeds. Marlee knelt sobbing by her dog as the siren grew louder. She prayed for the Lyle she had known, the Lyle who had not harmed her, had not harmed her dog. She hoped the siren's wail would smother the sound of the shot.

Dear Grant,
I really feel I should have written to you before this, but I've just felt kind of overwhelmed lately.

I'm not alone in that, as I'm sure you can understand.

First, let me say how sorry I am that we never got a chance to have much of a private talk before you went back to New York. I can't imagine more bizarre circumstances—or sadder ones. Can you?

Believe me when I say that Ed Delaney is sorry you were held at the airport and missed your flight. It's easy to see how it happened, in hindsight. Isn't hindsight great?

Anyhow, Ed understands how pissed off you were that he forgot to cancel the message for the police to pick you up. That's why he insisted on coming with me to drive you to the airport. It made for kind of an awkward situation, I admit. I like Ed's company, but I would rather have talked to you alone.

So—now that we've finally touched base after all these years, I hope we won't lose contact. Speaking for myself, as I get older I appreciate the importance of hanging on to the people one knows in life.

Oh, Ed had copies made of the tape you sent him, although I don't know what good it will do. God, can you imagine how Lyle must have felt pressured? I mean, once he got my copy of the tape, he had to not only get to New York but get *your* copy of the tape, too. At least he may have thought he did; if Ed Sperl hadn't had a big set of ears the night of my party . . .

Enough of that unhappy stuff. I need to go back to the point I was making, about keeping in touch, etc. Just because you're in New York and I'm in Bessemer doesn't mean we can't be friends. It's only an hour by plane, right? And I like the idea of having a friend in New York.

The office is buzzing about Will Shafer. I happen to know he confronted the publisher face-to-face and asked him what he had done to fix the case up for Lyle years ago. Knowing the publisher, he probably tried to tell Will that it was no concern of his. But I know Will stood on principles; he wouldn't be comfortable working for a publisher who did something like that, believe me.

So Will's days here are probably numbered, which is too bad. Too bad for the city and the newspaper, I mean. Will can latch on somewhere else. So can his wife, Karen.

One of the strange figures in all this is Ed Sperl's first ex-wife, Olga. She surfaced in Arizona, finally, and reportedly sold her story to one of those gossip tabloids for a hefty five figures. Well, good for her. Maybe she can take me to lunch sometime.

Will tells me your father is sick. I'm sorry to hear that, and I hope things don't go too badly. I know what it's like.

There's lots more I'd like to say, but I should save it for another time. And there will be another time, because from now on we must keep in touch.

As ever,
Marlee West

"'As ever,'" Grant said. "What the hell does that mean?" He wadded the letter and tossed it toward the wastebasket.

The phone rang, and for a moment he hoped, against all that was rational, that the call was from Bessemer.

"Grant? This is Lila Burlson. I've been trying for a couple of days to reach you at *Sleuth*."

"I took a couple of days off." What can she want, he thought.

"I hope you're not sick."

"No. I just needed some time." To think about my career, he thought. And my life.

"Can we get together soon?"

"Huh?"

"The reason I ask, I've been thinking. While your manuscript is, well, flawed, it does show . . . life. Talent. I mean, it stayed with me, warts and all, even though I sent it back."

"Oh."

"I mean, I thought it was too, too idiosyncratic to survive commercially, and yet . . . Let's talk, is what I'm saying. It might be possible to recast it in some ways that would at least get you in the marketplace."

"Oh. All right. That would be great."

"Good. I'll be in touch soon, and we can settle on a time and place. Maybe talk over a beer or two."

"Fine." Say more, a voice in his head said. Say more. "I'd like that."

Grant felt naked and vulnerable. For a moment, he thought he might cry. Damn, he thought. All these people trying to . . . reach me.

He put on dark glasses, fled his apartment, started walking uptown. He walked as fast as he could. hoping to tire himself. Penn Station was just ahead; he would buy newspapers at the stand in front of it.

"Disabled Vietnam veteran here. Won't you please help?"

Grant bought two papers and a magazine. He put his change into the man's cigarbox, whirled and walked away.

Back in his apartment, he had an impulse. Quickly, before he could talk himself out of it, he picked up the phone and dialed. "Doug? It's Grant Siebert. Still want to have a beer sometime soon?"

After hanging up, he saw that the wadded-up letter from Marlee West had missed the wastebasket. Grant laughed: the gods were telling him something.

He picked up the letter, smoothed it out, laid it flat on the kitchen counter. He read the end: " . . . from now on we must keep in touch."

Yes.

Will looked up to see Marlee.

"Can I come in?" she asked.

"Of course. How are you?"

"Not bad. Pretty good, actually. I just wanted to know if I can bring anything."

"Just bring yourselves and your appetite. Karen's putting chicken on the grill. We're looking forward to it."

Marlee beamed. "So is Ed. His daughter is a sweetie. I know your kids will love her."

"I'm sure. So we'll see you a few hours from now." Will felt an edge of sadness but chased it away. "I'm glad it's a warm day. This time of year, we never know how many days we have left to sit out on the deck and solve the world's problems over a drink or two or three."

"Will, do you ever think it would have been better if Lyle had, you know . . . ?"

"No. We'll probably never know, but I think he really wanted to live. Even as he was squeezing the trigger, I think he was changing his mind, pulling his hand away. I think that's why the bullet wasn't fatal."

"But the way he is now . . ."

"I know. But at least he'll have good care. And when someone in a life-or-death moment like that chooses life, I want to see him get his life back."

"Hmmm. That makes sense."

"Oh, I don't know if it does. It's just how I feel."

"Will he ever stand trial, do you think?"

"Doubtful. And if he does, for either killing or both, he'll have a good defense. Money will be no object, you know that."

"I thought I knew Lyle."

"So did I. We were both wrong."

"Will, I've thought a lot about that prowler at my place. At first, I wondered if it was Ed Sperl, trying to steal the tape to help his blackmailing. Then I thought it made a lot more sense if it was Lyle, trying to get the tape. See, I wasn't going to be at my place that night, and I changed my plans."

"So it could have been someone you knew, or someone who learned about you from someone you knew."

"Yes."

"Or maybe it was just a prowler, Marlee."

Marlee shook her head, made an expression that Will knew meant she was through with the subject. "I'll see you later on."

Hardly had Marlee left his office when the phone rang. It was Karen. "Home base to Will, urgent request from kids. They want Marlee to bring her dog. Do you think she'd mind?"

Will chuckled. "She won't mind. I'll ask her."

He hung up, started to leave his office and saw Jenifer Hurley standing there. From her expression, he knew at once why she had come.

"Can we talk a minute?" she said.

"Sure," he said, sitting back down.

Jenifer settled into her chair. "I'm leaving."

"Ah. Where?"

"The *Los Angeles Times*. I've been talking to them off and on for a while, and they've been following, you know, the case, and . . ."

"And they knew you had a role in it. Even though all the *Gazette*'s running is what official sources say."

"Yes. And it seems, it just seems like a good opportunity."

"It is, Jenifer. I'm very happy for you." How far away you'll be, he thought.

"Thank you. You've been wonderful to me. A lot of *Gazette* people have, but you especially. I've learned a lot from you."

"Jenifer, you have a lot of talent and you'll do well there. The *Los Angeles Times* has a reputation of letting its writers, especially its best ones, have a pretty free rein."

"I've heard that. I've learned to rein in myself a little, working with you. And to think more about the consequences of stories."

"Listen, you're a terrific reporter. Go get 'em. You get the stories, get the truth, and then worry about what happens. It's best that way."

"I'll try to remember that. We'll talk some more before I go. Okay?"

"Okay."

Will walked her to the door and put his arm over her shoulders, briefly. Then he went back to his desk, spun his chair around and blinked hard as he looked out the window. He allowed himself a minute or so of daydreams before spinning his chair around again and picking up the phone.

"Karen? Listen, check our beer supply, will you?"

He heard the footsteps behind him. He was not afraid, because he knew they were coming to wheel him in from the porch. It was getting dark.

Big strong hands took the rubber wheels of his chair and turned him around, pushed him inside and down the shiny hall into his room. He was not afraid of the dark anymore. When the window was open, he could hear the friendly noises in the grass. It was bad luck to kill a cricket. He never had.

Women who wore white and smelled nice put hands on his shoulders and talked to him as they changed his bandage. It didn't hurt much, and he was not afraid. They tucked him in and put his teddy bear in with him. The bear's name was Gary.

He was in the dark now, but he was not afraid of the dark. Now I lay me down to sleep . . .